PENGUIN BOOKS

HUNT THE MOON

Karen Chance is the *New York Times* bestselling author of two urban fantasy series. Her previous novels *Touch the Dark, Claimed by Shadow, Embrace the Night, Midnight's Daughter, Curse the Dawn* and *Death's Mistress* are all published by Penguin. Karen lives in Florida.

To find out more about Karen's books, please visit her website: www.karenchance.com.

SOUTHWAR
D0347737
SK 197

Hunt the Moon

A Cassie Palmer Novel

KAREN CHANCE

PENGUIN BOOKS

PENGUIN BOOKS

Published by the Penguin Group
Penguin Books Ltd, 80 Strand, London WC2R ORL, England
Penguin Group (USA) Inc., 375 Hudson Street, New York, New York 10014, USA
Penguin Group (Canada), 90 Eglinton Avenue East, Suite 700, Toronto, Ontario, Canada M4P 2Y3
(a division of Pearson Penguin Canada Inc.)
Penguin Ireland, 25 St Stephen's Green, Dublin 2, Ireland (a division of Penguin Books Ltd)
Penguin Group (Australia), 250 Camberwell Road,
Camberwell, Victoria 3124, Australia (a division of Pearson Australia Group Pty Ltd)
Penguin Books India Pvt Ltd, 11 Community Centre,
Panchsheel Park, New Delhi – 110 017, India
Penguin Group (NZ), 67 Apollo Drive, Rosedale, Auckland 0632, New Zealand
(a division of Pearson New Zealand Ltd)
Penguin Books (South Africa) (Pty) Ltd, 24 Sturdee Avenue,
Rosebank, Johannesburg 2196, South Africa

Penguin Books Ltd, Registered Offices: 80 Strand, London WC2R ORL, England

www.penguin.com

First published in the USA by Signet Select, an imprint of New American Library,
a division of Penguin Group (USA) Inc. 2011
First published in Great Britain in Penguin Books 2011

1

Copyright © Karen Chance, 2011
All rights reserved

The moral right of the author has been asserted

Printed in England by Clays Ltd, St Ives plc

Except in the United States of America, this book is sold subject
to the condition that it shall not, by way of trade or otherwise, be lent,
re-sold, hired out, or otherwise circulated without the publisher's
prior consent in any form of binding or cover other than that in
which it is published and without a similar condition including this
condition being imposed on the subsequent purchaser

ISBN: 978-0-241-95260-3

www.greenpenguin.co.uk

MIX
Paper from
responsible sources
FSC
www.fsc.org   FSC™ C018179

Penguin Books is committed to a sustainable
future for our business, our readers and our
planet. This book is made from paper certified
by the Forest Stewardship Council.

To my editor, Anne Sowards, for otherworldly patience!

LONDON BOROUGH OF SOUTHWARK	
SK 1975941 X	
ASKEWS & HOLT	26-Aug-2011
AF HOR	£7.99
3289255	CW

Chapter One

I hit the ground running—or stumbling or falling; it was kind of hard to tell when it felt like the earth was crumbling under my feet.

And then I realized that was because the earth *was* crumbling under my feet.

"*Craaaap!*"

I plummeted straight over a cliff and into thin air, arms waving and feet still moving uselessly, screaming bloody murder. For a long moment, there was nothing but me and crystal blue sky and acre upon acre of sparkling, snow-covered land way the hell too far below. I knew I was supposed to be doing something, but the wind was roaring in my ears and my eyes were watering from the cold and the ground was rushing up to meet me at a pace that promised one very mushed clairvoyant in the very near future—

And then I was jerked back up, fast enough to cut off my breath, to leave me dizzy. Or maybe that was the feel of the hard arms around me or the harder body behind me. Or the stunning relief of *Not dead, not dead yet*—

Because that never gets old.

My name is Cassie Palmer, and I've cheated death more times than anyone has a right to expect. In the past two months, I've been shot, stabbed, beaten and blown up a few dozen times, and that doesn't count all the magical ways I've almost been killed. I'd have been dead a long time ago if not for my friends, one of whom had just jumped off the cliff after me.

I'd have been a lot more appreciative if he hadn't pushed me first.

My nose was running, I couldn't see worth shit and my brain was still frozen in abject terror. So for a moment I just hung there, gulping ice-cold air and waiting for my heart to stop trying to slam through my chest. Out of the corner of my eye, I could see a small piece of what was holding us up, and it wasn't reassuring.

It was almost transparent, except for a faint bluish tinge that was largely invisible against the brilliant sky. It had a dome-shaped top and a few filmy tentacles streaming downward to wrap around us, making it look vaguely like a jellyfish—if they were as big as a bus and had a habit of drifting around over the Colorado Rockies. What it was was almost as strange: an expression of one man's magic, formed into a parachute that I didn't trust at all.

On the other hand, I did trust the man. Although I really wished he'd caught me from the front instead of from behind. That way I could have kneed him in the nuts.

"You did that on purpose!" I gasped when I was able to breathe.

"Of course."

"Of course?" I looked up, but had to crane my head back, leaving the features above me wrong-side up. The clear green eyes were the same, and, unfortunately, so was the spiky blond hair.

It didn't look any better from this angle, I decided.

"You have yet to learn to react reliably under pressure," I was told. "Until you do, you are vulnerable."

I tried swiveling my head around, because glaring at someone upside down doesn't work. But all I saw was part of a muscular shoulder in an army green sweatshirt. My sometimes friend, sometimes enemy, all the time pain in the ass John Pritkin wasn't wearing a coat.

Of course he wasn't.

It had to be subzero out here, and if it hadn't been for all the adrenaline pumping through my system, I'd have been freezing to death—but a coat wasn't macho. And if I'd learned one thing about war mages, the closest thing the supernatural community had to a police force, it was that they were always macho. Even the women. It was kind of scary.

Sort of like dangling about a mile above a lot of very pointy mountains.

"Your abilities will do you little good if you cannot learn to function under stress," he continued calmly, as we slowly drifted closer to the pointy bits.

"Stress?" I asked, my voice cracking slightly. "Pritkin, stress is a bad hair day. Stress is gaining five pounds right before swimsuit season. *This is not stress!*"

"Call it what you will; the point is the same. Remember what we discussed. *Assess*—determine what is happening; *address*—decide which of your abilities can best deal with the problem at hand; and then *act*—quickly and decisively. You must learn to do this automatically, without freezing up, and regardless of the circumstances. Or you will suffer the consequences."

"I'm trying!" I said resentfully. It was barely two months since I'd been pushed off another cliff, and the fact that it had been a metaphorical one hadn't helped at all. I'd been declared—over my loud and sustained protests—Pythia, the chief seer of the supernatural world.

It was a job that some people were willing to kill for, as I'd discovered the hard way. For my part, I'd spent a good deal of those two months trying to give back the power that came with the office, only to find that it didn't want to leave. After a number of very hard lessons, I'd finally accepted that I was going to have to make the best of it.

As a result, I'd been working my metaphysical butt off trying to make up for the lifetime of training the other candidates had received. It would have helped if Rambo up there hadn't demanded that I learn self-defense, too. I agreed that I needed it, but one thing I didn't know how to do at a time was enough.

"Try harder," Mr. Complete Lack of Sympathy told me.

"Look," I said, trying to reason with him despite extensive experience that this rarely worked. "This isn't a great time. I have my inauguration—"

"Coronation."

"—coming up, and I'm trying to raise my abilities from pathetic to just sad before then so I don't totally embarrass myself in front of the people I'm supposed to be leading. And then there're fittings for the dress they want me to wear, and about a ton of names to learn, and if I get a title wrong it could cause some kind of international incident—"

"I will make you a deal," he said, cutting me off.

"What kind of deal?" I asked warily. Wheeling and dealing was a vampire trait, something the other man in my life was much more likely to try. War mages ordered, threatened and bitched, depending on the circumstance. They didn't deal.

Except for today, apparently.

"We're directly over an area used by the Corps as a training ground," he told me, referring to the formal name of the war mages. "Stay ahead of me for fifteen minutes, using any abilities you like other than time shifting, and I won't bother you again for a week."

I didn't say anything for a moment. Because there were several types of shifting that came standard with my office—through space and through time. They might look the same to Pritkin, except that I moved from place to place instead of from era to era. But they weren't. His boss at the Corps, Jonas Marsden, was the one training me in my newly acquired abilities and he'd told me so himself.

So if Pritkin didn't specifically forbid me from *spatially* shifting, I could easily stay ahead of him—and buy myself a free week in the process. After the way things had been going lately, a little time off would be heaven. But it would be a bad mistake to sound like it.

"We've been out here half the day already," I complained. "I'm tired, I haven't eaten since breakfast and I can't feel my toes any—"

"I'll throw in a picnic."

My head came up. "What?"

"I hid a basket this morning. After the test, I'll take you to it."

"It'll be cold by now."

"I left it with a warmer," he said drily. Because war mages ate their fried chicken frozen to the ground and they *liked* it.

God. Fried chicken, potato salad, baked beans, maybe some apple pie or cookies for dessert—yeah. I could so use a picnic right about now.

"All right," I agreed, faster than I should have. But I really was hungry. "No time travel."

"You're sure? Because when I win—"

"*If* you win."

"—you'll stay until you've run the entire course. And you won't whine about it."

"I don't whine!"

"Then we have a deal?"

"I guess so," I said, trying to sound reluctant.

"Good," he told me pleasantly.

And then he let go.

A couple of hours later, I staggered into the Vegas hotel suite I currently called home and face-planted onto the sofa. There was already someone sitting there, but I didn't care. I was too tired to even open my eyelids and find out who it was.

Until someone pried one open for me with a finger the size of a hot dog. "Rough day?"

I rotated my eyeball—and, goddamnit, even that hurt—to see the leader of my bodyguards peering at me.

"No. I like being dropped from airplane height without a parachute."

Marco patted me on the ass, which I guess was fair, since I was draped over his lap. "You seem all right to me."

Marco, I reflected sourly, was getting awfully blasé where my health was concerned. He'd started out assuming that I was as squishy as most humans, and practically had a heart attack every time I got a hangnail. But after seeing me survive a few dozen attacks, he'd started to relax. These days, if I didn't come in with a gaping wound or spewing blood, I didn't get much sympathy.

"Because I managed to shift to the ground before I splattered on it!" I told him testily.

"Then what's the problem?"

I turned over so I could scowl at him. "The problem is that I just ran a marathon in freezing weather with a maniac chasing me."

"Why didn't you just"—he waved the ham-sized hand that went with his bear-sized body—"you know. Poof."

"You mean shift?"

"Yeah. Why didn't you shift?"

"I did! But Pritkin expected that, and he borrowed Jonas's necklace."

"What necklace?"

I sighed and sat up. "It's some sort of charm that allows him to recall the Pythia in times of emergency. As soon as I try to shift, wherever I am, whenever I am, it pulls me back." As Pritkin had known when he made that bet, damn him.

God, I wished I kneed him in the nuts.

Marco seemed to think that was funny, which didn't improve my mood. I got up and limped into the next room, still freezing cold and starving to death. Because Pritkin's idea of a picnic left a lot to be desired.

But my bathroom didn't. I knew it was stupid, but my bathroom made me happy. Maybe it was the size—which was huge bordering on sinful—or the soothing white and blue color scheme, or the rain forest showerhead over the Godzilla-sized tub. Or maybe it was because it was the one place in the whole damn suite where I could actually be alone.

Marco wasn't the problem. Over the last month, he'd gone from treating me like a burdensome pest to treating me like a slightly bratty younger sister, and most of the time, I found myself actually enjoying his company. But Marco was the tip of the iceberg where my bodyguards were concerned. And they'd only been growing in number since the date of the inauguration had been announced.

Everyone assumed there would be an attack. Even I assumed it. The supernatural world was at war, and killing off the opposite side's leadership was SOP. And whether I liked it or not, the Pythia was seen as one of our side's more important assets. Which explained Pritkin's stepped-up attempts to make me suck slightly less at self-defense, and the dozen or so golden-eyed master vamps constantly patrolling the suite.

They were there for my protection; I knew that. But it didn't make them any less creepy. They watched me eat. They watched me drink. They watched me watch goddamned TV. They even watched me sleep. I'd woken up more than once to find one of them just standing in the doorway of my bedroom, staring at me, like it was a perfectly normal thing to do.

If it hadn't been for my bathroom, I really might have lost it.

Too bad I couldn't sleep in there.

Marco stuck his head in the door as I was running hot water into my lovely big tub. "You need anything? 'Cause I go off duty in a couple."

"Food," I said, shrugging out of my coat.

"What kind?"

"Anything. As long as it isn't good for me."

He nodded and ducked out when I started to pull off my T-shirt. It was far too flimsy for where I'd been, but the saying on the front fit my mood perfectly: "I keep hitting escape, but I'm still here." I tossed it on a pile with the coat, my stiff-with-cold jeans and the expensive scrap of silk that had been wedged up my ass for the past half hour. Then I slowly climbed into the tub.

Oh, God.

Bliss.

It was actually a little too hot, but I figured the amount of ice clinging to me ought to even things out. I added a generous amount of bath salts, found my pillow under some towels and let my head sag back against the tub. After a few moments, my muscles began to unclench and my spine sagged in relief, and I seriously began to wonder if sleeping here was such a bad idea after all.

I think maybe I did drift off for a while. Because the next thing I knew, I was at the pink and pruney stage, the mirrors were all fogged up and the water was no longer hot. And a ghost was sitting by the tub, staring at me.

I'd have been more concerned, but this was a ghost I knew. I grabbed a towel and shot him a look; I don't know why. Billy didn't worry about his numerous vices. He'd cheated death like he'd cheated at cards in life, and he intended to keep it up. That made his morality a bit of a mixed bag, since he never intended to answer for any of it, anyway.

With an insubstantial finger, he pushed up the Stetson he'd been wearing for the past century and a half. "I've seen it before," he told me with an exaggerated leer.

"Then why are you looking?"

" 'Cause I'm dead, not senile?"

I threw the sponge at him, which did no good, because it

passed right through and hit the wall. "I can't feed you yet," I said. "Not until I eat."

Billy and I had a long-standing arrangement, dating from the time I'd picked up the necklace he haunted in a junk shop at the age of seventeen. I donated the living energy it took to keep him feeling frisky, and he did little errands for me in return. At least, he did if I complained enough.

He stretched denim-covered legs out in front of him, as if on an invisible sofa. "Can't a guy drop by without you immediately assuming—" He caught my expression and gave it up. "Okay, I'll wait."

I was trying to decide between getting out and running some more hot water when there was a knock at the door. "You decent?"

I pulled the towel up a little higher. "Yes, if my wrinkled toes don't offend."

Marco's swarthy head popped around the doorjamb. "Naw, they're cute."

I wiggled them at him since I could actually feel them now.

"Anyway, grub's outside and I gotta go." He grinned at me. "Big date tonight."

"Date?" I blinked in surprise, because master vampires don't date. Not unless forced, anyway.

"Witch," he said succinctly.

"Isn't that a little . . . unusual?"

"I'm like the master. I like to walk on the wild side."

It took me a moment to realize what he meant. "I am not the wild side," I told him flatly. "I'm about as far from the wild side as it's possible to get."

He raised a bushy black eyebrow. "If you say so."

I opened my mouth, then decided I was too beat to argue. "Well, have fun."

"Oh, I will." He paused. "And just FYI, there's a bunch of new guys on tonight. Well, not *new* new, but new to you."

I didn't know why he was bothering to tell me. The bodyguards were changed on a regular basis. Round-the-clock security meant that some of them got stuck on the day shift, which was hard on vampires. At least I assumed that was why, after a week or two, they started looking a little peaked.

I nodded, but Marco just stood there, as if he expected some kind of answer. "Okay."

"It's just . . ." He hesitated. "Try not to freak them out too much, all right?"

"I freak *them* out?"

"You know what I mean. It's those things you do."

"What things?"

His eyes darted around the bathroom. "Talking-to-invisible-people kind of things."

"They're ghosts, Marco."

"Yeah, only most of the guys don't believe in ghosts, and they've started to think you're a bit . . . strange."

"They're vampires and they think I'm strange?"

"And no popping out of nowhere in front of a guy. That takes some getting used to. I don't think Sanchez has recovered yet."

"The only place I'm popping is to bed."

"Good plan." Marco looked satisfied. "See you on the flip side."

I rolled my eyes at the slang, which as usual for the older vamps was decades out of date, and let my head sag back against the tub. I really didn't want to move now that I was warm and relaxed and actually starting to feel my extremities again. But the smells drifting in from the next room were making my stomach growl plaintively.

I couldn't immediately identify the source, but it didn't matter. If Marco had done the ordering, it had to be good. Unlike Pritkin, Marco didn't worry about things like trans fats and cholesterol. When Marco ate, he ate big: pasta dripping in cream sauce, huge peppery steaks, mashed potatoes with gravy, and cannoli sweet enough to crack teeth. Often at the same meal.

The fact that vampires didn't technically need to eat didn't appear to worry Marco. He'd told me that one of the best things about finally reaching master status had been the return of working taste buds. And he'd spent the time since making up for all those flavorless years.

I decided that maybe I was clean enough. "Turn around," I told Billy. "I'm getting out."

He made a pouty face but he didn't argue. Maybe he was hungry, too. I wrapped the towel around myself and started to get out of the tub.

But instead my hands slid off the porcelain, my knees bent and I slipped back into the rapidly cooling water.

For a second, I just lay there, more confused than worried. Until I kept on sinking. Then I snapped out of it and began to struggle.

And found that it made absolutely no difference.

The best I could do was keep my face above the bubbles for a few seconds while I struggled to move, to cry out, to do *something*. But my body was as frozen as the shout trapped behind my teeth, which my lips stubbornly refused to let out. The most I managed was a muffled grunt as my head slowly went under.

Immediately, all sound vanished. The whoosh of the air-conditioning, the almost silent footsteps of the guards, the soft clink-clink of someone dropping ice cubes in a glass in the dining room, all faded into a watery roar. Silence constricted around me, a heavy, cold hand that robbed me of breath as effectively as the water over my face.

The bubbles had half dissolved by now, with pockets of suds floating here and there, like the sky on a cloudy day. In between I could see the ceiling of the bathroom, rippling with my barely discernible struggles. But they weren't enough, weren't nearly enough, and my lungs were already crying out for air.

After what felt like an hour but was probably no more than a few seconds, the scene above me was obscured by Billy's indistinct shape. He was saying something, but I couldn't hear, and then his face passed through the water and he gazed at me curiously. "Time to get out."

No shit, I thought hysterically, trying to flail limbs that suddenly felt like they belonged to someone else. A frown appeared between Billy's eyes. But it was the impatient Billy look, not the panicked Billy look. He still didn't get it.

"Seriously, Cass. Your dinner's gonna get cold."

I just stared at him, my eyes burning from the soap, willing him to understand. Nothing happened, except that a chain of bubbles slipped out from between my lips, heading for the air a few inches away. It might as well have been a few thousand, for all the good it was doing me.

My toes were floating near the surface of the water, right beside the switch that controlled the drain. It was mounted just below the faucet, within easy reach—if I'd been able to move. As it was, I could only stare at it, stark terror creeping over my body, chilling my skin and threatening to paralyze whatever brain function I had left. I couldn't move and Billy was useless and I couldn't even take a deep breath to calm down because—

Because I was about to drown in the goddamn bathtub.

Chapter Two

The thought cut cleanly through the gibbering in my brain. People had been trying to kill me in elaborate ways for months, yet if I didn't get a grip, my epitaph was going to read: SHE DROWNED IN THE TUB. But it wasn't, *it wasn't*, because I was damned if I was going to go out like that.

Only it didn't look like I had a lot of choice.

The more I struggled, the more my body seemed to shut down. Trying to move was like battering against the lid of a coffin from the inside. I cried out furiously, but the shout stayed locked in my numb throat.

The worst part was the silence. Death was supposed to be loud—gunshots, explosions, screams and thunder. Not this eerie quiet that wrapped around me like a shroud. I couldn't hear anything but the water lapping at the sides of the tub, like a watch counting down the seconds I had left.

And a harsh voice echoing in my ears: *Assess, Address, Act.*

For a second, the words just hung there in my head, refusing to connect with anything. And then I remembered Pritkin's damn three A's. I grabbed at the thought like a lifeline, before it could skitter away into the white noise of my panic.

Okay, I thought wildly. Assess. What was the problem? That I couldn't fucking *breathe*.

Address. What could I do about it? Nothing. Not when

my own body refused to follow my commands, when it seemed almost like it was under someone else's—

Wait, wait. I didn't need to move physically to use my power, which was independent of my human form. And my power could—

I shifted before I finished the thought, ending up outside the tub, with my bare ass several feet above the bathroom floor. Gravity took care of that, dumping me onto the cold tile before I'd even managed to get a breath, along with about forty gallons of tepid water. In my panic, I'd shifted the entire contents of the bath, which foamed over the floor, drenching the fuzzy rug and breaking against the walls like a miniature tide.

I barely noticed. I lay on the water-slick tile, sucking harsh gulps of air into my screaming lungs, while Billy hovered around me. He looked a little panicked now, I noticed irrelevantly, right before a hand clenched around my throat.

It took me a second to realize that it was mine.

Fortunately, I have small hands, so the one trying its best to choke the life out of me wasn't having much success. It might have done a better job if it had had some help, but my other hand was locked, white-knuckled, around the standing towel rack and it wasn't letting go. I stared at it, dazed and uncomprehending, and my own wide blue eyes stared back at me from the bright chrome surface.

What the hell?

The question echoed the one in my head, but it hadn't come from me. It took me a second to realize that Billy had slipped inside my skin, the way he did when feeding. It gave him access to my power, something I'd learned to put up with but never to like. Today, I grabbed him in a metaphysical clench, almost sobbing from relief.

Help!

Help how? he demanded. *What's happening?*

Possession. The word stopped me, since my conscious mind hadn't connected the dots. But my unconscious seemed to be more organized, because that sounded about right. I'd had some experience with possession in recent months because it was one of the Pythia's chief weapons, but I'd never before had it turned on me.

I decided I wasn't enjoying the experience.

By what? Billy demanded.

Like I know! Just do *something!*

Yeah, only what I can do depends a lot on what exactly is—
Billy!

Okay, okay. Don't worry, Cass. I got this, he told me. Right before he was thrown out of me, across the bathroom and through the wall.

I watched him disappear, a look of almost comical surprise on his face, and belatedly realized who'd had control of my other hand. Because it immediately went numb and joined the choke party at my neck. But amazingly enough, that wasn't my biggest problem.

There were a limited number of things that could possess a human. Ghosts were one of them, but unless they were welcomed inside like I did for Billy, they had to fight their way through the body's defenses. And that meant a much-weakened spirit by the time it finally got in—if it did.

But that hadn't been weak. Whatever it was had exorcized Billy while maintaining its grip on me, and no mere ghost could do that. Which narrowed things down to the Oh, Shit list.

A fact that was demonstrated when the towel rack tipped over and tried to bash my head in. My hand wasn't on it anymore—no one's was—but it was going nuts, anyway. It shattered the mirror over the sink, then ricocheted off and slammed into the tub, sweeping the jar of bath salts onto the floor and turning the soggy tile fluorescent pink.

The result was enough noise to wake the dead, one of whom started hammering on the bathroom door. "Miss Palmer. Are you all right?"

I didn't know the voice, but it didn't matter. I couldn't answer, anyway. All I could think about was getting to the source. The vamps might not know any more about this than I did, but they could at least pry my damn hands off my neck.

I tried to shift, but this time, nothing happened. Maybe because the room was starting to spin and my vision was graying out and I was slowly sinking to my knees. And then Billy was back, looking pissed.

He slipped inside my skin, and immediately I felt a very familiar energy drain. *You're feeding* now? I asked incredulously.

I have to have energy to fight this thing, Cass! And I'm almost bottomed out.

And what do you think I am?

Billy didn't answer, and the drain didn't stop. But a moment later, my hands sprang away from my neck like they'd been burned. Suddenly, I could breathe again.

I stayed down because I didn't have the energy to get up, coughing and wheezing as my lungs struggled to drag in air through a throat that felt maybe half the right size. It was burning and my head was swimming, and I really, really wanted to throw up. But I would have cried in relief if my eyes had been under my control.

Unfortunately, they'd rolled up into their sockets and wouldn't come back down.

"Miss Palmer?" The vamp was sounding seriously unhappy now, but the door still didn't open.

Why isn't he coming in? Billy demanded angrily.

He doesn't want to upset me.

You and your damn personal space!

I didn't answer because he had a point. And because I suddenly realized that I could feel my legs again. It shouldn't have surprised me. Holding on to a body that isn't yours and doesn't want to be held is no easy task. And it looked like whatever had its claws in me couldn't keep all my appendages in thrall at once while also fighting off Billy Joe.

It wasn't much of an advantage, but it was the only one I had. I staggered to my feet, wincing when a piece of broken glass cut my heel, and almost tripping over the soggy, bunched-up rug. I was trying hard not to panic, but it felt a lot like drowning again—being naked and blind and at the mercy of an enemy I knew nothing about.

Except that it wanted me dead.

And it wasn't too particular about how I got that way.

I hadn't taken two hesitant steps when my legs suddenly went numb, my body turned and I ran—straight into the nearest wall. My head happened to be twisted slightly, which saved my nose, but my temple hit hard enough to leave me reeling. I staggered back, but only to get enough leverage to ram the wall again.

Eyes! I screamed mentally as I jerked out a hand to break my fall and almost broke the bone instead.

Working on it.

Work harder! I cried as the impact sent me stumbling into the side of the sink.

My hip hit the unforgiving marble hard enough to bruise, but a moment later, my eyesight returned. That would have been a relief, except that it freed up my attacker to grab back one of my hands. Luckily, it was the bad one, and it dropped the hair pick it had snatched up before it could stab me in the eye with it.

The pick went down and my other hand came up—along with a jagged piece of the mirror that it used to slash at my jugular. Billy caught it just in time, but the hand didn't drop. It hovered menacingly in the air in front of my face, shaking from the effort, while three different spirits battled for control.

I couldn't tell who was winning, but I didn't think it was us. I stared at the wickedly sharp triangle as it slowly edged closer, reflecting back to me wildly matted blond hair, a bone white face and dazed blue eyes—and the door to the dining room over my left shoulder. It was nearer now, and I was still on my feet.

I ran for it.

Halfway there, my body went into spasms and I went down. But I managed to snag a potted fern on the way. The pretty piece of blue and white delftware was on a pretty little stand, which made a pretty little crash when it tipped over and exploded against the hard tile.

And, finally, that was enough for the guards. The door burst open and three vamps rushed in, stopping in confusion when they saw nothing but a skinny white girl ripping the bathroom apart. And then it felt like something was ripping me, too, a burning, tearing sensation that mercifully only lasted a second before something *shot* out of me.

A wordless scream knifed through the silence, and some*thing* shivered through the air of the bathroom. The presence was oily and slick and wrong, but the smell was worse: sickly sweet, thick at the back of my throat, cloying, instantly nauseating. It sparked a feeling of primal revulsion deep in my gut, and it didn't look like I was the only one. The vamps ducked and pulled guns, despite the fact that there was nothing for them to shoot—except for me, and they managed not to do that even when I suddenly dove through the middle of them.

I wasn't driving, but I didn't think the entity was, either, because I could feel every inch of hide getting burnt off as I hit the carpet in the dining area face-first. *Not helping!* I told Billy, just as the remnants of the mirror shot by overhead and embedded themselves in the remaining guards.

I didn't have time to apologize, because the apartment was going nuts. A decanter set flew up from a nearby cart and slammed into the wall behind me in a wash of booze and expensive glass. The cutlery on the room service cart followed and would have skewered me if a vamp hadn't thrown himself in the way. And then the light fixture over the dining table ripped out of the ceiling, whirling for me like a crystal tornado.

Billy flung us into the living room and behind the sofa, which didn't help, and then rolled us under the coffee table, which did. At least for the moment. All I could see through the glass top were a few hundred crystals beating against it like an expensive hailstorm, but the view through the side was less obstructed.

I stared around, as much in disbelief as panic, because I'd never seen anything like it. Ghosts find it very difficult to move even tiny things, like a paperclip or a piece of paper. They don't rip curtain rods off the walls or toss heavy paintings at people's heads or throw chairs through plateglass windows.

Except for bleeding walls, it looked like something out of *The Amityville Horror.*

I blinked, finally making the connection. And then I squeezed Billy so hard he yelped. *Cut it out!*

We have to get to Pritkin, I told him quickly.

What? Why? What can he—

This isn't a ghost.

No shit!

So it's probably some kind of demon.

So?

So he'll know how to drive it out!

Billy didn't say anything, maybe because Pritkin was our resident demon expert. Or maybe because the coffee table had just splintered down the middle. He flipped us onto all fours and we scrambled out the other side, just as the chandelier burst like a crystal grenade all over the living room.

It might not have been made for this type of activity, but the dozen or so thick columns of wood flying around looked sturdier. They also looked familiar. I finally recognized one when it slammed through the piano while trying to get at me. I stared at one of the legs off the dining set and wondered why the entity would bother trashing that. We were on the other side of the apartment now, so it didn't seem to make a lot of sense.

Until I saw one of the guards run past, being pursued by the equivalent of a flying stake. He dodged it—mostly—and it hit his leg instead of his heart. That was lucky, because it punched through flesh and bone as easily as the other pieces did the walls, the furniture and the flimsy sides of the piano.

The vampires who formed my bodyguard were all senior-level masters and, presumably, they'd seen a lot of crazy stuff through the years. But it didn't look like they'd seen this. Vamps who prided themselves on strength and impassivity were running around wild-eyed, attacking the misbehaving furniture as if they thought it was the problem, or just trying to avoid being vamp shish kebab.

But other than for the sound of the suite imploding, it was weirdly quiet. I couldn't talk and the vamps didn't need to—at least not aloud. They could communicate mentally with each other as easily as I talked to Billy, something that usually gave them a hell of an advantage in a fight. Except, apparently, for right now.

But at least one guy had decided that they needed outside help, because he'd whipped out a cell phone. He was on the other side of the room from where I was hunkered down behind the baby grand, and I didn't have control of my vocal chords, anyway. So I poked the guy who did. *Tell him to call Pritkin!*

And Billy tried. But between my burning throat and the mortal peril and the deafening noise, nobody paid any attention. *These guys are new—I don't even think they know who he is!* Billy said frantically.

Then you'll have to go get him.

How? We'll never make it to the door through all that!

I won't, but you will. It isn't after you.

Yeah, except if I leave, that thing'll have its claws back in you!

And if you don't, it'll beat me to death! I wasn't seeing a whole lot of difference, really.

Okay, okay. Billy sounded like he was trying to calm down and wasn't doing so great. *Say I find the mage. Then what? He can't see me.*

Shit. Billy was so solid to me that I had a problem remembering that that wasn't true for everyone. But Pritkin wouldn't even know he was there.

It was hard to concentrate over the sound of the piano's death throes, but I tried. Only the three A's weren't doing me a lot of good right now. I knew what the problem was: I needed to get to Pritkin. But I didn't have any abilities to help me do that.

If I could have shifted, it would have been easy. But his room was five stories down and on the other side of the hotel. And I knew without trying that I couldn't make it that far. It was hard to shift after Billy had fed, even when I wasn't already exhausted. As it was, I'd be lucky to get five yards, and that wouldn't—

I stopped, my thoughts reversing. *Get to Pritkin,* I told Billy over the sound of the blood pounding in my temples.

I just told you, that won't—

Listen to me! He has Jonas's necklace. He used it to pull me back to him today when I tried to shift. You've got to get it!

And then what? It works on you only when you use your power, and you can't—

I only need to shift—it doesn't matter how far! A couple of inches should be enough to activate it. Now go!

For once, he didn't argue, maybe because he didn't know what else to do. I felt him leave, and braced myself for another onslaught. But the entity was having too much fun to notice Billy slipping away, and I didn't give it time to figure things out. I grabbed the top of the piano bench for a shield and started crawling.

A guard was on top of a tipped-over chair, batting at the flying shards of wood with a bloody table leg like a slugger at a baseball game. He saw me and his eyes went round, as if he assumed I must have been skewered ages ago. "Not dead yet," I croaked encouragingly, and crawled on.

The dining room had been destroyed, but the room service cart had miraculously survived, wedged in the doorway between the bar and the kitchen. I pushed it the rest of the way inside and peeked under the warming lid. Fried chicken, and it was still hot.

There was a God.

I hunkered down behind the kitchen table and concentrated on regaining enough strength to shift on my own if Billy failed. That basically involved stuffing down as much as possible as fast as possible without throwing up. I was making a serious dent in Marco's vast quantities when something caused me to look up.

Three vamps stood in the kitchen doorway, staring at me. They looked a little shell-shocked, and a glance at the stainless side of the fridge told me why. I was naked and bloody, with tufts of half-dried hair sticking up everywhere and a chicken leg distorting one side of my mouth. I looked startlingly like a mad cavewoman.

I removed the leg and licked my greasy lips. "Um. Hi?"

They didn't say anything. For a moment, we all just looked at one another. And then the creature attacked again, and I stopped worrying about the impression I was making and started worrying about getting my brains bashed out against the side of the table. I saw stars and red exploding things that probably came under the category of Not Healthy.

And then I saw Pritkin staring at me in utter shock.

I didn't remember trying to shift, but I must have, because instead of cold kitchen tile, my toes were suddenly sinking into the carpet in his hotel room. I'd landed by the bed, which he'd been in the process of turning back. His hair was damp and curling around his neck, and a few drops of water still clung to his shoulders. And either he hadn't bothered to put on pajamas yet or he slept in the nude, which might have been awkward if I hadn't been in the process of dying.

"Possession," I croaked, before my hands formed themselves into claws and my body launched itself off the floor, going straight for those clear green eyes.

I didn't succeed in scratching them out—Pritkin's reflexes are better than that, even when totally gobsmacked—

but I did tear an inch-long gash down one of his cheeks. "Sorry!"

"What kind of possession?" he asked grimly, one hand locked around each of my wrists.

"Not ghost, but I don't—"

I stopped talking, because my throat had closed up and my body started thrashing against his hold. Pritkin looked startled for a moment, like I was harder to control than he'd expected. But the next second, I found myself on my back on the bed with my hands pinned over my head by one of his. He used his other to summon a stream of little vials from a bookshelf he'd installed, apparently as a sort of filing system for nasty potions.

Most of which were soon all over me.

Some were sticky and some were sludgy and all of them were really, really vile. I wouldn't have cared if they'd done anything. But as far as I could tell, the most they accomplished was to stain my skin in blotches without affecting the thing inside me at all.

And then my entire body suddenly went numb and I had maybe a second to think—oh, shit—before the entity used my legs to send Pritkin sailing across the room. I saw him hit and pass through the wall, in an odd mirror of what Billy had done. Only Pritkin's much more material body took the flimsy Sheetrock and hard studs along with him.

And, to my surprise, the creature decided to follow. Maybe it assumed that I wouldn't be much of a challenge if it killed him first, or maybe he'd managed to piss it off. I didn't know, but I felt when it started to pull away, when all of the sensations of a seriously overtaxed body came rushing back at once, forcing out a whimper that I promised myself to deny if I survived long enough.

And then I felt its shock as I slammed my shields shut, trapping it inside.

I hadn't been able to expel the thing, but this was a different story. It had managed to possess me in the first place because I'd been exhausted and careless and I'd been expecting Billy any moment, so my shields were down. But they weren't now, and this was my body and ownership bestowed some privileges. And I was damned if I was going to let that thing finish off the one guy who had a chance of getting me out of this while he was possibly unconscious and—

And it had figured out that my body had become its prison and it *really* wanted out.

We apparently didn't speak the same language, but it didn't matter, because it started showing me a cascade of images like something out of a horror movie: my heart exploding in my chest, my lungs shredding like tissue paper, my brain—

If you could do all that, you already would have, I thought back viciously, sending the image of it trying to stab me in the eye with a freaking hair pick. I didn't know why it could trash the apartment and not me, but every single attack had been external or passive, like holding me underwater while I drowned. It was starting to look like maybe it wasn't all that strong inside the body.

Or like it wasn't so used to this possession thing, either.

That didn't make sense for a demon who, presumably, did this all the time, but I didn't have a chance to figure it out before it started thrashing around *inside* me. And if I thought I'd been in pain before, it was nothing compared to this. It was determined that I was going to let go, and I was determined I wasn't, because if it killed Pritkin I was dead, anyway.

And then he was back, bloody and bruised and reaching through the hole to grab something from his footlocker that he tossed at me. "Cassie, catch!"

My arm shot up automatically and I felt my fist close around something cold and hard. And then I didn't feel anything else for a long moment as I levitated completely off the bed.

Definitely Amityville, I thought blankly, and let go of my shields. My body gave a huge convulsion, and I was immediately surrounded by a storm of dark, flapping wings, a noxious odor and an infuriated, screeching cry.

And then I hit the bed and rolled off the side. That was lucky, because a second later what felt like a miniature cyclone burst out through the window and a shower of glass exploded *into* the room, in flagrant disregard for the laws of physics. But most of it didn't hit me, since I was huddled on the floor with my hands over my head, trying not to scream.

Pritkin had crawled back through the wall at some point, because when I looked up, he was crouched on the floor, staring at me. I stared mutely back, panting and limp, every limb shaking in reaction as confetti of dust and tattered bits of wallpaper rained down all around us. And then the door slammed open and Marco charged in.

He took in my naked, multicolored self, the hole in the wall, the broken window and the battered, bleeding war mage. "The *fuck*?" he said distinctly.

I swallowed, licking lips that tasted like dust and copper. "I think I freaked out the staff," I told him weakly. And then I fainted.

Chapter Three

Half an hour later, I was still naked and still not enjoying it.

"Goddamn it, Marco!" I croaked. "That hurts!"

"You don't hold still and it's gonna scar, too." The tone was harsh, but the large hand on my abused derriere was gentle.

"Just be careful, okay? That's living flesh back there." For the moment, anyway.

"I'll see what I can do."

I settled back onto my stomach and tugged at the sheet that was supposed to be protecting my modesty. It mostly wasn't, but I was too tired and, I suspected, too stoned to care. I knew the table I was lying on was level, but it felt a lot like it was floating on the high seas, thanks to the pills someone had given me and the two drinks I'd washed them down with.

"Can you get seasick lying still?" I wondered.

"If you're gonna hurl, you're gonna tell me," Marco said sternly.

"I'm not," I said with what dignity I could muster. Since I was sprawled naked on a massage table while he dug glass out of my ass, it wasn't much.

"Just so we're clear. We got enough to clean up."

This was true.

We were back in the suite, trashed as it was, because it had better wards than anywhere else in the hotel. Not that they'd done any good this time, but for the past month, they'd kept out most of the people who wanted my head on a stick. So livable or not, it was where I was sleeping tonight.

The vamps were trying to sort things out, but it was a hell of a task. I watched through the open door as a couple ran around, trying to catch the tattered curtains that were billowing in through the ruined living room window. At least, they were until one of the vampires muttered something vicious and snatched down the last remaining rod, bolts and all. He then tried to stuff it in a trash bag, but it didn't fit. So he crumpled it into a metal ball and *made* it fit. His buddy just looked at him with crossed arms and slowly shook his head.

Another time, it would have been funny. None of the guards were less than third-level masters, which made them pretty much vamp nobility. They were most definitely not used to carrying bags of trash, sweeping floors and hauling out debris. But they wouldn't let anyone else near the suite, including maid service, so there wasn't a lot of choice. And, to their credit, not a single one had complained.

Of course, that might be because they hadn't said anything at all. Most of them still looked a little paler than usual, and occasionally I caught one sneaking a glance at me as he passed. They were the kind of looks I might have given a dangerous animal in the zoo that was a little too close to the fence. Like they thought I might go for their jugular at any moment and just wanted to be careful.

"I think they're scared of me," I told Marco, as another one scurried past with the same little eye flick.

"Not of *you*," Marco corrected, tossing a blood-spotted paper towel into the overflowing bin.

"What does that mean?"

"It means you attract enemies like rotten meat does flies."

"That's a nice image!"

"And they're not normal enemies," he complained. "Someone a guy can really pound. They're ghosts or demons or a fucking *god*, and my boys are good, but they don't know how to deal with that shit. It makes 'em feel helpless, and they hate that."

I didn't exactly love it, either, I didn't say, because Marco was on a roll.

"And most of them thought this would be a vacation. Free trip to Vegas, stay in a luxury hotel, and all they gotta do is watch over the master's girlfriend. I mean, most of the time that means carrying her shopping bags and being asked which color shoes goes best with her purse, you know?"

I frowned. No, I didn't know. Their master and my significant other was pretty damn chary about his romantic past. I knew he wasn't inexperienced—at five hundred years old, that would be kind of hard—but I didn't have many details. In fact, I didn't have any, just some strong suspicions, any or all of which might be wrong.

For some reason, it had never occurred to me to ask Marco.

It occurred to me now.

"You sound like they've done this before."

"That wasn't my point."

"But have they? Have *you*?" It was unsettling to think that I might be just another in a long line of women Marco had babysat, at least until they grew too old to hold the attention of their perpetually thirtyish-looking boyfriend.

Really, really unsettling.

"I don't usually do the bodyguard thing," Marco evaded.

"But you've been around a while, right?"

"Yeah."

"So just how many girlfriends has Mircea had?" I asked bluntly.

Marco sighed. "You don't want to go there."

"Yeah, actually, I think I do."

"Then you want to go there with him," he told me flatly.

"But he isn't here and you are." And the fact that Marco obviously didn't want to discuss it made me wonder just what kind of numbers we were talking about. "I mean, how many can it have been?" I wondered aloud. "Five, ten?"

Marco didn't say anything.

"Twenty?" I asked, a little shrilly.

"You know, I forget," he replied. And then he stabbed me in the ass.

"Ow!"

"You want another drink?" he asked, as a vamp came in carrying a tray with a decanter on it.

"I want you to stop gouging me with that thing!"

He held something in front of my eyes. "See these? These are tweezers. They don't gouge."

"Tell that to my ass!"

"You want a drink or not?"

"I want some coffee," I said resentfully, since I obviously wasn't getting any answers. I clutched the sheet to my chest and tried to peer over my shoulder at my abused butt. And then I noticed the vamp looking, too. "Hey!"

"He don't mean anything," Marco said, as the man hurried out. "It's just there, you know?"

"And?"

"And we're guys. We look at women's butts."

"Are you looking at my butt?" I asked suspiciously.

"I gotta look or I can't dig all the pieces out."

"Then maybe we should call for a doctor."

Marco patted my shoulder. "It's okay. You aren't my type."

"What is your type?"

"Someone who gets in less trouble," he said, as a sliver of glass rang in the ashtray he was using as a receptacle. "I decided I was wrong. I don't like the wild side. I ain't got the master's stamina."

"I don't require stamina."

"Babe, you require a freaking tank."

I didn't know what that meant, but it didn't sound complimentary. But before I could ask, Pritkin came in with a mug that smelled like heaven. He handed it to me, and I braced myself for his usual caffeine hammer to the brain. This batch didn't disappoint; after two sips I could already feel my heart racing.

"It wasn't demon," he told me, without preamble.

"The hell it wasn't." Marco tossed another little sliver into the ashtray, more forcefully than necessary. "The guys said it was like *The Exorcist* in here."

"*Amityville,*" I muttered, but no one was listening.

"They were wrong," Pritkin said shortly. He looked at me and frowned, then reached over and brushed my curls out of my eyes. I smiled at him blearily, which got a bigger frown for some reason. "You are certain it wasn't a ghost?"

I nodded. It was about the only thing I was sure about. "Can you describe it?"

"Didn't you see it?"

He shook his head. "A dark cloud, nothing more."

"I didn't see much more than that."

"Tell me what you can. Anything would help at this point."

I tried to think back, but my head really hurt and the room was still swimmy and there just wasn't that much to remember. "It was dark colored," I said slowly. "Black or gray. Or really dark blue. And it had feathers—I think." I racked my brain, but I wasn't getting anything else. "It was big?"

"What about your servant? Did he see anything?"

It took me a second to realize that he meant Billy Joe. Pritkin had this weird idea that Billy was for me what an enslaved demon was for a mage—a capable, obedient servant who stayed unruffled in the face of adversity. When the truth was pretty much exactly the opposite. As soon as the crisis was over, Billy had fled into his necklace and I hadn't seen him since.

I gave him a little poke, just for the hell of it, and got back the metaphysical version of the finger. "Billy doesn't know anything," I translated.

"Are you certain?"

Tell him to suck my balls!

"Pretty certain."

Pritkin ran a hand through his hair. It was sweaty, and although he'd put on a pair of old jeans, they didn't cover the marks from being hurled through a wall. He looked about as beat up as I felt.

A particularly livid bruise trailed up his rib cage and wrapped around his back—where he'd hit the wall, I assumed. He was standing close enough that I could reach out and touch it, so I did. It was hot under my fingertips—Pritkin was always a little warmer than human standard—for the instant before he moved away.

I let my hand drop. "You should get that seen to. You might have broken a rib."

"It's fine," he said curtly, as another vamp came in carrying a phone.

"For you," the man told me, his eyes already sliding south.

"Is there anyone in this apartment who hasn't seen me naked?" I demanded, grabbing the sheet and the phone.

"I genuinely hope so, Cassandra."

I sighed and let my head thunk down against the padded surface of the table. I could always tell how Mircea was feeling based on what version of my name he chose to use. When he was in a good mood, it was *dulceață*, the Romanian endearment that colloquially translated as "sweetheart" or "dear one." When he was less happy, it was plain old Cassie. And when he was royally pissed but not showing it because he was Prince Mircea Basarab, member of the powerful North American Vampire Senate and allaround cool guy, it was Cassandra.

"Cassandra" was never good.

But this time, it wasn't my fault.

"This time, it isn't my fault," I told him, wincing as Marco found another heretofore untortured cut.

"I am not calling to assign blame."

"Then why the 'Cassandra'?"

"You frightened me. For a few moments, I could not feel you."

I frowned at the phone. "You're in New York. How are you supposed to feel me?"

"Through the bond."

"We have a bond?"

A sigh. "Of course we have a bond, *dulceață*. You are my wife."

By vampire standards, I didn't say, because that *always* got a Cassandra. The ceremony, if you could call it that, had been over before I fully knew what was happening. But that didn't matter, because little things like the bride's consent aren't required in vampire marriages.

Except, that is, by me.

That was why Mircea and I were dating—or, at least, that's why I was doing it, to figure out whether this whole relationship thing was something I could handle. He was doing it to humor me, when he remembered, although he clearly thought the whole thing was ridiculous. Mircea had been born in an era when men took what they wanted and kept it, as long as they were strong enough. And strength had never been one of his problems.

Listening, on the other hand . . .

"I listen," a velvet voice murmured in my ear.

I bent my head and let my hair fall over the phone. It wasn't much as privacy went, but around here, it was as good as it got. "Uh-huh."

"And what does that mean?" he asked, sounding amused.

"It means 'that's bullshit,' but I'm too high to think of a good comeback right now," I said honestly.

"High?"

"Blitzed, baked, stoned . . ."

"I understood the term," Mircea said, his voice sharpening. "My question was why?"

I hesitated. The truth was, I'd been pretty near hysterical when I woke up. I was getting better in crises, mainly because I'd had a lot of practice lately. But afterward . . .

I still had problems with afterward.

"Marco thought it best," I finally said.

Mircea didn't seem to like that answer. "I will speak with Marco," he said grimly. "But for the present, I am more concerned about the attack this evening. I have heard my men's report, such as it was. I would like to have yours."

It was my turn to sigh. "I don't know. It wasn't a ghost; that much I'm sure of. And Pritkin swears it wasn't a demon."

"There are thousands of types of demons, Cassie. He cannot possibly be certain—"

"He's pretty certain," I said drily.

"—and you have recently had problems with several of them. A demon is the most likely culprit."

"I think we should trust Pritkin's judgment on this one," I said, because I couldn't say anything else. That Pritkin was half demon himself wasn't exactly universally known, but what type he was wasn't known to anyone but me.

I intended to keep it that way.

"I am not so certain," Mircea said, sounding sour. "But I would speak with the man. Can you put him on?"

I really didn't think that was a great idea, considering that Pritkin and Mircea mixed like oil and water, only not as well. But I passed the phone over, anyway. I didn't get much of the resulting conversation, both because it was pretty terse on Pritkin's end, and because Marco had started the extraction process again.

"There can't possibly be that many pieces of glass in my ass," I gritted out, after a couple of agonizing minutes.

"Babe, it's like you rolled in it."

"It was all over the floor!"

"And when that's the case, it's best to avoid the floor," he said drily, digging what felt like an inch into my tender rear.

"I'll keep it in mind the next time I get possessed by an evil entity!"

"Demon," Marco said, sounding final.

"It wasn't a demon," Pritkin argued, but I couldn't tell if he was talking to Marco or Mircea. "Yes, I'm bloody well sure!"

Mircea.

"Okay, this is going to sting a little," Marco told me, right before he set my butt on fire.

"Shit, shit, shit!"

"Gotta disinfect it," he said imperturbably. "You're not a vamp. You could get an infection."

"In what? You just burnt my ass off!"

"He wants to talk to you," Pritkin said, looking grim.

I took the phone back. "What?"

"Cassie?"

Mircea wasn't accustomed to getting that tone from women, but I was too sore—in several ways—to care. "If Pritkin says it wasn't a demon, then it wasn't a demon. Goddamnit, Mircea! He ought to know!"

"And why is that, *dulceaţă*?" Mircea asked smoothly. And, okay, maybe I was going to have to revise that list. Because sometimes Mircea also used my pet name when he was being sneaky.

"He's a demon hunter," I said, forcing myself to calm down before I said anything stupid. Well, anything stupider, anyway. "It's his job to know."

"I will have my people check into all possibilities," Mircea said, and I really hoped he was talking about the entity. "In the meantime, I need your promise that you will not leave the hotel."

"Mircea, I was *attacked* at the hotel. How is staying here going to—"

"The guards will be doubled."

"You could have tripled them—you could have had a

guard per square foot—and it wouldn't have made a difference! No one could have predicted—"

"We should have predicted it," he said harshly. "We
knew there would be an attack. I simply did not expect it so
early. The coronation isn't for another ten days."

"But why wait until the last second?"

Mircea didn't say anything, but the very pregnant pause
made it clear that he didn't think that was funny.

Of course, he didn't find too much funny these days. He
was currently trying to negotiate the first worldwide alliance of vampire senates. It was what he'd been working on
all month, what he was doing in New York, where a lot of
the senators had gathered for some kind of meeting prior to
the coronation. But as formidable as his diplomatic skills
were, there was no doubt that he was up against it. The senates had had centuries to plot and scheme and piss one another off, and they'd apparently done a pretty good job of it.

And nobody holds a grudge like a master vamp.

Add to that the ongoing war and now the coronation
that was scheduled to be held at his estate, and it would
have been enough to give anyone a headache. I didn't want
to add to his problems. And what he asked was easy enough.

It wasn't like I'd be safer anyplace else.

"I'll stay put," I promised.

"Good. Then I shall see you tomorrow night."

"Tomorrow? I thought you wouldn't be back for a
week."

"That was my intention, but . . . I have obtained the information you requested." For a moment, it didn't register, because I couldn't recall asking Mircea about anything.
Except—

I suddenly sat up.

And just as suddenly regretted it. I gasped and Marco
cursed. "Hold still!" he told me, pushing me back down.
That was okay, because it gave me a chance to get my face
under control.

"About our date," Mircea's voice clarified unnecessarily.

"Oh. Right." My voice sounded normal enough, but I
felt my palm start to sweat where I clutched the phone. Because what I'd asked him for wasn't the usual dinner and a
movie. I hadn't really thought he'd be able to pull it off—or

that he'd be willing, for that matter. But Mircea never ceased to surprise.

I wanted details, wanted specifics, but I couldn't ask for them. Not with Pritkin's eyes on me from across the room. If he knew what I planned, I had no doubt at all that he'd try to stop me. And while that would probably be the smart thing, it wasn't the right thing. Not this time.

"What should I wear?" I asked, hoping that was safe.

"Classic formal attire."

"Okay. I look forward to it," I told him, and rang off.

Marco finished his little torture session a moment later and bandaged me up. I cautiously moved into a sitting position, and it still wasn't fun. But I was too distracted to really notice.

"We'll get you one of them little doughnut things," he told me, as Pritkin walked over. And, shit, his eyes were narrowed.

"So if it wasn't a ghost and it wasn't a demon, what was it?" I asked, to forestall any inconvenient questions.

To my surprise, it worked. "I have a theory, but I would prefer some confirmation."

"What theory?"

"Do you remember how we defeated it?" he asked, as I tucked the sheet around me and slid to the floor.

"I remember you threw something at me."

"It was half of a nunchuck. I've been intending to get the chain re-soldered, but haven't had time."

"Half a nunchuck?" I frowned. "Why would you give me that?" It wasn't like I could bash a spirit over the head with it.

Green eyes met mine, and they were serious enough to stop me. "Because it was the only thing I had within reach that was made of cold iron."

Chapter Four

I don't remember falling asleep, but I must have. Because the next thing I knew, I woke up to a dark, quiet room and hot, tangled sheets. My head was throbbing, my mouth was bone dry and for one brief, panic-stricken moment, I thought I was possessed again. Because nothing seemed to work.

I finally realized that I was just really, really sore. It looked like Marco's little pills had worn off, except for a thickheaded feeling that made me have to try three times to turn on the light. It didn't help that the room was like an oven. The suite was supposed to be temperature controlled, but there was obviously something seriously wrong.

After a minute sweating in already damp sheets, I gave up on sleep and rolled out of bed. I threw on a worn-out tank top that had been purple but was now a soft mauve and a pair of loose, old track shorts. Then I staggered out the door in search of aspirin and cold water.

I didn't find them.

Light from the hallway cast long shadows across the bathroom, sparkling off broken glass like so much spilled ice. The floor was still wet, and the bunched-up rug was crouched in the middle like a wounded animal. The mirrors were the worst. The right one was cracked, but the left one was obliterated, the cheap wood backing showing through in chunks, making a mockery of the expensive fixtures. Like scars on a pretty woman's face.

I suddenly realized that my hands were shaking and stuffed them under my armpits. My nice, safe bathroom didn't seem so safe anymore. Not that it ever had been, really, but it had *felt* that way.

And now it didn't.

I turned around and went down the hall.

When I flicked on the chandelier in the suite's second bathroom, the black-and-white tile reflected the light with a cool, mirror shine. Soft, luxurious towels were stacked here and there, all blindingly white. The black marble counters gleamed, and the complimentary toiletries were still in their cellophane wrappers. It was as pristine as if housekeeping had just left.

Or as if nothing had ever happened.

I relaxed slightly, washed my face and hands and then used one of the casino's toothbrushes to scrub my teeth. My reflection showed bags under my eyes, no color in my skin and a truly epic case of bed head. I poked at one of the larger clumps and found it stiff and vaguely green.

I briefly wondered what the hell Pritkin had dumped on me. And then I wondered what it would take to get it out. A bath, obviously, at least for starters.

The thought had barely crossed my mind when the first shiver hit, hard enough to make me tighten my grip on the sink. I stared at the gleaming white tub behind me, reflected in the gilt-edged mirror, and told myself I was being stupid. It was a *bathtub*; it couldn't hurt me.

But my body wasn't listening.

The shivers turned into shudders and I sat down before I fell down. I put the cabinet at my back, wrapped my arms around my knees and prepared to wait it out. At least it wasn't as hot in here. Nobody ever used this bathroom— the vamps had their own rooms and showered there, and visitors used the half bath off the living area. So nobody had bothered to put a rug down over the cool checkerboard tile.

But it wasn't helping. The door on the cabinet was moving with me, in little click-clicks as the magnet on the catch caught and released, caught and released. I finally scooted an inch or so away and it stopped, even if the shaking didn't.

I knew what this was, of course. I'd spent most of my teen years on the run from my homicidal guardian, Antonio Gallina, who had brought me up from the age of four. Clairvoyants—real ones, not the sideshow variety—didn't grow on trees, and when Tony found out that one of the humans who worked for him had a budding seer for a daughter, he just took me. After removing my parents from the picture in the most final way possible.

He thought he'd covered his tracks, but he forgot: clairvoyant. My parents died in a big orange and black fireball, courtesy of an assassin's bomb. And ten years later, I felt the wash of heat across my face, smelled the smoke, tasted the dust in my mouth.

I ran away an hour after the vision, with few preparations and no destination in mind, and it hadn't taken long before the stress had caught up with me in the form of panic attacks.

The worst one had been in a bus terminal, when I'd been sure I saw one of Tony's thugs in the crowd. I'd had a ticket, already purchased and in hand, but suddenly I couldn't remember where I was supposed to go. It gave the bus number on the ticket; I knew that. But my hands had been shaking and my eyes hadn't wanted to focus, and when I finally did manage to read it, it didn't make sense. Like the words were written in a foreign language I didn't understand.

I'd gotten lucky that time. I'd missed the bus, but I'd also missed Tony's goon—if it had been him. I never found out, but I kind of thought not. Even the not-so-bright types Tony employed could hardly have missed me, standing in the middle of the terminal, shaking like a leaf.

I hadn't had a panic attack in years; had thought I'd outgrown them.

But I guess you don't really grow out of fear.

The shaking finally lessened, my eyes slipped closed and my head tilted back against the slick wood. I was bone tired, but I knew I wouldn't sleep. Not like this. But I didn't really feel like doing anything else, either—except taking a bath, and that was obviously out.

But I really needed one. My body ached, my hair reeked

and my skin felt itchy, probably from the dried soap I hadn't had a chance to wash off. Only it didn't feel like soap. It felt like somebody was touching me, here and there, brief brushes of sandpapery fingertips as they tested my shields, as they tried to find a way *in*—

A hand touched my arm and I screamed, jumping up and hitting my head on the bottom of the counter. I tried to scramble away, but someone had me by the upper arms and I couldn't break free. I felt another scream building, a keening, desperate cry in the back of my throat, before I finally heard someone calling my name—

And looked up into Marco's startled black eyes.

I stopped struggling and just breathed for a minute. I wasn't sure who was more freaked-out—me or him. Finally, he pulled me in, tucking me under a huge arm and rubbing my head in what he probably thought was a gentle way. It felt more like it was going to take off another layer of skin, but I didn't mind.

"You okay?" he asked cautiously.

I didn't know how to answer that, because clearly not.

"Sorry about the other bathroom. We were gonna clean up, but we thought you'd sleep till morning."

I nodded but didn't look up, because I didn't have my face under control.

"You're gonna have to say something," he said after a moment. " 'Cause otherwise there's gonna be phone calls and doctors and all kinds of drama, and I think we've had about enough of that for one—"

"My butt hurts," I blurted out. It was completely inane, but it was true. It also got a chuckle out of Marco.

He'd been squatting beside me, but now he sat down, somehow wedging that huge body between the sink and the tub. He was big and hot, but felt reassuringly solid, too. It was suddenly impossible to believe that anything bad could happen with Marco around.

"You and me both," he said conversationally. "I think the master chewed most of mine off."

It took a moment for that to sink in. "He did *what*?"

Marco laughed, a deep rumbling in that barrel chest. "That's better. You've got some color in your face now."

"You were lying?" I demanded.

"No, but I like seeing you pissed off. It's cute."

I just sat there for a moment because, as usual, I felt like I needed to catch up. "You weren't lying?"

He shook his head.

"Then Mircea *did* tell you off?"

A nod.

"What on earth for?"

"For giving you drugs."

It took me a moment to realize what he meant. "Marco, you gave me *Tylenol.*"

"Yeah, but it was the kind with codeine. And it seems Pythias aren't allowed to take that shit. Or anything that leaves them too groggy to use their power. He said I left you defenseless."

"That's ridiculous! I couldn't have shifted any more tonight, anyway."

"Yeah, but that ain't the point."

"Then what is the point?"

He shrugged. "It's like I told you: vamps don't like feeling helpless. And that goes double for masters—and maybe triple for Senate members."

"That doesn't make it okay to take it out on you!"

"Maybe not, but I know where he's coming from." Marco settled back against the sink, as if prepared to stay there all night. Like he regularly counseled hysterical women in bathrooms. "He's got you in the most secure place he knows, right? I mean, the Senate's just upstairs, and they got guards and wards out the butt, plus all the extra ones on the suite here. And he's got some of his best people protecting you. Hell, he's got me."

I smiled a little at that, as I was supposed to. "So what's the problem?"

"The problem is that it don't work. Every time he turns around, somebody or something is able to get to you. And it has him scared. And he's not used to feeling scared. It's been so long, I'm not even sure he knows what it is."

"Must be nice," I muttered.

"I don't think he's finding it so nice," Marco said drily.

I didn't say anything, because there was nothing *to* say. I didn't know how to reassure Mircea; I didn't even know how to reassure myself. I was supposed to be this great clairvoyant, but I never saw anything good, just death and destruction.

I really hoped that wasn't because that was all there was to see.

"I'm teaching the new guys how to lose at poker," Marco said. "Want me to deal you in?"

I shook my head. "I suck at it."

"Even better. They could use a chance to win some back."

"So you can take that, too?"

He stood up with the liquid grace all vampires have, which was always surprising on a man of his size. "That's the plan."

"I'll take a rain check," I told him as he helped me up. But I followed him into the lounge.

Before I moved in, the suite had been used for whales, people with more money than sense who were comped expensive rooms because they lost a hundred times the price at the tables every night. This particular one had been popular because it included a small lounge area off the dining room with a pool table, which the guards had all but confiscated for themselves. They were usually there when they weren't watching me paint my toenails or something, playing pool or, like now, clustered around a card table.

Marco rejoined the poker game and I passed through into the kitchen. There was no aspirin to be had, because vamps don't get headaches. There was beer, but the way my head felt, I was already in for it tomorrow, so I left Marco's Dos Equis alone.

I wandered around a bit, because it was too hot to sleep, and found a sofa-shaped hole in the living room window that was trying to air-condition Nevada. No wonder it was hot. A couple of the guards must have heard me swearing, because they stuck their heads in the door and stared at me for a moment, their fire-lit eyes glowing against the dark.

I went out onto the balcony.

It wasn't nearly as large as the one on the penthouse upstairs, which had room for a pool, a wet bar and a dozen or so partyers. But I'd managed to squeeze in a lounge chair and a small side table, and had hung a set of wind chimes from the railing. They were tinkling now in the breeze blowing off the desert. It was hot, but marginally better than the slow roast I'd been doing inside.

We were too far up to hear traffic, so it was still eerily

quiet. But, then, it always was here. The vamps didn't need to talk aloud and often no one did for hours, unless I asked them a direct question. I didn't watch TV much, unless it was in my room, and the one time I'd turned on the radio, several of them put on such pained faces that I'd quickly turned it off.

On a good day, it felt like living in a museum, but not as a visitor. It was more like being one of the exhibits a bunch of silent guards watched in case some bandit makes off with it. Tonight it was slowly driving me crazy.

After a few minutes, I went back inside, glancing at the clock on the way. It had somehow survived the carnage, and it said nine thirty. I hadn't slept long at all, then. Technically, it was still too late to be calling anyone, but maybe—

The phone rang.

I jumped back, barely stifling a yelp, because my nerves were just that bad. And then I stared at it, hoping someone would pick up in the next room so I wouldn't have to be all cheerful. But no one did pick up. And then Marco appeared in the doorway, a longneck in one hand and five cards in the other.

"You gonna get that or what?" he asked, his tone more curious than annoyed.

I got it. "Hello?"

"What are you doing up?"

Pritkin's irritated voice made me smile and I turned away so Marco wouldn't see it. "Answering the phone."

"Very funny. Why aren't you asleep? It's after one."

I glanced at the clock again. I guess it hadn't survived, after all. "It's hot."

"It's always bloody hot here," he agreed, to my surprise. I'd never heard him complain about it, but I guessed for someone used to England's climate, Vegas in August would kind of suck. And thanks to me, his bedroom had a big hole in it, too.

"Don't you have anything cold to drink?" he demanded.

"Beer."

He snorted. "You're going to have a murderous hangover as it is. Call room service."

"I could do that," I agreed.

He waited. I didn't say anything, because I wasn't that pathetic. There was no emergency, and what was I going to tell him? I'm hot and bored and freaked-out, and I want to talk to someone with a pulse?

Yeah, that sounded mature. That sounded like a Pythia. I didn't—

"That the mage?" Marco asked impatiently, like he couldn't hear every word we uttered.

"Yeah."

"He coming over?"

"Yes," Pritkin said, surprising me again.

"Then tell him to bring beer," Marco said. "We're almost out, and the damn room service around this place sucks ass."

"He said—"

"I heard." Pritkin rang off without saying good-bye, or anything else at all. So I didn't know why I was smiling as I went to the kitchen to make sure we had enough clean glasses.

"Damn it," Marco said. "You didn't tell him what kind. He'll probably bring one of those weird English beers."

"Ale," one of the other vamps said darkly.

"Shit."

They went back to their game while I washed up. Because, apparently, master vampires would carry out garbage, but they drew the line at dishpan hands. Not that there were a lot, since most of my meals came on room service carts these days.

I finished up and went to try again to get a comb through my potion-stained curls. I was still working on it when the doorbell rang. I gave up, pulled my hair back into a limp ponytail and went into the kitchen. Pritkin was already there, unpacking a couple of brown paper grocery bags.

"Foster's," he told Marco, who was peering into one suspiciously.

The vamp looked relieved. "It's even cold."

"Why wouldn't it be?"

"I thought you Brits liked it hot."

"Hot beer?" Pritkin looked revolted.

"That's the rumor."

"Because we don't drink it iced over, thereby leaching right out whatever flavor you Yanks accidentally left in?"

"Ooh, touchy," Marco said, and swiped the beer.

I looked in the other bag, but saw only a bunch of little

boxes. I pulled one out, and it was tea. After a moment, I realized that they all were: peppermint, chamomile, green, black . . . It was like he'd bought out the store.

"You need something to calm your nerves that isn't going to knock you out," he told me.

"I don't think tea is going to cut it," I said drily. "Not with my life."

A blond eyebrow rose. "You'd be surprised."

He came up with a kettle I hadn't known we possessed and proceeded to do tea-type things with it. I took an apple out of a bowl and set it on the table. "So you think it was Fey?" I asked, because I hadn't gotten many details before I passed out.

"I don't know what it was," Pritkin said, looking like the confession pained him. "The Fey do not have a spirit form, yet your attacker was incorporeal. And you were able to give me a description—a fairly good one for so short a glimpse."

"Why does that matter?"

"It matters because if it *was* Fey, you should have seen nothing."

"You saw something," I said, concentrating. A fragile bubble closed over the fruit, no more substantial than the ones the dish soap had left in the sink. And by the look of things, no more effective.

"I have a small amount of Fey blood," Pritkin said, glancing at it. "It sometimes allows me to detect when they are near, although it isn't a reliable skill. In some instances, however, a Fey under a glamourie might look like what I saw—a dark cloud. That's why I threw the nunchucks to you." His lips twisted. "That and the fact that I was out of other ideas."

"Maybe I have a little Fey blood." I didn't really know enough about my family to know what I might have.

"You don't."

"How do you know? Can you see that, too?"

"I don't have to. If you had so much as a drop, the Fey family you belonged to could claim you. And then you wouldn't have just the Circle and the Senate fighting over you; you'd have them, as well."

He was talking about the Silver Circle, the world's leading magical association, which ruled over the human part of the supernatural community the way the Senate did the vamps. It was used to having the line of Pythias firmly under its protective thumb. That had been fairly easy, as the power of the office usually went to whomever the previous Pythia had trained, and that was always a proper little Circle-raised initiate. Or it was until me. The last heir to the Pythian throne, a sibyl named Myra, had also turned out to be a homicidal bitch, and the power had decided on another option.

The Circle had been less than thrilled by its choice, but we'd finally come to terms. As in, they were no longer trying to play Whac-A-Mole with my head. Only now they seemed to think they had the right to make sure that nobody else did, either. That was a problem, because the vampires felt the same way and the Senate didn't share well.

The last thing I needed was another group in the mix.

"I have absolutely no Fey blood," I said fervently.

"Trust me, they have checked," Pritkin told me. "And you don't. But that means you should have seen nothing."

"Okay, I get that. I saw it, so it can't be Fey. But it also wasn't demon or ghost or human or Were. So what's left?"

"That's the question." He leaned one hand on the table. "But the fact remains that it was driven off by cold iron. And only one species, to my knowledge, is so affected. Of course, it could have been a coincidence that it chose that precise moment to leave, but—"

"But that's a hell of a coincidence."

"Yes." He looked at the bubble, which was shivering as if someone were blowing on it. "What are you doing?"

The fragile shell burst, dissipating without so much as a pop. I sighed. "Nothing." Obviously.

"What were you trying to do?"

I repressed a sudden urge to pound the fruit into pulp. "Age it," I said tersely. "Jonas said Agnes could take an apple from a seed to a shriveled mass and back again, running through its whole lifetime in a few seconds."

Pritkin took in the apple, which was plump and round and perfect and had a healthy red blush. Just like all the others in the little bowl. Just like I'd never done anything at all. "You're tired."

"And I'm never going to be attacked when I'm tired."

He frowned. "Taking yourself to the brink of exhaustion is not a good idea."

"So says the man who ran me halfway around a mountain today."

"That was before we knew you have a threat that can walk through wards. You should have been safe to recuperate here."

Safe. Yeah, like I'd ever been safe anywhere. I turned around and abruptly left the kitchen.

Chapter Five

The balcony was still hot and still creepy, the latter mostly due to the sign flickering on and off overhead, not in any pattern, but like it was about to go out. It wasn't broken; the hotel had a hell theme, and the sign was supposed to do that. Sort of a Bates Motel pastiche, which was usually a little disturbing. But tonight, it fit my mood perfectly.

Pritkin followed me out. He didn't say anything, just handed me a cold Coke he'd dug up from somewhere. I guess the tea wasn't ready.

I took it without comment, feeling absurdly grateful. I didn't really want to talk. I'd wanted him here, but I wasn't sure why. Maybe just to have someone to drink with. Actually, that sounded pretty good at the moment. I sat on the seat of the chaise and he sat on the foot, and we just drank at each other for a while.

After a few minutes, he leaned back against the railing, like maybe he wanted a backrest, and I shifted my feet over to make room. But I guess I didn't shift far enough, because a large, warm hand covered my right foot, adjusting it slightly. And then it just stayed there, like he'd forgotten to remove it.

I looked at it. Pritkin's hands were oddly refined compared to the rest of him: strong but long fingered, with elegant bones and short-clipped nails. They always looked like they'd wandered off from some fine gentleman, one they'd probably like to get back to, because God knew they weren't getting a manicure while attached to him.

There were potion stains on them tonight, green and brown, probably from the earlier encounter. I wondered if they'd wash off skin faster than hair. Probably.

I laid my head back against the plastic slats and looked up at the horror-movie sign. A breeze blew over the balcony, setting the wind chimes tinkling faintly. It was still hot, but I found I didn't mind so much.

"Are you going to tell me what's wrong?" he finally asked.

"How do you know anything is?"

He shot me a look. "You're up at one a.m. after a day that would have put most marines down for the count. You're pale and restless. And something unknown tried to kill you a few hours ago and almost succeeded. Have I missed anything?"

Actually, yes, he had, but I didn't want to talk about it.

I rolled the can around in my palms, trying to cool off, which might have worked if it hadn't already gotten warm. I put it down, but then I didn't have anything to do with my hands. And that wasn't good, because any minute now, they were going to start shaking again.

I picked up a battered old tarot deck off a side table. "I'm fine," I told him tersely.

"Of course you are. You're one of the strongest people I know."

It took me a second to process that, because he'd said it so casually. Like he was talking about the weather or what time it was. Only Pritkin didn't say things like that. His idea of a compliment was a nod and to tell me to do whatever it was I'd just done over again. Like that was usually possible.

But that had sounded suspiciously like a compliment to me.

God, I must look bad.

I flipped the deck for a while. It was old and faintly greasy, but it felt good in my hand. It felt right.

Pritkin looked a question at me. "It's . . . sort of a nervous habit," I told him.

He held out a hand, and I passed the cards over. He

turned the pack around a few times, concentrating. "It carries an enchantment."

"A friend had it done for me as a birthday present, a long time ago. It's . . . a little eccentric."

"Eccentric?"

I took the deck back. I didn't try to do a spread—that was just asking for trouble. I merely opened the top and a card popped out—thankfully, only one. Otherwise, they tried to talk over each other.

"The Moon reversed," a sweet, soothing voice told me, before I shoved it back into the pack.

"Was that . . . it?" Pritkin asked, looking a bit nonplussed.

"It doesn't do regular readings," I explained. "It's more like . . . like a magical weather vane. It gives the general climate for the coming days or weeks."

"And what kind of weather can we be expecting?"

"The Moon reversed indicates a pattern or a cycle that is about to repeat itself."

"A good cycle?"

"If it was, I sure as hell wouldn't see it," I muttered.

That got me a cocked eyebrow.

"I don't see the good stuff," I explained briefly. "Anyway, the cards can be read a number of different ways. But normally the Moon reversed points to a dark time, like the dark side of the moon, you know?"

"How dark?"

"That depends. From a personal standpoint, it often indicates a time of deep feelings, confusion, long-buried emotions coming to the surface—"

"And from a larger perspective? A national perspective?"

"People with dark purposes, order moving into chaos, wars, revolutions, riots."

"Fairly dark, then," he said drily.

"Usually," I admitted, before adding the standard disclaimer. "But tarot is an indicator, not an absolute. Nothing about the future is decided until it happens. We create it every day by the choices we make, good or bad."

Pritkin's lips twisted cynically. "But so does everyone else. And not all of them are striving for the same things, are they?"

"No," I said, thinking of the war. I picked up my Coke and took a sip before remembering that warm Coke tastes like battery acid. I set it down again.

"There's a calendar on the fridge," I commented, after a while.

Pritkin didn't say anything.

"I don't know how they got it to stay up there. I mean, it's stainless. Nothing sticks to that stuff."

He drank beer.

"But it's there. And I see it every day. Right after I get up, I go get a Coke or whatever, and it's—" I licked my lips.

"The coronation." It wasn't a question.

"Yeah."

Sort of. In fact, it was a lot of things: problems learning about my power, the refusal of the Senate or the Circle to take me seriously, the lack of any useful visions about the war and now the fact that someone was trying to kill me. Again.

But the coronation would do. It had become a symbol for everything, the whole damn mess coming to a head, the fast-approaching day when I, Cassie Palmer, would be presented as the seer of seers to the supernatural world. Which would probably take one look and laugh their collective asses off.

Not that I blamed them. Two months ago—a little less, actually—I'd been a secretary in a travel agency. I'd answered phones. I'd filed stuff. I'd picked up the boss's freaking dry cleaning.

On my days off, I worked as a tarot reader, because a couple of bucks an hour over minimum wage doesn't pay the bills. Only that hadn't paid them all that well, either, because people didn't like my readings. Nobody really wanted to know the future; they wanted reassurance, hope, a reason to get up in the morning. At the time, I hadn't understood that; I'd thought forewarned was forearmed.

Now I understood why I hadn't had too many repeat customers. Now I'd have liked a little reassurance myself, even if it was a lie. And I really, really didn't want to see tomorrow.

Ironic that it was my job now.

"It's a formality," Pritkin said firmly, watching my face. "You've been Pythia since your predecessor's passing."

"Technically. But I haven't really had to do anything yet, have I?"

He frowned. "You haven't had to *do* anything?"

"Well, you know. Nothing important."

"You killed a god!"

I rolled my eyes. "You make it sound like I dueled him or something. When you know damn well we flushed him down a metaphysical toilet."

Pritkin shrugged. "Dead is dead."

He tended to be practical about these things.

Of course, so did I when the creature in question planned a literal scorched-earth policy, starting with me. But that wasn't the point. "I just meant that no one's expected me to do anything as Pythia," I explained. "But the coronation is coming up, and you know as soon as it's over . . . and I can't even age a damn apple!"

I started to get up, but that hand tightened on my foot. I wanted to pace, needed to let off some of the nervous energy that kept me from eating half the time, kept me from sleeping. And just when I told myself I was being paranoid and everything would be fine, something tried to drown me in the goddamned bathtub.

But I didn't get up. Because then I'd lose that brief, human connection. A connection that shouldn't have been there, because Pritkin wasn't the touchy-feely type. He touched me in training, when he had to, and grabbed me in the middle of crises. But I actually couldn't recall him ever touching me just . . . because.

I sat back again. The damn balcony wasn't big enough for pacing, anyway.

"And yet, from what Jonas tells me, you shift with more alacrity than Lady Phemonoe ever did," he said, using Agnes's reign title. "And the power is the power. If you can use it for one application, it would seem logical—"

"Yeah, except it doesn't work that way. At least not for me."

"It's only been a month, whereas most heirs—"

"Train for years. And that's just *it*. I don't feel like I'll ever catch up. And even if I do, nobody is going to listen to me!"

"And why not? You're Pythia."

"No, I'm some kind of . . . of trophy to be fought over. At

least that's how I'm treated. So if I do get a flash of something, something useful, something important, who the hell is going to pay attention?"

"The opposition, apparently. They seem to insist on paying you a great deal of attention."

"I've noticed."

"And you don't find that strange? If you're so powerless?"

I shrugged. "I'm still Pythia. Killing me would—"

"Would what?" he demanded. "Say they had succeeded tonight. What would it have gained them? When the power leaves you at your death, it simply goes to another host, probably one of the Initiates. There's no gain for the opposition there; in fact, they might have reason to view it as a loss. For the moment, the Initiates are probably better trained."

"Thanks," I said, even though it was true.

"Then the question remains: why you?" he asked, leaning forward with that sense of pleased urgency he always got when debating. I tried not to take it personally; Pritkin just liked to argue. "Why are they still concentrating on you?"

"Why have they been for the last two months?" I countered. "Apollo—"

"Was focused on you, yes. But only because he had to be. He wanted to use your pentagram ward as a direct line to your power. It was the one thing that would allow him to break through the barrier and exact revenge on those who had banished him."

I unconsciously rolled my shoulders, stretching the skin between the blades, where my ward had sat ever since my mother put it on me as a child. The big, saucer-shaped thing had never been pretty, and had somehow ended up lopsided and droopy, like something a tattoo artist had done after a late-night bender. But it had felt like a part of me.

It didn't now. Ever since Apollo's attempt to find a way back into the world his kind had once misruled, everyone had been freaked out about it. They were afraid I might be captured with it on my body, allowing our enemies to use it to drain my power. So it remained in a velvet case on my dressing table, like a discarded piece of jewelry.

I'd thought I'd get used to its absence after a while, the way you get used to a tooth that's been pulled. But so far, that hadn't happened. It was funny; I'd never been able to feel the ward, which had no more weight than the tattoo it resembled. But I could feel its absence, could trace the path where the lines ought to have been, like a brand on my skin.

"But that also didn't work," I said, because Pritkin was waiting for a response.

"Which is my point. His allies have to know that we wouldn't put the ward back on you. You're safer without a direct conduit to your power plastered on your back. And yet they remain focused on you, despite having a thousand other targets."

"A thousand other targets who didn't just help to kill their buddy," I pointed out. "This could be about revenge."

"If they knew about the role you played, yes. But how would they? The Circle contained any mention of the aborted invasion in the press, to avoid a general panic. And no one was there at the end but us."

"There was Sal," I reminded him. She'd been a friend—or so I'd thought—who had chosen the wrong side. Or been ordered onto it by Tony, my old guardian, who also happened to be her master. It had cost her her life and given me one more reason to hate the son of a bitch.

Like I'd needed another one.

"Yes, but she was dead before Apollo was," Pritkin reminded me. "She couldn't have told anyone anything. Of course, by now, his associates must have realized that he was defeated, but there is no way for them to know that you were the cause."

I shook my head. Pritkin knew a lot about a lot of things, but his understanding of vampires was . . . pretty bad, actually. He'd picked up a few things from hanging out with me, but the gaps in his knowledge still showed once in a while. Like now.

"Sal was a master vamp," I told him. "Not a very strong one, but still. It carries certain privileges—like mental communication. I don't know if she could contact Tony all the way in Faerie, but she might have told someone else—"

"Say she did. Or that they otherwise learned or guessed.

If we presume revenge as a motive, why now? They've had all month."

"The coronation is coming up—"

"And if they wished to send a message, they would have waited to attack during the ceremony itself. Not now, not here, where there was no one to see. Where, even if they were successful, it could be passed off as a tragic accident, not a victory for the other side."

I crossed my arms. "Okay. What's your theory?"

"That this might not have to do with the war at all. That it could be personal."

I didn't have to ask what he meant. I'd had the same thought as soon as I heard the word "Fey." Because in addition to all the people on the other side in the war—the Black Circle of dark mages, a bunch of rogue vampires and whomever the god had been buddies with—I'd also managed to make an enemy out of the Dark Fey king.

I'm just special like that.

"But there's no way to know for certain," he said, "not without more information. Which is why I need permission to go away for a day, perhaps two."

There were several things wrong with that sentence, but I latched on to the most pressing one first. "You're going away *now*?"

"I don't have a choice," he told me, searching in his coat for something. "I've already called my contacts here, but given the limited description we have, they wouldn't even venture a guess as to what we're dealing with."

"If you've already contacted them, then why do you—" I stopped, a really nasty idea surfacing. "You're not going back there!"

"That is exactly what I am doing. Cassie." He caught my wrist as I started to rise. "It will be all right."

"That's— Do you *remember* last time?" I asked incredulously.

Mac, one of Pritkin's friends, had died defending me on the one and only time I'd ventured into the land of the Fey. Pritkin, myself and Francoise, a human woman who had been stuck there for years, had barely escaped with our lives—and only after I'd promised the Fey more than I could deliver.

"We made a deal," I whispered furiously. "If you go

back, they're going to expect you to honor it. And you know we can't—"

"I'm not going to court. I'm merely slipping in to speak with some old contacts."

"And if they catch you?"

"They won't."

"But if they do?"

"Listen to me. The ability to possess someone is a rare talent, even among the spirit world, and few manage it so easily. This thing, whatever it is, must be very powerful."

"Yes, but—"

"If I don't know what it is, I cannot fight it. Neither can you." He pressed something into my hand. "But this may help."

I looked down at a small, gathered bag made out of linen. It had a red thread wrapped around the top, with enough length to allow it to be used as a necklace. Only nobody would bother, because the thing reeked like old Limburger.

"A protective charm," Pritkin said unnecessarily, because I'd worn something like it once before. Only I didn't recall it being much help the only time I'd run up against the Fey.

I didn't recall anything being much help.

"If this creature is so powerful, you think this will stop it?" I demanded.

"No. But it will buy you time. Seconds only, but that is all you need to shift away. Keep your servant on watch when you sleep; when you're awake, keep your shields up at all times. You'll know if an attack comes. If it does, shift immediately—spatially, temporally, I don't care. Just get out. It cannot hurt you—"

"If it can't find me," I finished dully.

"I'll be back as soon as I can manage it. And then we'll formulate a plan for killing this thing."

I stared at the little sachet, talisman, whatever it was in my hand. It felt heavy, like there might be something made of iron in there. And faintly greasy, as if some of the contents were sweating through the material. Or maybe that was my palm.

"And if I order you to stay?" I asked, after a few moments.

Pritkin didn't say anything. I looked up but I couldn't see him very well. He'd leaned forward, out of the sign's bloody light, and only a little filtered in from the lounge. But when he finally answered, his voice was calm.

"I would stay. And protect you as best I can."

And possibly get killed in the process, because he didn't know what he was fighting. It wasn't said aloud, but it didn't need to be. I'd felt that thing go after him. I might have been the chief target, but he'd been on the list somewhere, too.

And that wasn't acceptable.

But neither was the alternative. I hugged my arms around myself and stared out at the night without seeing it. I was seeing another face instead, the cheerful, scruffy, laughing face of another war mage, one who hadn't come back. One who would never come back.

I didn't realize Pritkin had moved until he crouched in front of me. Green eyes, almost translucent in the darkness, met mine. "I wouldn't be going if I didn't think you would be all right," he told me. "It is doubtful that this thing will try the same approach again, now that it knows—"

"I'm not worried about me," I whispered viciously. And as soon as I said it, I knew it was the truth. Apparently, the surefire antidote for your own fear is concern for someone else.

Pritkin looked surprised, the way he always did at the idea that anyone might actually care about him. It made me want to hit him. Of course, right then I wanted to do that anyway.

"Nothing is going to happen," he repeated. "But even if it did, you don't need me. You don't need—"

"That isn't true!"

"Yes, it is." He looked at me and his lips quirked. "You can't fire a gun worth a damn. You hit like a girl. Your knowledge of magic is rudimentary at best. And you act like I'm torturing you if I make you run more than a mile."

I blinked at him.

"But I've known war mages who aren't as resilient, who aren't as brave, who aren't—" he looked away for a moment. And then he looked back at me, green eyes burning. "You're the strongest person I know. And *you will be fine*."

I nodded, because it sounded like an order. And because, all of a sudden, I believed it. And because right then I couldn't have said anything anyway.

We stayed like that for a moment, until Pritkin stood up, as if something had been decided. And I guess it had.

I got up and walked him to the door.

"You never told me what you're going to do," he said, pausing on the threshold.

"About what?"

"The bloody heat."

The question surprised me, because for a while, I'd forgotten all about it. Like the sweat trickling down my back, and the soap scale drying on my skin.

You're the strongest person I know.

I looked up at him. "I thought maybe . . . I'd go take a bath."

Chapter Six

"Ze Fey?" Francoise looked doubtful.

"That's one theory," I said, as yet another guy elbowed me in the ribs.

It was the next afternoon. Mircea was in New York, doing important stuff for the Senate. Pritkin was in Faerie, risking his life to find information. And where was I?

I was shopping.

But at least I wasn't enjoying it.

I glared at the rude guy, but I don't even think he noticed. I was in baggy jeans and a sweatshirt to cover the bruises, with my green curls in a ragged ponytail. I hadn't bothered to put on makeup when I got up this morning, so the dark circles under my eyes and the bruise along my cheekbone were perfectly visible.

Of course, on my best day, I couldn't compete with Francoise, who was tall, dark, lovely and very, very French. And at the moment, she was also almost naked, which explained why I was having a hard time getting close enough to ask her anything.

Francoise had recently taken a job as a sales clerk for the designer she occasionally modeled for. His posh shop was the crown jewel of the hotel's main drag, mainly because he had refused to go along with the Wild West–meets-hell theme the rest of the place had going on. Augustine was better than that.

But he wasn't too good to dress his models like strippers to lure in additional customers. Francoise and the three other sylphlike beauties currently on the clock were modeling his latest creation, which as far as I could tell wasn't a dress at all. It was more like an eighteen-inch-wide satin ribbon—red, in her case—that wrapped around the body and ended in a flourish behind the head.

It was obviously magicked to cover strategic areas, because no matter how much she turned and twisted, getting down items from the shelves behind her for the salivating horde of customers, she never flashed anyone. But the guys were clearly living in hope. And while they did, they bought things from the tacky tourist line Augustine made fun of, but never actually got around to deleting.

I browsed through the T-shirts and found one that showed a frazzled-looking 'toon with bulging eyes. The caption read "There's too much blood in my caffeine system." I bought it for Pritkin, knowing he'd probably never wear it, just to see his face.

Assuming I saw his face again. Assuming—

I snatched the shirt off the rack and told myself to stop being an idiot. If ever there was a guy who could take care of himself, he was Pritkin. And he knew Faerie better than most. He'd be fine.

He'd be fine, or I'd kill him.

"When you get a chance, I could use some help," I told Francoise, as she handed back my credit card.

"Some 'elp?"

"I need to talk to you. And I need a dress."

She shot me a look. "You 'ave a dress. Or you would, if you evair came for a fitting. Each day you do not, you make him more of a . . ." She waved a hand to indicate an English word that wouldn't come to her. *"Salaud."*

"Asshole?" I guessed.

"Zat, too."

We were talking about Augustine, and the dress he was supposedly designing for my inauguration. I say "supposedly," because I'd never seen it. Nor had I been given a sketch, a mock-up or even a description. The ceremony was a little over a week away, and all I'd seen of my outfit so far was a bunch of brown paper, the kind patterns are made of.

Considering my past history with Augustine, it was mak-

ing me very nervous. I was going to have to stand up in
front of the leaders of the magical world with no pedigree,
little training and few skills. I couldn't afford to look crappy,
too.

"I'm boycotting until I get some details," I told her.

"You 'aven't seen eet?" Francoise looked puzzled.

"No."

" 'Ave you asked?"

"Of course. But he won't show it to me. He says I
wouldn't understand the artistic process, or something.
Anyway, I'm afraid if he gets a chance to fit the damn thing,
they'll make me wear it, no matter what it looks like—"

"Augustine is a good designer," she protested.

"And he hates me. You know he does."

Francoise didn't argue. She just pursed her lips and
rolled her eyes, and because she was French, actually made
it sexy. A nearby guy groaned.

"If you saw eet, you might change your mind," she told
me.

"I might. Can you ask him for me?"

"I do not sink zat would do any good," Francoise said,
looking thoughtful. " 'E is very strict wiz his designs."

"But?" I said, because there'd clearly been one in her
tone.

"But 'e is on lunch at ze moment...."

"And?"

She pulled something out of a drawer and dangled it off
one finger. "And I 'ave his keys."

She waved one of the other girls over to cover for her,
and in less than a minute, we were past the back counter
and into the fitting area, where I had to stop to deal with
my shadows. The two golden-eyed vamps had been loitering nearby all morning, pretending to be part of the scen-
ery. They weren't doing it particularly well. Everybody else
was in shorts and T-shirts, in respect for the 120-plus-degree
heat wave outside, while they were impersonating the Men
in Black.

Still, we had a truce; I pretended I didn't notice them,
and they didn't crowd me too closely. But enough was
enough. "Out," I told them abruptly.

"We have to do a check first."

"Then do it and leave."

"Why?" One of them demanded. He was one of the new guys and I didn't know his name. "What are you planning to do in here?"

I blinked at him. "It's a dressing room. What do you think I'm planning to do?"

"That doesn't explain why we have to go."

"Because I might be trying on some clothes."

"And?"

"And I might have to get naked!"

He just looked at me for a moment. "You are aware that we've seen it, right?"

"OUT!"

As soon as they'd left, Francoise unlocked the door to Augustine's workroom and we scurried inside. It was a lot like the man himself, a flamboyant sprawl of creative excess, which in this case involved bolts of expensive fabric, bins of precious trims, heaps of glossy furs, and assorted sparkly things. There were tables holding materials, whiteboards covered with sketches and some half-assembled mannequins looking like war victims in the corner.

But I didn't see any sewing machines or other nonfabulous equipment. Only a couple of tomato-shaped pin cushions that buzzed around our heads as soon as we entered. Like they knew we weren't supposed to be there.

Francoise waved them away and they floated over to the back wall, where they huddled together ominously. Then she pulled back a curtain, and I promptly forgot about them and the vamps and even my aching body. Because Augustine was a bastard, but he was a brilliant bastard.

"Ze spring line," Francoise said with a flourish worthy of a TV spokesmodel.

I didn't say anything, because my mouth was busy hanging open. Okay, I decided, maybe I'd misjudged the guy. Because obviously he'd been busy.

I recognized some of his staples: a nude sheath dress with black lace fans embroidered on it that opened and closed every few seconds; a bunch of kicky little origami dresses that constantly reworked themselves into new shapes; and a selection of jeweled columns of what looked like liquid ruby, sapphire and diamond, the last so bright it was hard to look at.

But the real story this season was obviously the seasons themselves.

A nearby pale blue gown was printed with a swirl of autumn leaves—russet, gold and rich, earthen brown. But the leaves didn't just move; they also didn't see any need to actually stay on the fabric. They tumbled down the garment and spilled out into the air, swirling around the dress in one last, brief, ecstatic dance before finally vanishing.

The same was true for a shimmering white gown that shed glistening snowflakes whenever I touched it, and a grass green one with sleeves formed of hundreds of fluttering butterflies. But the real showstopper was a pale pink kimono with a Japanese landscape hand painted onto the silk.

Francoise had been watching me with an amused tilt to her red lips. " 'E is good, no?"

"He is good, yes," I breathed, as the kimono shimmered seductively under the lights.

It would have been beautiful on its own, but the scene had been magicked to change as I watched. Snow melted from the bare branches of a tree, which sprouted leaves, and then delicate pink and white blossoms. They hung there, trembling, until blown off the surface of the dress by a summer's breeze.

But unlike the images on the other dresses, these didn't almost immediately disappear. They hung in the air for a long moment, creating a sort of train effect that gradually vanished maybe three feet behind the dress. And when I caught one on my hand, I swear it was petal soft, with weight and substance, before it melted away into nothingness.

"Zees is one of ze special orders for ze ceremony," Francoise said, reaching up to flip over a little card affixed to the hanger.

"Is it . . . is it mine?" I asked, fervently promising every deity I could think of unswerving devotion if only it said my name. I could look like a Pythia in that dress. I could take on the world in that dress.

"*Non,*" Francoise said, squinting at the card.

"Whose is it?" I asked, breathing a little harder. And wondering whether said individual might be open to bribery. There was still a week and a half to the big day. Maybe Augustine could make another dress for whomever—

"Ming-duh," Francoise read, scrunching up her face. "Or 'owevair you say eet."

"What?" I snatched the little card and stared at it, hoping she'd just mangled the pronunciation. But no. The card bore the name of the leader of the East Asian Vampire Court.

Goddamnit.

"But ... but she's Chinese," I protested. "Why would she want a kimono?"

Francoise gave a Gallic shrug. "You wanted it," she pointed out. "And she ees also ze head of ze Japanese vampires, is she not? Perhaps eet is—'ow you say?— diplomacy."

I looked at the dress, which had cycled back to the winter stage again. It was no less lovely, despite the relative bleakness. The black branches were a beautiful contrast to the shell-pink silk, and on the one slashing across the skirt, a bluebird had paused to delicately preen its feathers.

It was achingly, desperately beautiful, and there was no way, no way at all, that anything I wore was going to compete. That wouldn't have bothered me quite so much if it had been going to someone else. But Ming-de wasn't just one of the world's most powerful vampires. She was also one of the women I strongly suspected of having been among Mircea's lovers.

And if that wasn't bad enough, she was also an arresting, delicate porcelain doll of a woman. Even in her normal clothes, she made my five-foot-four frame look Amazonian and cloddish, and my reddish blond coloring look washed-out and common. And in this—

Okay, it was official. My life *sucked*.

Francoise noticed my expression and frowned. "We 'aven't seen your dress yet," she pointed out. "It may be even better."

I shook my head. "It won't be."

"You don't know zat," she said impatiently, sorting through the other gowns and sending a cloud of multicolored magic into the air.

There were a lot of them—it looked like business was booming—and I didn't know when Augustine might be back from lunch. I plowed in to help her. "I came by for a couple of reasons," I said, as we furiously flipped tags.

"Vraiment? Qu'est-ce que tu veux?"

I explained about the night's events. "I wanted to ask about what Pritkin said," I finished. "You were in Faerie a while, right?"

"Too long," she said darkly.

I hesitated, not wanting to poke at old wounds, because Francoise's trip to the land of the Fey hadn't been by choice. One of the things the old legends got right was the Fey's poor reproductive record, which you'd think wouldn't matter so much to beings who lived as long as they did. But apparently that wasn't the case, because they had no compunction at all about kidnapping anyone they thought might be able to give them a little help.

But Francoise didn't change the subject. "I only saw a leetle of ze Light Fey lands before I escaped," she told me. "But I 'ave 'eard about zem. And I know ze Dark Fey court well. And nevair do I hear of any Fey who does ze possession."

"Neither have I," I admitted. "I always thought they were flesh and blood, like us. Well, more or less."

"Zey are. And zere are no spirits in zeir world, and no ghosts. So 'ow could zey possess?"

"I don't know. But Pritkin seemed pretty adamant."

"Qu'est-ce que c'est 'adamant'?"

"Sure. He was pretty sure."

"Adamant," she rolled it over her tongue thoughtfully. "I like zees word. Eet ees fun to say, no?"

"I suppose." I paused to take a look at a crimson silk evening dress that was doing something strange—just hanging on the rack. I poked it, but nothing flew up or off or morphed into anything else. Either Augustine hadn't gotten around to fiddling with it yet, or it was designed for his nonmagic customers.

It was pretty and fairly classic, with a low-cut top that ended in a little jeweled belt and a flouncy hem. I put it to the side. "So you never heard any stories, legends, anything like that, about the Fey being able to possess anyone?" I asked.

"*Non.* I am adamant." She looked pleased with herself. "What did Pritkin say?"

"Not a lot. Just that he thought it might be Fey."

"I do not sink so," she said, and frowned. We'd come to

the end of the rack and hadn't found a little white tag with my name on it.

"Maybe he hasn't started mine yet?" I wondered.

"*Non.* 'E 'as been working on ze enchantment for weeks. Eet is all he talks about."

Her bright red nails drummed on a tabletop for a moment, and then she looked up and smiled. "Of course. 'E must still 'ave it in back."

"I thought this *was* the back."

She shook her head. "'Is private workroom is through zere." She nodded at a small door I hadn't noticed, over by the hovering pincushions.

"Well, let's go." I started forward, only to have her put a hand on my arm.

"You can't. No one ees allowed in zere, ozzair than ze employees."

"But he won't know."

"Eet ees warded. 'E will know. And zose things, zey launch pins," she said, nodding at the Tomatoes of Doom.

"Then how—"

"I weel go and bring it out."

I nodded and folded my hands behind my back to keep them from shaking. I didn't know why I was so nervous. Okay, I did. Because this whole thing had gotten entirely out of hand.

Normally, the ceremony installing a new Pythia was no big deal. The guests typically included a handful of dignitaries from the major groups in the supernatural community: vamps, Weres and the Silver Circle. It generally took the form of a short meet and greet, sometimes followed by dinner. Last time, there'd been a brief photo op. And that was it.

Fast forward to today.

Last time I'd seen the guest list, it had almost two thousand names on it. That included the elite of the vampire world, who suddenly had a renewed interest in the Pythia, since I was the first in anyone's memory who was not a Circle-raised Initiate. It also helped that I was dating—or married to, in their eyes—one of the senior members of the North American Vampire Senate.

Add that to the war, which had everyone more than usually worried about politics, and the fact that I was currently the darling of the magical tabloids, and suddenly the simple little ceremony was the hottest ticket in town. To make matters even more fun, someone had decided that it might help morale to broadcast the damn thing live. So in addition to however many people they finally managed to squeeze onto Mircea's estate, at least half the magical community was expected to tune in via a simple spell.

I really, really wanted to call in sick. But since that wasn't possible, I at least needed to look the part. For once in my life, I really needed to look good.

It suddenly occurred to me that Francoise had been gone a long time. A long, long time. I was actually starting to get worried when she finally reappeared, looking a little pale.

"What is it?"

"I . . . I don't sink Augustine 'as started eet yet," she told me.

I frowned. "But you just said—"

"I know what I said! But . . . but 'e must be behind." She started to close the door, but I got a foot in it. The tomatoes dipped menacingly lower.

"Let me see."

She shook her head. *"Non, Cassie. Vraiment—"*

"Let me *see*."

"You don't want to see."

"How bad can it be?"

She just looked at me, her dark eyes huge. "I was wrong. 'E 'ates you."

"Francoise, *move*!" I pushed past her, ignoring the kamikaze pincushions and the static tingle of a ward. And there it was, in solitary splendor on a dressmaker's form in the center of the room.

For a moment, I just stared, not sure what I was seeing. Because it didn't look like a dress. It looked like a bunch of wire hangers that had had a drunken binge with a load of paper bags. Cheap paper bags. The brown kind they give you at the grocery store that have been recycled a couple dozen times. It wasn't just hideous; it was sad. A sad, brown-paper-bag dress with what looked like—

"Uh," Francoise said faintly.

I didn't say anything. I narrowed my eyes and moved closer. And saw a banana peel masquerading as a shoulder pad, a line of bottle caps on a string for a necklace and a hollowed-out tin can as a belt buckle. There were coffee grounds on the shoulder and red wine on the hip and what looked like a desiccated mouse pinned to the bodice. The whole thing looked like it had taken a roll through a Dumpster before—

And then I got it, and speechless became furious.

"Okay," I said, my voice trembling slightly. "So I trashed one of his dresses—all right, a couple—in the line of duty and through no fault of my own. So he makes me a trash heap of a dress? *Is that what this is?*"

Francoise just looked at me, a terrible kind of pity on her face. "Zere is a card."

And there was, attached to the dress form above the desiccated rat. I yanked it off and stared at it.

I thought I would save you some time on this one. You'll get the real dress when it's finished, and not a second before. And get out of my workroom.—A

I said some creative things about the creative genius, until I ran out. "Eet is not nice," Francoise agreed. "But what can you do?"

For a moment I just stood there, contemplating Augustine's face if I showed up wearing another designer's creation. But I didn't know any other designers, any magical ones, at least, and it wasn't like I could just go out looking for them. And, frankly, I doubted anyone else would stand up to the competition I would be facing.

I needed a dress, and I needed a good one. Fortunately, I was surrounded by them. "How long until he gets back?" I asked quickly.

Francoise's eyes narrowed. "Why?"

"Because I feel like doing some shopping."

Chapter Seven

"That's more like it," Marco said approvingly, as I staggered through the door of the suite half an hour later.

"I thought they were supposed to help," I gasped, nodding my head at my shadows. It was the only thing I *could* move, since every other appendage was laden with bags, boxes and packages.

"Need our hands free for weapons," one of them said blandly.

"*Both* of you?"

"You have a lot of enemies."

"I have a lot of pulled muscles now, too!" I snapped, lurching into the living room.

"That mage is here," Marco warned me.

"Pritkin?" I asked, my head coming up.

"Naw. That old one. And some slick-haired guy."

I didn't know who Slick Hair was, but That Old One was Jonas Marsden, acting head of the Silver Circle. Of course, Marco knew that perfectly well, but the vamps were never happy whenever a mage showed up. And that went double for their leader.

Jonas rose to help me after I stumbled into the lounge, and I shot Marco a look. That got a kiss blown in my general direction and a promise to be right outside aimed at the mages. In case they intended to use some nefarious wizard trickery to make off with me or something.

"Sorry I wasn't here, but I thought we weren't meeting until three," I panted.

"No matter. I should have called," Jonas said genially. "But I did want to talk to you, if you have a moment."

"About last night?"

"Oh, I do truly hope not," he said, which would have sounded odd coming from anyone else. But Jonas was always odd.

For one, he was the only person I knew with hair worse than Pritkin's. It was extra poufy today, a magnificent silver-white ball of static electricity that appeared to have a life of its own. Like some alien creature had happened to light on his head and decided to stay a while. In contrast, his face was surprisingly normal, with pleasant features, rosy cheeks and fewer lines than one would expect for his age, whatever that was. Jonas usually just described it as "damned old."

"And Niall did so want to meet you," he added, as I stumbled toward the bedroom.

"Niall?"

"Niall Edwards." A sharp-faced brunet with slicked-back hair came forward, and I managed to get a hand out. But either he didn't see or he ignored it. "Have you thought about losing five to ten?" he asked, circling me.

I turned, trying to keep him in my field of vision, and dropped a heavy shoe box on my foot. "Five to ten what?" I asked, wincing.

"Pounds. The camera adds at least that much and, frankly, you could use some more definition in your face."

"I—what?"

He pulled out a computerized notepad. "What do you weigh?"

"That's none of your business!"

"It is if I have to sell the idea of you as Pythia to the masses," he said sourly, his fingers flying over the keys.

"Niall is our leading public relations expert," Jonas explained, as I limped into the bedroom and tossed the packages on the bed.

"I don't need a PR person," I said, sitting down to examine my toe.

"Oh, of course not," Slick said, following me in. "You were brought up by a vampire mob boss, you go around looking like a cross between Paris Hilton and a homeless person—"

"I do not look like Paris Hilton!"

"You're wearing sparkly pink nail polish," he pointed out. "On your toes."

I looked down at the offending digits, which were sticking out of a pair of sandals. "I don't see anything wrong with—"

"Exactly. And if that weren't bad enough, you're suspected of being a dark mage. But you don't need PR."

"I'm only suspected of being a dark mage because you people told everyone I was!" I said furiously.

Until recently, the Circle had been headed by a mage named Saunders, who had been cooking the books in favor of himself and his buddies. And he hadn't wanted a Pythia in place who wasn't firmly under his thumb, in case she outed his little moneymaking scheme. So while his operatives were busy trying to hunt me down, he was planting nasty stories in the press about my family background.

It didn't help that most of them were true.

"And we did our usual good job," Slick said proudly. "Everyone now knows that your mother was a ruined Initiate, your father was a dangerous dark mage and that you yourself have received absolutely no training for the position you hold."

"I wouldn't say *no* training," Jonas demurred.

"It will be the triumph of my career to bring you back from that. But I will. Make no mistake."

He disappeared into the walk-in closet, leaving me staring at Jonas. "You have got to be kidding."

"Niall is a bit abrupt, I grant you—"

"A bit?"

"But he does have a point, Cassie. Your public image"— Jonas shook his head, causing the alien hair to waft about luxuriously—"it would be difficult to imagine how it could be worse, you know."

"Then why haven't you guys worried about it before?"

"Because we were waiting for things to cool down," Niall told me, emerging with a heap of my clothes. "The public has a very short attention span and they forget details easily. Trying to eradicate or even amend their impression of you right after the story broke would have been impossible. Now it's merely impractical." He threw my clothes out the door.

"Hey!"

"Considering the damage, I would prefer another fortnight to pass, at the very least, before the ceremony," he said, going back for another load of my belongings. "But I was told that we were at war and it couldn't wait."

"I just bought that!" I said, snatching an off-white slip dress out of his hand.

"For what?" he demanded.

"If you must know, I have a date tonight!"

"Really?" Jonas looked delighted. "May I ask with whom?"

"Mircea," I said, only to see his face fall.

"Ah."

"What does that mean?"

"Nothing, nothing. None of my business, after all."

"Well, it is *my* business!" Slick said. "We can't afford any more bad press. Such as you being seen with a vampire, particularly dressed like that!"

I looked down at the dress. It had a draped front and little spaghetti straps, but no sparkles, sequins or any decoration at all. Unless you counted what looked like the vague outline of tree branches that swayed across the silk, like shadows on a wall. It was beautiful and tasteful and one of my favorite purchases.

"And just what is wrong with this?" I demanded.

"On the hanger? Nothing. On you?" Slick looked me up and down and shook his head.

"What the hell does that mean?"

"Two words: 'foundation garment,'" he said, and snatched it back.

"There are such things as strapless bras, you know!" I told him furiously.

"And do you own one?"

"That's also none of your—"

"That would be a no, then," he said, and swept out.

I was about to chase him down and possibly beat him to death with a shoe—assuming he'd left me one—when Jonas piped up. "Of course, there are those who will agree with Niall," he said diffidently.

I narrowed my eyes. "What is this?"

He took off his thick glasses and polished them on an already rumpled sleeve. Maybe they really were dirty, but it looked like a stalling tactic. Like he knew I wasn't going to like whatever he'd come to say.

"This is my pointing out, however clumsily, that when one is Pythia, personal relationships are often . . . tricky."

"Like yours was with Agnes?" I asked archly. Because Jonas and the former Pythia had apparently been an item back in the day.

"Yes, in fact. That was why we kept it a secret, from all but a few very close associates. Had we openly been a couple, people might have thought that she was under the influence of the Circle."

"People already thought that," I pointed out. "They think that about every Pythia."

"No, they suspect. Which is a very different thing."

"So you're saying what? That I can't date Mircea?" I asked, and heard someone outside smother a laugh. I suspected Marco.

Jonas apparently heard it, too, because he shot an irritated glance in the direction of the living room. "No, dating can be spun as savvy intelligence gathering on your part. Or as an attempt to bring the vampires into a closer alliance with the Circle. Or as a way of showing your impartiality toward the species."

"Then what's the problem?"

"There isn't one. As long as your liaison doesn't become more . . . permanent."

My hand went unconsciously to the marks on my neck, the two little scars that were the physical manifestation of Mircea's claim. Because we were already about as permanent as it got. Wedding rings could be taken off, just as marriages could end in divorce, annulment or separation. But the marks I wore, I would wear for life.

Diamonds might not be, but a vampire's claim? Now, that was forever.

"A formal claim is about as permanent as it gets," I admitted, not really wanting to get into it, but not seeing an alternative. I'd known this was bound to come up sooner or later.

"A formal claim?" Jonas sounded as if he'd never heard the term.

I pinched the bridge of my nose, wondering for something like the hundredth time how the different supernatural groups had survived this long when they knew almost nothing about each other. And, frequently, what they did know was wrong. It was no wonder they were at each other's throats half the time.

"It's sometimes used to bind nonvampires to a vamp family," I explained.

"For what purpose?" Jonas asked narrowly.

"For a lot of purposes. Say there's a particularly strong magic user that the family has relied on for a while to do its wards. They want to make sure he stays around, that some other family doesn't steal him away. But they can't just absorb him, because mages lose their magic when Changed."

"It is also illegal!" Jonas said hotly.

"Not if the person involved agrees to it. But—"

"As if any mage in his right mind—"

"—but if the mage can't be Changed," I said, talking over him, because I wasn't in the mood for that particular conversation today. "Then the next-best option is a claim. It makes him a formal part of the family, and vampire laws don't allow poaching from other people's families."

It also had another use, being the method traditionally used for marriages between two highly ranked vampires. It united them and their families but left them as equals, with neither having to be blood bound to the other. But if Jonas wanted to know about that, he was going to have to do his own damn homework.

Jonas frowned. "Then why haven't I heard of this before, if it's so common?"

"I didn't say it was common," I said, taking an armful of my clothes back where they belonged. "It isn't."

"And why not, if it's so useful?"

"Because a master vampire is accountable for his family members, whether claimed or Changed. Their actions reflect on him, and he's answerable for them to the Senate. But someone who has been claimed doesn't have the blood tie to him that ensures obedience, giving him a lot less control over that person's actions."

"But senior-level masters within a family can also challenge their sire, can they not?" Jonas asked, surprising me.

I turned from hanging the stuff back up. It had been quick, since my old governess had always insisted that the hangers all go the same way, and I'd never gotten out of the habit. "Yes. Which is why a lot of senior vampires are emancipated by their masters. Most of them, in fact."

"Except in Lord Mircea's case," Jonas said darkly. "There seem to be quite a few upper-level masters in his service. In fact, I have yet to meet a low-level one!"

"The low-level ones wouldn't be much use here," I pointed out. "And Mircea is a senator. He needs more senior vamps to help with his work. But he's the exception, not the rule. Most masters cut loose anyone strong enough to challenge them, just like they think twice before putting a claim on someone."

Jonas sat a while, absorbing that, while I tidied up the rest of Niall's mess. "If I understand you correctly," he finally said, "the vampires consider you Lord Mircea's servant, almost his property."

There was no "almost" about it, I didn't say, because he looked ruffled enough. "In a sense," I said, knowing where this was going.

"And property is expected to work for the good of its owner, is it not?"

"Yes."

"Then they believe they'll control the office of Pythia!" he said, as if he'd suspected this all along.

I shrugged. "Probably."

"And this doesn't concern you?" he demanded, as outraged as if he weren't planning to do the same thing himself.

"Jonas, I'm expected to work for the good of the *family*. Not the Senate."

"And you really think they're going to make that distinction? You think that Lord Mircea will make it?"

"*I'll* make it."

"And you believe you can divide your loyalties so easily?"

"Why not?" I asked, suddenly angry. "Every Pythia has had a family, hasn't she?"

Jonas looked taken aback for a moment. "Well, yes. But this is hardly the same—"

"It's exactly the same!" I thought of the vamp who'd had

half his leg taken off last night. It would eventually grow
back, but others hadn't been so fortunate. One of Mircea's
older masters, a vampire named Nicu, had died protecting
me barely a month ago, and Marco nearly had, too.

If that wasn't family, I didn't know what was.

"They're my family," I repeated flatly. "And I'll treat
them as such. But it doesn't mean that I'm going to be the
Senate's happy little puppet." Or the Circle's.

Jonas looked far from satisfied. "That's easy to say, but I
think you may have more of a struggle establishing your
independence from the Senate than you seem to think. But,
in any case, we're talking about appearances, not esoteric
facets of vampire law. And the fact is that you . . . belong-
ing . . . to a vampire, however you define it, is not going to
sit well with the supernatural community as a whole."

"So what do you expect me to do about it?" I demanded.

"I'm not saying don't date the man, Cassie—"

"Then what are you saying?"

"Merely that it would be helpful if you were seen to be
dating others, as well. A Were, perhaps, or a mage. It would
make it far easier to sell the idea that your private life has
little to do with your decisions."

"Yeah, well, I don't really know any—"

"I could send you some."

I blinked. "Some what?"

"Some . . . suitors . . . if you will."

"You could send me some suitors," I repeated slowly,
while outside, it sounded like someone was choking to
death.

"You wouldn't have to date any that you didn't like, of
course," Jonas said, without the faintest hint of irony. "I
could send a selection, and you could choose one."

I had a sudden, crazy image of recruitment posters plastered on the walls at war mage central: BOYFRIEND WANTED.
HAZARDOUS-DUTY PAY. Only it really wasn't funny. Because I
could see Jonas deciding that that was a perfectly reasonable way to proceed.

"Or you could choose two," he said, warming to the
idea. "A mage and a Were. Covering all the bases, so to
speak."

"How about half a dozen?" I asked sarcastically, only to
have him blink.

"Oh, no. That might get you a bit of a reputation, as it were."

"And we wouldn't want that."

There was some sort of commotion going on outside, and I decided I'd had enough. I went to the door and stuck my head out. Marco was gasping for breath on the sofa, and two of the other guards were bent over a cell phone.

"What are you doing?" I demanded.

"Trying to record this," the smart-ass from the shopping trip told me. "Nobody is going to believe us otherwise."

"Well, cut it out. It isn't funny!"

"On what planet?"

I glared at him, which did no good, because he simply went back to tinkering with the phone. So I looked at Marco. "Can't you do anything with them?"

Marco flopped a hand at me, tears streaming down his reddened cheeks, and tried to say something. But all that came out for several moments were asthmatic wheezes. I bent over his prone form, starting to worry about him, and he put a hand on my neck and pulled me down.

"It ... is ... funny," he gasped.

I stood back up and smacked him on his rocklike shoulder. "Bastard."

Jonas was coming out of the lounge when I turned around, dragging Niall by the arm. "Now, now," he told the younger mage. "Don't fuss."

"We have *ten days*, Jonas," he said. "When I frankly doubt that ten months would be enough! She looks about twelve, except for the, uh ..." he gestured up and down at my offensive curves. "Her clothes are wrong, her makeup is wrong—"

"Those are bruises!" I told him indignantly.

"And her hair is ..." He bent closer, squinting at it in the lights. "Why is your hair green?"

"It's a fashion statement."

"It's hideous. And even if it weren't ... tinted ... or whatever you did to it, it still wouldn't do. We haven't had a blond Pythia before; it's simply not what people expect to see. And, frankly, it doesn't suit you."

"It's my natural color!"

"Then it's naturally hideous. And this"—he tugged at my curls—"will have to go."

"If you touch me one more time—" I said softly.

"I'll make you an appointment with a hairdresser who understands that we need suave. We need sophisticated. We need—well, someone else, obviously, but—"

"Niall. I really think that will do for today," Jonas said, watching my face.

"And what is this?" He took the fine, starched handkerchief out of his pocket and used it to fish Pritkin's amulet from my shirt. "And if all that weren't enough, she smells!"

"Let it go," I told him, my voice low and even.

"I'll let it go," he told me grimly, ripping it off my neck. "Straight into the nearest trash bin, along with whatever other hippie-dippie nonsense you—"

"Oh, dear," Jonas said.

I blinked, staring at the spot where the officious mage had just been. Because he wasn't there any longer. "Damn," one of the vamps said.

"What happened?" I asked, feeling myself start to panic. Because the mage wasn't anywhere in sight.

"Well, on the bright side, we weren't scheduled to cover that for another month," Jonas said. "We're making fine progress, it would seem."

"Jonas! What happened?"

"Hm? Oh, well, as you know, you can move through space as well as time. What you haven't yet learned is that you can move other things, too. And people."

"But . . . but where did I move him *to*?"

He blinked at me owlishly from behind his thick glasses. "I haven't the faintest. Can you see him?"

"Can I—" I broke off, because suddenly I could. A furious little mage in the middle of a great, big desert, a black snake of a highway a few hundred yards off. And nothing else but dirt and scrub for what looked like miles.

"I think he's in a desert."

"Would you happen to know which one?"

"I . . . no. There's a road, but—"

"Oh, well. That's all right, then." He patted my arm.

"Jonas! How do I get him *back*?"

"Yes, well, we'll get to that, of course. But for right now"—his glasses gleamed—"it might be as well to leave him be. Agnes had to do that a time or two, as I recall, to his predecessor. It's no end of use in teaching them manners, you know."

He tucked my arm in his and we walked to the door, my head still spinning. "By the way, you haven't had any visions about a wolf, have you? Or a large dog?"

"You mean a Were?"

"No, no. I don't think so. Of course, it could be, but that would be a little too easy, wouldn't it?"

"I'm . . . I'm not really sure what you—"

He took my hand and bent over it with old-fashioned courtesy. "If you do see anything like that, anything at all, you will let me know, won't you?"

"I— Yes. Of course."

He looked up and those vague blue eyes were suddenly anything but, and the expression on that usually jovial face was almost scary. "Right away, Cassie."

I nodded, a little freaked-out, and suddenly he was all smiles again. "Enjoy your date," he told me, and left.

Marco closed the door and we stood there, staring at each other. "Mages," he said in disgust. "They get weirder every year."

And I couldn't really argue with that one.

Chapter Eight

"You are sure you're ready?" Mircea asked me.

It was seven hours later and several decades earlier, and I wasn't sure of a damn thing. My hands were sweaty and my stomach hurt and I was starting to rethink my dress choice for the evening. I'd already rethought it once, going with the red silk, which had seemed chic and sophisticated in the shop. But now I thought the top might be a little low, and I hadn't had time to have it altered, so it was too tight in some places and too loose in others, and I wasn't sure that the color looked that great with my hair, especially since I hadn't gotten all the green out yet, and—

"I'm fine," I said tightly.

Mircea gave me a look that said I wasn't fooling anyone. But he pressed the doorbell nonetheless. And at least he looked like he belonged here.

His dark hair was sleek and shining, confined in a discreet clip at his nape. His black tuxedo fit his broad shoulders like a glove, the material soft and sheened as only truly fine wool can be. He'd paired it with a crisp white French-cuff shirt with small gold links that glinted under the lights. They were carved with the emblem of a royal house, although he hardly needed them. Nobody was ever going to mistake him for anything but what he was.

Apparently the butler agreed, because despite not having an invitation, we were ushered straight into the party taking up most of the ground floor of a swanky London mansion. There were a lot of gleaming hardwood and glittering chandeliers and softly draped fabrics and fine carpets, and I barely noticed any of them. Because across the main salon was a small, dark-haired woman in red. And by her side was . . .

"She is beautiful," Mircea said, snagging us champagne from a passing tray.

I didn't say anything. I clutched the flute he handed me, feeling a strange sense of detachment. I could feel the cool crystal under my fingertips, taste the subtle bite of the alcohol, but it seemed distant, unreal, like the people crowding all around us. I heard the soft sounds of their laughter and the conversation that swelled and ebbed, like the notes someone was playing on a distant piano. But none of it mattered.

Not compared to the tall girl in the bad eighties ball gown, standing by the side of the former Pythia.

Her dress was electric blue satin with big, puffy sleeves and a peplum. There was a lace overlay on the top and little jeweled buttons down the front. Her shoes were dyed to match. It was absolutely awful, like something a bridezilla would stick on a too-pretty bridesmaid. Yet somehow she carried it off. The blue matched the color of her eyes and complemented her dark hair and pale skin. And when she laughed, you forgot all about the dress, didn't even see it.

Because you couldn't take your eyes off her face.

An arm slipped around my waist. "*Dulceaţă*, I do not think you want to get so close."

I suddenly realized that I was halfway across the room, although I couldn't remember moving. Mircea pulled me off to one side, near a row of floor-length windows that looked out into the night. The one in front of us was as good as a mirror, allowing me to stare at the girl's reflection without being so obvious.

Mircea is right, I thought blankly. She was beautiful. And delicate and fragile and poised.

She looked nothing at all like me.

"I don't agree," he murmured. A warm finger trailed down my cheekbone, tracing the track of a tear I couldn't remember shedding. "There's a similarity in the bone structure, in the shape of the eyes, the contour of the lips. . . ."

"I don't see it," I said harshly, gulping champagne and wondering why I was suddenly, blindingly angry.

"You said you were prepared for this," he said, pulling me against him.

His chest was hard at my back, but his arms were gentle. I felt myself relax into his embrace, even knowing what he was doing. All vampires could manipulate human emotions to a degree, but Mircea could practically play me like a violin. It was a combination of natural talent and more knowledge of what made me tick than I probably had. But for once, I didn't care. I clutched the familiar feeling of warmth and comfort around me like a blanket and told myself to stop being an idiot.

I didn't know why I was reacting this way. I'd known in advance what she looked like. I'd seen a photo of her once, a faded, grainy thing taken at a distance. But it had been clear enough to show me the truth.

I didn't resemble my mother in the slightest.

"I'm fine," I told him, my throat tight, only to feel him sigh against my back.

"You are not fine, *dulceață*. You are feeling anger, loss, betrayal—"

"I don't have any reason to feel betrayed."

"She abandoned you when you were a child—"

"She died, Mircea!"

"Yes, but the fact remains that she left. And hurt you in the process."

"I wasn't hurt. I was barely four."

"You were hurt," he insisted. "But you do not deal with such emotions, Cassie. You ignore them."

"That isn't true!"

"That has always been true. It is one of the defining aspects of your character."

I scowled at his reflection in the window, but if he saw, he didn't react. He took the empty champagne glass from my hand and sat it on a nearby table. Then his arms folded around me again, trapping me, although it didn't feel that way. I didn't want to talk about this. But suddenly I didn't want to move, either.

"Do you recall when I visited Antonio's court when you were a child?" he asked.

"Of course." He'd been there for a year, from the time I

was eleven until I was almost twelve. It had been a lengthy visit, even by vampire standards. At the time, I hadn't thought much of it; Tony often had visitors, and it had made sense to me that his master would eventually be one of them. It was only later that I found out Mircea had an ulterior motive.

He'd discovered that the little clairvoyant Tony had at court was the daughter of the former heir to the Pythian throne. My mother had run away from her position and her responsibilities to marry a dark mage in Tony's service. That effectively barred her from any chance of succeeding, but made no difference as far as my own odds were concerned.

"You hoped I'd become Pythia one day."

Mircea didn't bother to deny it. He was a vampire. Utilizing whatever resources were available within the family was considered a virtue in their culture, and a possible Pythia was a hell of a resource. "Yes, but you were also interesting in your own right."

I snorted. "I was eleven. No eleven-year-old is interesting."

"Most eleven-year-olds do not wander about talking with ghosts," he said wryly. "Or pipe up at the dining table to casually mention that one of the guests is an assassin—"

"I think Tony would have had heart failure," I said, remembering his face. "You know, if he had a heart."

"—or lead me to a cache of Civil War jewelry hidden in a wall that no one else knew about."

"The guy who put it there did."

"My point is that you were a fascinating child, not least of which for the way you dealt with pain. Or, more accurately, the way you avoided dealing with it."

"I deal with it fine."

Mircea didn't comment, but a hand covered the fist I'd bunched at my waist, finger pads resting on sharp knuckles. "I had been there perhaps a month," he said softly, "when I chanced to be passing your room. It was late and you were supposed to be asleep, but I heard you cry out. I went in to find you sitting in bed, your arms wrapped around your knees, staring at the wall. Do you recall what you told me when I asked what was wrong?"

"No." I'd been watching images flickering on the wall

and ceiling, like reflections of headlights on a road. Only there was no highway near Tony's farmhouse, which was set well back from a two-lane dirt track in the Pennsylvania countryside. But the scenes had washed over the room nonetheless, like the stuttering frames of a silent movie.

They'd looked sort of like one, too, the colors mostly leached away by the night. Except for the blood. For some reason, it had been in bright, brilliant Technicolor, standing out starkly against the blacks and browns and dull, asphalt gray.

But as horrible as it had been, it hadn't been particularly unusual. I'd had visions almost every day, until I grew up enough to learn to control them, until I learned how not to see. I probably wouldn't even remember that one, except that Mircea had been there, jolting me out of it.

Tony's people didn't do that. They had standing orders not to interrupt, because I might see something he'd find profitable. So it had been the strangest of strange sensations, to suddenly feel a touch, human soft and blood warm, on my shoulder.

"It was just a nightmare," I told him.

"You said you had seen a multicar accident. Or, as you described it, blood leaching into puddles of oil; broken bodies lying on shattered glass; and the smell of gasoline, burnt rubber and charred meat. The next morning, the news reported a ten-car pileup on the New Jersey Turnpike."

"Did it?" I asked, suddenly wishing I had another drink.

"I wondered then what it would be like, to grow up as a child who saw things no child should ever see. Who, every time she closed her eyes, was surrounded by pain, by horror, by death—"

"That's a serious exaggeration."

"—by sights that kept her up at night, shivering in fear, and staring at a blank wall."

"It wasn't blank," I said shortly. "Rafe drew things on it."

Our resident artist at court had been none other than the Renaissance master Raphael, who had been turned after unwisely refusing a job for Florentine up-and-comer Antonio Gallina. It had been the last time he'd refused one of Tony's commissions, not that he'd been given many. Appreciating art required a soul, something I was pretty sure Tony had been born without.

"Yes," Mircea agreed. "Because I asked him to."

I frowned. I hadn't known that. "You asked him? Why?"

"I thought a child should have something to look at besides death."

Dark eyes met mine in the window for an instant, until I looked away. "I want another drink," I told him, but Mircea's arms didn't budge.

"Of course you do," he said. "I wish to discuss your feelings about your mother, so naturally you become thirsty. Or hungry. Or suddenly recall an errand that you need to perform."

I struggled, Mircea's hold no longer feeling quite so comforting. "Let me go."

"To get a drink, or to avoid the conversation?"

"I'm not avoiding it!" I snapped. I just hadn't expected this to be so hard.

Mircea and I had crashed the party, if walking in escorted by a gushing butler can be termed such, because I'd wanted to see my mother. Not talk to, not interact with, not do anything that might possibly mess up the timeline. Just see.

Because I never had, other than in that one lousy photo. But now that I was here, seeing wasn't enough. I wanted to get close. Wanted to find out if she still smelled like honey and lilac, with a hint of waxy lipstick.

Wanted her to see me, too.

But even more, I wanted to ask her things. Why she gave up a job most people would have killed for to marry a man most people would have liked to kill. Why she'd had me. Why she'd died and left me with fucking Tony.

If she'd ever loved me at all.

"Let me go," I said unevenly. Mircea released me and I moved away, needing space, needing air.

I hugged my arms around myself and stared across the party, an almost physical ache gnawing at my insides. Her hair was dark, as I'd assumed from the photo, but it wasn't brown. The lights were shining on it now, and it was a deep, rich, coppery bronze, as rare and striking as her sapphire eyes.

I wondered if that was where the red threads in my own hair came from, if maybe it ran in the family. I wondered if I had a family, distant cousins or something, floating around. . . . I'd never really thought about it before, maybe because I'd grown up surrounded by people who never mentioned theirs.

Vampires usually acted as if their lives started with the Change, instead of ending with it. And in a real sense, they were right. Most masters Changed an individual because they possessed a talent they needed, or strength or intellect or wealth they wanted, none of which included a human family. And few were willing to Change a bunch of hangers-on who could be of no real use and who might be a danger, since a master was responsible for the actions of his children.

As a result, most families got left behind when a baby vamp joined his or her new clan. And I guessed that, after a while, you must stop wondering about people long dead, whom you probably had nothing in common with anymore, anyway. After a while, you must stop missing them.

Only I didn't think I was going to live that long.

"My mother was also quite beautiful."

I'd been so lost in thought that it took me a moment to realize that Mircea had spoken.

And then another few seconds for what he'd said to sink in. "Your mother?"

He smiled slightly. "You look surprised."

"I just . . . you never mention her." In fact, I'd never thought about Mircea having a mother. Stupid; of course he had. But somehow I'd never imagined him as a boy.

It was surprisingly easy.

The mahogany hair had a faint wave to it that might once have been curls. The sculpted lips, so sensual in an adult, had probably been a cupid's bow then. And the dark, liquid eyes must have been irresistible in a child's face.

"I bet you got away with murder," I said, and he laughed.

"Not at all. My parents were quite strict."

"I don't believe it." I tried to be strict with Mircea, I really did, but somehow it never worked. And I doubted that anybody else had better luck.

"It's true," he insisted, settling us into chairs by the wall. I didn't stay in mine more than a few seconds. I felt too antsy, too oddly keyed up.

Mircea started to get up when I did, but I pushed him

back down. "A gentleman doesn't sit while a lady is standing," he admonished.

I put a knee on his leg to keep him in place. "And if the lady insists?"

"Hm. A quandary." A strong hand clasped my thigh through the silk. "Since a gentleman always accedes to a lady's wishes."

"Always?" That could come in handy.

He laughed and kissed my hand. "Unfortunately, I am not always a gentleman."

"Close enough," I told him honestly, and slipped the clip out of his hair.

A dusky wave fell over his shoulders. He looked up at me, dark eyes amused. I'd always had this weird fetish about his hair, which we didn't talk about. But he knew.

It felt like cool brown silk flowing over my fingers. And, as always, touching him felt more than good. It felt right, steadying. And right now, I could really use some of that.

"You were talking about when you were a boy."

"Ah yes. The trials of childhood," he mused, that hand slowly stroking my thigh. "One of my first memories is of being thrown out to play in the snow, completely naked."

"Naked?"

"Hm. It was not too bad when the sun shone, but after dark—"

"After *dark*?"

"—it became somewhat . . . frigid."

I stared at him. "How old were you?"

He shrugged. "Three, perhaps four."

"But . . . but why would anyone *do* that?"

"To demonstrate my fitness to the people. I was my father's heir, and although he had no throne at that time to leave to me, he had absolute confidence that it would one day be his."

"Yes, but to risk a *child*—"

"Life was about risk then. And there was no childhood, in the modern sense, when I was young. Not for peasant children, who started work in the fields by age seven. And certainly not for those of us in the nobility."

"That doesn't sound like much fun."

"Some of it was. There were puppet shows on feast days and sledding in the winter. And I could ride an unsaddled horse at age five at a full gallop, as could my brothers. Well, except for Radu," he said, talking about his youngest brother. "He was deathly afraid of the creatures and took rather longer to come to terms with them. I should know; I taught them to ride."

"Them?"

"He and Vlad," Mircea said, his smile fading. I didn't say anything, but inwardly I cursed. It was rare enough for Mircea to talk about his family, and that particular topic was almost certain to make him shut down. But to my surprise, this time it didn't.

"Radu had absolutely no seat at all," he said, after a moment.

"Neither do I," I admitted. Rafe had tried to teach me, but had finally given up in despair.

"But you do not need to lead charges in battle, *dulceață*. He did! My father finally solved the problem by tying him onto the largest horse in the stable, and promising that he should remain there until he could ride it properly."

"And did he?"

Mircea looked up at me, baring the long line of his throat as he leaned back against the chair. It exposed a vulnerable area, a traditional vampire sign of trust. "With amazing alacrity."

I stared down into those velvety dark eyes, fascinated by the pleased humor on the handsome face, by the crinkle of the eyes, by the white, even teeth and the glimpse of tongue behind them. Without thinking, my hand stopped combing through the thick silk of his hair and dropped to his nape, before sliding forward to curve around his throat.

Most vampires would have moved away or at least flinched. Mircea just looked up at me, eyes bright, but no longer with amusement. There was something dark in those depths, something fierce and possessive that made my breath come faster and my hand tighten over the pulse that beat strong and steady under my fingertips.

His heart didn't need to beat, of course, but he knew I liked it, so he rarely forgot. Like he always remembered to breathe when I was around, to blink, to do all the things that made him seem human, even though he hadn't technically held that title for five hundred years. But he was human to me.

He would always be human to me.

"You shouldn't look at me like that when we are in public, *dulceaţă*," he murmured, stroking his hand up and down my leg. "It makes me wish to cut the evening short."

"How short?"

Those fingers suddenly tightened. "Very."

And for a moment, that sounded like a really good idea. Really, really good. But if I left with Mircea now, I knew how the rest of the evening would go. And it wouldn't involve a lot of talking.

I licked my lips and stepped away a few paces. "You were telling me about your mother?"

Mircea didn't say anything for a moment, but when I looked back, he didn't appear annoyed. If anything, his body seemed to have relaxed, and he was smiling. "Princess Cneajna of Moldavia," he said easily. "Tall, with raven hair and green eyes. Radu took after her, not in coloring but in a certain delicacy of feature."

"What about you?"

"They said I resembled her more in temperament, although I never saw it. She was more . . . fiery. More highly strung. I remember her as beautiful and passionate, proud and ambitious."

I bit my lip. I thought that described Mircea perfectly.

"I always thought I was more like my father," he told me.

"How so?"

Mircea's head tilted. "He was a . . . prudent sort of man, a diplomat, for King Sigismund of Hungary. He was around your age when he was sent as a special envoy to Constantinople to discuss a possible merger between the Roman Catholic faith and the Orthodox. It never happened, of course, but he impressed the Holy Roman Emperor with his tact and judgment." Mircea smiled. "Although probably not for his piety."

"He wasn't religious?"

"No more so than was politically expedient. My mother was the devout one in the family. Forced her poor sons into the care of the Dominicans for part of our education." He shuddered.

I smiled. "You don't like monks?"

"I always have suspicions of any man who can willingly turn his back on the finest of God's creations."

Brown velvet eyes met mine, and a shot of something warm and electric shot right through me, making my pulse pound harder in my throat—and other places. I decided I really wanted that drink now. Luckily, another of the ubiquitous floating trays was headed my way.

I moved forward and reached for a glass, at the same time as a man on the other side. My hand brushed the flute, toppling it and sending a splash of golden liquid onto his pristine white shirt. He looked down and I looked up, an apology on my lips. And that was where it stayed, as both of us froze in stunned recognition.

Because we knew each other, and neither one of us was supposed to be there.

Chapter Nine

I stared at the thin, vaguely horsey features and pale blue eyes of the mage in front of me, and hoped I was imagining things. He looked a little different in a well-fitted tux instead of seventeenth-century slops, his sandy blond hair slicked back instead of falling messily around his face. But it was him. The guy I'd once helped Agnes apprehend before he could blow history to kingdom come.

If I'd had any doubts, they were erased when he suddenly gave a screech, knocked the tray of drinks at me and bolted. A choking mass of thick, blue-black smoke boiled through the room as I stumbled back. Someone fired a gun and someone screamed. And then everything slowed down—literally.

The whole room suddenly looked like it was on slow-motion replay. I fell back into Mircea, my gown fluttering lazily around me, as the serving tray arced high in the air above. Glasses scattered, golden liquid sloshed and the silver surface flashed in the candlelight for a long moment. . . .

And then sped back up and hit the floorboards with a crash. But it was barely audible over the sound of rapid-fire gunshots, breaking glass and the collective panic of a crowd unused to danger. Not that I was having much of a different reaction, and I was plenty used to it. I hit the ground instinctively, only to have Mircea grab me around the waist and jerk me back.

That was lucky, because the crowd took that moment to decide on the better part of valor, and there was a stampede. Ladies in fine gowns and men in tuxes forgot about elegance, threw away decorum and fought to be the first out the door. The place where I'd been kneeling a second ago was suddenly a mass of swirling hems and pounding feet.

"What happened?" Mircea asked, pushing me behind him.

"Agnes," I gasped. The smoke burned at the back of my throat, making it hard to talk, hard to breathe. "She can manipulate time for short periods, stop it ... slow it down ... and she must have recognized him—"

"Recognized who?"

"The guy from the Guild," I said, desperately trying to spot him in the crowd. But the smoke made it difficult to see anything, and most of the guests were taller than I was. I hiked up my skirts and scrambled onto a nearby table.

"What guild?" Mircea asked, but I didn't answer. I could see over the crowd now, but not through the smoke. But there was something going on near the back of the room— spell fire lit up the haze in spots, like strobes on a dance floor. And most of the colors were in the red and orange range—offensive magic, war spells; not the soothing blues and greens of the protective end of the spectrum.

I hopped off the table and ran.

Mircea grabbed me before I'd gone a yard—and then flung us to the floor as a stray curse blistered the air overhead. It crashed into the window behind us, shattering the glass and sending fire running up the brocade curtains. More smoke, thick and smothering, added to the mix, threatening what little air was left in the room.

"Let me go!" I choked. "He'll kill her!"

"Kill who?"

"My mother!"

"Who will?"

"The asshole from the Guild!"

"Listen to me." Warm hands framed my face and dark eyes met mine. I felt the usual reassurance Mircea's presence caused ramp up a few notches, soothing my fears, calming my mind—and depriving me of my edge. "Whatever is going on, it doesn't succeed," he assured me. "Nothing of importance happened tonight. My men were told specifically—"

"Nothing *did* happen," I said, furious because I no longer was. "But something *is* happening. And if you don't *listen*—"

But Mircea wasn't. He'd pulled me to my feet as we argued and slipped an arm around my waist. And now he started to push his way through the crowd toward the nearest exit.

And then, just as suddenly, started to back up again.

I found myself walking backward, too, unable to control my body's movements despite the fact that they were the exact opposite of what I wanted to do. I tried to talk but I couldn't do that, either, except for some garbled sounds that didn't make sense. For a moment, I panicked, sure I was possessed again—until I caught sight of the drapes.

A minute before, the dark red damask had been a border of flame around the window, embroidered designs standing out harshly against the rapidly darkening fabric, fat tassels writhing as they were quickly consumed. Now the opposite was true. Clean, whole cloth blossomed out of flames that were shrinking, falling back, forming into a ball that flew through the air back to whoever had cast it.

The fleeing crowd was also moving the wrong way, panicked faces streaming away from me as I jumped on the table, jumped off, hit the floor and then was back on my feet, staring at a wide-eyed mage with champagne on his shirt. And then I was in Mircea's arms, facing the window as if nothing had ever happened. Because it hadn't yet.

Time juddered and shook, trembling around me for a long second before reversing again. And this time, I didn't hesitate. I threw off Mircea's hold and tackled the mage.

We went down in a thrashing heap, my arms around his waist and then his leg when he tried to shake me off. Smoke bloomed around us, harsh and stinging, as he threw something to the ground. But I held on—until a shiny, booted foot caught me upside the face, sending me reeling. But by then Mircea had him by the collar and jerked him up—

And was blasted through the air as if shot out of a cannon.

I didn't see Mircea hit the wall, recover and launch himself back at our attacker, because it all happened faster than I could blink. But I did see him freeze in the air, midleap, as time shuddered to a halt. At least it did for me, Mircea and everybody else—except the goddamned mage, who shrugged it off like an old coat and bolted into the crowd.

I started after him, pushing hard against the power freezing me in place, but it felt like trying to swim in a river of cold molasses. Time swirled sluggishly all around me, weighing my limbs, slowing my breathing, keeping me back. Away from him. Away from *her*.

Until I *pushed*, breaking free in a rush that sent me sprawling into the statuclike crowd, disoriented and breathing hard. A woman toppled over, stiff as a board, her red, red lipstick smearing across the shirt of the man beside her. Another woman teetered back and forth on her high heels, but was unable to fall because of the people pressing her hard on all sides.

They were pressing me, too, but that was a good thing, because they were also slowing down the mage. I could see his blond head bobbing through the crowd, shining under the lights. He was easy to spot, being a good three inches taller than most of the guests and the only one moving. But even if I caught him, I couldn't take down a crazy dark mage on my own.

And Agnes couldn't help me. I didn't know what kind of weird shit was going on with time, but I knew this maneuver. Stopping time was the biggest weapon in the Pythia's arsenal, a trump card. But it was also a one-shot deal. The only time I'd done it—by accident—it had completely wiped me out for the rest of the day.

And I was a lot younger than Agnes.

It frightened the hell out of me, because she knew the cost better than I did. She wouldn't have used it if the danger to her or her heir wasn't acute. But it wouldn't work this time, and might even backfire. Because if the mage could throw it off, he could hunt them while they thought they were safest, and while she was weakened with her power diverted elsewhere.

I had to follow him, and I had to have help.

And there was only one place to get it.

I looked up to where Mircea was still suspended in the air, amber eyes slitted, staring at the place where the mage no longer was. I grabbed the front of his shirt, the only thing I could reach, and gave a pull. And like a big, Mircea-shaped balloon, he floated a little closer to the ground. But he was still frozen, still useless.

It hadn't worked.

I stood there with tears of pure fury burning in my eyes. I hated the fact that I didn't know how to use my power, that no matter how much I studied, how much I practiced, what I needed was always something I didn't know how to do. But if I'd done it once, goddamnit, I could do it again. No stupid mage from some squirrelly little cult was going to beat me at my own damn game.

I fisted my hand in Mircea's shirt, and fisted my power in the current swirling thickly between us. And *pulled.*

For a long moment, nothing happened. He didn't even move toward me this time, not an inch. But while he wasn't moving in space, he was moving through something. Because I could feel the resistance dragging on him, tugging him back, wanting to fix him in place while I was doing my best to yank him out of it.

It was unbelievably difficult, far harder than it had been in my own case. I started to shake, and sweat broke out on my face, and for a second, I almost lost him. It was like time was slippery and he was oiled, and along with the sheer physical strain was the stress of keeping my wobbly grip. But I could feel time peeling away from him, layer after layer, as if he were shedding some kind of strange skin.

And then suddenly I was hitting the floor, with a hundred and eighty pounds of freaked-out vampire on top of me.

Mircea jumped back to his feet and then ducked into a crouch as I lay there, panting and half-sick. God *damn*, that had sucked. He seemed to think so, too, because he was staring around, minus his usual sangfroid. Mahogany silk whipped around his face as he took in the motionless crowd, the frozen clouds of smoke and a glass that had been caught midfall a few feet away, the contents spilling out like a champagne waterfall.

He put out a tenuous hand and touched it, and then jerked back when it wet his fingers. He looked at me, dark eyes wide. "What did you do?" he asked in wonder.

"Never mind that." I staggered back to my feet, wondering why I felt like throwing up. "We've got to get to him before he finds her."

"The man who attacked you?"

"Yes."

"He's trying to harm the Pythia?"

"Yes!"

"Why?"

"Because Agnes and I stopped him on his last mission. And because that's what the Guild does—they disrupt time!" And killing a Pythia and her heir would definitely do that.

It would also do something else, I realized. My mother was still the Pythia's chosen successor, still the good little Initiate preserving her virginity until the all-important transfer ceremony. She had yet to meet my disreputable father, yet to run away with him.

Yet to have me.

Suddenly, my skin was too cold, too tight, and my lungs couldn't seem to pull in any air. "Mircea—" I grabbed his sleeve.

But I didn't need to explain. I saw when he got it, and I'd never been more grateful for that whip-fire intellect, which rarely missed little details. Like the fact that if the maniac succeeded, he wouldn't take out two Pythias tonight.

He'd eliminate three.

Mircea didn't ask any more questions. He caught me by the waist and surged ahead, cutting a swath through the motionless crowd faster than I'd have thought possible. But the mage had a sizable lead, and in the few moments it had taken to get Mircea on board, I'd lost sight of him.

It didn't help that smoke hung heavy in the air like a thick, dark fog. I thought it would get better as we moved farther from the source, but the opposite seemed to be true. The far end of the room was a sea of clouds, darker in some areas and lighter in others where lines of spell fire criss-crossed in the gloom.

The clouds were annoying, but it was the spells that had me worried. They were frozen in place like neon tubes at a bad '80s disco, but there were a lot of them. And while they wouldn't slam into us with time the way it was, if we hit them—

I didn't know what would happen if we hit them. But I didn't think it would be fun.

"Can you shift us across?" Mircea asked grimly.

"Not without seeing where I'm going." And the smoke pretty much excluded that.

"Then we'll go around."

"There's no time! He's already—"

"Then I'll go," he said, putting a heavy hand on my arm as I dropped to the floor, preparing to crawl under the nearest beam.

"You can't manipulate time, and he can! He can freeze you and kill you before you know what's happening."

"I'll take that chance."

"Well, I won't!"

His jaw clenched stubbornly, and I felt like screaming. "Mircea, you're going to protect me to death!"

He stared at me a moment longer, and then cursed inventively and dropped beside me. I took that as assent and started forward. But it wasn't nearly as easy as it sounds.

A bright beam sparkled in the air above our heads like a frozen column of raspberry ice. Frost spell, cold enough to burn, cold enough to freeze any skin it touched. Cold enough to kill. I made very sure to hug the floor as I slithered below.

It was marginally safer down here, because most of the spells were higher up, forming a brilliant lattice above our heads. But even though the smoke was thinner down here, visibility was actually worse, with gowns caught in midswirl everywhere and a forest of men's trouser legs. I scurried forward anyway, careful not to topple any of the living statues in my path.

"I thought only Pythias could manipulate time," Mircea said, from behind me.

"So did I."

"Then how is he doing it?"

"I don't know," I said, aggrieved. "Agnes didn't say anything about the Guild being able to do something like this. They're supposed to be time travelers, but she said that most of them are losers who manage to blow themselves up attempting dangerous spells they can't control."

"And yet this one is different."

"He didn't seem that way," I complained. "At least not when Agnes and I were after him. He was kind of an idiot. He couldn't shoot worth a damn, and he kept running around screaming, and running into—"

I stopped because I'd slammed into something, hard enough to hurt. It turned out to be the faint green bubble of a protection spell, so dim against the glowing colors that I hadn't seen it. An older man was underneath, his hand up, projecting the shield over himself and the woman lying beside him. Her gray chiffon evening gown, silver hair and colorless pearls blended perfectly with the frightened pallor of her face.

"Let me," Mircea said, taking the lead. I didn't argue, because his sight was about ten times keener than mine. "And tell me about this Guild."

"I don't know much," I said, hugging his heels. "Just what Agnes told me. She said they're some kind of freaky cult. They think they can make history better, solve humanity's problems, if they can identify where we screwed up and then go back in time and change it. Only they're the ones who get to decide what was a mistake and what wasn't."

"Fanatics." Mircea sounded disgusted.

"She called them utopians."

"Same thing under a different name."

"She said they could be dangerous—"

"They always are. Anyone who can only see their point of view is. Once a group decides that their way is the only way, it is an easy progression to vilifying anyone who doesn't agree with them. And once someone has been demonized, has been characterized as opposing the good, killing him becomes a virtue."

He sounded like he knew firsthand, but I didn't get a chance to ask. Because we'd reached the middle of the room, where a dark red stain spread over the floor, like someone had dropped a bucket of paint. But paint didn't simmer like the top of a boiling pot, with potion bubbles rising from the surface to spill into the air. They were sluggish now, like gas trapped in viscous oil, but they wouldn't stay that way for long.

"What is it?" Mircea asked.

"It's fading."

"What is?"

"The spell. It takes a lot of energy, and no one can hold it for—"

"What spell?" Mircea asked sharply.

"The one I pulled us out of."

"The time spell?"

"Yes."

"You're telling me that time is about to start back up?" he demanded.

"Yes."

"When?"

"Now?" I said, watching a crimson bubble rise almost a foot before bursting with a little pop.

And then I wasn't watching it anymore, because Mircea had thrown me over his shoulder and taken a flying leap over the puddle. He landed hard and I gasped, partly because it had hurt and partly because we'd hit a woman in a bright pink evening gown. I grabbed her by the hair before she could topple into the stain, and Mircea thrust her back into the arms of a mage behind her. And then we were sprinting over and under and through the maze at a pace that was definitely not safe.

But then, neither was this.

A spell flashed across our path, hit somebody's shield and ricocheted back, striking the parquet floor in front of us and sending a hundred little wooden slivers whirling up into the air. Another brilliant beam slammed into the ceiling, causing a cascade of plaster dust to sift down like snow, and a third exploded through the French doors at the end of the room. And then we were bursting through what was left, into darkness and crisp autumn air and the night sounds of a city.

And the sight of a mage dragging a girl in a tacky blue dress.

They were halfway down the street and moving fast, probably because they were being chased by four war mages. The men must have been outside, sneaking a smoke or something, because they obviously hadn't been caught

in the time bubble. They were still half a block back from
the running couple, but then they put on a burst of magically enhanced speed, blurring their figures as they tore
through the night, hands outstretched, bodies leaping for
the fleeing mage and his captive—

And then the whole group disappeared in a flash that lit
up the surrounding buildings like a single strobe.

For a moment, I just stared in disbelief. Because I might
not know everything about my office yet, but I damn well
knew a shift when I saw one. And the entire group had just
fled, not through space but through time, shrugging off the
fragile grasp of the moment as easily as most people would
walk through a door.

But while their bodies were gone, something else remained. I clutched at it desperately as Mircea cursed behind me. "What the devil . . . ?"

"I can still feel her." My hand clenched on his arm, hard
enough that it would have hurt a human.

His head whipped around, scanning the empty street.
"You're saying they're hiding under some kind of glamou-
ric?"

"No. I'm saying I can *feel* her."

And I might even know why. The holders of my office
had to train replacements somehow, and one method was
on the job. But that required being able to locate an heir
who had landed herself in trouble, no matter when she happened to be. At least, I assumed that was why I could sense
where she'd gone, like a glimmering golden thread in my
mind, tying us together.

A thread getting rapidly thinner as she moved farther
away.

"What does that—" Mircea began, but I shook my head.

"Hold on," I told him. And shifted.

Chapter Ten

We landed on the same street, but suddenly there were no electric lights, no cars, no milling crowd of freaked-out party guests. And no crazy mage and his captive. Just dirty snow melting in between cobblestones, the moon riding a bunch of dark clouds overhead, and a few dim puddles from gas lanterns placed too far apart.

Some dry leaves rattled along the gutter, but nothing else moved.

"Did he take her into a house?" I asked Mircea, who had his eyes closed and his head tilted back.

"I do not think so," he murmured. And then he rotated on his heel and opened his eyes, looking straight at a group of three-story row houses lining the left side of the street.

They were painted some light color that glowed ghostly pale in the moonlight. Their windows were mostly dark, shrouded by heavy curtains, which wasn't much help. But the shadows rippling across their fronts were more useful.

There was nothing to throw them—nothing that I could see anyway. And there were no soft-voiced commands, no sounds of running feet, no faint rustles of clothing to give anyone away. But Mircea didn't need all that. He could hear their hearts beat, smell the sweat on their skin, feel the faint currents of air from their passing. Glamouries, even good ones, have a hard time fooling vampire senses.

"That way," he told me softly, but I didn't need it. The

shadows had disappeared into the dark mouth of an alley, and I shifted us right in behind them.

Silver moonlight was sifting in the far end of the passage, lighting up the kidnapper and my mother disappearing around a corner. And the figures of three war mages, who must have been right on their tail, but who were now stumbling out of thin air, dropping their glamouries as they turned and tripped and staggered and ran—right back at us.

For a second, I thought that they'd mistaken us for enemies and decided to take us out before going after Mom. Except that they weren't looking at us. Judging by the whites showing all around their eyes and the way they kept running into each other, they weren't looking at much at all.

I'd never seen war mages look that unprofessional—or that panicked. I looked past them, but there was nothing to explain it, not even a rat nosing at the garbage littering the alley floor. But clearly, something had them spooked.

And then they blew by us, one of them shoving me brutally aside in his hurry. I hit the brick wall hard enough to knock the breath out of my lungs, and Mircea hit the mage. The casual-looking blow sent him flying out of the alley and into the street, but, amazingly, the man didn't even try to retaliate. He just staggered to his feet and limped off as fast as he could, disappearing from view around a corner of the building.

I gazed after him for a second, confused, and then shook my head and started the other way, desperate not to lose the tenuous connection to my mother. Only to have Mircea jerk me roughly back. I didn't ask why, because I hadn't gotten my breath back and couldn't talk yet. And because I knew him well enough to know that he'd have a good reason.

And because what looked like a piece of the night had broken off from the rest and was flowing our way.

It surged along the sides of the alley like water, turning the dark red brick gray and chipped and flaking, leaving a pale stripe on the wall like a flood line. It disintegrated a few pieces of trash that had been blowing on the breeze, turning them brown and curled and then dusting them away. It ate through a wooden rain barrel, sending a wash of dirty runoff foaming across the alley floor.

And it did all of that in a matter of seconds.

I stared at the path of destruction, knowing what I was seeing but not really believing it. Because this wasn't a time bubble; it was a time wave. One that had just engulfed the fourth mage.

I hadn't seen him until his glamourie melted like dripping paint, showing pieces of him scrambling through the garbage on the alley floor. He was still trying to run, but it wasn't going well. He kept tripping over his feet, getting up, taking a few awkward steps, and then falling back down again. Until he abruptly stopped, threw back his head and screamed.

Suddenly, I was grateful that there was so little light, that he'd made it into the shadow of the building, that I couldn't see details of what was happening. Because what I could see was bad enough.

A wave of hair sprang from his head, going gray streaked and then solid gray and then pure silver-white as it snaked over his shoulders, pooling in the mud and grime caking the cobblestones. At the same time, the body under the long leather coat began to move in odd ways, bucking and writhing, although his hands stayed on the ground as if glued. And then the wave ate through the coat, disintegrating it like it had been dumped in acid, and what was underneath—

"Don't look at it," Mircea said harshly, pulling me back.

But I couldn't not look. Skin darkened and then peeled away in patches, muscle thinned and browned, nails sprouted long as talons and a cascade of what I recognized dully as ropy intestines hit the cobblestones with a splat. And then the face lifted, the mouth still open but no sound coming out anymore.

No, of course not, I thought blankly.

It's kind of hard to scream with no vocal cords.

And then my paralysis broke and we were pelting back toward the street, just ahead of the tidal wave boiling toward us. Mircea threw us into the road and then slammed us back against a building all in one quick movement. I stayed there, nails biting into the cold stones, as the wave shimmered through the air right past us.

I still couldn't see it, other than as a vague distortion against the night. But I didn't have to. I could see what it did well enough.

The sidewalk in front of the alley cracked and splintered, and the section of roadbed beside it suddenly rippled like an angry sea. The individual stones began moving up and down like keys on a piano, the whole expanse to the other side dancing as the mortar between the pieces crumbled and age pushed them out of place. It was like watching hundreds of years of wear happening in seconds.

But it didn't stop there. A lamppost across the street began to writhe, the metal twisting and groaning as rust surged up the sides. The lamp on top cracked and then shattered, before what was left of the structure tumbled into the road, exploding against the uprooted stones.

But it didn't stop there, either. The fence around a grassy area disintegrated in a pouf of bronze rust, glimmering in the moonlight like fairy dust. Flowers in a small bed bloomed and died and bloomed again, pushing upward against the snow as the sticklike sapling they hedged suddenly shot toward the sky. Limbs bulged, bark flowed and leaves sprouted in abundance. Acorns rattled down like rain as the leaves changed and fell and sprouted again, piling up around the rapidly thickening trunk like a mountain.

I blinked, and when I looked again, it was at a fully grown tree, branches huge and rustling, spreading luxuriantly against the night where a moment before there had been only sky. I stared up at it, the breath coming fast in my lungs, because no way. No *freaking* way.

I'd been willing to take the shifting thing on faith, to believe that maybe the mage had somehow learned a spell the others hadn't, or had a special talent that allowed him to control the needed power, or had just gotten really lucky. But that? That was the sort of thing that only a Pythia could do—and a damned well-trained one at that.

Or a well-trained Pythian heir.

My head turned on its own, and I found myself staring at the darkened mouth of the alley again. It looked a little different now, the bricks on either side of the entrance cracked and discolored and in some cases missing altogether, crumbled into dust. But there was no sign of the mage, nothing to show that a man had ever been there, much less that he had suffered and died on those stones. It was almost like nothing had ever happened.

But it had.

And my mother had done it.

"I believe it has stopped," Mircea said softly, examining a nearby fountain. As far as I could tell, the wave had done nothing more than add a little to the verdigris etching over the elaborate metalwork. It should have made me feel better, because I'd had no clue how to counter it if it had just kept going.

But it didn't.

"Why would she help him?" I asked harshly.

Mircea looked up. I couldn't see him very well with the only nearby lamppost now a bunch of rusted shards in the street. But he didn't sound surprised when he answered; he'd probably been thinking the same thing. "He must have her under a compulsion."

"But . . . why bother? If he could make her do anything, he could order her to kill herself! He doesn't need—"

"If he wished to kill her, why not do so at the party? Why take the risk of trying to control power like that?" He sounded slightly awed, as if he'd never before seen precisely what a Pythia could do. And maybe he hadn't.

It sure as hell was news to me.

"Why take her at all, then?" I demanded.

"As you said, the Guild exists to disrupt time. But their power is insufficient to allow them to travel where they wish. And even when they manage to collect enough, through whatever means, for a shift, there remains the problem of controlling it. Perhaps they decided—"

"That it would be easier to get themselves a pet Pythia," I rasped. "To act as their goddamned cab ride!"

"It would make sense."

I didn't say anything. But I had a sudden, vicious image of the mage, kneeling in place in that alley, hair shooting out of his head as his body slowly disintegrated along with his clothes. It was surprisingly satisfying.

"What do you wish to do?" Mircea asked, as a lone figure darted across the end of the street. One of the remaining mages, no doubt. I was going to have to get them back to their own time before they screwed up something here, whenever this was. But that would have to come later. Right now, my mother was top priority, or there wouldn't *be* a later.

"I want to find her," I said savagely.

"Then let's go find her."

Two streets over, we came to another alley that looked a lot like the first, except that the light spilling in the end of this passage was a dim, hazy gold. The sun hadn't suddenly come up, so I assumed that the light was man-made. It went with the sound of horses' hooves on cobblestone, the rattle of wheels, and the shouts of people hawking something nearby.

I didn't see my mother, but I kind of thought she might have been by.

"What is that?" Mircea demanded, staring at a mage loping along in the shadows beside us.

His arms were pumping, his legs were working, and his long coat was flapping out behind him as if caught in a stiff breeze. Only he wasn't going anywhere. He also wasn't paying any attention to us, which wasn't surprising.

As far as he was concerned, we weren't there yet.

Mircea frowned and reached out a hand, as if to give him a push. Until my fingers tightened over his wrist. "Don't do that."

He looked a question.

"Time loop," I told him shortly, moving closer to the mouth of the alley. I was cautious, staying well inside the shadows provided by some stacked crates. I didn't think my mother could manage another wave like that so soon—if she could, the man behind us likely wouldn't be alive. But I wasn't sure. And that little demonstration earlier wasn't something you just forgot.

I kept telling myself that it hadn't been her, that she hadn't chosen to kill him like that, that she hadn't known. But it still sent chills rippling over my flesh. God, what a horrible way to—

"Time loop?" Mircea asked, putting a hand on my shoulder.

I jumped and almost screamed.

He lifted an eyebrow at me, cool as always. Like he regularly saw people disintegrate into puddles of flesh. I licked my lips and told myself to get a grip.

"He's stuck on repeat," I explained, glancing back at the mage running his personal marathon.

"And that means?"

"That he'll keep reliving the same few seconds over and over until the bubble fades or he breaks out of it."

"He's encased in a time bubble?"

"Yes."

"Then why can't I sense it?" Mircea asked, wrinkling his nose, as if he expected to be able to smell it or something.

I thought that unlikely. All I could smell was pee. The alley must serve as the local latrine.

"Did you sense the other one?" I asked.

"Not . . . precisely. But I saw something, like a current in the air—"

"Probably caused by the different weather patterns that piece of air was shifting through," I told him, figuring it out as I spoke. "Rain, sleet, snow—on fast forward, they're going to make it look a little weird."

"Then you're saying I didn't actually see anything."

"You can't see time, just what it does."

His fingers tightened. "Then your mother could throw a bubble over us and we would never see it coming?"

"Something like that," I said grimly.

Mircea abruptly pulled me behind him.

"That won't help," I said, peering between the crates at a busy street. "If she hits you with something, I probably won't know how to counter it. And without you, the mage can take me out easily." He'd managed to throw a master vamp at a wall, so that was sort of a given.

"Then how do we fight something we cannot see?" Mircea demanded.

I glanced back at him. "By not getting hit with it in the first place."

"And how do we do that?"

"I'm open to suggestion," I told him honestly.

I actually had no idea what to do. I'd assumed that my mother would be resisting her captor, and that when we caught up with him, the fight would be three against one. I'd liked those odds; I'd been all about those odds. I wasn't so thrilled with these.

Because I couldn't manipulate time like that. I hadn't known that anybody could manipulate time like that. And while I had to get only a finger on her to shift her away, I had to stay alive long enough to do it.

I also had to find her. But the light was lousy and the

street was packed with people rushing home through the cold. Most were in dark colors—brown or black or dark gray—not electric blue. But outside the illumination of shop doors and gas lamps, pretty much everything looked the same. If she stayed in the shadows, she'd blend in perfectly.

But while I couldn't see her, I could feel her rapidly getting farther away, the golden cord between us stretching like an elastic band. "She's moving," I said, and ducked out into the street.

Mircea didn't try to stop me, but he looked less than thrilled. I didn't say anything, because I wasn't any happier. As if I didn't have enough other reasons, I was freezing to death. Unfortunately, my coat was a century or so away.

He must have noticed me shivering, because he stripped off the jacket of his tux and put it around me. It was thin, but the wool was top quality and still warm from his body. I clutched it around me as we dodged a street preacher, a hawker selling roasted nuts and a seemingly endless line of wagons.

Despite the weather, it looked like half the damn city was out tonight.

And then I saw why when we came to a crossroads. Four streets, all of them busy, converged here. I was sure we were in the right area, but there was no way to know which road they'd taken. And if I guessed wrong, by the time we backtracked—

"Can you shift to her?" Mircea asked, as we stood on the street corner, trying to look four ways at once.

"No." Spatial shifts had more restrictions than the time variety, and if I couldn't see her, I couldn't shift. "Can you track her?"

"I can try." He did the eyes-closed, head-back-and-mouth-slightly-open thing again while I huddled inside the coat and tried to be optimistic. But it wasn't easy. Even in the cold, the place reeked. The streets were packed with horse manure, garbage rotted in the gutters, and the joys of deodorant were apparently unknown to most of the crowd. Add that to the smell of spilled beer radiating out of a nearby pub, and it wasn't looking good. My only hope was that she would shift through time again, and I could catch up that way.

At least, I hoped I could.

The fact was, I was getting pretty tired. The stuff at the party hadn't been fun, and then there'd been the small matter of shifting a century or so and taking someone else along for the ride. I didn't know how many more shifts I had in me, especially of the time variety. And if I ran out of juice and she shifted again—

I decided not to think about that. Besides, she had to be getting tired, too. I didn't know if she'd had anything to do with what happened at the party, although it seemed likely. But even if not, she'd just shifted herself *and five other people* more than a century.

I didn't know how the hell she'd done that. Or, rather, I understood it technically—the mages had been too close when she shifted, and had ended up trapped in the backwash of the spell. That was what happened when I took someone along with me, only I usually had to be touching them to do it. But I'd accidentally taken Pritkin on a shift once without touching him, so I knew it was possible. But six?

Carrying just one person this far had felt like it was wrenching my guts out. I couldn't even imagine doing five more. Not that the power couldn't handle it; the Pythian power was pretty much inexhaustible, as far as I'd been able to tell. But the person channeling it was not. And then there'd been the time wave and the time loop and the haring across London and—

And I didn't know why she wasn't passed out on the damn sidewalk. But she had to be tired. She *had* to be.

Because if she wasn't, we were screwed.

"This way."

I hadn't realized I'd closed my eyes, half dozing despite the cold, until a tug on my arm woke me up. I followed Mircea down the street, not saying anything because I didn't want to distract him. But apparently he could track and talk at the same time, because he glanced at me before we'd gone five yards.

"Do we have a plan?"

"I need to touch her."

"That is not a plan, *dulceață*; it is an objective."

I frowned. "Okay, your turn."

"If I get close enough, I can drain the mage and end this."

He was referring to the ability of master vampires to

pull blood particles through the air, without the need to do the Bela Lugosi thing. I'd seen Mircea drain a guy dry in a few seconds once, but while it was damned impressive, it wouldn't work here. "He'll have a shield up—"

"I can drain a man even through a shield. But it takes longer."

"How long?"

"For the average mage . . ." He shrugged. "Thirty seconds to incapacitate; perhaps a minute to kill. But with stronger shields, war-mage strength, for instance, multiply that by five."

I didn't think the mage had that kind of shield, but what did I know? I hadn't thought he'd be able to kidnap my mother, either. "So worst-case scenario, two and a half minutes to unconsciousness."

"From across a room, yes. But if I am right on top of him . . . perhaps cut that by two-thirds."

I didn't stop moving, but I stared at him incredulously. "You can drain a war mage to unconsciousness in fifty seconds *through his shields?*"

"It depends on the mage, and I do not know this one's capacities. But normally—"

"Normally?"

His lips quirked. "Let us say, it is what I would expect."

I decided not to ask what he was basing that on.

"Still, two and a half minutes isn't bad," I said hopefully. "We might be able to keep them in sight for that long."

"Yes, but if I try it from a distance, he will almost certainly notice before I can incapacitate him. And then they will either shift away or attack."

"And we can't afford for them to do either."

"No." He looked frustrated. "Normally, I would call on the family to assist, but I have never cared for London and do not keep a residence here. And while I could borrow people from another senator—"

"We don't have time."

"No."

"Then we're on our own." And for some reason, I felt the tension relax in my neck.

It must have in my voice, too, because Mircea looked at me narrowly. "Is there a reason you suddenly sound relieved?"

"It's not . . . relief exactly. It's just that . . . well, it's fly-by-the-seat-of-our-pants time, isn't it?"

"And that is a good thing?"

"No, but it's . . . sort of familiar."

He closed his eyes. "Do you know, *dulceață*, there are times when I truly believe you are the most frightening person I know."

I blinked. "Thank you?"

"You're welcome."

And then we didn't say anything else. Because we spotted them.

Chapter Eleven

It wasn't hard, considering that they almost ran us down. There were a lot of vehicles on the street—mostly small, two-wheeled contraptions with a covered area in front, a driver perched high on a seat in back, and a single horse. But there was only one being driven by a girl in an electric-blue party dress.

And barreling straight down the middle of the sidewalk.

For once, Mircea didn't have to pull me out of the way; the crowd was already doing that for him. It parted into two halves, surging into the road or back against the pub. Mircea and I ended up in the road, and then had to shuffle back even farther because the little carriage was weaving drunkenly all over the place.

I didn't know how much my mother knew about horses, but I didn't think her driving was the problem. That was more likely the two war mages in the coach behind her, firing spells that she was doing her best to dodge. She wasn't entirely successful, which probably explained why the roof of her carriage was on fire, and why her horse had the wall-eyed look of the totally panicked.

Although the horse looked positively calm compared to the kidnapper, who was sitting in the covered area of the coach, hands braced on either side, screaming his head off.

"Those idiots! Are they *trying* to kill her?" I demanded,

as another bolt of what looked like red lightning flashed between the carriages.

It missed her, but only because she'd jumped the sidewalk at the same moment, scattering pedestrians and overturning a vendor's cart. Apples rolled across the street like oversized marbles, tripping people and sending them sliding on the icy road. Unfortunately, the mages' horse managed to avoid them just fine, and thundered after her.

"It would appear so," Mircea said grimly.

I stopped staring at the chaos long enough to stare at him. "What?"

"From what you know of the Circle, *dulceață*, which do you think they would prefer—a fully trained heir in the hands of a dark mage, or the same heir deceased?"

A finger of ice ran down my spine. Because I didn't have to think. I'd just spent more than a month dodging the Circle of my time, who had been convinced that I was a threat thanks to my parentage, my vampire connections and a couple of dozen other things. And their solution had been what it always was—kill it, then kill it again.

Goddamnit!

There was a walkway over the road ahead, and I shifted us onto it, putting us momentarily ahead of the chase. It wouldn't be for long. The light weight of the vehicles allowed them to zip past the larger ones lumbering down the road, most of which were trying to get out of the way, anyway. But one wagon, piled high with barrels, was too heavy to move fast enough. And a spell that missed my mother by a fraction didn't miss it.

Whatever was in the barrels must have been pretty flammable. Because they exploded in a wash of light and heat and eardrum-threatening sound, setting the wagon ablaze and sending several of the smaller casks shooting heavenward, like wooden cannonballs. And if I'd thought the street had been chaotic before, it was nothing compared to this.

Horses don't like fire, noise or unexpected events, and every horse on the street had just experienced all three. Pandemonium broke out, with bolting animals, running people and fiery barrel parts raining down from the heavens. One of the latter took out an awning over a tobacconist's shop, which the owner hadn't remembered to roll up for the night. The dark green material went up in flames, right by a couple more horses.

That might not have been so bad, except for the fact that they were hitched to a double-decker bus. It had been about to let off a group of passengers, only they had to cling to the railings instead as the spooked horses took off at a dead run. I caught sight of my mother again as she and the bus raced side by side for the bridge, and Mircea grasped my arm.

"Can you shift us onto her coach?"

I stared at him, wondering at what point he'd lost his mind. But he looked perfectly serious, maybe because he thought this was as good a chance as we were going to get. It didn't help that I agreed with him.

"I'm not . . . I don't . . . It isn't so easy shifting onto moving things," I explained. Particularly ones that were all over the road and on fire.

"Then we'll have to do it the old-fashioned way," he told me. And before I could ask what that meant, his arm went around my waist and we were running for the side for the bridge, and then we were—

"Oh, shiiit!" I screamed, as Mircea threw us over the side just as mother's coach thundered underneath.

Only she must have moved again, because when we landed, hard enough to rattle my teeth, it was on the top of the bus.

Mircea managed to keep his feet, but I went sprawling into a big woman clutching a little dog, which tried its best to bite my nose off. And then I was pushed backward onto the lap of an astonished-looking man, who appeared less flabbergasted by my sudden appearance than by the brief outfit I was wearing.

"What? You've never seen a calf before?" I demanded, as Mircea pulled me up. Only to get us almost trampled by a crowd of panicked people trying to get down the stairs.

Several managed it by falling off, several more almost did and a lot of parcels and umbrellas and hats went flying. That included someone's bicycle, which bounced riderless off the back of the bus and continued down the street, looking oddly steady. Or at least it did until the mage's vehicle crashed into it, sending it sailing into a storefront and then careening into us.

The bus shuddered under the impact, and most of the people who had gotten back to their feet were thrown onto their butts again. But the mages hadn't emerged unscathed from the crash, either. The light gray horse pulling their ride broke free of its harness, neighed in terror and then took off back down the road.

So they grabbed the next convenient means of transportation.

Which happened to be ours.

It was Mircea's turn to swear as they jumped onto the bus, knocking people aside, and, in some cases, off the side as they vaulted up the stairs and onto the roof. And then flew off it again as Mircea grabbed the backs of two seats, swung up and *kicked*. A couple thousand bucks' worth of fine leather left muddy imprints on their shirts as they rocketed backward, arms flailing and bodies flying.

They landed what looked like half a block down the street, which should have ended that. But they'd no sooner hit pavement than they were back on their feet. I saw them shake their heads, dart into the crowd and kick into enhanced speed—and then I didn't see anything else, because Mircea was dragging me toward the front of the bus. "Did they have shields?" I asked, confused, because I hadn't seen any.

"No."

"Then how did they—" I began, only to stagger and go down when the bus suddenly swerved dangerously.

It was racing down the road like there was no driver, which was sort of true, since I didn't think the guy in the driver's seat was supposed to be there. A third mage had appeared out of nowhere and knocked the real driver aside, just in time for Mircea to vault down the length of the bus and do the same to him. Only when a master vampire knocks you aside, you don't end up on the floor.

The guy sailed off the bus, flew through the air and slammed face-first into the second story of a nearby building. Which I'd kind of expected. And then he twisted, kicked off the bricks like gravity didn't apply to him *and jumped back on the bus*. Which I hadn't.

I had a second to think that the guy looked a lot like the mage I'd last seen running a marathon inside a time bubble—tall, dark hair, red face—only that couldn't be right. And then he lunged for Mircea, who had turned his back to grab the reins, and I decided to worry about it later. I jumped after him, yelling a warning I doubted even vampire ears could hear over the galloping horses and the creaking bus and the screaming people.

But it didn't matter, because some of the passengers had clearly had enough. One fine-looking gent with a monocle tripped the mage with his cane, a burly-looking guy in a butcher's apron smashed him in the face, and a couple of other men helped flip him over the side and into the street. Which all things considered, probably didn't hurt him much.

And then he was run over by a speeding coach, which probably did.

At least, I didn't see him vault back on board before Mircea pulled the real driver back into his seat and grabbed me. "We aren't going to catch up to her this way," he yelled.

I nodded, feeling a little dizzy. The Clydesdales pulling the bus were already going as fast as they could, and they weren't bred for speed anyway. We weren't going to catch up to Mom on a heavy bus loaded with people, and neither were the mages.

"What's the alternative?" I yelled back.

"This!" he told me. And flung us over the side.

It happened so fast I didn't have time to scream before we landed in a mostly empty wagon. The lack of weight was probably why it was beating the bus in the race to get the hell out of Dodge. But it wasn't beating it by much, particularly after the driver turned around to shout at us and rammed into the next vehicle in line.

But it looked like Mircea hadn't planned on staying long, because before I could get a breath, we were jumping onto another wagon and then into a four-wheeled cab, which had gotten close enough for him to grab the door. And then through the back, trying not to step on the occupants' toes, and out the other side into—

Well, I guess it was a car. Except it looked more like a roofless carriage with no horses and a big stick coming out of the floorboard. It also had a huge, bulbous horn, a couple of foot pedals and a freaked-out driver who was currently dangling from the hand of a master vampire.

"You know, I could use a little more warning next time!" I told Mircea breathlessly, as he dropped the man gently into the road.

He shot me a glance. "Now you know how I feel whenever you shift."

"I tell you when we're about to shift!"

"When you remember." He picked me up and deposited me in what I guess was the passenger's seat, since it didn't have a stick. "Fair warning: this is going to be a bumpy ride."

Yeah, like it hadn't been so far, I didn't say, because my ass had no sooner touched leather than we barreled onto the sidewalk, slung around a bunch of people, clipped the side of a shop and then shot ahead.

"Are you sure you know how to operate this thing?" I demanded, trying to get my limbs sorted out.

"This is a Lutzmann. I used to own one."

"Yeah, but did you actually *drive* it?"

He just raised an eyebrow and shot ahead, as I frantically searched for a seat belt. Which I didn't find, because, apparently, they hadn't been invented yet. Maybe because the car's top speed appeared to be about thirty miles an hour, which sounds like nothing unless you're in a vehicle with no sides, a high center of gravity and a stick for steering. I don't think all four wheels were ever on the ground at the same time as we careened down a street littered with obstacles, half of them living and all of them disapproving.

But however pathetic, our speed was constant, while it looked like the horses pulling Mother's coach were getting tired. Because a moment later I spotted them, just up ahead.

Mircea must have seen them, too, because he floored it, taking us up to maybe a whopping thirty-five. But it was lucky he had. Because a second later, red lightning lit up the night, shooting just behind us to explode against a building, blackening the bricks and taking out a window.

I whipped my neck around and saw what I'd expected— three damn mages in a coach they'd stolen somewhere. It had two horses and a lightweight body, and damned if they weren't gaining. And it looked like they held a grudge, because a lot of the bolts blistering through the air were aimed at us.

One took out a row of streetlamps, popping them one after another as a bolt leapt from light to light to light, burning through the night right alongside us. Another hit a swinging pub sign, appropriately named the Fiery Phoenix. The Phoenix went up in smoke and then so did we, as a spell crashed into the back of the car, picking it up and sending it sailing through the air, straight at—

I screamed and grabbed Mircea, shifting us just as he grabbed me back and jumped. The result was a confusing few seconds of shifting and then flying through the air, as his jump ended up taking place on the other side of the shift. And then we landed in a heap, half in the street and half in the gutter, before rolling onto the sidewalk and a lot of unhappy pedestrians.

I barely noticed, too busy watching the car smash into the front of a church. And wedge between two of the pillars. And explode.

And then the bastard mages zipped by us, splashing us with filthy water from a ditch in the street. The one we'd already rolled through. And the next thing I knew, we were clinging to the back of their vehicle as it pelted down the road, past the remains of the little car and into a street on the right.

Mircea must have done it, moving us with that vampire speed that sometimes seemed almost as fast as shifting. Because I sure as hell hadn't. I wasn't up to doing much, frankly, except clinging to the leather-bound trunk on the back of the coach and trying not to puke. And then it started raining.

Of course it did.

Mircea was making some kinds of signs at me, probably afraid the mages would hear if he said anything. Which would have worked great, except that my eyes kept crossing. But I guess he must have meant *I'm going to leave you for a minute to go do something insanely stupid.* Because the next second, he vaulted around the side of the coach, kicked in the door and disappeared into the small, covered area.

And then things started to get interesting. At least, they did if you consider cursing and kicking and a wildly rocking coach and a spell that blew off the roof to be interesting. It wasn't doing so much for me, but I didn't have time to worry about it, because a fist punched through the back of the coach, almost in my face.

Since it was a left one and wasn't wearing Mircea's OMEGA watch, I had no compunction at all about slipping off the one shoe I hadn't yet managed to lose and using the stiletto heel to try to sever it at the wrist. It didn't work as well as its namesake, but it must have been a distraction, at least. Because somebody cursed and somebody grunted, and then somebody went sailing out the side of the carriage to splat against one thundering along right next to us.

Which would have been great if it hadn't happened to be Mom's.

The mage grasped hold of the coach with one hand and flung a spell at me with the other, but it didn't connect— thanks to the kidnapper, of all people. I could see him, because there was no covered area of the coach anymore, due to the fire. The rain had put it out, or maybe it had burnt out after it consumed all the cloth over the cab. But either way, only the wire frame remained in place, which didn't hinder the kidnapper at all from slamming his heavy-looking suitcase upside the mage's head.

That sent the spell flying off course, missing me but setting the hem of my dress alight. Fortunately, the mud puddle I'd just finished wallowing in had pretty much soaked the material, and that and the pelting rain took care of the fire before it took care of me. I was left with a ruined dress, a burn on my thigh and a serious case of Had Enough.

If my mother could shift seven people through most of a century, I could shift five a few hundred yards, like to the next street over. It would get them off her ass, and once Mircea and I shifted back, we'd have only the mage to deal with. I just needed to get the damn war mages all in one place in order to—

And then I didn't, because Mom did it for me.

She slammed her coach into ours, almost knocking me off my perch. It did more than that to the mage, who had been trying to grab her while the kidnapper tried to grab him. The sudden movement sent him flailing back, and he fell through the missing roof of our coach, splintering the wood forming the back of it in the process. That left me looking at Mircea, who had a mage under one arm and another by the throat, and was trying to get a foot in the new arrival's stomach.

He looked up at me and I looked at him, and then to the side, where a gap in the buildings showed a nice, broad street running parallel to this one. "Fair warning," I told him. And shifted.

And immediately regretted it.

It felt like my body was coming apart at the seams, a searing, tearing pain that shot down every nerve. It hurt badly enough to have wrenched a scream from my throat, if I still had one. I didn't, because it was streaming in molecules across space, like the rest of me, like my brain, which was nonetheless informing me that this was too far, too much. That maybe I should have remembered that the two horses would count as people, too; like maybe I should have thought about how tired I already was; like maybe this would be my last shift ever because my freaking head was going to explode.

At least, it would if I had the energy to rematerialize it long enough, which I wouldn't if this went on much longer. What was going to happen instead was a quick unraveling of me and the horses and the coach and everyone inside it into particles blowing on the breeze that the rain would wash away, like we'd never existed at all. I knew it with the absolute conviction of someone who could already feel it happening, feel pieces and parts beginning to break away from their patterns, to jumble up, to distort—

And then I thought, No.

And then I thought, *Stop*.

And we did.

Really, really abruptly.

I hadn't known it was possible, mainly because I'd never had reason to try. But somehow, I had aborted the shift. Right in the goddamned middle.

It had been that or die, so it had seemed the lesser of two evils. Until we rematerialized not a street over, but still on this one. Sort of.

The street was a posh-looking curve of neoclassical

buildings fronted by pale stone that the gaslight turned gold against the black sky. Along both sides of the street ran a covered colonnade, which I hadn't really noticed because I'd been kind of busy. I noticed it now since we landed up close and personal—as in, right on top of it.

That put us well above the street, flying along a narrow roofline barely wide enough to accommodate the coach, the horses and the heads that popped out of the side of the coach to look down at the street below. And then turned to look at me. And then one of the mages managed to get an arm up, and I had absolutely no doubt what he planned to do with it.

But I couldn't stop him. I could barely even see him, wavering around in front of my blurry vision along with everyone else. Which was why it took me a moment to realize that he suddenly wasn't there anymore. That Mircea had just bailed with him and the rest, throwing the whole kicking, fighting knot over the side of the colonnade.

Which would have been fine if I'd still been able to shift. But I wasn't and I couldn't, and the end of the colonnade was coming up and I was trying to bail, too, because falling from the back of a galloping coach wouldn't be fun, but it was a lot better than the alternative. But my goddamned foot had gotten wedged behind the goddamned box and it wasn't coming out, and I didn't have time to figure out what was wrong with a brick wall staring me in the face and—

And then I was staring into a lovely pair of lapis eyes instead.

I blinked, stunned and confused and more than a little sick, as one of the mages ran up alongside the carriage. It was the one my mother was driving, in the middle of the road like a sane person, and which I was now somehow on top of. The mage grabbed for her and she broke eye contact with me long enough to glance at him, and then he was gone, popping out of existence like Niall had back in the suite. I knew that was what had happened, because a second later he showed up again in the middle of the street in front of us.

And then she ran him down.

"Damn, Liz!" the kidnapper said, staring up at her.

"Who are you?" she asked, turning those amazing eyes on me again.

And for some reason, I couldn't answer. I stared into that lovely face, so close, closer than I'd ever thought it would be, and I couldn't say anything at all. My throat closed up and my eyes filled and my face crumbled and I probably looked like a complete, blubbering idiot. But try as I might, I couldn't seem to *say* anything—

And then the kidnapper answered for me.

"Agnes sent her," he said harshly. "It's a trap!"

"I don't think so," she said, her eyes never leaving my face. I don't know what expression I was wearing, but she looked stunned, disbelieving, shocked. She put out a hand to touch my cheek, and it trembled slightly. "I don't think so," she whispered.

"I'm telling you, they're working together!" he hissed. "She's the one who helped that bitch drag me back—"

"Agnes is a good woman."

"She's a *bitch*!" he shrieked. "And this one's just as bad. You have to—"

I never found out what he wanted her to do. Because four mages jumped on the coach at the same time, which was impossible, since at least two of them were supposed to be dead. But they all looked pretty lively to me, including the one who grabbed the kidnapper around the throat and jerked him back off his feet. I didn't see what the others did, because the next moment we were shifting, flowing through time with an ease I'd never before experienced.

Shifting was usually metallic and electric and vaguely terrifying, like the thrilling ride of a roller coaster you suspect might just be out of control. But this wasn't. It was warm and soft and natural, like breathing, a light caress that picked us up and gentled us along toward . . . somewhen. I didn't know; I didn't care. I just wanted to stay here, right here—

"But this isn't your fight," she told me simply, as the tide washed us toward an unknown shore.

I shook my head, trying to tell her that she was wrong, that it was my fight; it so very definitely was. But I still couldn't talk, even as I felt her hand dissolve under mine, as the current washed us in two different directions, as I cried out and tried to hold on to something that simply wasn't there anymore—

And the next thing I knew, I was standing on a street

corner, surrounded by flashing neon lights and falling snow and shimmery, delicate nets of hanging stars, watching a Victorian coach veer across modern traffic lanes—for an instant. Before vanishing again into nothingness.

And just like that, she was gone.

Chapter Twelve

I stood on the street corner, swaying slightly, while bits of snow gathered in my hair. It's a beautiful last view, I thought blankly, watching what looked like Christmas crowds rushing about. The stars overhead were banners of lights draped across the openings of each street feeding into the intersection. Other streets farther down had them, too, so that the whole from the air probably resembled a great, glittering wheel. Or maybe a wreath. That would be more Christmassy, wouldn't it?

They look pretty against the black sky, anyway, I thought, as water dripped into my eyes from rain that had fallen however many decades ago. I didn't bother to brush it away. It didn't seem to matter now.

The lights on passing cars blurred together in long streamers of gold and red, appropriately festive. I watched them, feeling wobbly and cold and numb, and waited for oblivion. And waited. And waited.

And then I heard running footsteps coming up behind me, and before I even had a chance to turn around, hands grasped my shoulders, spinning me about. I stared dizzily up at Mircea, who was looking a little crazed. His hair was wild and so were his eyes, and there was a smudge of mud on his cheek. "You're still here," he said blankly.

I nodded cautiously, half expecting not to be at any second.

His fingers tightened on my shoulders, almost painfully. And then he picked me up and spun me around, heedless of my filthy dress or my dripping hair or the safety of the passersby. "You're still here!" he said, laughing, and kissed me.

And either it was a damn good kiss or not fading away into oblivion was a hell of an aphrodisiac. Because after only a second, those lips melted the cold shock that had all but paralyzed me, and my hands clenched on his shoulders and my leg curled around him and the next thing I knew, I was climbing his body and doing my best to climb down his throat. Mircea gave as good as he got. His hands found my ass and he lifted, and my legs fastened around him and he spun us around again, as snow fell and cars honked and somebody laughed, and I didn't give a damn because I was alive to experience all of it.

We broke apart only when it was that or asphyxiation. I clung to him, panting and light-headed from passion or relief or lack of air or all three, and the crowd we'd managed to collect applauded politely. Somebody donated a sprig of mistletoe, "not that you two need it," which Mircea jauntily stuck behind his ear. And then he kissed me again.

I think he only stopped because I started shivering. We were both soaked and it was freezing, and I'd managed to lose his jacket somewhere along the way. Even with Mircea's warmth, the cold, damp night air was already making its way in underneath my clothes, seeping down my neckline and slithering up my legs.

And there was no point even trying to shift back home. I'd be lucky to be able to do it in the morning, assuming I got some food and rest between now and then. But that posed a problem.

I looked at Mircea, who was staring up at the swirl of snow seemingly in fascination. "Mircea?"

"It's beautiful, *dulceață*," he said, his tone awed. "Do you see? Beautiful."

"What is?"

"The snow. The night." His arms tightened. "You."

I eyed him warily. "Thanks?"

Warm lips found my neck. "You are welcome."

"Mircea. It's freezing."

"I will keep you warm," he told me, those lips sliding down to my cleavage.

And, okay, it *was* getting warmer out here. "We can't stay on a street corner all night," I protested.

"Of course we can't." And before I fully realized what was happening, we were at the end of the street, my arm tucked in his as he looked this way and that, curious and bright-eyed and obviously delighted. With what I didn't know, but a second later he laughed. "Oh yes. Yes, that will do splendidly."

And then snowflakes falling around us were caught in headlights. They froze like crystals hanging in the darkness, a thousand tiny flashes of gold, as a limo pulled up at the corner. I looked at Mircea. "How . . . ?"

"I borrowed it from a friend," he told me, bundling me inside. And then immediately covered my body with his own.

He kissed me slower this time, a tender movement of his lips and then his tongue against mine, deliberate, caring, and carnal. And for a few moments, I forgot everything, except the silky hair falling around me, the smoothness of the lips on mine, and the feel of his hands on my body. Their calluses came from handling a sword regularly, hundreds of years ago, but vampires stayed as they were when they died, so they had never softened. They were the only remnant of the half-barbarian prince he'd once been, except for the hair he refused to cut.

I took the opportunity to bury my hands in it now, a spill of deep, silky mahogany, the color of oak leaves in autumn. And, okay, that was corny, but Mircea made a girl poetic. Only this so wasn't the place.

"Mircea. We can't," I gasped, glancing at the driver, who was watching us unashamedly in the mirror.

Mircea didn't even look up. "Drive," he said, and smashed a hand down on the button for the partition.

By the time it was up, my top was down and things were progressing at a rather frightening rate. "People can see us through the windows," I protested, as the soaked silk was unzipped and my bra unhooked, all in one smooth motion.

"Tinted."

"But . . . I'm hungry."

"So am I," he growled, and pulled off my dress.

Somebody had left a fur coat on the seat, something black as midnight and soft as a cloud, and the sensation against my bare skin was a hell of a distraction. Although not as much as the warm hands smoothing over me, the hard-muscled thighs pressing against me, or the tongue sliding over mine, liquid and warm and increasingly demanding.

I came up for air, minutes later, to find that Mircea's coat was off, his shirt was open and his tie was barely clinging to one shoulder. That was a little disturbing, because I couldn't remember how he got that way, or how my panties had ended up flung against the opposite seat. All I knew was that I was naked except for that sinfully soft fur coat, most of which was trapped beneath me.

I tried to tug it around, to give me some possibility of coverage should any of the passing cars get too close, but Mircea had other ideas. "Leave it," he said hoarsely. "I like the contrast with your skin."

And then he proceeded to show me exactly how much.

"What's . . . what's gotten into you?" I gasped, as that dark head worked its way down from lips to neck to body. Not that Mircea wasn't usually . . . affectionate . . . but he didn't normally care for public displays—or even semipublic ones.

It didn't seem to be bothering him right now, though.

The lips on my skin were warm and soft and pliable, unlike the prick of fangs behind them. But he didn't bite down, he just scraped them lightly over sensitive flesh, until I was hard and peaked and desperate. "It has been a while, so I cannot be certain," he murmured. "But I believe I may be drunk."

I blinked at him. "What?"

"The blood of those creatures. It was . . . intoxicating."

"You mean the mages?"

"Mmm-hmm." He rolled a nipple between tongue and teeth, making my hands fist in his shirt.

"But . . . but they were human."

"Mmm, no," he said thoughtfully. And then he bit down.

I gasped and clutched his head between my hands, holding him as he drank from me. The sensation of warm lips, sharp, sharp teeth and deep, intimate pulls had my body tightening, my skin flushing and my pulse pounding in my ears. I felt my grip on the moment slipping away.

"Then what were they?" I asked breathlessly, before I forgot what the hell we were talking about.

"They were human, but stronger," he told me, sitting back on his heels. "Like you."

"Like me?"

"Your blood is richer than normal, due to the power of your office," he explained, tossing the tie aside.

"Why does that matter?"

"It matters because your power used to belong to a god." He started to pull off the shirt, but I put out a hand.

"Leave it," I said huskily. He wasn't the only one who liked a contrast. And the white, white fabric against the honey-drenched skin was . . . pleasing.

He quirked an eyebrow, but did as I asked. Then he slid back over me, grinning wickedly. "Perhaps that is why you taste divine."

"You're saying those mages were—were some kind of demigods?" I asked as he nuzzled my neck.

"I do not know, having never before had the opportunity to sample a god. But their blood was like yours—thick, rich, like old cognac."

I had another question, but then his head dipped and his mouth closed over me again and I forgot what it was. I pretty much forgot everything as his tongue laved the small puncture wounds he'd made, the gentle, tender probing sending shudders through my whole body. I arched up mindlessly and he sat up, pulling me, naked, onto his lap.

My lips opened to protest, because if I'd been visible before it was nothing compared to now. But then strong hands grasped me and a magnificent hardness pressed against me and he started to suck not so gently. And my protest turned into a moan as my legs tightened around him, my skin flushed a deeper shade of pink, and my body squirmed, craving friction, craving more. I buried my fingers in the raw silk of his hair and forgot the passing cars and the curious driver and everything except the pull of that mouth and the feel of those hands, smoothing up and down my back and clenching—

And, okay, I thought dizzily, maybe this could work, after all.

But the next second Mircea was drawing back. "You're hungry," he announced, as if this were news.

"What? Do I have low blood sugar?" I asked facetiously.

"Yes." He rapped smartly on the partition, which lowered so fast I barely had time to snatch up the mink. The vampire driver wasn't a family member or a high-level master, so Mircea had to talk to him directly. "The Club," he said succinctly.

"We are already there, my lord," the driver said softly. "I took the liberty of anticipating your wishes."

"Good man," Mircea said, and before I quite knew what was happening, he'd pulled me out into the snow.

Even with the mink, the shock of cold air was a little stunning after the cozy warmth of the limo. But we weren't out in it for long. My toes barely had time to register the frozen sidewalk before Mircea swung me up and ran with me up the stairs of a beautiful old row house.

A plain red door, like a dozen others on the street, gave way to a narrow little hallway boasting a priceless chandelier, a mahogany welcome desk and what looked suspiciously like a Cézanne, its bright colors glowing against the dark wood paneling.

A rotund little vampire bustled around the side of the desk and then disappeared. It took me a second to realize that he'd bowed, so low that even peering over the edge of the mink, all I could see were the lights gleaming off his shiny bald head. He bobbed back up after a minute, and then he did it again, like one of those drinking bird toys that just can't stay upright.

But eventually he did, leading the way up the stairs. And I guessed he must have been a lot older than the driver, because not a word was said until his slightly shaking hands had opened the door to a magnificent suite. It was saffron and coral and deep chocolate brown, with a fireplace in caramel-colored marble and a huge window overlooking the city lights.

"I—I hope it is to your liking, my lord," he murmured, and turned pink-cheeked with delight when Mircea casually nodded.

"Yes, it's fine. We'll eat up here."

"Of course, of course. Right away." The little vamp bowed himself out—literally—bobbing three times as he withdrew backward into the hall. And then Mircea finally let me down, only to get his hands inside the coat and push me against the wall.

"I'm dirty," I protested.

He waggled his eyebrows. "Promise?"

"Mircea!" I laughed in spite of myself. "I want a bath before we eat!"

His eyes, glinting in the discreet light of the suite, met mine. "If you'll indulge me."

"I'm not bathing with you," I told him firmly. I'd never get any dinner that way.

"Of course not," he said, in pretend shock.

"Then what?"

He let a single finger trace down my cheek to my jaw, to my neck, to my . . . necklace? "Is your ghost in residence?"

"No." I hadn't felt the need for a chaperone. "Why?"

"Because I have a recurring fantasy of you dining with me wearing this." That warm finger slowly traced the outline of the baroque monstrosity. "And only this."

I made a small sound and closed my eyes.

Goddamnit.

Despite appearances, I was trying, I was really, really trying, to have a relationship with Mircea, not just to jump his bones every time we had five minutes alone together. And I'd been doing pretty well lately, mainly because he'd been in New York and I'd been in Vegas and my plans always sounded a lot more doable when he wasn't pressed up against me and—

"Stop that," I told him, as he rotated his hips sinuously, because the damn man had no shame at all.

"Then give me an answer," he said, laughter in his voice.

I looked up, intending to say no, but those dark eyes had an unmistakable glint of challenge sparkling in their depths. As if he thought I wouldn't do it. As if he was sure I wouldn't do it. Because I wasn't a vampire, wasn't adventurous like . . . certain other people. Who probably didn't have a problem sashaying around covered in nothing but that long, silky black hair, those almond-shaped, dark eyes peeking coyly back over her dainty shoulder as she—

Goddamnit!

But it wasn't that easy for me. Not because I had a problem indulging him, although nudity wasn't my favorite thing. But because I was human. And Mircea, like a lot of vampires, had the bad habit of assuming that whatever he wanted from a human, he would get.

It didn't help that he was usually right.

And centuries of that sort of thing had messed with his head, to the point that he rarely saw the need for debate with said human, or compromise or negotiation or any of the sort of things he would do with one of his own kind. He'd claimed me; therefore I was his. End of discussion, had there been a discussion, which there hadn't been because I was human and some days, most days, that attitude just really made me want to tear my hair out.

So here I was, trying to see if a relationship would maybe, possibly, in some sort of way work despite the fact that the mages were absolutely going to hate it and the Weres weren't going to love it and I was also going to take flak from the vampires after they realized that "relationship" didn't mean "ownership" in my vocabulary, and what was Mircea doing?

Acting like there was nothing to discuss, of course.

Only there was. There so very definitely was, like five hundred years of history I knew next to nothing about. Like the fact that almost all I did know was that he was fiercely loyal to his family, had a horrible sense of humor, and when he walked into a room, he made my breath catch.

And, yeah, that was definitely something, but was it enough to base a lifetime on? I didn't know yet. All I did know was that if I kept giving in, kept doing what he wanted, kept acting like we were already together and the decision had been made . . . then pretty soon, it would be.

And I didn't know yet if it was one I could live with.

"Cassie?"

I looked up to find him regarding me with exasperated eyes. "Do you really have to think so hard about this?"

"It's . . . complicated," I said fretfully.

"No, it really isn't."

"Yes, it is! It really, really is, and you know it is and—"

He stopped me with a hand on either side of my face. "When are we?"

"What?"

"The year."

I frowned. And my power sluggishly called up the date: "Nineteen sixty-nine."

"And that means you haven't been born yet, doesn't it?"

I nodded.

"We haven't met yet—am I right?"

"Well, not unless you count that time in—"

"Cassie."

"No. Not . . . technically. But I don't get what you're—"

"I'm saying that nothing that happens, or doesn't happen, tonight will have any bearing on our relationship once we return. No implications. No consequences. Think of this as . . . a night out of time."

"A night out of time?" I repeated doubtfully, because I didn't get those. Time caused me problems; it didn't solve them. Not even for one night.

His forehead came to rest against mine. "A night out of time."

I licked my lips and thought it over. "The servers will see."

"And if I arrange it so they won't?"

I looked up at him, and it was a mistake, because he was grinning that little-boy grin, the one he never showed in public because it would completely trash his image as big, bad Vampire Senate member. But I got to see it every once in a while. And it never failed to be devastating.

"Just dinner," I heard myself say, before I could bite my tongue.

"Just dinner," he agreed softly, stroking the lines of my cheekbones with his thumbs.

And then he let me go.

Chapter Thirteen

The bathroom of the suite turned out to be as impressive as the rest. Golden marble with thin veins of burnt umber running through it covered everything from the floors to the ceiling to the double sinks to the spa-like tub, all polished to a high gloss. There was a plush dark orange rug, matching towels, and a basket of expensive toiletries all done up in cellophane like the Easter bunny had just delivered it.

And there were mirrors, lots and lots of mirrors.

Almost every surface that wasn't covered in marble had one, and all of them informed me that I looked like hell. My makeup was long gone, my hair was a freaking disaster, and my body was smeared with mud and various other substances I didn't want to think too hard about. I sighed and peeled the laddered foot of what had been an expensive pair of stockings off my filthy feet. My polish was chipped and my toes ... well, they looked like you'd expect after being dragged across cobblestones.

I contemplated my shredded toes and sighed. One day, one fine, fine day, I was going to be in peril in a damn pair of sneakers. Of course, I'd settle for not being in peril at all.

Not being in peril at all would be good.

I grabbed a couple of sinfully plush towels and got my beat-up, grimy self into the nice, clean shower. I didn't even try for a bath, because I'd immediately turn the water black. Kind of like the evening's entertainment had done to me.

After I got clean enough to be fairly sure that whatever was left wasn't dirt, I took stock. I had a swelling bruise on my ankle, another on my hip and a third, long and horizontal and rapidly darkening, on my lower stomach, probably where I'd hit down on the damn carriage ride from hell. Add that to the bruises I was still carrying from the bathtub incident and, oh yeah, I looked sexy.

Not that I wasn't happy to be alive in any shape. I just didn't understand why I was. Particularly not if Mircea's theory was correct about what we'd been fighting.

It had seemed crazy when he said it, because demigods weren't exactly thick on the ground. The gods, or the creatures calling themselves that, had been banished a long time from Earth, and most of their by-blows had either gone with them or been rounded up by the Circle. And because I couldn't imagine what a bunch of half gods could want with my mother.

But now that I had a chance to think, it did explain a lot. Like how resilient the mages had been, not bothering with shields but bouncing back from blows that should have left them a smear on the concrete without them. And why they'd seemed so damn strong.

Pritkin had once told me that war mages never used a hundred percent of their power for attack. In battle, the standard ratio was seventy-thirty, meaning that seventy percent of a mage's power went to defense—to the shields and wards needed to keep him or her alive—with maybe thirty percent leftover for offensive stuff. Particularly powerful magic users could hedge on that a bit, maybe taking the total needed for defense down to sixty-five or even sixty percent, because their excess power made up for it. But nobody went completely unprotected. If they did, the first spell to so much as nick them might take them out of the fight—permanently.

Pritkin himself regularly used only about a quarter of his power for defense, although he didn't admit as much to the Circle. But what if someone could shrug off being trampled under horses or slung against buildings or dragged half the length of a street, despite not using shields? Being able to put everything toward attack would make even a low-level mage look pretty damn impressive. And if he or she was already extra-strong to begin with ...

Well, that mage might look something like what I'd just seen. But as reasonable as that sounded, it couldn't be right. Because my mother couldn't have fought off four demigods and a crazy-ass kidnapper all by herself.

Could she?

It seemed ridiculous. But, then, if the answer was no, why was I still here? If the mages had killed her or the kidnapper had carted her off, or anything had happened to keep her from meeting my infamous father, then I should have vanished. And other than for the rather large amount of skin I'd left in the road, I hadn't.

And that was ... well, that was kind of an epiphany. The whole damn night had been, really. Because I'd never seen the Pythian power used like that. In fact, I'd rarely seen it used at all, which was one of the reasons I'd been having so much trouble mastering it.

Jonas did his best to help me, but he wasn't a Pythia. He'd overheard some of the stuff Agnes had said when training her heirs, and he'd seen a lot of what she could do. But trying to harness time with his help had been like building a car from a set of oral instructions when you've never seen one and the guy giving them has only a vague idea of what one is supposed look like.

It had been the blind leading the blind all month.

It had gotten frustrating enough that I'd actually thought of going to the Pythian Court for help. But I hadn't, and not just because one of their number had already tried to kill me. They probably weren't all homicidal maniacs, but I doubted I was real popular with a group who had zero chance of advancement as long as I lived.

Which might explain why I hadn't heard from them all month. Not a "congrats," however insincere; not a "fuck you"; not a peep of any kind. I didn't know what that meant, but it was more than a little ominous. And Jonas sure as hell hadn't suggested stopping by for a chat.

So I'd been on my own.

And being on my own sucked ass.

But then had come tonight. And ... damn.

Somehow, I'd gotten into the habit of thinking about my power as defensive—shifting to get out of a tight spot, throwing time bubbles to ward off attackers, stopping time to give me a chance to run like hell. Maybe because that was mostly how I'd been using it. But my mother . . . she hadn't been real big on defense. She'd been real big on kicking some demigod butt.

The war mages might have been running a full-on offensive, but she'd been right there with them. She'd sent them screaming in terror. She'd imprisoned one like a bug under glass. She'd run one the hell down.

Mom, I realized in shock, had been kind of a badass.

And so was the Pythian power in the hands of somebody who actually knew how to use it. And while I didn't realistically think I'd ever be anywhere near that good . . . still. It gave me a lot to think about.

Only this wasn't the place, because I was going all pruney. I hadn't known a shower could do that, but this one was hard and hot and enthusiastic, to the point that my fingers and what was left of my toes were wrinkling up. I got out of the shower, dried my hair, and swiped a hand over the nearest mirror.

It showed me what I'd expected: a thin, pale girl with scraggly blond hair, dark circles under her eyes and a bruise in her hairline. I leaned in, pulling my hair back, searching my own face. I had a lot more to go on now than a grainy photo taken at a distance. I'd stared her right in the face from barely a foot away. Yet try as I might, I couldn't see even a distant echo in me.

My eyes were blue, but they were just blue. My hair was reddish, sort of, in the right light, but nothing like that beautiful bronze color. And my face was . . . just a face.

It looked back at me now, too-round cheekbones, a too-stubborn chin and a scattering of unfashionable freckles over a tip-tilted nose. It wasn't a bad face, as faces go, but it wasn't going to be launching a thousand ships anytime soon. I stood there, searching it anyway, desperate to find some trace of that ethereal beauty. . . . And it suddenly hit me. If I hadn't taken after my mother, then I must look like—

Him.

The dark mage who had wooed her away from the court, from her rightful place in the succession, from everything she'd ever known. Agnes had told me once that my mother had been a natural with the power, the best she'd ever seen, and I'd had plenty of proof of that tonight. And yet she'd left it all behind for an evil man, a onetime member of the notorious Black Circle, who looked like . . . me?

I leaned closer. Was this the face that had commanded an army of ghosts to spy on the Silver Circle, who had almost seized control of the Black and who had somehow seduced the virgin heir to the powerful Pythian throne? My reflection didn't answer; it just dripped at me, looking vaguely like a drowned Kewpie doll.

I scrunched up my face and tried to look menacing.

Now I looked like a Kewpie doll with gas.

I sighed. Maybe I'd taken after some distant relative or something. I might never know, since I didn't have even a grainy image of my father. Not that I wanted one, at least not as a keepsake, but it would have been nice to know what he'd looked like.

It would also be nice to get dressed before the rest of the hot air leaked out of the bathroom. My clothes had been left in the limo, and, frankly, they'd been no big loss. But there were some plush terry cloth robes on a rack beside the door, and I had an arm in one before I remembered.

Oh, dear God.

Had I really just agreed to walk out there *naked*?

I just stood there for a minute, clutching the robe and staring blankly at the mirror, which was mercifully fogging back up. I told myself that it didn't matter, that I'd just been naked in the freaking *limo*, for God's sake, flashing who knew how many people on the way here. But it had been dark and I'd been half-crazy with relief and Mircea . . . Well, Mircea could make a girl forget her own name when he put a little effort into it. But that was a lot different from walking out there cold and naked and bruised and pruney and—

Shit. How did I get myself into these things?

I bit my lip and stared at the door. I didn't *have* to do it. Mircea might be disappointed, but he'd live, and I could say—

What? That I was a freaking coward? That I knew I wouldn't live up to the standards of his—very many—other women? That most of them had been among the world's great beauties, and here I was, with cracked toenail polish and rat's-nest hair and no makeup and a body that looked like it had been used as a punching bag?

I ran a comb through my hair while I stood there debating it. Okay, okay. There was no denying that I didn't look my best. But honestly, even polished to a high gloss, I wasn't going to compete in the looks department with a porcelain doll like Ming-de. Or the Grace Kelly look-alike I'd seen with Mircea at the theater once. Or the sloe-eyed countess who had been willing to fight a duel over him. Or the athletic-looking brunette with the big boobs that he'd kept a freaking photo album of until it was destroyed in an accident, and wasn't that just too goddamned bad?

Yeah. So. I had what I had, and it might be a little beat-up, but it was pretty much the package. And it had been really dark in the limo, but that wouldn't bother a vampire's sight, and he hadn't seemed exactly put off then.

And, hey, at least I was clean now.

I took off the robe and looked at the door again. I felt cold. And really, really naked. Like, super-ultranaked. Which was stupid, because naked was naked and goddamn it! Just do it already.

I grasped the doorknob, feeling nervous and jittery and silly and kind of turned on and—

I took my hand off again.

How often do you get a free pass? the less cowardly part of my brain demanded. I didn't answer, because talking to yourself is a little too close to the scary side of crazy, and I was teetering on the brink as it was. But I knew the answer anyway. If I didn't do this, if I let myself chicken out, I knew damned well I'd regret it. Maybe not now, but soon, and I had enough regrets. Tonight I wanted to live.

I put my hand back on the knob. It's like pulling off a Band-Aid, I told myself sternly. Just do it fast and the hard part will be over. Before I could talk myself out of it again, I took a deep breath, grabbed the doorknob and flung it open.

And burst out into a room full of vamps.

The fat little manager was standing over by the fireplace, along with Mircea and a couple of young guys dressed like waiters. Another waiter type was by the door, wheeling out a room service cart, but of course he turned to see what the commotion was about. And I didn't doubt that he got a good view. The room was dim, lit mainly by a couple of low-burning lamps in the corners and the bright white light flooding in behind me.

Spotlighting me like freaking Gypsy Rose Lee.

For a moment, I stared at them and they stared at me and it was like Agnes's party all over again, after it had been frozen in time. Nothing moved except the flames somebody had stoked in the fireplace. And then I gave a shriek and the paralysis broke.

One of the guys jumped and one of them grinned and Mircea held out a hand, and then I don't know what happened because I ran back into the bathroom and slammed the door.

Oh, God.

Oh, God, oh, God, oh *God*.

Tonight *sucked*. Tonight sucked so damn hard I just didn't even know—

Someone rapped on the door.

I could feel it in my shoulder blades, because I had my back to the damn thing and I wasn't moving. I might never move again. "*Dulceață?*"

Shit.

"*Dulceață?* Are you all right?"

I didn't say anything, because he knew damn well I was all right. He could hear me breathing through the door. This close, he could probably feel the heat from my flaming cheeks, which a glance in the mirror informed me were bright, lobster red. As was my neck and a good bit of my chest, all of which was perfectly visible, and oh, *God*.

"*Dulceață?*"

"I'm fine," I choked out, hoping he'd just go away. If there was some kind of disaster scale for dates, this one had just hit ten. Or maybe twenty. Or maybe some number heretofore unknown in the history of dating, and I really didn't think I could take a conversation on top of—

I heard a door close outside, with a discreet snick. "They've gone, *dulceață*," Mircea said, his voice sounding a little funny.

Somewhere in all that, I had slid down to my haunches, with my arms over my head, hoping the floor might be merciful and swallow me up. But that tone got me back on my feet. I grabbed one of the damn robes and jerked it on, and then stuck my head out the door.

"Are you laughing at me?" I demanded incredulously.

"No," he said, and pulled me against his chest.

It was vibrating.

"You *are* laughing at me, you complete and total—"

"I'm not," he said, but he had a hand on the back of my head and he wouldn't let me look at his face.

"This was your fault!"

"Dulceață—"

"Don't call me that!" I was feeling anything but sweet at the moment. In fact, if I could have gotten an arm free, I'd have probably hit him. But his had gone around me and they were holding me tight, although at least I could move my head now. I looked up.

His face was absolutely and suspiciously sober, but his eyes were dancing.

"You're a *bastard*," I said with feeling.

"I assure you, my parents were properly wed. And I was merely going to say that you're right."

"I know I'm right!" I blinked. "What?"

"I should have warned you that they were here, but I did not expect you to be quite so . . . bold."

And no, he probably hadn't, I realized. He'd probably expected me to come out in a robe or a towel, or at least to poke my head around the door first. Not to storm out like the bathroom was on fire. Or like a really, really inept stripper.

I winced and let my head fall forward. "That's me," I told him miserably. "I'm bold."

"To a frightening degree at times," he murmured, combing his fingers through my wet curls.

"I don't try to be."

"I know."

We just stood there a while, and it felt really good. He was freshly washed, with his dark hair still damp and combed back from his face, and he was wearing a robe like mine. I guessed that either the suite had a second bathroom or, considering how the hotel manager had been pretty much genuflecting, they'd opened another room for him. Or possibly the entire floor.

Anyway, this was better. This was the best part of the date so far.

Not that that was saying much.

"Cassie?"

"Hm?"

"You can't stay in the bathroom all night."

"Why not?"

"It's wet."

"Don't care."

"It's going to get cold."

"Don't care."

"And you'll miss dinner."

I looked up, feeling a slight bit of hope creeping in past the utter mortification. "Dinner?"

"Dinner," he said, and pulled me out the door.

Chapter Fourteen

We reentered the living room and I figured out what everyone had been doing over by the fireplace. Flames danced on a row of silver chafing dishes, which had been strung out along the hearth to keep them warm. In front of them was a picnic area, if picnics featured silk cushions, bone china, linen so white it gleamed and napkins tortured into little birds of paradise. There was a single rose in a crystal vase that reflected the firelight. It was lovely.

It was also less interesting than the contents of those dishes, which smelled heavenly. My stomach growled, reminding me that I hadn't eaten since lunch and it had been a busy night. I knelt in front of the fire and picked up the first lid, happy and hopeful and starving and—

"What's this?" I asked, perplexed.

Mircea looked over my shoulder. "Pan-seared foie gras with cherries and foie gras caramel."

I put the lid back. Duck liver had never done a lot for me, no matter what they cooked it with. "And this?" I was staring into the second offering.

"Poireaux vinaigrette aux grains de caviar."

I did a quick translation. "Leeks and fish eggs in vinegar?"

He grinned. "It sounds better in French."

Yeah, but did it taste better? Door number three had crab and artichokes in Pernod, which would have been fine, except that I hated two out of the three. Door number four offered up more artichokes—must have been a sale—with gnocchi and herbed cheese. Door number five had more foie gras, this time stuffed into a duck breast. Door number six had—

"What is this?" I looked up at Mircea hopefully, because the stew had potatoes and onions and some kind of meat in a rich sauce and smelled awesome.

"Hossenfeffer. It's one of the house specialties."

"Hossenfeffer?" It sounded familiar, but I couldn't—

"Rabbit stew."

I looked up at him tragically.

"Is there a problem?" Mircea asked carefully.

"I used to have a pet rabbit," I said, seeing Honeybun's black eyes staring at me accusingly.

Mircea bit his lip. "This date isn't going so well, is it?" he asked, half-amused, half-despairing. I recognized the look because I felt pretty much the same way.

"It's . . . well . . . you know," I said, and then realized I didn't have anything else to say, so I shut up.

My stomach growled.

We regarded the last little dish in forlorn hope.

"You look," I told him. I probably wouldn't know what the hell it was anyway.

He leaned over and removed the lid, and some really wonderful smells steamed out. But I wasn't going to get excited, not this time, because it was probably Bambi in shallots or Nemo with fennel or—

"It's some kind of pork," he told me.

That didn't sound so bad. But then, neither had the others until I did a little translating. I moved closer and peered inside. And saw—

"It's ribs and fries," I said, in something approaching awe.

"Amish roasted pork loin with potatoes and apple-baked cabbage," he said, reading off a little menu card I hadn't noticed before.

"It's ribs and fries," I said, so happy I could have cried.

Mircea slanted me a glance. "It does look delicious. I believe I may—"

"Don't even think about it." I grabbed the dish and a plate and chowed down, while he watched with ill-concealed amusement. He started on the rabbit. I tried not to notice.

The ribs were succulent and falling-off-the-bone tender, the apple-baked cabbage was a little sauerkraut in a hollowed-out apple that I pushed aside as the garnish it was, and the fries were the English kind, thick-cut wedges of golden potato that went great with fish but turned out to be pretty good with pork, too. And so was the wine, some Riesling or other that was crisp and fresh and tart on my tongue, and oh yeah . . .

This was more like it.

Mircea laughed, and I looked up. "What?"

"It's merely . . . good to see someone enjoying their meal."

"Bet you wish you hadn't had that gourmet stuff now."

Gleaming dark eyes regarded me over his wineglass. "You didn't give me a choice. And I'm surprised you don't care for that 'gourmet stuff.' I recall Antonio having quite a good chef."

Yeah, till he ate him, I didn't say, because we were having a nice dinner. "How did you end up changing that bastard anyway?" I asked instead. "I always wondered. I mean, he was just a chicken farmer, right?"

Mircea shook his head. "Not when I met him. He had inherited the farm, such as it was, when his father died, and used the money from its sale to move to Florence. There he became . . . I suppose you would call him the strongman for a small money-lending operation."

"A thug, in other words."

"As you say. But a thug with ambition. He eventually gained control of the business—"

"Imagine that."

"—and under his hand, it grew considerably in size. By the time I met him, he was a man of some means."

"That doesn't explain why you changed him."

"You might say that we had . . . complementary problems," he said, refilling his glass with the red wine he preferred. He tilted the bottle at me.

I shook my head. "I'll stay with this one. And what kind of problems?"

"In Tony's case, it was the plague. The Black Death cut a swath through Italy every few decades in those days, and at the time it was raging in Florence. There was no cure; the only way to combat it was to flee. And Antonio tried, moving himself and his household to the country as soon as he heard."

"But he got it anyway?"

"No, but several of his servants did and he was afraid he would be next. He therefore moved again—and again and again. But everywhere he went, it was already there or it broke out shortly afterward. He told me it was as if the plague was following him."

I nodded. That sounded like Tony. He was paranoid even when he didn't have a reason.

"He finally ended up in Venice, hoping to get a ship to somewhere without the disease. But he was told by the sailors he talked to that it was everywhere that year."

"And he started freaking out."

Mircea smiled. "To put it mildly. He was in a taverna, drowning his sorrows, when I met him. At the time, I was in dire straits myself—financially speaking. I had left my home with little some years before and had . . . someone with me for whom I was responsible. I needed money for living expenses, and also to allow me to avoid a certain first-level master who had decided to add me to her family—by force if necessary. She had tracked me to Venice, and I had narrowly avoided her twice in as many days. I wanted to get away; Antonio wanted to avoid the plague. We struck a deal."

"He gave you money and you Changed him," I guessed. "Because vamps can't get the disease."

"Yes." Mircea swirled his wine around. "He was the first child I ever made. It came as . . . quite a shock . . . when he threw in his lot with our enemies."

"You thought him better than that?" I asked incredulously.

Mircea snorted. "I thought him smarter than that. I also thought it out of character."

"Because it was a gamble."

He nodded. "And Antonio doesn't. Not with his neck, at any rate."

I'd thought as much myself, more than once. Tony only liked to gamble when it was a sure thing. It made me wonder what he knew that we didn't.

Mircea finished his meal and then lay on his side, a hand under his head and the other toying with his wineglass. "Why the sudden interest?"

"I don't know. I was thinking about my parents and how Tony is probably the only person who could tell me much about them."

"What about the venerable mage Marsden? He must know something about the former Pythian heir. I would be surprised if he hadn't met her on occasion."

"He did. But all he could tell me was that she was a charming young woman. As far as facts go, all I got was the standard bio stuff they'd give to a newspaper or something. Born Elizabeth O'Donnell, adopted by the Pythian Court at age fourteen, named the heir at age thirty-three. Ran away with Ragnar, aka Roger Palmer, my disreputable father, for reasons unknown, at age thirty-four. Died five years later in a car bomb set by Tony the Bastard. The End."

"That is . . . somewhat terse," Mircea agreed. "Surprisingly so, considering the Circle's intelligence network."

I shot him a look. "Has yours done any better?"

He grinned. "Now, why would we be checking on your mother?"

"Because you check on everyone?"

"It's Kit, you know," he told me mournfully, talking about the Senate's chief spy. "I can't do a thing with him."

I ignored that for the bullshit it was. "What did you find?"

"Little more than that, I'm afraid," he admitted. "Your mother was extremely . . . elusive. My people even had difficulty finding a venue for tonight. She rarely went out, and when she did, it was usually to small dinner parties of ten or twelve people, which wouldn't have allowed you to see without being seen."

"What about her background?"

"She was adopted by the Pythian Court from a school in Des Moines, one of those for magical orphans run by the Circle."

I nodded; Jonas had said the same. And it wasn't too surprising. The Circle ran a bunch of those schools, and not just for kids with no parents. They also locked up—excuse me, benevolently housed—kids who had families but who also had talents of which they disapproved—necromancers, firestarters, jinxes, telekenetics, etc. I assumed the orphans got out at age eighteen or whatever; the others . . . sometimes they never did.

It was something I was working to change, and not just because it was appallingly unfair to be locked up simply for the crime of being born. But also because if I hadn't ended up at Tony's, I might have been in one of those pseudoprisons myself. Nobody was afraid of clairvoyants, most of whom were assumed to be frauds, anyway. But the talent I'd inherited from my father was another story.

Having ghost servants who hung around, feeding off you and occasionally doing an errand or two in return, was seen as Highly Suspicious Behavior. Maybe because my father had refined it to an art form. According to rumors, he'd had his own ghost army, which he'd used in an attempt to seize control of the notorious Black Circle. The coup hadn't worked and he'd ended up on the run, but that didn't change the fact that he'd been powerful enough to try. And power like that would have gotten me put away real quick.

But my mother hadn't had it. Which made me wonder what she'd been in for. "What was she in for?" I asked Mircea, who was savaging some poor bunny, apparently with relish.

He swallowed. "Nothing. Her records merely said that she was dropped off as an infant by person or persons unknown, with a note giving her name and birth date. The administrators assumed that a teenage mother had wanted to get rid of an embarrassing responsibility."

"And the name?"

"There were no magical families by the name of O'Donnell in the area at that time. There were several in other parts of the country, but Kit found none who fit the requisite profile. He thinks the mother might have given the child the father's last name, and that the father might have been human."

I didn't have to ask why that was a problem. Humans outbred the magical community by something like a thousand to one. Even assuming O'Donnell wasn't a wholly made-up name to begin with, sorting through the number of possible human fathers would be—

Well, it wasn't likely to happen. Not to satisfy my curiosity, anyway.

"Okay," I said, moving on. "So the court finds her, probably because they keep a lookout for particularly strong clairvoyants."

Mircea nodded and stole a fry.

"And then she joins the Pythian Court. And then the record scratches, at least according to Jonas."

"And according to Kit. The Pythian Court is a separate, self-governed entity and does not have to vet its members through the Circle—or anyone else. The court tells us what it wants, when it wants, and has traditionally been . . . less than forthcoming." Mircea shot me a suspiciously innocent look. "I think Kit is waiting impatiently for your accession, when he will finally have a conduit to all that lovely information."

I snorted. Yeah. He could keep on waiting. I wasn't his freaking all-access pass.

Mircea smiled. "This should prove . . . entertaining."

"Something like that." I drank wine. "So, anyway, Jonas dated Agnes, or whatever you want to call it, for thirty years, yet he never got the story about what happened with my mother. He said she became angry whenever he brought it up, so he mostly didn't. Which means the only thing I have to go on is what happened afterward."

"When she and your father went to live with Antonio."

"And that's what I don't get." I said, swirling a rib around in the gooey sauce. "My father was some big-time dark mage, right? So how does someone like that end up working for a rat like Tony?"

He pursed his lips. "It wasn't a bad choice. Many of the mages who work for us have needed to disappear for one reason or another. Admittedly, most of them are running from the Silver Circle, not the Black, but the same rule applies: if someone is looking for you in one world, go to another. And the Circle often forgets that our world exists." He smiled a little ferally. "Or it would like to."

"But *Tony*? He couldn't have done better than *that*?"

"With his abilities, doubtless. But you forget, *dulceață*, a more prominent court would also have been more risky, as it might have come under scrutiny by one or both of the circles. Whereas Antonio . . ."

"Wasn't worth their time."

One muscular shoulder rose in a shrug. "He was to the local branch, but I doubt he so much as registered at the national level. It was why I left you with him, if you recall."

I nodded. After Mircea had found out about my existence, he'd considered bringing me to his court. But as a senator, he was watched constantly, and he'd been afraid that the Circle might get curious about me. And since I was a magic worker, not a vampire, he could have been forced to hand me over.

"Okay, I understand that," I said, chewing thoughtfully. "My parents wanted to fly under the radar, so they hid out with a loser nobody cared about. I just don't understand why they chose *him*."

"Ah, now, that I can answer."

It was so unexpected that it took me a moment to react. I'd hit so many brick walls trying to find out something about my parents, that I almost expected it now. "You *can*?"

"Yes. Well," Mircea hedged. "I can tell you what Antonio told me. He said that he and your father had had business dealings for some years before Roger asked him for refuge."

"What kind of business dealings?"

"You know that Antonio remained in the money-lending business?"

"He was a loan shark," I corrected. Among a lot of other things. If he could make a buck off it, Tony had wanted in.

"As you say. In any case, many of his clients found that they could not repay their debts, and he was ruthless about confiscating whatever had been put up for collateral."

"Yeah. We always had stuff sitting around," I said, remembering. "Cars, boats—even a light airplane once. And then there was all the junk from the houses. I got in trouble for finger-painting on a Chippendale sideboard once, but how did I know? It was just another scarred, old table."

"But antiques—even finger-painted ones—are easy to move," Mircea pointed out. "That wasn't true of magical devices, particularly unstable ones. They had to be disposed of properly, and such disposal is not cheap."

I nodded. "You have to call in a Remainder." They'd occasionally come to the farmhouse, men in stained coveralls who carted away boxes of suspicious charms, amulets and potions before they blew up in anyone's face.

"And you know how fond Antonio was of spending money," Mircea said. "But he couldn't leave the items in place and risk having them burn down his investments, and he couldn't abandon them somewhere without possibly coming to the attention of the Circle, which monitors that sort of thing. For a long time, he had to pay up."

"I don't see what this has to do with my father."

"Antonio told me that Roger contacted him offering to dispose of any such volatile devices for free."

I frowned. "For free? But isn't that work kind of . . . risky?"

"Very. One of my cooks likes to tell the story of the time he bought a growth charm to use on his kitchen garden. But he didn't monitor it properly, and it went past the expiration date. Shortly thereafter, he woke up to a garden of giants—squash as long as canoes, watermelons the size of small cars, tomatoes as large as beach balls—all of which had burst because of too-rapid growth. He said the mess was . . . astonishing."

"He's just lucky he didn't have it in his room," I said, getting a vision of a head swollen to the size of a beach ball.

"Indeed. Remainders earn their money."

"Yet my father offered the service for free. Didn't that make anyone suspicious?"

"Yes. But Antonio was not the type to turn down a good deal. After your father came to work for him, he developed the theory that he was using the leftover magic to feed his ghosts."

I shook my head. "Ghosts require human energy. Some old charm wouldn't do them any more good than it would you or me." Less, really. It wasn't like they needed to grow hair or lose weight or whiten their teeth.

"Then it remains a mystery, I'm afraid."

Like everything else about my parents. I sighed and contemplated my almost-empty plate. I couldn't possibly eat another thing. Except maybe that one last rib . . .

"You met him, didn't you?" I asked, slathering on the sauce.

Mircea nodded. "Antonio sent him to court a few times

as his representative." His lips quirked. "I think because his manners were somewhat more refined than those of most of Antonio's stable."

"You mean he didn't drink straight out of the bottle?"

"Or use the tablecloth for a napkin. Or lick the butter knife. Or drink from the finger bowl, and then complain that the tea tasted just like hot water."

I blinked. "Who did that?"

"Alphonse."

"Ah." I grinned, thinking of Tony's second, a seven-foot hunk of muscle who was great with the guns and the knives and the things that went boom. Not so much with the dainty table manners. "What was my father like?"

Mircea thought about it for a moment. "Somewhat reserved, as might have been expected. But articulate, well-read, even amusing at times. I tried to steal him away from Antonio, but he said he liked the good air in New Jersey!"

I nodded. Tony had business interests in Jersey. My father must have worked in some of them. "He was probably afraid you'd do a background check."

"Probably. I have employed mages on a number of occasions who were at odds with the Silver Circle, whose punishments are often out of proportion to the crime. But the Black . . . no. I do not deal with them."

I drank wine and didn't comment. I didn't want to think about what my father might have done as a member of the world's most organized bunch of evil mages. I didn't know why I was curious about the damn man at all. Maybe just because, while I knew a little about my mother, he was almost a total blank.

For years, all I'd known was that he'd been Tony's "favorite human" until he refused to hand me over. Tony had been so incensed by this "betrayal," as he saw it, that killing him hadn't been enough. He'd had a mage construct a trap for my father's soul, capturing it at the point of death. Tony had used it for years afterward as a paperweight—and as a subtle reminder to anyone else who thought about crossing him.

But as far as memories went, I had almost nothing—just the vague impression of a pair of strong arms tossing me into the air as a child. I couldn't even picture him in my head. "What did he look like?" I asked, pushing a fry around because I was too stuffed to do anything else with it.

"It is odd, now that you mention it," Mircea said.

"What is?"

"He was slightly swarthy, handsome enough, with dark hair and eyes."

"Why is that odd?"

He shrugged. "Merely that, having seen your mother, I would have expected him to have been a blond."

Chapter Fifteen

I gave up pretending to eat a few minutes later. There was a cart with dessert—chocolate hazelnut sponge cake, crème brûlée and pavlova with raspberries and kiwi. But by the time I finished the ribs and the fries and most of a bottle of wine, I couldn't walk that far. I kind of doubted I could walk at all. I flopped onto my back and stared at the ceiling, lost in a food haze.

It was glorious.

Mircea leaned over to refill my wineglass, and a section of his bare chest showed under the robe, along with a hint of a dusky nipple. It's a good thing I'm too stuffed to move, I thought hazily. I would so have jumped that.

He laughed, and I looked up and met amused, dark eyes. "What?"

He started to say something and then stopped himself. "You have sauce everywhere," he said instead.

"Of course I do. I had ribs."

"And apparently enjoyed them."

I sighed. "They were really, really good."

He reached over, picked up my hand. And before I could ask what he was doing, a pink tongue flicked out and—

And he licked my fingers clean.

"You're right," he told me. "It's delicious."

"Don't do that," I said, as he nipped the mound below my thumb.

"Why not?"

"Because it feels too good."

Mircea just smiled. And then he did it again.

Bastard.

The firelight gleamed on dark hair and wine-reddened lips. The robe had come apart some more, showing off most of a hard chest and a thigh thick with muscle. And I was tired of fighting.

I tugged him over.

His bent his head and I raised mine. A warm sigh caressed my face for a moment before our lips met. I made a soft sound and pulled him closer.

He kissed me slowly, leisurely, like a man who knows he has all night and intends to use it. It felt ... strange. My life wasn't about slow these days. It was all hurry, hurry, hurry and go, go, go, constantly full speed ahead because something was always about to go fantastically wrong.

But slow could be nice.

Slow could be very nice, I decided, as his tongue slid over mine, liquid and warm, a patient, gentle seduction that matched the lingering caress of his hands. His hair fell around my face, gleaming with a few strands of red where the firelight shone through it. My fingers ran though the thick mass—like silk, just like silk—and down the long line of his back.

I sighed, tension I hadn't even known I had leaving my body.

"How is the date going?" he asked, nuzzling my neck.

"It's ... trending up."

He laughed and slid a knee between my legs.

"You should go around like that all the time," I told him sincerely, sliding my hands up his chest. God, he felt good. Warm, sleek skin over hard, hard muscle, nipples already peaked under my hands. I let my mouth close over one, my tongue circling it gently, and he made a sound of appreciation deep in his chest.

"I might shock a few people."

"And make a lot more very happy. Of course, then I might have to beat the women off you with a stick." I kissed my way over to the other nipple, which was looking sad and unattended and not half so rosy. "But, then, according to Marco, I may have to do that anyway."

"Marco talks too much."

"Marco doesn't talk enough. I couldn't get anything out of him about my competition."

"You don't have competition."

I rolled us over for better access, and rested my chin on the hard surface of his chest. "You're telling me you don't have any mistresses?"

"Not at the present."

I frowned.

"That was evidently not the right answer," he said ruefully.

I kissed my way down his body, consciously keeping my nails out of his skin. It was a bit of a struggle. "How many have there been? And don't tell me you forget," I added, as he got that look on his face. The one that said he was wondering how big of a lie he could get away with.

"I haven't forgotten a single one, I assure you," he said, and then he winced.

And, okay, my nails might have sunk in just a little there.

"So you're not going to give me a number."

He suddenly rolled me onto my back again and nuzzled my neck. "Numbers are meaningless. Particularly when they are in the past."

"All of them?"

"All of them."

"Even Ming-de?"

"I never admitted Ming-de."

"Hmm." He'd never denied it, either. And then he cleverly got out of the argument by the underhanded trick of sitting back on his heels and starting to strip off the robe.

The white terry cloth had made his skin look darker than normal, a deep, rich caramel, but I didn't miss it. Not with the fire painting intriguing shadows on a body that was already intriguing enough. It gilded his muscles, cast a very incongruous halo around that dark head and licked at the smug smile hovering about his lips.

He took longer undressing than strictly necessary, because he was a bastard and a tease and because he clearly did not have a problem with nudity. I kind of suspected that Mircea liked nudity. Of course, if I had a body like that, I probably would, too.

I must have said that last aloud, because he grinned as

he crawled back over me. "If you had a body like mine, we would have a problem."

"You don't like men?" I asked, running my hands up hard-muscled arms.

"I like them well enough, just not in my bed," he said, nibbling on my lower lip.

"Have you tried it?"

"I didn't need to try it, *dulceață*," he said, kissing his way downward. "I know what I like. I have always been very clear on that point."

I was, too, and Mircea pretty much hit every button, with smooth lips and rough fingers and cool, cool hair that he deliberately dragged across my body as he worked his way down. The silken caress followed the warmer, more insistent one, making me crazy, making me writhe, lighting up nerves I hadn't even known I had. Until I arched up—in pain, because his mouth had fastened over the livid bruise below my belly button.

"That hurts," I protested, as he sucked at the already tortured flesh.

"Not for long."

And sure enough, the size of the mark began to fade as I watched, the edges dissipating like a cloud in a windstorm, the color thinning and then breaking apart and then disappearing altogether, letting the clear, pale skin show through. I suddenly noticed that a lot of my other scrapes and scratches had vanished as well, soothed away by the healing ability that was one of Mircea's gifts as a master.

"Doesn't that take a lot of power?" I asked, amazed.

He smiled, licking the last of the bruise away. "I have it to burn tonight."

"Because of those creatures."

He nodded. "It pleases me that their blood should heal you, since they were the reason you require it in the first place."

And, okay, yes. Healing had its place and it was nice of him to make the effort and I was suitably grateful not to be hobbling around like a ninety-year-old for the next week. But at the moment, I'd have been a lot more grateful if he would just move that talented mouth a few more inches south. . . .

He must have read my mind. Because the next moment,

rough hands slid up my inner thighs, silky hair cascaded over my stomach, and a warm, wet tongue went to work. Along with lips and teeth and God knew what else, but whatever was happening definitely wasn't normal. Because it suddenly felt like there were maybe a few extra tongues down there, which my brain kept telling my body was clearly impossible, and my body told it to get bent, because it was busy arching and writhing and thrashing and screaming. And then it didn't matter anyway, because the next instant my brain stuttered and short-circuited and all but blew out the top of my head.

Maybe I passed out or maybe I just lost a few minutes there. Either way, I came around to find him just barely stroking, too light to give any friction at all, too light to do more than tease. And I writhed anyway, every tiny movement sweet torture, shuddering down nerves still raw with pleasure.

He looked up at me teasingly. "How about now?"

"What?"

"The date."

It took me a moment to even realize what the hell he was talking about. "Oh . . . it's fair . . . I guess," I said, trying for joking, but mostly sounding breathless.

"Fair." Dark eyes narrowed. "I'll have to try a little harder, then, won't I?"

I stared at him. I thought a little harder might just kill me.

And then I was sure it would, when the bastard moved on—to my thigh.

"What—what are you doing?" I gasped. I wanted him in me. I wanted him in me *now*.

"Healing you," he said innocently, mouthing a completely inconsequential bruise.

"It can wait!"

"No, no. I like to be thorough."

I noticed, I thought grimly, as he licked away a tiny, almost-not-there scratch on my knee. I started to reach for him, hot and aching and desperate. But then rough fingers slipped over the skin of my outer thighs, smoothed up to my buttocks, and then back down to tease the softness behind my knees.

And, God, he knew how I loved that.

He did it again and I sighed and gave up, because clearly Mircea was going to take his time whether I liked it or not. Although I couldn't imagine what he thought he was doing—

Nibbling on my foot? It would have been more surprising, except that Mircea liked feet the way I liked long, beautiful hair. In a quasi-fetishy sort of way that we didn't talk about, but that I indulged by doing a lot more pedicure-type things than I ever had before dating him.

Of course, he usually preferred the objects of his affection encased in silk stockings, the old-fashioned kind with the seam up the back, which he kept sending me in alarming quantities. Or useless wisps of leather, preferably beaded and be-crystalled to within an inch of their life. Or those weird satin mules with the marabou feathers that I drew the line at because I kept tripping over them.

Not cracked and bruised and torn and battered.

Not that that seemed to be slowing him down any.

He licked the underside of the big toe, curling his tongue all the way around it, and I made a small sound. Teasing, dark eyes regarded me from over pink skin and chipped polish. "How did you manage to get barbecue sauce on your toes?"

"I didn't," I said indignantly.

He just laughed. "You taste good."

I would have answered, but he'd started mouthing the mound below the toes and I forgot how. I laid my head back instead and stared at the ceiling, trying not to go completely out of my mind as he took his sweet time. Halfway through, I decided that if I survived this, I was going to kill him. It wouldn't be easy, him being a master vamp and all, but I would *find a way*.

He licked a long swath up my instep and I shivered helplessly. "Are you cold?" he asked innocently.

"Mircea, seriously—"

I broke off because he'd started sucking on my heel. Which should have been no big deal, but which, for some reason, felt positively sinful. Who the hell knew that a heel could be an erogenous zone?

"Anything can be, if you never get a chance to see it," he murmured.

"People see feet all the time."

"Today. But they even swathed the piano legs in Victoria's London."

"That makes no sense at all."

"Humans rarely do," he told me, and bit down.

I made a sound that was absolutely not a whimper, but might have been edging that way. Because the sensation had shot straight to an area that definitely *was* an erogenous zone. And that had already been pretty damn stimulated.

"Mircea, I swear to *God*—"

"All done," he told me, releasing my foot. I sagged in relief.

And then he grabbed the other one.

And that was it.

I let the pink, silky-skinned foot he'd left me with come to rest on that taut chest. Mircea paused what he was doing to look at me narrowly, which I took as a good sign. Getting his attention hadn't been so hard, after all. Let's see if I could keep it.

I let my foot caress a flat little nipple, rubbing it to a peak between my toes, and then sliding down a ridged stomach to a hard thigh. Mircea hadn't said anything, hadn't even moved. I smiled.

My toes slid lower, across satiny skin and crisp hair to a velvety hardness that jumped eagerly under my touch. I felt a little clumsy—I wasn't nearly as dexterous as with my hands—but my foot was surprisingly sensitive. I hadn't expected to feel . . . quite so much. My own breath picked up a little as I went exploring, sliding my toes slowly up and down that rigid column. And I guess I must have gotten something right, because it swelled impossibly bigger under my touch.

"That isn't . . ." He stopped and licked his lips. "That isn't going to work."

I laughed. "Yeah. That was convincing."

Particularly since Mircea could put a halt to this at any time. Unlike a human male, a vampire has perfect blood control. He could have willed all that lovely hardness away, could have refused to play. But that would have been admitting defeat, something that his stiff-necked pride, the kind he liked to pretend wasn't there, would never permit. So I gently fondled the superb length of him, so thick, so silky soft, so good against my skin.

And sighed.

"This isn't going to get you anywhere, either," I was informed tightly.

"That's okay." I ran a single digit over the smooth head, watching it blush like a girl in pleasure. "I'm pretty comfortable where I am."

Mircea shuddered at the implicit threat, that I could keep this up all night. But I honestly thought I could. It was fascinating, what something so simple did to him, reversing who was in charge with amazing speed. I experimented, putting a foot on his chest and giving a little push. He fell back with almost no resistance at all, allowing me to crawl up his body.

Okay, then.

"That wasn't fair," he said hoarsely.

"Like you didn't use power on me earlier? And stay still."

"Give me a reason," he challenged, smoothing a hand over my curls.

I didn't need to be asked twice. My lips covered the sensitive tip of him, and he suddenly looked like maybe he was having trouble focusing. Been there, I thought cynically, only it was usually me losing my train of thought around him, instead of vice versa. I decided I liked vice versa, and twirled my tongue around the head.

Mircea groaned and his eyes slid to half-mast. Which was all very well, but that wasn't what I wanted. Hm.

I swirled my fingers over the tip of him, getting them wet, and then trailed them lightly up my own flesh. Stomach, breasts, pausing to paint the nipples, feeling his fingers tighten on my skin, up to my neck, lingering over those two little marks, his brand of ownership—we'd see who was owned—and up to my lips. I traced my bottom one with the salty taste of him, and his own tongue flicked out, unconsciously mimicking my movement.

Then I sucked the whole finger into my mouth and his eyes closed.

"You taste good, too," I told him, smiling, and felt his body shudder against me.

And then the next thing I knew, I was on my back, one of my legs crooked over Mircea's shoulder, and even with the preparation, he was too big for there not to be a burn.

But that was okay, that was perfect, because tonight I wanted to *feel* it. I wanted to know I was alive.

And it looked like Mircea felt the same, because he was driving into me hard enough that my breath caught and my body writhed and my fingers dug into his shoulders, and then he found just the right angle and *stayed* there. Sparks of intense sensation flashed up my spine and coiled in my belly, regular as clockwork, and then arrhythmic, treacherous, as Mircea modified his stroke to torment me all over again.

"Bastard," I hissed, even as my spine was arching helplessly, trying to meet his thrusts and continue that extreme high. I would have come in seconds, but he wouldn't let me, the man's ungodly stamina keeping me hungry.

"You'll live."

"Make me *want* to," I moaned, and Mircea was laughing as he gave in to my hunger, taking me deep and fast. Just the way we needed.

"Is this better?" he teased, but I didn't have breath to laugh because I was coming, even as the hard thrusts inside me turned erratic. I was still riding the aftershocks as Mircea shuddered above me, sagging against the tight hold of my legs as he came, both of us grinning like fools.

After a moment, he pulled me up and poured us more wine, and we settled down in front of the fire. He nestled up against me, cradling my body against his and sliding his hands up and down my legs, while the logs hissed and the snow fell and I wished I did know how to freeze time. Because I'd have liked to stop it right here.

It was times like these that I thought he was right, that I made things too hard, too complicated. Tony had elevated paranoia to an art form, and I'd absorbed a healthy dose of it growing up. And occasionally it had been really useful. It had kept me alive more than once, causing me to double- and triple-check things for no reason, or to abruptly leave somewhere just because of the ants running up and down my spine.

But sometimes it could be pretty stupid, too. More than once it had caused me to be too careful, to automatically say no when maybe I should have said yes, to guard myself and my heart so closely, I never let anyone in. I didn't know everything about Mircea; I would probably never know everything about Mircea. But I knew the important thing.

I knew I loved him.

I had always loved him. Loving him was as natural as breathing, as essential as water. It had defined my life in a real way ever since I was a child.

Before I met him, I had lived in constant fear, even without realizing what it was. When you've never known anything else, fear just seems . . . normal. Jumping at shadows because of what might be in them; staying carefully out of sight, because attracting attention was never A Good Thing; monitoring every word, in case it caused offense that would have to be made up for somehow. Of course, there were those I didn't have to act that way around—Rafe and Eugenie and a few others who came and went through the years.

But as much as I'd loved them, I'd always known the truth. They couldn't protect me. They couldn't, as it turned out, even protect themselves. Because they weren't the master there.

The most powerful vampire I knew was Tony, and even without realizing that he had been responsible for my parents' deaths, there'd been plenty to fear, including the rooms downstairs that none of the vamps talked about but that the ghosts in the house informed me were essentially torture chambers. People Tony didn't like went down there, and most of the time, they didn't come back up.

But I never saw those rooms, other than in a flash of vision I'd experienced years later. And after Mircea's visit, I had known instinctively that I never would. Because Tony, as mercurial, deadly and downright crazy as he could be at times, wasn't the most powerful vamp I knew anymore. Mircea was. And Mircea liked me.

And during his visit, it was impossible not to notice that Tony's attitude changed. He wasn't exactly jolly—despite his shape, Tony was never jolly—but he was . . . careful. He didn't raise his voice to me anymore, didn't threaten, didn't menace. In fact, it had been a real revelation, seeing him, the always-feared head of house, practically groveling on his master's perfectly shined Tanino Criscis.

And even after Mircea left, Tony didn't treat me as he

had before. If I didn't get a useful vision for a week or two, there was a definite chill in the air, or he might confine me to my room or cancel one of my rare forays outside the house. But I wasn't going downstairs. I was never going downstairs.

Mircea had meant security, protection, sanctuary. He had many other attractive attributes, ones that other women would probably value much more highly. But nothing came close to that sense of security for me. It had been the greatest gift anyone had ever given me.

It still was.

"I'm thinking you just hit good," I told him, when I could talk again.

He thought about that for a moment. "Let's try for excellent," he said, and rolled me over.

Oh, boy.

Chapter Sixteen

"I knew it!"

I jumped, because the angry voice spoke at almost the same moment that I rematerialized back in my bedroom in Vegas. I spun around, sending my aching head sloshing unpleasantly against my skull, and saw Billy lounging on the bed. A pack of playing cards hung in the air in front of him, laid out in a vertical game of solitaire. But they were ghostly cards, no more substantial than their owner, and I could clearly see his scowl glaring through.

For someone who regularly was up to as much crap as Billy Joe, he did disapproval really well.

"What?" I said defensively, clutching the mink and my dignity. Since I was barefoot, mostly naked and completely hungover, I was pretty sure I grasped only one of them.

"You slept with the goddamned vampire!"

"I— How did you know?"

Billy rolled his eyes.

"Well . . . even if I did, it's none of your business," I informed him haughtily. And then I ruined the effect by limping to the bathroom.

I flicked on the lights, but they hurt my eyes so I flicked them off again. But then I couldn't see. Until Billy's softly glowing head poked through the wall, like a pissed-off night-light.

"I thought you were gonna give it some time," he said

accusingly. "I thought you were gonna get to know him first. I thought—"

"Does anybody ever really know anybody?" I asked. And, okay, it was lame, but my head hurt like a bitch.

"Oh, man." Billy looked disgusted. "He must really be something. One night and he's got you wrapped."

"He does not!"

"Like hell." He crossed his arms. "What did you tell me right before you left?"

I sighed, wondering why I never had any damn aspirin. "I know. But—"

"But what? You told me you're absofuckinglutely, posi-fuckingtively, not getting horizontal. 'Cause vamps aren't like regular people, and you're in the middle of negotiating the relationship and he'd take it as a sign of surrender, and—"

"It wasn't like that," I said, running some cold water onto a washcloth. And then slapping it over my aching eyes. Dear God, I was never drinking again.

"Oh, okay. So what was it like?"

"A . . . time-out," I mumbled incoherently.

But apparently not incoherently enough.

"A time-out." Billy did sarcasm pretty well, too.

"Yeah."

"Which means what?"

"Which means it didn't count," I snapped, and then wished I hadn't, because it hurt. I stifled a groan and put my elbows on the counter, supporting my throbbing head.

"And who decided this?"

"We did."

"And which part of 'we' came up with the get-out-of-jail-free card?"

I didn't say anything.

"Yeah," Billy said. "That's what I thought."

I took the washcloth off so I could glare at him. "I don't recall appointing you my conscience!"

"You don't need a conscience. You need some goddamn common sense! You used to have some, remember? You're the one who told me what those things are like—"

"Mircea isn't a thing."

"Oh, so he's not a monster all of a sudden? He got up-graded? I guess I must have missed the memo!"

I turned and walked out of the bathroom. Billy's faintly glowing backside was sticking out of the wall above the dresser, framed in the mirror like a bizarre trophy. But all things considered, I liked it better than the other half right now. Get him wound up and he could go for hours, and I was so not up for it tonight. Or this morning. Or whenever the hell it was. The room was dark, but there were blackout shades under all the drapes in the suite, so that didn't mean much.

"Okay, 'monster' is out," Billy said, getting himself sorted. "So what are we calling him now? Sugar Tits? Baby Cakes? Angel Boy?"

I got a sudden image of a very naked Mircea, fire-warm skin backlit by flames, the same ones that had formed a vague halo around his head. He wasn't an angel, I knew that. But regardless of what Billy thought, he wasn't the devil, either. And it had been only one night, and he'd sworn it wouldn't make a difference—

"Why are you here, anyway?" I demanded, going on the offensive, because my defense kind of sucked right now. "I fed you before I left."

"Yeah, and that's all I care about! You were supposed to be back hours ago!"

"Well, I would have been, but . . . there was a delay."

"A delay that left hickeys all over your neck and made you walk funny?"

"I'm not in jail, you know," I snapped. "I can come and go whenever I—" I stopped. "What hickeys?"

He pointed silently at my neck. I pushed the old-fashioned collar of the coat aside and leaned closer to the mirror. And saw—

"Son of a bitch!"

"You didn't *notice*?" Billy demanded.

I winced. "No. And keep your voice down."

"Why? No one can hear me but you."

I rested my forehead on the cool top of the dresser. "That's kind of the point."

He snorted. "And to top it off, you're hungover!"

"It was the wine. It always does this to me."

"Then why'd you drink it?"

"Because after the night I'd had, I thought I deserved it," I muttered.

Billy sighed, and a moment later I felt a ghostly chill on the back of my neck. It felt good. "What went wrong this time?"

"Short version: everything."

"And the long version?"

"I'm too hungover for the long version."

"Gimme the CliffsNotes, then."

I pried myself off the dresser and started sorting through a drawer. "Let's just say, it looks like my luck runs in the family."

"Ouch."

I went back into the bathroom to change, and this time, Billy left me alone. I pulled on an old pair of khaki shorts and tried a couple of different shirts, finally settling on one with orange and white stripes. It was soft, thin cotton with a mock turtleneck and no sleeves. It had been part of my work wardrobe, worn under a jacket to keep me from dying of heatstroke in the Atlanta summers, and it looked a little dressy for the shorts. But it was better than announcing my evening's activities to everybody I met.

Only now that I was dressed, I found that I didn't really feel like meeting anybody. I kind of felt like going back to bed. I walked into the bedroom, yawning. "What time is it?"

Billy looked up from his card game. "Four a.m."

I sighed in relief and fell face-first onto the bed. Jonas was coming at one for our lesson, and I had nothing to do until then. And nothing sounded pretty damn good right now.

"Move over," I told Billy, because he was hogging the bed as usual. He gave me maybe another two inches of space, also as usual. I turned onto my side, since it was easier than arguing.

The room was dark but the bed was spotted by watery blue-white rectangles, the light shadows from Billy's cards. They moved across the duvet as he played, silent, intent. For about half a minute.

"You can call him what you want, but he's still a monster," Billy said, because of course this wasn't over. "They all are."

"I don't know why you hate vamps so much," I said sleepily. "What'd they ever do to you?"

"They're creepy."

"They are not."

"Like hell."

I didn't point out the irony of this coming from a guy who would send most people screaming in terror if they could see him, because the door cracked open. A thin sliver of slightly less dark leaked in from the hallway and fell over the bed. It highlighted dust particles dancing in the air and a massive head poking around the doorjamb.

"Hey," Marco said softly, like he thought I might already be asleep.

"Hey, yourself."

"You okay?"

"Yeah."

"You have fun?"

"Yeah."

"Thought so." I couldn't see his expression, but his voice was smug.

It would have been weird coming from a human, but vamps got a lot of their self-worth from their masters. Anytime Mircea did something well—negotiated a treaty, got recognition from the Senate, banged the Pythia—their egos all got a boost. In a real sense, when you dated a master vamp, you dated his entire family. All of whom thereafter took a proprietary interest in your business.

It was something I tried hard not to think about.

"You hungry?" Marco asked. "We got pizza."

Actually, I thought one more bite of anything, and I might just pop. "I'm good."

"Beer?"

"Just gonna get some sleep."

"Yeah, you probably need it," he said, sounding satisfied. The door closed.

"No, that's not creepy at all," Billy said sourly.

I sighed and pulled the pillow into a more comfy position. "It's just the way they are."

"And I don't like the way they are."

It wasn't surprising. Billy had never liked any of the guys in my life, not that there had been many. It wasn't jealousy so much—not the physical type, anyway—but more of a natural distrust. I guess getting drowned like a sack of kittens would do that to a person.

"You don't like anybody."

"Not when they look at you like he does," he said sharply.

"Like what?"

"Like the way hardened gamblers on the riverboats used to look at young rich guys. Like *here comes dinner*." He glanced at me. "I don't want you to be dinner."

"I won't."

"For anybody," he added. "He's no worse than the rest of them; they all want a piece of you."

"That's how the game is played."

"Yeah, well the game *sucks*." He wiped a hand across his own game and it dissipated like mist, leaving only a lightly glowing cloud above the bed. It made the room darker, but not cozier. Someone must have fixed the window, because the air conditioner was running like it was trying to make up for lost time.

I pulled up the comforter.

"What is wrong with you tonight?" I asked. Billy could bitch with the best of them, but usually he had a better reason than my missing curfew.

"It's . . . I don't know," he said, turning to face me. The scruffy features under the Stetson were unusually sober. "It's nothing I can put my finger on. But lately . . . it feels like there're ants running over my skin, all the time."

I didn't say anything, but I had to consciously refrain from smoothing my hands down my own arms. Because I'd had the same feeling for days. Not localized on anyone or anything; just a general impression that something wasn't right. And that had been before somebody tried to kill me.

It was one reason it had been so damn hard to leave that warm hotel room this morning. Last night really had felt like a moment out of time. For once, no one had been after me, no one had wanted to hurt me, no one had even known who the hell I was. It had been really nice.

But I couldn't hide in the past forever. And now that I was back in my time, that antsy feeling was setting my skin to crawling again. It was less than reassuring to know that Billy felt it, too.

How bad did things have to be before the ghosts started freaking out?

"I thought after that son of a bitch Apollo died, things

were gonna calm down," he said fretfully. "But it doesn't feel that way. It feels like it used to, when Tony's bastards got too close. If we were still back in Atlanta, I'd be bugging you to start packing."

"And if we were still back in Atlanta, I'd probably be doing it," I said honestly. "But I don't think running is going to help now."

He waved a hand. "I'm not talking about running. Plenty of people ran; he always caught them. You got away because you're . . . I don't know. Not smart, exactly—"

"Thanks."

"—but clever, resourceful, stubborn—and freaking lucky." He saw my expression. "What?"

"It's just . . . someone else said that to me recently." Well, minus the stupid part.

"What's wrong with that?"

"Nothing." Except that I didn't want to have to be resourceful. I didn't want to need to be lucky. I wanted to sleep late. I wanted to get up and putter around the suite. I wanted to go light a fire under Augustine before I ended up going to the damn coronation naked.

I didn't want to have to figure out what was trying to kill me this week.

But while I didn't know who or what had it in for me, at least I knew what didn't. "All that stuff with the gods . . . it's over," I told him. "They can't hurt us if they can't get back to Earth, and they can't."

"You sure about that?" he asked skeptically.

I didn't answer, because no, I wasn't. Not entirely.

It had been a shock to find out recently that a lot of the myths I'd grown up with were all too real. But not nearly as much as discovering that some of them were still alive. And that they were plenty pissed.

Their bitch was that they'd been banished from Earth, aka the land of milk, honey and slavishly devoted worshippers, by one of their own, Artemis. She'd turned traitor, teaming up with some of the less-devoted types, because her fellow immortals viewed humans as disposable. And they had been disposing of a lot of them.

So Artemis gave humankind the ouroboros spell to solve the problem. It banished the gods back to their home world and sealed off Earth so that they couldn't return to their favorite playground. The Silver Circle, named after the alchemical color sacred to Artemis and in the shape of her symbol, the moon, had been formed to furnish the power needed to fuel the barrier.

It was still doing so, all these millennia later. But no one believed that the Circle or the spell were foolproof any longer. Not since one of the self-styled gods had found a way past them barely a month ago.

Fortunately, it had been a short trip.

"Apollo got in," Billy said, like he'd been reading my thoughts.

"And he's dead," I said harshly.

"Yeah." Billy fell silent, and I rolled over, pushing the conversation away.

It was surprisingly easy. The bed was extra soft, just the way I like it, with a duck-down mattress pad and matching comforter. They were usually too hot, and the comforter often ended up on the floor. But tonight it was perfect. I felt myself start to relax, start to sink into the warm cocoon between all that squashy goodness, start to drift off—

"Where do you think they go when they die?"

Billy's voice jolted me back to unwelcome consciousness. I turned my head to frown at him. He'd stretched out on his back, hands behind his head, and was staring at the reflection of his own ghost light on the ceiling.

"Where does who go?"

"The gods." He turned his head to look at me. "They have to go somewhere, don't they? Everybody goes somewhere."

"I don't know." Somewhere nasty, hopefully. "Why?"

"I was just thinking about that thing that possessed you. It wasn't demon or Were or human or Fey, right?"

"Jury's still out on Fey."

"But not any Fey we ever heard of."

"No."

"So what about a god?" Billy gestured, throwing leaping patterns like blue candlelight on the walls. "They were said to be able to possess people, weren't they? In some of the old legends?"

I frowned. So much for sleeping. "Apollo's dead," I said irritably. "He couldn't possess anybody."

"I'm dead. And I possess people all the time."

"You're a ghost."

"So? Maybe he's a ghost now, too. You killed him—"

"And now he's come back to haunt me?" I asked incredulously.

He shrugged. "I know it's far-fetched, but compared to some of the other shit that's happened to you—"

I pulled the pillow over my head. This was so not what I needed to hear tonight. Or any other night.

"I know you don't wanna think about it," he said impatiently. "But we gotta figure this out—"

"It wasn't Apollo," I said, my voice muffled by the pillow.

"How do you know?"

"Because he wouldn't have waited this long to attack me."

"Maybe he learned something last time. He underestimated you, and look where that got him. Straight down the metaphysical crapper."

"And I haven't had any more visions—"

"Maybe he figured out you were spying on him and blocked you somehow. He was the source of your power, wasn't he? So he should be able to—"

"And he wasn't human," I said, throwing off the pillow. Because obviously Billy wasn't going to let me sleep until we had this out. "And nonhumans don't leave ghosts!"

"That we know of."

"In a century and a half, how many nonhuman ghosts have you seen?" I demanded.

"None. But we're talking about gods here. Who knows what they can do?"

"Well, they can't do this. Whatever went after me was driven off by cold iron. That wouldn't have bothered a god at all."

"That could have been a coincidence," Billy said stubbornly. "Pritkin even said so—"

"Stop eavesdropping on my conversations! And the spirit also didn't know English. We could barely communicate."

Billy thought for a moment. "Maybe he forgot?"

I snorted. "Yeah. And then he grew feathers."

"Damn."

I stared at him. "Did you just say 'damn'?"

He grinned, unrepentant. "It was a beautiful theory, you gotta admit."

I didn't have to admit anything of the kind. "Look, the gods are gone. Finished, kaput, out of the picture. Okay?"

He held up his hands. "Hey. Preaching to the choir here."

"Beautiful theory," I muttered, and swung the pillow at him.

It was a wasted effort, because he disappeared before it landed, fading away until only his laughter remained. It was the last thing I heard as I finally drifted off.

Chapter Seventeen

I walked into the living room sometime that afternoon, yawning and bleary-eyed from too much sleep, to see Marco coming out of the lounge. At least, I assumed it was Marco. It was a little hard to be sure, because while the height and girth were the same, the face was completely covered—in flowers.

"Hey," I said, as a perfect red rose dropped off the towering stack he was carrying and plopped at my feet.

"Hey, yourself," Marco's voice told me, heading out of the apartment. "Get the door, will ya?"

I got the door. "What are you doing?"

"Taking out the trash."

He strode over to the elevator and punched the button, shedding blossoms all the way. One had a little card attached. I bent and picked it up. *Cassandra Palmer.*

I frowned. "Marco?"

"Mmm-hmm?"

"Are you throwing out my flowers?"

"Yep."

"Why?"

"Go look in the lounge."

The elevator arrived before he could say any more, assuming he'd planned on it, and a man got off. He was dressed in a crisp blue suit and shiny black shoes and was carrying more roses. "Thank you," Marco said, plucking them out of his hand and stepping into the elevator.

"Hey!"

The elevator doors shut before the man could retrieve his bouquet. "Goddamned vampires," he muttered, and then he turned around—to see three of the guards loitering in the open doorway of the suite.

He lost what color had been in his face, which wasn't much, since he was a pleasant-looking white blond. The vamps came forward and started circling him like sharks in water. "I liked the last one better," a brunet said. "This one's a little weedy."

"And please tell me that's not your best suit," another commented, eyeing the man's pinstripe with a moue of distaste. "I'm thinking what? One ninety-nine ninety five?"

"And they throw in an extra shirt," the third vamp added.

They all laughed.

The man flushed but stood his ground. "See here, I have an appointment with—" he caught sight of me and his expression lightened. "Ah, you must be—"

"Too busy to talk to you," the first vamp said, putting an arm around him and turning him back toward the elevator.

"Get your hands off me, vampire," the man snarled, pushing the vamp's hand away. "And I think I'll let her tell me that!"

"Ooh. This one's spunky."

"What's going on?" I demanded.

The man—or, I guess, the mage—came forward, holding out a hand. The hand had a box in it. The box was full of candy, judging by the glossy photo on the front.

"For you," he said, obviously proud to have rescued part of his offering.

"Uh, thank you?"

He brushed it away. "I'm not sure what to call you," he said frankly. "Lady Cassandra isn't technically correct until after the ceremony, and it sounds too formal in any case. And Miss Palmer is little better. Would you like for me to call you Cassie?"

"I'd like for you to tell me who you are."

The man blinked. "David Dryden."

I just looked at him.

"Your one o'clock?"

"My one o'clock what?"

"Date," the third vamp said, grinning.

"For what?" I asked, confused.

"Well, you know." The mage looked a little awkward suddenly. "The usual."

"I think we've got a contender here, boys," the brunet said.

"Smooth operator," the second vamp agreed.

"Can you do something about them?" the mage asked me angrily, as the elevator dinged.

"They're supposed to be here," I pointed out.

"As am I! The Lord Protector sent me."

The Lord Protector and his hair got off the elevator. "Ah, Dryden, my boy. There you are." Jonas beamed at him, and then leaned over to dust a minute speck off his coat. "Have you met our new Pythia yet?"

"I'm trying!" the mage said, exasperated.

"Jonas, can I see you a minute?" I asked mildly.

"Of course, my dear, of course. It's why I'm here."

"Can you repeat that pickup line for me?" I heard one of the vamps ask. "I want to write it down. Something about the usual?"

"Go to hell," the mage told him.

I preceded Jonas into the apartment, but stopped in the doorway to the lounge. Or what had been the lounge. It looked more like a greenhouse now, with what had to be four dozen vases of flowers, loose bouquets and potted plants sitting around.

"Jonas." I narrowed my eyes at him. "What is this?"

"Options, my dear," he said, surveying the sea of flora approvingly. "It's always nice to have options."

"It's nice to have a place to sit, too. And we discussed this."

"Did we?" he asked vaguely.

"Yes. We did. And you promised—"

"I didn't, in fact."

"Jonas!"

He held up placating hands. "But truly, very little of this is my doing."

"Then what—"

"It was Niall. I believe he was ... perturbed ... about the desert incident. He returned in time to insert a piece in this morning's *Oracle* about our eligible new Pythia and, well ..."

"Well what?"

"The power of the press," he said, patting my hand. "But don't worry. I'm sure it will blow over in a week or two—"

"A week?" I stared around. I'd be able to open my own florist shop by then.

I sneezed.

"Smells like a New Orleans cathouse in here," Marco agreed, coming back in and handing me a handkerchief.

I took it gratefully. "How would you know?"

He just raised an eyebrow at me and gathered up another load. "I'm heading to bed after this," he told me, glancing at Jonas. "It's about to get surreal up in here."

"About to?"

He just grinned and sashayed out. I sneezed.

"Can we do our lesson in the living room?" I asked Jonas, wiping my streaming eyes.

"Oh, I think we can postpone that for today," he said genially.

"We don't need to postpone. I'm not going out with—with that man," I sniffed, trying and failing to recall the guy's name.

Jonas regarded the mage, who was standing by the kitchen door, looking about the way you'd expect. "Why? What's wrong with him?"

The man twitched.

I sighed. "Nothing."

"Then perhaps a late luncheon—"

"No!"

"Tea?"

"Jonas!"

He sighed and gave up. "Handsome boy ... very good family," he muttered, reentering the living room.

I blew my nose and followed. And almost ran into an old-fashioned blackboard that was taking up most of the space beside the new sofa. I blinked at it, because it hadn't been there a minute ago.

"Well, in that case, perhaps you could help me with a

few small matters," Jonas said, feeling around in his coat for something. "I used to do this with Agnes, you know. We had tea every Thursday, and I would go over any affairs of interest in the magical community, in case she saw something of significance."

"I haven't seen anything lately," I said, eyeing the blackboard suspiciously. I poked it. It was solid.

"Which is rather the point," Jonas said. "Agnes sometimes had dry spells, too, and other times she had visions about all sorts of things, but most were entirely unrelated to what we needed to know. But if we'd recently discussed something . . . well, it seemed to help focus her energies. I thought it might do the same for you."

"Okay." I edged around to the sofa.

"Good, good." Jonas had been turning out his pockets as he spoke, one after another, leaving him looking like he had little gray tongues all over his suit. But I guess he hadn't found what he wanted, because he made a gesture and plucked a small package out of thin air.

I stared at it, because I'd never seen anyone do that before, except on TV. But I didn't think Jonas had used sleight of hand. Particularly not when he had trouble getting the cellophane off whatever it was.

"Now, I realize that visions can't be made to order, as one might wish," he said, fiddling with it.

"What is that?" I demanded.

He looked at me from behind heavy glasses. "What is what?"

"That." I pointed at the package.

Jonas peered down at it. "This?"

"Yes, that! What is *that*?"

"Chalk."

"Chalk?"

"Yes."

"For what?"

"For the chalkboard," he said, looking a bit bewildered.

"But . . . where did you *get* it?"

"Where did I get what?"

"The chalk!"

His forehead wrinkled slightly. "Ryman's. They had a sale."

I opened my mouth to say something else and then

closed it abruptly. I wasn't doing this with him. Not again. Not today. I sat down on the sofa and crossed my legs. "All right."

Jonas regarded me warily for a moment, as if I were the one acting strange. But in the end, he didn't say anything, either. He just fished out a piece and started scribbling on the board, like a more than slightly batty professor.

"Now, as I was saying, visions can be a bit ... dicey. Agnes often described them as less of a narrative than a kaleidoscope or puzzle, with pieces here and there that, without context, made little sense. Would you agree?"

I shrugged. "I've had both kinds. The jumbled ones are the most irritating."

He nodded. "Yes, so she said. She also told me, however, that having a starting point, some clue as to what she was seeing, often went a long way in helping her sort them out. And once she knew to focus on a particular piece, the others that went with that puzzle often presented themselves."

"So what puzzle piece do you want me to focus on today?"

"One I've been working on for some time now. I've been doing some fascinating research into the—"

He stopped and looked at something over my shoulder. I turned my head to see the mage peering around the chalkboard. He looked back and forth between the two of us. "I, er, I was wondering—"

"No, no, we're past all that," Jonas said.

The man looked at him for a moment and then decided to focus on me. "Are we having lunch?"

"No."

"Dinner?"

"No."

"It's just ... I haven't eaten."

I just looked at him.

"Could I have my chocolates back?" he asked after a moment.

I silently passed them over. He disappeared back behind the blackboard. Jonas looked at me. "Where were we?"

"I have no idea."

He thought for a moment. "Oh yes. I was telling you

about my research into the old Norse sagas—the mythology of ancient Scandinavia. Have you read them?"

"Uh, no."

"You'd like them, Cassie." He waved the hand with the chalk in it. "All sex and violence."

I frowned. "Why would you think that I'd—"

"And in a real sense, they're very like visions, in that they give us pieces. Not necessarily the best pieces, you understand, nor in the right order, nor with the right emphasis, but pieces nonetheless. It's up to us to decode what those pieces mean."

"Pieces of what?" I asked, trying to figure out where he was going with this.

"Our current situation, I hope. As we recently had demonstrated somewhat . . . vividly, many of the world's ancient myths have a basis in real events. Take the ouroboros legend, for instance."

"The ouroboros?" I repeated faintly. Artemis's protection spell wasn't my favorite topic of conversation.

"Yes. As with most cultures around the world, the Norse have a legend about a giant snake who grasps its own tail, and in doing so somehow protects the planet. In their case, the snake was Jörmungandr, one of three children of the god Loki, who could shape-shift into a reptile."

He stepped away from the board so that I could see what he'd been drawing. Only that didn't help much, because what I saw looked a lot like a lopsided soccer ball with eyes. Or maybe some kind of deformed squid—

"The legend states that eventually Jörmungandr grew so large that he was able to surround the Earth and grasp his own tail. He was believed to be holding the world together, and that when he let go, it would end."

He added a line across the top of the board and wrote "Loki" in the middle. Then he made three branches coming down from it, like an abbreviated genealogical table. The soccer ball was attached to one of them. He underlined it helpfully.

"That's Earth?" I asked, just to be clear.

"Yes."

"And that thing wrapped around it, that's Jor—whatever?"

"Yes." He frowned. "Can't you tell?"

"Not really."

He leaned over and did something to the drawing. "Is that better?"

I didn't see any difference. Until I looked closer. And saw that the thing with eyes now also had a tiny, forked tongue.

"Jonas—"

"Now, the interesting thing about the Norse myth," he told me, "isn't so much how it differs from the others, but what it adds." He drew a little line down from the soccer ball and scribbled a name below it. He looked at me expectantly.

"Thor?" I guessed, because Jonas's handwriting wasn't any better than his art.

"Yes."

"God of thunder, big guy with a hammer?"

"Quite. And Jörmungandr's archenemy. The legend says that in Ragnarok—" He saw my expression. "That is the Old Norse term for the 'Twilight of the Gods,' the great war that will decide the fate of the world."

I nodded, mainly because I wanted him to get to a point already.

"The legends say that Thor will defeat Jörmungandr during Ragnarok, only to die himself shortly thereafter," he told me. And I guess that was it, because he just stood there, rocking back and forth on his toes and looking pleased.

"I'm kind of still waiting for the interesting part," I confessed after a few moments.

Jonas blinked at me. "But don't you see? That is essentially what we have just experienced. The ouroboros spell *was* defeated, allowing the return of one of the old gods, who died almost immediately afterward."

"But that was Apollo," I said, my stomach falling a little more. Because if there was one thing I liked discussing even less than the ouroboros, it was the guy who had defeated it.

Apollo had been the source of the power that came with my office, gifting it to his priestesses at Delphi so that they could help him keep an eye on those treacherous humans. But once the ouroboros spell kicked him out along with the other gods, the power had stayed behind, bound to the line of Pythias who continued their work, only on behalf of the Circle and the humans he had despised.

Or at least it had until I came along. Apollo thought he had it made when a clueless wonder inherited the Pythia position instead of one of the carefully groomed Initiates the Circle kept under its watchful eye. He'd intended to use me to help bring back the bad old days of gods and slaves and nothing in between by helping him get rid of the barrier once and for all.

He'd been less than pleased when I'd declined.

In the end, I'd been the one left standing, although I still wasn't quite sure how. But I suspected that a heck of a lot of luck had been involved. Now, as far as I was concerned, I could happily go the rest of my life and never hear that name again.

"You know, it's really quite fascinating," Jonas said. "But many of the old Norse gods have parallels in the myths of other cultures. From Scandinavia through Ireland, India and even beyond, their names may change, but they are essentially the same entities with the same powers and, in many cases, the same symbolism."

"Are they?" I asked, waiting for the other shoe to drop. And it was coming; I could feel it.

"Oh yes. Take Thor, for instance. As you say, he is best known as the god of thunder. But would it interest you to know that, when famine threatened, it was Thor to whom the ancient peoples of Scandinavia prayed to send a good harvest—a role traditionally allocated to a sun god? Or that sun gods the world over have customarily been depicted holding axes—which look a great deal like Thor's famous hammer? In fact, some scholars have suggested that they were the prototypes for it."

"But what does that have to do with—"

"And that, according to legend, of the four horses that drew Apollo's chariot, one was named Lightning and another Thunder? Or that Apollo was said to have used lightning and thunder—the elements, not the horses—to drive away marauding Gauls who threatened his sanctuary at Delphi?"

"Um, okay, but—"

"The ancient Gauls also considered the god of thunder and the sun god to be one," Jonas said, really getting into it now. "Images have been found in France of a god resting one hand on a wheel, the symbol for the sun, and holding a flash of lightning in the other. And the Slavonian god of thunder, Perun, was honored with an oak-log fire."

"Oak?"

"In Greece, oak was the wood dedicated to the sun god."

I stared at the chalkboard, and the queasy feeling doubled. I swallowed. "So . . . so what you're trying to say is that—"

"And then there's the Hindu god Indra. He had early aspects of a sun god, riding in a golden chariot across the heavens to bring the day. But he is more often known as the god of thunder, wielding the celestial weapon Vajra—a lightning bolt."

"Jonas—"

"And then there's the fact that Thor's home was said to be in Jotunheim, in the east, connecting him again to the rising—"

"Jonas!" That was Pritkin.

I looked up at the sound of his voice to see him standing in the doorway to the foyer, arms crossed and green eyes narrowed. He looked pretty pale, for some reason, and instead of his usual ramrod posture, he was leaning against the wall. But he was alive and looking pissed off and I'd never been so happy to see him.

"Hm? Yes?" Jonas blinked at him.

"Are you trying to tell us that Thor and Apollo are two names for the same being?"

"Well, yes," Jonas said, as if that went without saying. "And once I realized that, well, naturally I began to wonder. . . ."

He and Pritkin stared at the board for a long minute. "Wonder *what*?" I finally blurted out.

Jonas looked at me. "Well, if we aren't fighting Ragnarok right now, of course."

Chapter Eighteen

"Breathe," Pritkin told me, and I tried. But suddenly, that seemed a lot harder than normal.

"It's merely a theory," Jonas said, fussing about the kitchen. We'd moved after that little revelation, because he'd declared that we needed tea. Personally, I didn't think tea was going to fix this.

"Even if we accept the identification of Thor with Apollo," Pritkin said, "which many scholars do not—"

"They don't, you know," Jonas assured me. "Really they don't."

"—there remains the fact that the creature in question is dead. Whatever his name, he is no longer an issue."

"That's very true." Jonas and his hair nodded emphatically.

"Then why did you bring it up?" I asked harshly.

"Why, because of the others, of course."

Pritkin and I looked at each other, while Jonas kept opening cabinets. He paused slightly when he came to one that had a fork sticking out of it, half-buried in the wood, but he didn't comment. "You haven't any tea?" he finally asked me, looking as if he knew that couldn't be right.

"No."

He blinked. "None whatsoever?"

"In there," Pritkin said. He nodded at one of the lower cabinets.

"Oh, good." Jonas looked vastly relieved, as if a major crisis had been averted.

I started to wonder if I was insane.

After a moment, I cleared my throat. "What others?" I asked, as Jonas began examining Pritkin's little boxes and tins.

"Hm? Oh, the other two gods, of course," he said absently. "Ah, Nuwara Eliya. Yes, very nice."

"Nuwara Eliya is a god?" I asked, confused.

He regarded me strangely. "No. It's a town in Sri Lanka." I looked at him.

"Where they grow tea. Very good tea, too."

Pritkin put a heavy hand on my shoulder, which was just as well. It probably wouldn't have looked good to choke the head of the Silver Circle to death right before the coronation. Then again, my reputation was shot to hell anyway. . . .

"What other two gods?" Pritkin asked quickly.

"Oh, didn't I say? Ah, well that's where it really becomes interesting. According to the sagas, Ragnarok involves the deaths of three main gods: Thor, Tyr and Odin. The legends state that the war will end only when all three are dead, and that the three children of Loki are the ones fated to kill them."

"Meaning?"

"Well, that's just it," Jonas started filling up the kettle. "I'm not sure. But I did locate some clues that might be useful. The first child of Loki was Jörmungandr, which we now know stood for the ouroboros spell. The snake was opposed by Thor, or Apollo if you prefer. He defeated the spell, but died soon afterward. This, of course, has already happened."

"Of course," I said faintly.

"Now, the second child of Loki was Hel," Jonas said. He reached across the counter to draw what looked like a crooked smile or possibly a banana on his blackboard, which he'd set up just outside. "She was thrown into the underworld by Odin and became the goddess of death."

"Hell?" I repeated. "You mean, like the place?"

"Yes, in a sense. Our modern word derives from her name. She was said to have power over the nine hell regions—"

"Nine?'

"Yes, the same number that Dante would later record in his *Inferno*. Fascinating how the myths intersect on so many—"

"Jonas." That was Pritkin.

"Yes, well. In any case, she was said to have control over the hells, as well as the pathways between worlds. Quite a powerful figure."

"Like the Greek goddess Persephone," Pritkin said.

Jonas wrinkled his nose. "No, not exactly. Persephone was queen of the underworld, yes, but only because of her marriage to Hades, who already ruled it. Hel was queen in her own right. She was one of those powerful virgin goddesses you find sprinkled throughout the pages of mythology who lived independently of the authority of any man. Which is why I don't think Persephone quite fits the bill. And, of course, the moon wasn't her symbol—"

"Hel's symbol was the moon?" I asked, finally figuring out what the banana was supposed to be.

"Yes, the dark side, at least. She was—"

"The dark side?"

I guess my voice must have changed, because Jonas looked up sharply. "Yes, why?"

"It's probably nothing," I said, wishing I'd kept my mouth shut. I wasn't thrilled with the idea of explaining my little toy to Jonas. But he was standing there, looking at me intently, and I didn't really have a choice now. "It's just . . . I have this tarot deck and—"

"You saw something?"

"Well, no. I mean, I didn't have a vision or anything, you know, magic—"

"Forgive me, my dear, but the tarot in the hands of the Pythia *is* magic. Yes, indeed. What did you see?"

"Well, it's not a normal deck," I explained awkwardly. "So I didn't have a spread to go on, just the one card—"

"The Moon, I take it?"

"The Moon reversed."

"Ahhh." Jonas slowly sat down.

"Like I said, it probably doesn't mean anything—"

"Oh, I wouldn't be too sure about that," he said mildly, staring off into space. "No, no. I shouldn't at all, really."

I just sat and looked at him for a while, but he didn't say anything else. Pritkin tried to ask something, but Jonas just waved a hand. "Talk amongst yourselves," he said vaguely.

I looked at Pritkin helplessly. Most of the time I thought Jonas was a sharp old bastard who was playing some kind of weird mind game with everyone for his own amusement. But there were days when I honestly wondered if the magical world was being led by a complete nut.

"It isn't even a real deck," I told him, trying again.

Nothing.

"It's a toy I was given as a child."

Nada.

"I don't even choose the card. It chooses for me!"

May as well have been talking to the wall.

"I'll be right back," Pritkin said, apparently giving up. He headed out of the kitchen and I went along because, frankly, it was getting kind of creepy in there.

"I'm just going back to my room for a moment," he told me, when he realized I was following him. Which would have been fine, if he hadn't turned around and tripped on the stairs leading from the living room to the foyer.

He caught himself before he face-planted, and for anybody else, it would have been no big deal. I tripped over that same step an average of once a day. But Pritkin wasn't me and he didn't regularly fall over his own two feet.

I grabbed him before he could escape, and I didn't need to ask what the problem was. Blood was seeping through the lower part of his shirt, staining the soft gray cotton. Of course it was, I thought furiously. Of course it bloody well was.

"Damn it, Pritkin!"

"I'm fine," he told me, which was less than comforting, considering he'd probably say the same thing after losing a limb. I crouched down and pushed up his T-shirt.

"Fine?" I said, staring up at him angrily. The blood was leaking out of a bandage that covered half his stomach.

"Well enough," he said, trying to push his shirt back down. I slapped his hands and started to pry up the edge of the soaked bandage with a fingernail. It had already come loose and would have to be replaced, and I needed to see—

A steel-like grip caught my wrist. "I'm *fine*," Pritkin repeated. "It will be healed by tonight, by the morning at the latest—"

"And what kind of a wound takes you that long to heal?" I demanded. I'd seen him shrug off a knife to the chest in a matter of minutes.

"A Fey one," he admitted.

I said a bad word and started to pull off the bandage with my other hand, but he caught that wrist, too. And then he tugged me to my feet. "You said you were going to see friends!" I accused.

"Acquaintances."

"Do your acquaintances usually want to kill you?"

"It's not completely unknown," he said wryly. And then he saw my face.

"Let me go," I told him dangerously.

"So you can slap me?"

"So I can get you a new bandage!" I'd slap him later.

Pritkin let go and I stalked off. We didn't have a medicine cabinet in the suite; we had a medicine closet. I didn't know what the guys were preparing for, but they could have stocked a small clinic out of there. Usually, I thought it was a big waste, since I was the only person around here who could benefit from that stuff, and if I needed that much I was a goner, anyway. Today, I was grateful for it.

I grabbed what I needed and went back to the living room, but it was empty. I found Pritkin in the lounge, seated at the card table. I guess he didn't want to bleed all over the new sofa. The vamps had cleared out, leaving us alone except for a forest of plants and a guy eating chocolate in a corner.

"What are you still doing here?" I demanded.

The blond mage jumped slightly and looked up. "I— No one told me to leave."

"Leave." I slammed the medical supplies down on the table.

He scurried off.

I glared at Pritkin. "You swore you'd be all right!"

"And as you can see—"

"You lied!"

"I didn't lie. I merely didn't anticipate walking into a— What are you doing?"

I'd knelt on the floor and now I was pushing his legs apart so I could fit between them. "I'm going to rebandage you. If you're smart, you'll sit there and let me."

"I can do that my—" He stopped when my fingernails sank into his thighs.

"Open your legs and hold your shirt up," I snapped. And to my surprise, he did.

The bandage came off easily since it hadn't been put on right to begin with, and underneath was—

I sucked in a breath.

Pritkin started to say something, but stopped when I glared up at him, so angry I could barely see. "*Don't.*"

He didn't.

The thing about having superhuman healing abilities is that you're seriously out of practice when you actually need to do some first aid on yourself. At least, I assumed that was why the bandage had merely been slapped into place, why the cleanup job underneath had been half-assed and why the line of black stitches holding an ugly red wound together might have been done by a farsighted three-year-old. Or maybe he was just trying to piss me off.

If so, it was working really well. I was so mad my hands were shaking, but I didn't know if it was at him or at me for letting him go. Damn it, I'd *known* this was going to happen. He was *Pritkin*. He couldn't walk across a freaking street without getting shot at, and I'd let him go into goddamn *Faerie*.

I must have been out of my mind.

"I suppose you had to sew yourself up?" I asked harshly, going into the kitchen to run some water into a bowl.

"It seemed . . . advisable."

Yeah. If the alternative was spilling your guts everywhere.

I brought back the water and the hand soap. Marco had told me that hydrogen peroxide wasn't a good idea in deep cuts. Apparently, it could cause bubbles to form in the bloodstream that would kill you a lot faster than whatever had caused the cut in the first place.

I sat everything down on the floor and knelt back in place. I thought about asking him to unzip, because his jeans were in the way, but he usually went commando so I didn't. I just tugged the fabric, which was soft and old and loose, down enough that I could see to work.

It looked like he'd showered before he came over, which, ironically, had left him clean except for the large patch of skin that had been covered by the bandage. I started on the dirt and the grass and the God knew what that he had somehow ground into the wound. And for once, he just sat there, without trying to give me orders or critique me or tell me a better way to proceed. It was odd but nice.

"What happened?" I asked after a few moments.

He cleared his throat. "I was ambushed."

"Why didn't you go back through the portal?" I was assuming he'd used the one the Circle had recently opened, since it was pretty much the only option available right now.

"I would have, had I been near it at the time. But I'd already made my way to the village where one of my contacts lives—or I should say, where he used to live."

Some blood had dried around his belly button. I scrubbed at it with a fingernail until it came off. "Is he dead?"

"What?" Pritkin sounded a little strange.

"Your friend. Associate. Whatever."

"Er . . . no. At least . . . I'm not sure."

He fidgeted, and I tightened my hand on his thigh. "Don't." I was about to start cleaning the actual stitches now and I didn't want to rip any out. He froze.

I pushed his jeans down enough that I could see the bottom of the wound, and it wasn't a pretty sight. He'd already started to heal around the thick black cord he'd used as thread, but the wound itself was ugly and looked infected. And when I gently put the back of my hand against it, it was like a line of fire against my skin.

"Are you supposed to be this hot?" I asked, frowning.

He didn't answer, and I looked up. And found him staring at me with a strange expression, part tender, part exasperated, part . . . something. I didn't get a chance to figure it out before he looked away.

"Yes. When I'm healing."

I decided to take his world for it, since I didn't have a lot of choice. Pritkin had a severe allergy to doctors, and I knew better than to suggest one. I rinsed out the rag and carefully started cleaning the angry red line.

"What did you mean, you're not sure?" I asked. "About your friend?"

"I meant . . . his village was deserted. There were clothes dropped in the road and many doors and windows had been left wide-open. I went into a few houses, and found half-eaten food on the table in one and a dog tied out back of another. I let the dog loose, and it took off down a road. I followed it—"

"Of course you did," I said sourly.

"—and picked up the trail of the villagers almost at once. That in itself was strange enough—"

He broke off, probably because I'd gotten the rag a little too wet that time. "Sorry," I said, wiping up the dribbles below the wound before they wet the front of his jeans. He closed his eyes.

"The Fey are excellent hunters and trackers," he told me roughly. "They are usually very difficult to follow."

"But not this time."

"No. I found a number of personal items that had been discarded along the way, haphazardly, as if they had fallen out of . . . of peoples' arms while they ran. It had rained and the forest had a number of muddy areas, and the footprints I saw were running, too. Clearly, the villagers were fleeing some—" He looked down suddenly, his face a little flushed. "Are you almost done?"

"Almost. So you followed them?" I prompted.

"Yes. And that was when I was ambushed. I foolishly hadn't considered that they might leave some of their number behind, to slow down whoever was pursuing them. That is, I hadn't considered it until—" He sucked in a breath.

"I'm being as careful as I can," I told him, patting him dry.

"Just hurry it up, will you?" he said harshly.

"I wouldn't have to do this if you'd done a better job yourself," I pointed out. "Having sped-up healing won't do you any good if you get an infection."

"I'm not worried about a damn infection!"

"Well, you won't have to be now," I said, smacking on a new bandage. And this one, I decided grimly, wasn't going anywhere.

Pritkin watched me work for a moment in silence. "That's adhesive tape," he finally said.

"Mm-hm."

"That's . . . rather a lot, wouldn't you say?"

"Never hurts to be sure."

"But it's going to hurt like the devil when I have to take it off."

"Is it?" I looked up innocently and slapped on another piece.

His eyes narrowed, but before he could say anything, Jonas poked his head out the door. "Are you two done, then?" he asked politely.

"Yes," I told him, cleaning up the cleaning supplies. "Pritkin is about to tell us what happens when you follow a bunch of panicked Fey into an unknown forest all by yourself."

"Oh yes?" Jonas said curiously.

Pritkin closed his eyes and leaned his head back, looking martyred. "I ended up swinging from a rope, upside down, while some of the village men poked at me with poisoned spears," he said dully. "I managed to convince them that I was not one of their enemies, but not before—"

"They gutted you like a pig?" I asked brightly.

He flushed and cracked an eye at me, but whatever brilliant riposte he'd managed to come up with was ruined by Jonas. "Who were these enemies?"

"The Alorestri," Pritkin said, sitting up and wincing.

"The Green Fey," Jonas translated for me. "They share a border with the Dark and have had an on-again, off-again struggle over land, resources, hunting rights"—he shrugged—"what have you, for millennia."

"And currently it appears to be on again," Pritkin said. "According to the villagers, the Green Fey broke through the border defenses a few days ago and overwhelmed the local Dark Fey forces. They were fleeing ahead of a contingent of Green Fey said to be coming their way."

"There was an invasion?" I asked, my stomach sinking. I had a friend at the Dark Fey court, and I liked the idea of him remaining in one piece.

Pritkin noticed my expression. "This sort of thing isn't unusual," he told me. "The Dark Fey army will regroup and likely battle them back within a few weeks. But in the meantime, there is no way to reach my contacts, or even to know for certain where they are. And without them, there is no way to know what attacked you."

Frankly, I couldn't have cared less. I was just grateful to have him back, beat up and bloody or not. "It may not even be Fey," I reminded him. "Billy's decided it's Apollo's ghost come back to haunt me!"

"Oh no," Jonas said, apparently serious. "I shouldn't think so."

"Well, yeah. I wasn't actually suggesting—"

"This world leeched the gods' power; it did not feed them. That is why all the old legends speak of them visiting Earth but living elsewhere: Asgard, Vanaheim, Olympus. And if they could not feed while alive, they certainly could not do so dead."

"Yeah, well. Like I said—"

"No, I believe the gods we are dealing with are still quite alive."

"Jonas, please!" I looked at him impatiently. "This isn't freaking Ragnarok, all right?"

"It would be nice to think so," he said mildly, the same way someone might say that it would be nice if it wasn't raining, while standing in the middle of a deluge.

I was about to reply, but the kettle started whistling its head off, so we trooped back into the kitchen. Jonas made tea, and I waited for some kind of an explanation. A coherent one, preferably, but I wasn't hopeful. Which was why it was a shock when a suddenly brisk Jonas sat down at the table.

"Three children of Loki; three gods to be overcome," he told us. "Apollo has already been dealt with, leaving two. The difficulty was in knowing which god would be opposing us next, but I believe your tarot may have shown us that, Cassie. It is an invaluable aid, but it leaves us with a daunting challenge."

"Jonas—"

He patted my hand. "Almost done. Now, I believe that the second child of Loki, Hel, may be another name for the

Greek goddess Artemis. Not only was she a virgin goddess with the moon as her symbol, but she was also associated with hunting. Not personally, in her case, but in the form of the Moon Dogs she loaned Odin for the Wild Hunt every year."

"Okay," I said wearily, not because I understood what he was talking about, but because it was simpler just to go with it.

But, of course, Pritkin had to argue. "But Artemis wasn't a death goddess."

"Oh, but she was, dear boy," Jonas said. "Most certainly. If you wanted a quick death in ancient Greece, you didn't pray to Persephone or Hecate, but to Artemis, who would give you 'a death as swift as her arrows.' "

"But Hecate is more traditionally associated—"

"But we don't care about tradition," Jonas interrupted, a little sharply. "Hecate has nothing to do with our current situation, whereas Artemis has been deeply involved from the beginning. I think there is little doubt that the goddess we are searching for is Artemis."

"Searching for?" I asked. "When did we decide ''

Jonas leaned over the table. "If we assume that Artemis and Hel are the same individual, as Thor and Apollo were, then she becomes a person of the utmost importance. According to legend, she is protected by a fierce guard dog named Garm, and together they are destined to defeat Tyr in Ragnarok."

"Tyr?" I asked, feeling more confused by the minute.

"Ares," Pritkin said. "If Jonas's reasoning is correct."

"Yes, the identification is a bit easier there," Jonas agreed. "As far back as ancient Rome, it was assumed that the war gods were one and the same. They even celebrated Ares, or Mars as they called him, on Tuesday."

"Why Tuesday?" I asked, my head spinning.

"Because it means 'Tyr's day.' Just as Thursday was named after Thor." He looked at the chalkboard. "There is, of course, a third child of Loki, the wolf Fenrir. He was shackled by Odin, king of the gods, but eventually escaped and killed him. But I do not believe we are there yet."

I stared at the wildly decorated chalkboard for a moment, and the sick feeling in my stomach settled into a familiar, ulcer-inducing burn. "Wait. Are you trying to tell me that to win the war, we have to *kill two more gods*?"

"Oh, no, nothing like that," Jonas said, and I felt my spine unknot slightly. "We have to help the children of Loki kill them."

Chapter Nineteen

"That what you call lunch?"

I looked up to see Marco loitering in the doorway of the kitchen, massive arms crossed over an even bigger chest. When Marco fills a doorway, I thought vaguely, he does it right. I wiped chocolate off my mouth and swilled some now-tepid tea. "Only thing here."

"Gonna make you sick."

I shrugged.

He sighed and swung a massive thigh over a kitchen chair. It groaned. "Wanna tell Papa Marco about it?"

"You're not my papa."

"Coulda been. I had a little girl once."

I looked up from sorting through the mage's abandoned candy box, trying to find another cream. "I didn't know that."

He nodded. "Kinda looked like you. 'Cept she smiled more."

I thought briefly about asking what had happened to her, but that sort of thing was risky with vamps. The answer usually didn't make anybody happy. "I smile," I said instead.

"Just not today."

"The damn mage ate all the creams."

One bushy eyebrow rose. "And here I thought it was that old coot pissing you off."

"That, too."

He sat back and the chair shrieked for mercy. "What is it this time?"

I crunched a toffee. "Well, Marco, apparently we're in the middle of the Norse version of Armageddon and just didn't know it. Ares, god of war, is out to get us, and the only way to defeat him is to find Hel—the goddess, not the place—who may or may not also be known as Artemis, and may or may not actually be a person instead of a spell or a weapon or a jelly doughnut. But we have to find her, because, despite the fact that the old legends say *she* defeats Ares, they said the same thing about the ouroboros spell and Apollo, so, clearly, the old legends are whacked."

"Uh-huh."

"So Jonas needs to know who or what or where, and expects me to tell him." I threw my chocolate-stained hands up. "Somehow. See how that works?"

"No."

"Yeah, me neither."

"So you're sittin' here, eating candy."

"Chocolate."

"And that's different?"

"Candy is candy. Chocolate is therapy."

"Got plans for this afternoon?"

"Eating more chocolate."

Marco just shook his head. "You shouldn't let that old guy get to you. He's nuts."

"Yeah." I was kind of coming around to Marco's way of thinking.

"Where'd he go off to, anyway?"

"Home." Or wherever he went when he wasn't blowing my mind.

"And the mage?"

"Same." At least, Pritkin had said he was going to his room. I chose to believe him, because if I shifted down there and didn't find him resting, I was going to lose it. And I was close enough anyway.

"Well, I'm going to bed," Marco announced, placing massive hands on the table and levering himself to his feet. He didn't need the help, even in the middle of the day, but vamps like to play martyr when they have to be up past sunrise.

"I thought you went an hour ago."

"Wanted to wait till everyone cleared out."

I rolled my eyes. Yeah. Because Jonas or Pritkin might suddenly decide to take a cleaver to my head.

He ruffled my hair and left. I found a coconut cream hiding in the second layer and sucked out the ooey-gooey innards. Things were looking up.

And Marco was probably right about not paying too much attention to Jonas. The guy told me one minute that he knew visions couldn't be made to order, and then the next he asked for exactly that. I was supposed to hand him Artemis on a silver platter with nothing, absolutely nothing, to go on except a name that might not even be hers.

I'd tried to explain how unlikely that was. Like really, really unlikely. Like not-going-to-happen unlikely. But all he'd done was tell me that he was sure I'd come up with something.

Yeah, right.

To find someone, I'd need at least a photo, preferably something she'd owned and touched, or, even better, a trip to her last known place of residence. And even then, I wasn't a damn hound dog. I might get a flash of something; I might not. But under the circumstances—

No. Just no. Even assuming Artemis actually existed, even assuming she was a person and not a metaphor, even assuming Jonas hadn't made up this whole crazy thing in that brilliant but cracked head of his, the answer would still be no. There were no photos, nothing she'd personally owned, and she hadn't been at her last known place of residence for something like three thousand years.

Not that I wasn't going to try, because what the hell. But my track record for made-to-order visions wasn't great. Actually, my track record for made-to-order visions was zero, but Jonas had looked so hopeful, I hadn't wanted to tell him that.

He'd find out soon enough.

I sighed and sat back, hearing my own chair creak. Probably not a good sign. Probably should lay off the creams, not that there were any left.

I scrubbed my face with my palms, feeling a little light-headed from all the sugar. Maybe ordering some real food might be smart, after all. The phone was on the counter, all of five feet away, but it seemed really far for some reason. I sighed again and followed Marco's example, putting my hands on the table to lever myself up—

And went in the other direction instead.

The room spun wildly, my legs collapsed underneath me and I dropped like a stone. Something shot overhead as I hit the tile, and a loud crack reverberated around the kitchen. I looked up, dizzy and confused and wondering why there was a knife bisecting the back of my chair.

I stared for a split second at the shiny, shiny blade, which was still quivering, slinging little shards of light around the room. And then I shifted.

Or I tried. But the woozy feeling that had sent me to the floor made it hard to concentrate, and when I finally did feel the familiar swoop catching me, it stuttered and jerked and wobbled and fractured. And the next thing I knew, I was kneeling by the fridge, staring at a familiar pair of glossy black shoes.

The vamps should have told him, I thought vaguely; they were totally the wrong color for the season.

And then one of them kicked me in the head.

It hurt like a bitch, despite the fact that I'd dodged at the last second and it only clipped my ear. I grabbed the fridge door and swung it open, hard, just as three more enchanted knives ripped through the flimsy material. Stainless steel, my ass.

I'd have been dead, but I was on my knees and the knives burst through overhead, shattering plastic and breaking condiments, before slamming into something behind me. I couldn't see—literally—because I'd just gotten a face full of pickle juice. I blinked it away to find that the knives had also exploded some hot sauce, forever ruining my blouse, which concerned me less than the eyes peering at me through the lacerated fridge door.

They had been my would-be date's best feature, a soft, melting, cornflower blue that had looked a little girlie for a war mage. That wasn't so much a problem now. I stared into something cold and black and boiling, and then I threw the rest of the hot sauce at them and scrambled away on all fours.

The mage screamed and it was nothing human, but a

high-pitched, keening cry of pure rage. The eyes had been a big clue, but that sealed it. Whatever had possessed me before must have hitched a ride in a new body, obviously with the idea of finishing what it had started.

Awesome.

I scrambled for cover behind the table, eyes burning, head spinning and fingers fumbling for the little pouch Pritkin had made for me—only to remember that I didn't have it anymore. Goddamned Niall! If I lived, I was going to send him back to the desert—this time the freaking *Gobi*.

I jerked open a cabinet door and crawled inside.

It wasn't as crazy as it sounds. I had to find something made of iron and I had to do it quick. It was either that or use the only weapon I had on me, and while I'd killed when I had no other choice, it had never been some poor schmuck who nobody had bothered to tell that dating me was a hazardous occupation.

I really didn't want to send him back to Jonas in a body bag. I really, really didn't. Even when knives started slamming through the cabinets and ricocheting back and forth in the small space like BBs in a jar. They also let in slivers of light that glinted off pots and pans and colanders and bowls, all nice, modern, worthless stainless without an iron skillet in the bunch.

And then a knife bisected a water line under the sink, spewing me in the face.

I was only blinded for a second, but it was long enough for a hand to reach in and jerk me out—by the hair. It hurt bad enough to bring tears to my eyes, but it also left me with an opportunity. Fucking *Sahara*, I thought viciously, and then I grabbed a knife out of a block and slashed—my own curls.

The sudden loss of his handhold caused the mage to stumble. And then my foot in his ass caused him to sprawl on the floor. And then I stepped on his shoulders and heard his face smack against the tile as I ran full out for the hall, screaming for Billy and my useless, useless bodyguards—

I didn't make it.

Halfway there, a blast picked me up and sent me hurtling toward the far wall of the lounge. My feet left the floor, my head hit the wall and pain lanced through my skull. But that wasn't the main problem. That would be the film of what felt like hard plastic flattening me against the dark red wallpaper like a bug under cellophane.

Make that shrink-wrapped cellophane, because in another second it had molded to every inch of my body, including my nose and mouth and eyes. I struggled furiously, feeling the possessed mage approach, even though I couldn't turn my head to see him. I also couldn't twitch a finger or contract my throat to swallow or blink my drying eyes or—

Or anything.

Suddenly, it was like being in the bathtub all over again, unable to move or breathe or even to cry out for help. And isn't that just the wrong analogy? I thought, as stark terror hit me like a fist. My heart sped out of control, my palms started sweating, and my stomach twisted violently, until I was sure I was going to be sick right here.

In desperation, I tried to shift, because I needed to go only a foot or so. But this time, nothing happened. I could close my eyes and see the bright, familiar energy, like an ocean of power sparkling in the sunlight. But I couldn't reach it. It was trapped by the weird, cottony feeling in my head, just like the bracelet that formed my only weapon lay locked tight and useless between me and the wall.

And then the mage came up alongside.

The pleasant-looking face didn't look so pleasant anymore, distorted by the thick, wavy barrier like an image in a fun house mirror. But I could see him pretty well anyway, because he bent close, close, so very close. Like he wanted to see my expression at the end.

Only the end didn't come.

Of course not, I thought blankly. Why waste the energy to kill me when all he had to do was stand by and watch me suffocate? I was trapped like an animal, splayed out like a trophy already mounted on the wall. Any minute now I was going to go from living human being to useless piece of meat, those pitch-black eyes watching as my spirit finally gave up the fight and left my lifeless—

My spirit.

Some idea skittered across my brain, just out of reach. I couldn't grasp it, could barely think at all, because I was panicking—oh yes, I was—even though someone had warned me about that, had said it was the very best way to die in a situation where you didn't have to. And he'd said something else, something he'd pounded into my head so many times I'd gotten sick of the very word—

An image of a pair of furious green eyes floated across my vision. *Assess. The problem. Now.*

Okay, okay. For some reason, help couldn't get to me, so I needed to get to help.

Address.

But I *couldn't*. I couldn't *move*. Not an inch, so how could I—

But that wasn't right. My *body* couldn't move. My spirit was a totally different thing. Because I was Pythia. And Pythias could leave their bodies, could shift into other people's, could—

But I couldn't shift, at least not now. And that meant I couldn't reach the safety of another body, couldn't do anything except . . .

Step out.

Yes, I could do that. I could just leave my body behind as if I'd already died. But since I hadn't yet, it should serve as an anchor holding me to this world. But I didn't really see the point, as it would leave me merely an unhoused spirit, no better than a ghost. Worse, in fact, since a ghost had a renewable source of energy, and mine would be left behind as soon as I—

As soon as—

As soon—

I couldn't think, couldn't finish the thought, because I was losing consciousness. And that meant end and that meant fail and that meant death, and whatever I was going to do, I had to do it, I had to—

Act.

And then I was stumbling backward, dizzy and disoriented and sick, but not as sick as when I caught sight of my body. Tiny and pale and helpless, it lay huddled against the wall, hair smushed around distorted features, face bleached bone white out of fear. The same fear that had one hand locked, white-knuckled, on the edge of a door, a door it couldn't go through.

But I could, and I didn't waste any time, diving past the mage and my own almost corpse and into the blessed darkness of the hall.

I called for Billy, desperately, because if anyone knew about these kinds of things, it was him. But either he was out for the count or he'd gone off somewhere, because I didn't even get a blip in response. This time, it looked like I was on my own.

That was true even when I finally found my bodyguards hanging out in a spare bedroom, playing poker. And weren't they just looking relaxed. Ties were loosened, collars were popped and a bucket of ice sat on the floor with a dozen frosty longnecks poking out of the top. I guess so they wouldn't have to make the huge trek all the way to the kitchen.

Where, you know, they might have seen someone *trying to kill me.*

"Comfy?" I asked harshly, but of course nobody heard.

I watched them play cards for a second, happy and carefree and unconcerned about the knife-wielding mage prowling the apartment or my trip to la-la land or anything but their stupid, stupid game, which I sent flying with a sudden swipe of my hand. Bills fluttered, chips flew, and cards reshuffled themselves all over the floor. And that was before I tipped over their damn card table.

Of course, I knew this wasn't how it was supposed to work. The name of the game for ghosts was to preserve energy. To guard every tiny scrap carefully, jealously, spending it in little dribs and drabs and only when absolutely necessary. Because to run out was to die.

But I was about to die anyway, and I didn't give a crap about the rules. I wasn't trying to conserve energy; I was spending it all in one last, crazy spree. At least I'll go out with a bang, I thought, laughing hysterically. And then I grabbed a beer and threw it at the nearest vamp's head.

I missed, but it made a satisfying thump when it hit the wall, so I did it again. And again and again as the vamps stumbled back, knocking over chairs and staring around wildly. Several pulled guns, but they had nothing to shoot.

"Why do I have bodyguards, huh?" I yelled, throwing a bottle against the dresser, which exploded with a satisfying crash.

"What is the freaking point?" Another hit the mirror, leaving a big web of cracks radiating out from the center.

"We have to watch you sleep, Cassie!" Thud.

"And eat, Cassie!" Bang.

"And paint your freaking toenails, Cassie!" Smash.

"And dog your every step, Cassie!" Splinter.

"But when someone is *actually trying to kill me*, what the hell are you doing?" A bottle took out the overhead fixture, shattering the decorative shell and raining sparks down onto the already freaked-out vampires.

And then I stopped, not because I'd run out of things to say, but because one of the vamps had caught sight of the mysteriously floating beer bottle. And it seemed to piss him off. "I have had enough of this shit," he announced viciously, lining up a shot.

I didn't bother moving; I just waggled the bottle provocatively. "Want it, motherfucker? Want it? Then come *get it*!" And then I ran like hell.

A bullet smashed into the wall beside me, another shattered a hallway light and a third tore through a pretty little painting, drilling the girl on the swing straight between the eyes. I didn't care; I was more concerned about the girl on the wall, who was looking pretty damn blue and pretty damn dead. I stopped for a split second, staring in horror at my slack features and my lifeless face, and then I was merging with my poor abused body and—

Nothing.

Blackness.

Cold.

So cold.

Silence.

Until someone started screaming. "Don't you die, don't you die, don't you fucking die on me—"

And someone was pounding my chest and someone else was forcing smoke-flavored breath down my throat, and he really needed to gargle because that was just gross, and then I was choking and gasping and flailing weakly and Marco was dragging me against his huge, rapidly moving chest. "Are you all right? Are you fucking all right?" he yelled right in my face.

"Urp," I said brilliantly. And then I threw up on him.

Chapter Twenty

I thought there was a good chance the fridge was possessed.

It was subtle about it, but I had its number. I knew its ways. Oh yes.

"How the hell did nobody hear him?" someone demanded harshly. I couldn't see who it was because he was outside the kitchen. But it sounded sort of like Marco. Or like Marco might sound if he wanted to bite someone's head off their body.

One of the vamps must have thought so, too, because he was awfully tentative when he answered. "He . . . apparently, the mage threw a silence spell over the lounge. We couldn't hear any—"

"I'm more interested in why you couldn't *see*. All of you congregated in one place, with not a single fucking one watching your fucking charge—"

"The apartment was supposed to be empty!" Another, slightly less cowed voice said. "And she hates it when we hover—"

"Then you play pool, you play cards, you watch without making it obvious. But you fucking well watch!" Something crashed into a wall.

Nobody said anything that time. Or maybe I just wasn't listening. After all, someone had to keep an eye on the fridge.

There were slash marks in the front, spaced evenly like evil eyes, glowing with yellow light from the inside. And that couldn't be the usual fridge light, could it? Wasn't that supposed to go out when the door was closed? I thought I saw something move behind one of the slashes, but then I blinked and it was gone.

Oh yes. I knew.

Pritkin came in and knelt by my chair. "You can't go to sleep yet, Cassie," he told me, handing me a heart murmur in a mug. It smelled good, but not good enough to wake up for. I mumbled something and turned over, burying my face in the nice, warm shoulder someone had thoughtfully provided.

Only to be hauled up again.

So I sighed and snuggled into a nice, warm chest instead.

"Drink." My hands were wrapped around the mug.

I pushed it away. "Don' wanna. Wanna sleep."

"Not yet."

"Then why am I in bed?"

He sighed and pulled me to a sitting position, putting the mug firmly in my hands. "A healer is coming and he wants you to stay awake until he arrives, all right?"

I drank some too-hot coffee and scowled at him, annoyed although I couldn't remember why. The light from the lounge was leaking in, highlighting his spiky blond hair. I decided that must be it.

"You really hate my hair, don't you?" he asked, a smile flickering over his lips so fast I might have imagined it.

"Yeah."

"Why?"

I reached out to touch it, and was surprised as always to find it mostly soft. Just a little stiff in places from whatever product he used on it. It felt weird, imagining Pritkin having anything in his hair but sweat. But he must have; nobody's did that all on its own.

"It's like ... angry hair," I said, trying to pat it down and failing miserably.

He caught my wrist. "Most people would say that suits me."

"I'm not most people."

"I know."

I went back to watching the fridge. I could see the door over Pritkin's shoulder, and it wasn't closed after all. It was very slightly open, like a panting mouth. And some kind of multicolored mucus was dripping out the bottom.

Condiments, I told myself firmly.

Or so it wanted me to think.

"Dryden's finished hugging the toilet," one of the vamps said, walking into the kitchen. "Do we need to dose her, too?"

"She took care of that herself," Marco said, joining the party. He'd pulled off the barfed-on shirt but hadn't yet bothered to go to his room for another one. That left him in dark gray slacks, a pair of Ferragamo loafers and a lot of hair.

A *lot* of hair. It was even on his shoulders. It was like a pelt.

He crouched down on the other side of me. "You're really hairy," I told him, impressed.

"And you're really stoned."

I thought about that for a moment. It seemed like an outside possibility. "Why am I stoned?"

"It was the goddamned chocolates. I always taste everything before you eat it, yet I sat right there and watched you scarf half the damn—"

"You couldn't know."

"It's my goddamned job to know!"

I sighed and pulled his curly head to me. He was warm and fuzzy, like a big teddy bear. A big teddy bear with fangs.

I patted him softly.

"Why didn't the wards detect that shit?" one of the other guards demanded angrily. He was a redhead, his fiery hair worn in a slick style that went with his natty blue-plaid suit. He was one of the ones who had made fun of the mage when he first arrived, but who'd let him follow us in. I wondered if he'd caught flak for that.

Probably.

"They detect poison," Pritkin told him. "This was a narcotic."

"What the hell was the point in that?"

"Probably hoped she'd eat enough to kill her," Marco said savagely. "Don't have to be poison to do the job if you consume enough of it! But even one or two pieces would make sure she couldn't shift away from that asshole."

"That asshole ate half the box himself," Pritkin said, "hoping he'd pass out before that creature could make use of him."

"Then why the hell didn't he?"

"He doubtless would have, given more time. Unfortunately, our meeting broke up too soon and Cassie found the box—"

A phone rang. Marco pulled it out of his pocket and looked at the readout. "I gotta get the rest of my ass chewed off by the master," he told me. "Think you can maybe not die for five minutes?"

"I'll try," I told him seriously.

"You know, if anyone else said that, it would be funny." He left.

"What I don't get is how that thing knew that particular mage would get in," another vamp said. He was a tall brunet in nice tan jacket that was now covered in beer. "We'd been tossing them out on their fortune-hunting asses all day. He'd have gone the same way if he hadn't shown up with the Lord Protector."

"Maybe that's what it was waiting for," a third vamp said, glancing around. He was another brunet, in shirt-sleeves and dark brown slacks. A bright blue tie was askew under one ear, but he didn't appear to have noticed. "It could have been there all morning, watching us, waiting for someone to get in. . . ."

"Someone who just happened to have poisoned chocolates?" the redhead asked sarcastically.

"They weren't poisoned," the brunet said, scowling. "And he could have gotten them—"

"Where? At the gift shop?" The redhead rolled his eyes. "Yes, I'll take the drugged kind, please. Do you have any in mint?"

"Very funny!"

"Well, you sound like an idiot! Obviously, the bastard brought them with him, meaning this wasn't random opportunity. It was planned."

"I agree," Pritkin said, causing their heads to swivel back his way. "But not by him."

"You would say that," the redhead sneered. "Then where did he get the damn things?"

"He brought the candy with him, but it wasn't drugged. He said he did that later, under the influence of the entity."

"With *what*?"

Pritkin reached into a pocket and tossed something to the vamp, who caught it easily. It was a little vial, the type war mages wore in bandoliers or on their belts. A lot of them were filled with dark, sludgy substances that sometimes moved on their own, but this one was just plain, colorless liquid.

"And this does what?" the vamp asked, wisely not opening it.

Pritkin didn't reply. He just knelt beside me, green eyes assessing. He held up a finger. "Cassie, can you tell me how many—"

I grabbed it and laughed.

He looked over his shoulder at the vamp. "That," he said drily.

"What the hell was he carrying this shit around for?" the second vamp demanded.

"It's useful in making captures, subduing difficult prisoners." Pritkin shrugged.

"Then . . . this is a weapon."

"Yes."

"But he was going on a *date*."

Pritkin looked confused. "Yes?"

The redhead threw his hands up.

"How do we know the mage was really possessed?" a skinny blond asked, leaning over the counter. "Maybe somebody hired him—"

"He's been in the Corps for seventeen years," Pritkin said.

"And mages can't be bribed?"

"He also comes from a wealthy, prominent family. He has no need—"

"*That* guy?" the blond asked incredulously.

"He didn't dress like it," the redhead sniffed.

"Not everyone cares about such things," Pritkin said.

The redhead looked him over. "Obviously."

"Blackmail, then," Tan Jacket put in. "Maybe somebody had something on him."

"There will be an investigation," Pritkin told him. "But his actions speak for him. If—"

"His actions? He tried to kill her!"

"He tried to save her. Not only did he attempt to eat the chocolates whenever he was lucid enough, but he also slowed down his reflexes in the fight, skewed his aim. And when she ran, he threw a nonlethal spell instead of a fireball. He fought it every step of the way—"

"And we know this how? Because he told you?" Tan Jacket interrupted.

"We know this because she's still alive!" Pritkin snapped. "Essentially, he and Cassie were both fighting it. He bought her time, and she used it, brilliantly."

He bent over and topped off my coffee cup. Pritkin hadn't shaved for a few days, and I put my hand to his cheek. "Fuzzy," I told him seriously.

He sighed.

"I don't understand why this thing needed to hitch a ride in the first place," the redhead said. "If it's powerful enough to possess a war mage—"

"Anyone can be possessed if his guard is down," Pritkin said curtly. "And no one's is up every minute."

"It didn't possess one of us," the vamp pointed out snottily.

"Vampires are more difficult," Pritkin admitted. "You *can* be possessed, but it takes considerably more energy than possessing a human. The creature might not have had the strength to manage it and also force you to attack."

"But why did it need someone else to attack at all? If it's such a big, bad evil entity, why not go after her itself?"

"It already tried that—" Pritkin said.

"It tried to possess her, not simply attack her. If it can get past the wards, why not go for an all-out assault?"

Pritkin shrugged. "In Faerie, it doubtless would have. But outside its own world, its power is weakened."

"We still don't know that it's Fey," the vamp said.

"Yes, we do," a new voice said hoarsely.

I looked up to find a slim blond figure standing in the doorway to the kitchen. For a frozen second, I looked at him and he looked at me, and then I screamed and threw my coffee, which hit him square in the groin. And I guess that didn't feel too good because he screamed, too, and for a minute there was a whole lot of screaming going on.

Then Pritkin put a heavy hand on my shoulder and I belatedly noticed that Dryden was flanked by a couple of vamps, each of whom had one of his arms. It looked less like they were restraining him than holding him up. And then I noticed other things, like the fact that his eyes were back to blue and his nose was all bloody and he was pale and shaky and his nice suit was torn and dripping coffee.

He smelled like hot sauce.

"Sorry," I told him.

Dryden didn't say anything. He just stood there and shook at me.

Pritkin handed him some paper towels. "How do you know?"

Dryden swallowed and dabbed at his crotch. "My . . . my great-grandmother was Fey," he said shakily. "Somehow, it knew that. It tried to talk to me—"

"About what?"

"I'm . . . not sure. I—"

"You don't know the language?"

"A little, but—"

"Then take a guess!"

"That's what I'm trying to do, if you'll give me a chance!" he snapped, tossing the wet paper towels in the trash. "I only caught maybe one word in ten, but I think . . . I think it was trying to apologize."

"Apologize?" The redheaded vamp sneered. "For what?"

Dryden scowled and flailed a hand angrily. "For *this*? For almost getting me killed? For almost making me—" he broke off and glanced at me, and his lips tightened. "I don't know. I didn't get that much. Just something like 'they made me do it,' and that she was afraid of them—"

"She?" the vamp asked.

"Yes. It . . . She . . . I think it was female. It was using the female form of address, anyway. Like I told you, my grasp of the language isn't good and that goes double for the High Court dialect—"

"High Court?" That was Pritkin.

"It's the version of the language spoken at court—"

"I know what it is," Pritkin snapped. "How did you recognize it?"

"Because my grandmother spoke it!"

"And your grandmother was?"

"A Selkie noblewoman."

Pritkin cursed. "Dark Fey."

The mage didn't deign to respond to that. He looked at me and took a deep breath. "Before I left, I just wanted to say . . . thank you." It came out a little strangled.

I thought about it for a moment. "You're welcome?"

"Do you know what I'm thanking you for?"

Damn. I'd hoped he wouldn't ask that. It couldn't be for lunch, since we'd never had any.

And I guessed we wouldn't now, what with a possessed fridge and all.

"No?" I said, figuring I had a fifty-fifty shot.

He knelt in front of my chair, or maybe his legs collapsed; I don't know. He wasn't looking so good. "I know what that is," he said hoarsely, nodding at my wrist, where my bracelet of interlocking knives lay hard and cold against my skin. "It's my job at the Corps to disenchant confiscated dark objects and . . . I've seen one like it before."

His eyes searched my face. He seemed to be waiting on some kind of response. So I nodded.

"You could have killed me," he said. And then he kissed my hand. "Thank you."

He just stayed like that for a while, head down, on one knee, like a supplicant in front of a priest. Or like a guy making a marriage proposal. I started to get nervous. Because the last thing I needed was another one of those.

I decided to let him down easy.

"You seem like a nice guy," I told him. "I mean, you know, when you're not trying to kill me. I just . . ." I sighed and came out with it. "I just really don't want to date you."

He suddenly looked up. His eyes were wet, but his smile was blinding. "Then it seems I have something else to thank you for."

Chapter Twenty-one

According to the alarm clock on my nightstand, I slept for seven hours, despite already having slept for most of the day. It was almost midnight when I rolled out, groggy and thickheaded and gritty-eyed and yucky. And saw a man in the corner of my room.

I didn't scream, because the man was a) sitting down, b) reading a paper and c) had the golden-eyed glow typical of Mircea's masters. I just snatched up the sheet, because I'd been too high to worry about pj's, and scanned the room for more. But I didn't see any, unless they were hiding in the closet or under the bed.

And wasn't that just a fun thought?

"What are you doing here?" I demanded after a moment.

He didn't bother to reply, just flipped over another page.

"You're not supposed to be in my room!"

Nothing.

Talking to a vamp who's not in the mood is one of life's biggest time wasters, so I didn't try. I also didn't attempt to budge him, because master vamps go wherever they damn well please. I just wrapped the sheet around me and dragged myself off to the bathroom.

I stood in the cool air for a minute while my eyes adjusted to the brilliant light on all that tile. But even after they did, I still stayed where I was, one hand on the door-

knob, like I was waiting for something. It finally occurred to
me that I was expecting another freak-out, only my body
didn't seem interested. It felt chilly and kind of achy and
kind of high. But not particularly panicked. I gave it a little
longer, until I started to feel stupid; then I dropped the
sheet and checked out the damage.

It wasn't all that bad. Other than putting a new bruise on
my ass and a lump on my head, I'd come out pretty good
this round. Whatever is trying to kill me is obviously going
to have to step up its game, I thought viciously, and looked
in the mirror.

And swore.

I might not have been too beaten up, but I still looked
like hell, especially my hair. Not only was it still faintly
green, but it was now missing a large chunk. I pushed it
around for a while with clumsy fingers, but nothing seemed
to help. I tried parting it different, but the only way that
kind of worked looked suspiciously like a middle-aged
guy's comb-over. And it still left me looking like something
had taken a bite out of my head.

Damn it all! Not so long ago, my hair had been a shimmering red-gold wave that cascaded down my back like a
cloak. It had been my one claim to real beauty, and I'd cried
like a baby when I had to cut it while on the run from Tony,
because it was too recognizable.

I didn't cry this time. I was too freaking mad. I just
brushed my teeth, washed my face and dragged my big wad
of fabric back to the bedroom.

The vamp still didn't say anything, and neither did I. I
also didn't turn on a light, which was stupid, because he
could probably see about the same either way. But it made
me feel more naked to have it on, which was why it took
five minutes of hunting and grumbling and falling and cursing around in the closet to find what I wanted.

I finally emerged with an old Georgia Bulldogs baseball cap, a pair of silky blue track shorts and a faded pink
tank top from my comfort-clothes stash. None of it
matched, but right then, I didn't give a damn. I hauled
everything back to the bathroom, and after dressing and
combing and slapping on some mascara, I decided I
looked mostly normal.

If normal people had green hair and wore hats indoors.

The vamp folded his paper and got to his feet when I started out the door, even though there was another guard just outside. He was leaning against the wall, smoking a cigarette, looking bored and butt-sore. He didn't say anything and neither did I. I just padded across the hall to the living room, because stomping doesn't work so well in bare feet and on carpet.

The rest of the crew was in the lounge, playing cards. Of course they were. I felt like asking them if that's how they'd envisioned spending eternity, but I had other things on my mind.

Marco was sitting at the card table, doing one of his fancy shuffles. He looked up and a smile quirked at the corner of his mouth. "What?" I demanded.

"You and the bulldog got the same expression."

"Very funny! What the hell—"

He held up a hand. "First of all, how you doing?"

"I'm fine! Or I would be if—"

"You sure? We got the doc on standby."

I scowled. That was where that sadist could stay, too. "No, thanks. And can we—"

"You hungry? 'Cause we got Chinese coming."

"Marco—"

"Not from room service; from that little place around the corner. Kung pao chicken, ginger beef—"

"Marco!"

He sighed and gave it up. "I told the master this was how you were gonna react. But you gotta see that it makes sense, at least until we figure this thing out."

"It does not make sense! There's nobody in the apartment but us, and the creature can't possess a vamp—"

"We don't know that."

"—or it would have already done it instead of hanging around the foyer, waiting for Mr. Mage to show up."

"Mr. Mage," one of the vamps said. "I like that. I'm gonna start calling all of 'em that."

"I can think of a few things to call them," another one muttered.

"And if you think it *can* possess a vamp, this makes even less sense," I pointed out. "You just left me alone in my room with one for hours!"

"You're right," he told me.

"I am?"

"Yeah. We obviously need two."

"Marco!"

He held up placating hands. "Just kidding."

"This isn't funny. It's like being a freaking prisoner!"

He started to answer, but the phone rang. It wasn't the main line, but a black cell phone sitting on the card table. Marco picked it up, glanced at the readout, scowled and hung up. He looked at me. "Better than being a freaking corpse."

"Didn't you hear me? This isn't going to help!"

"It will if that thing goes after you. It already possessed you once—"

"And won't again." I pulled out Pritkin's little amulet. He'd left me another one before he took the mage off to the Corps' version of a hospital. It might be stinky, but I liked it a lot better than the alternative.

"That only works on Fey," Marco pointed out, wrinkling his nose.

"Which this thing is."

"Which this thing may be. That ain't been decided yet."

"It spoke in a Fey dialect—"

"And demons don't know that shit? If it's trying to throw us off, of course it's gonna pretend to be something else."

"Or maybe it really was trying to communicate."

"For what? To apologize?" Marco's tone said clearly what he thought about that. He dealt another round. "Anyway, until we get some solid proof of what we're dealing with here, the master don't want to take chances."

"That isn't his call. It's my life!"

"Yeah, well. You're gonna have to take that up with him."

I put my hands on my hips. "Fine, I will. Get him on the phone."

"Can't."

"And why not?"

"He's in a high-level meeting—"

"How convenient."

"—and told me not to disturb him until morning."

"Then get a note to him."

"That would be disturbing."

"Damn it, Marco!"

The phone rang. He glanced at it, sighed and put it back down again. "Look, it's only for a little while—"

"Oh, please!" I couldn't believe he was trying that. "Sell it to someone else. I know how these things work!"

He took his smelly cigar out of his mouth and rested it on the ashtray. "And how do they work?"

"I go along with this now, and I'll have Mutt and Jeff here dogging my every step for the rest of my damn life!"

The taller vamp looked at the shorter one. "Guess that makes you Jeff."

"I ain't no Jeff. He was a crazy little bugger."

"Well, Mutt was an idiot."

"They were both idiots, and shut up," Marco told them. He looked at me. "You know I don't have any say over this. But you're already up now, so it don't matter anyway. And you can talk to the master in the morning."

I just stood there for a moment, debating options. Because giving in, even for a few hours, wasn't smart. Give a vamp an inch and he wouldn't take a mile; he'd take the whole damn continent.

My stomach growled.

"Kung pao chicken," Marco wheedled.

The bastard.

Mircea and I clearly needed to have a conversation, but I also needed to eat. And only one was currently available. And I was *starving*.

"Sweet-and-sour pork—"

"Oh, shut up," I told him.

He grinned.

I sighed. "You order egg rolls?"

Marco spread his hands. "Please."

I decided that I'd bargain better on a full stomach, and swiped a beer. He dealt me in, and I grabbed a chair before looking at my cards hopefully. Nothing—not even a pair of twos.

Typical.

The phone rang.

"Can't you turn that off?" one of the guards groused. He was an attractive blond I didn't recognize. Probably one of the new guys.

"It's my private line. Could be important," Marco told him tersely.

"Your private line? How the hell—"

"I don't know, but I'm getting it changed tomorrow. Just play your cards."

"I would if I ever got any worth a damn," the guy muttered.

They anted up. I folded. The phone rang.

"Damn it, Marco! I can't play with that thing going off every five seconds!"

"Then don't play," Marco told him.

"Just tell the mage to go fuck himself—"

"What mage?" I asked, and everyone froze.

"Thank you," Marco told the guy viciously.

The phone rang. Marco had left it on the table, and it had jittered its way over to me. So I picked it up. "Don't," he said.

I flipped it open and checked the readout. PRITKIN. I shot Marco a look and put the phone to my ear. "Hel—"

"Goddamnit, Marco, you're supposed to be—" He cut off abruptly. "Cassie?"

"What is it?" I asked, feeling my heart rate speed up.

"There's no emergency—not right now," he said, apparently hearing the alarm in my voice. "But I need to see you. I'm coming up."

"The hell you are," Marco said, grabbing back the phone. "I already told you—"

"I want to see him," I said, crossing my arms.

Marco looked at me, clearly frustrated. "You need to rest!"

"I'm playing cards and drinking beer. How is that not resting?"

"You were gonna go back to bed soon."

"I slept all day!"

The doorbell rang.

Marco got to his feet, looking conflicted.

"What are you going to do—bar the door?" I asked, also standing up.

"I got orders," he said defensively.

"Mircea told you to lock Pritkin out?"

"Just for tonight. He don't want the mage here while you're vulnerable."

"He's my bodyguard! When I'm vulnerable is when I need him!"

"Look, you really gotta—"

"Take that up with Mircea," I finished for him.

"Yeah."

"Fine. I will." I pressed the menu button on Marco's phone.

"Cassie—"

And there it was. I hit the button. The phone rang.

"Yes?" The familiar voice was smooth, with no sign of irritation. Not yet.

"You said you weren't going to do this."

There was a pause. "Cassandra."

"Wow, we just leapt right to it there, didn't we?" I asked, furious.

"You are supposed to be asleep."

"I was. And then I got up to discover that I'm a prisoner."

"You are not a prisoner."

"Then I can leave?"

Another pause. "In the morning, when you can shift."

"So I'm only a prisoner for the night, is that it?"

"It is for your protection."

"And how does that work, exactly? I've been assaulted twice. And where have they both been again?"

"You were vulnerable the first time due to our ignorance of the threat. You were vulnerable the second because a *mage* provided a conduit for the creature—"

"And that explains why I can't see Pritkin?"

A third pause. That had to be some kind of record. Mircea usually had the defense prepared.

"No. Considering the probable nature of the entity that has been attacking you, I consider the warlock to be a threat in his own right."

"The what?"

"He had a demon servant at one time, did he not? Encased in that battle golem he devised?"

I frowned. "I guess."

"Then he is a warlock, not merely a mage. Only warlocks can summon demons to their aid."

"Is there a point?"

"Merely that warlocks are a notoriously unstable class.

They are prone to strange behavior, increasingly so as they age, with some going mad over time. It is one reason that many mages avoid the specialization, despite the added power it gives them."

"But Jonas had a golem once," I protested. "He told me so."

"Forgive me, Cassie, but Jonas Marsden is hardly an example of well-adjusted behavior!"

Point.

"And we are discussing the warlock Pritkin."

Actually, we weren't. Because Pritkin wasn't a warlock. His ability with demons came not through some arcane magic, but because he was half demon himself. His father was Rosier, Lord of the Incubi, which made Pritkin sort of a demon prince. Or something. I really didn't know what it made him, since he hated that part of his lineage and almost never talked about it. But I didn't think mentioning that I was being guarded by the son of a prince of hell was likely to go well.

Of course, neither was this.

"He's a friend."

"Those creatures are not friends, Cassie! They are self-serving, power-hungry—"

"They say the same thing about vamps."

"—and unpredictable. Not to mention that this one may well be part demon himself."

"What?"

"That is the rumor Kit has been hearing. And it would explain why he heals so quickly, how he has lived—"

"A lot of people are part one thing, part another—"

"But most of them don't bother to cover up large areas of their past. Yet despite all of Kit's efforts, he has been unable to discover anything about the man before the last century—"

"Because he wasn't born then!"

"We both know that isn't the case."

I didn't say anything. Mircea had recently seen Pritkin on a trip we'd taken back in time. And while mages tended to live a century or more longer than most humans, it was kind of hard to explain why he'd aged maybe five years in a couple hundred.

Of course, I didn't intend to try. I didn't think that ex-

plaining that Pritkin had been in hell for much of his life
was likely to make him seem more trustworthy.

"I would like you to consider dismissing the man," Mircea said suddenly. It caught me off guard, which I suspected
was the point.

"I can't do that."

"Cassie—"

"I need him," I said flatly. "If he hadn't been training me,
I might have died—"

"Or you might not have been in danger at all. Have you
noticed that your problems with demonkind always seem
to come when the warlock is around?"

"What are you suggesting?"

"That perhaps he is the source of the threat, rather than
its solution."

"That's ridiculous!"

"Is it? I know only that every time you have trouble
with demons, he is there."

"He's my bodyguard! He's supposed to be—"

"You have bodyguards."

"Yeah, only I think most of them would like a new as-
signment. And this wasn't a demon."

"According to him."

"Well, I trust him!"

Pause number four. "And I do not."

And there it was, as plain as any challenge ever given.
And to underscore it, as if anything else was needed, Marco
quietly took the phone out of my hand and put it in his
back pocket. His expression said clearly that it wasn't coming out again.

All right, then.

The doorbell rang.

I glanced around the room. One thing about Vegas hotels, especially those built before the widespread use of cell
phones, is that they put land lines everywhere. Busy executives needed instant access to the empires they were gam-
bling away and wouldn't stay anywhere that didn't offer it.
As a result, there were no fewer than three telephones in
sight—one in the living room, one in the bar and one sitting
on the counter in the kitchen.

And a vamp was casually loitering near every one of
them.

Okay, then.

I turned on my heel and went back to my room.

Unsurprisingly, there was no cell phone in my purse. I hadn't really expected one. When a master vampire gave an order, his men were thorough in carrying it out. And Marco had never been a slouch. But there were things that a vamp might not notice, especially one who had been around as long as he had.

I went back to the bathroom, turned on the exhaust fan and the shower and blasted Led Zeppelin from the built-in radio.

Vampires don't use bathrooms all that much, especially the toilet facilities. And, of course, housekeeping kept the place clean. As a result, I was willing to bet that the guys outside had never bothered to so much as crack the door on the toilet cubicle.

And then I knew they hadn't, when I opened it and saw what I'd expected—yet another phone, this one mounted on the wall. It was big and kind of complicated-looking, like something that ought to have been on the desk of an executive secretary, not sitting above the toilet-tissue dispenser. But it was there, and when I lifted the receiver, I got a dial tone.

Pritkin picked up on the first ring, like he'd been expecting a call. "Do you still have Jonas's keys?" I asked quietly.

There was silence for a beat, as if he hadn't been expecting that. But he recovered fast. "See what I can do."

He hung up and so did I. After waiting another few minutes, I turned off the water and went back to my room. I couldn't change clothes, because somebody might notice. But I put on a bra, jammed my feet into an old pair of Keds and shoved some cash and my keys into my pocket. Then I went back into the lounge.

The guys were still playing poker, quietly now, as there was no need to keep up audible patter for the human. So they didn't fall silent when I entered and picked up my half-finished beer. But ten pairs of eyes watched as I made my way across to the living room and then to the balcony.

The wind chimes were tinkling in the breeze blowing off the desert. It was hot, but after the deep freeze the vamps had going on inside, it felt good. I hung over the rail and drank my beer and waited.

"Is there a problem?" Marco asked, sticking his head out the door.

"Need some air."

He looked at me suspiciously, but I guess his orders stopped short of actually confining me to my room. He went back to the game, and I went back to my beer. I hadn't even finished it when my ride showed up.

"Best I could do on short notice," Pritkin told me, grabbing my arm as I scrambled over the railing. And into the front seat of a beat-up green convertible that was idling in the air twenty stories up.

"No problem," I told him, hanging on for dear life as the rattletrap belched smoke into the startled faces of half a dozen vamps, who had taken a fraction of a second too long to figure out what was going on.

"Cassie!" I heard Marco's infuriated bellow behind me. But by then we were out of there, soaring away into the star-shot indigo high above the Strip.

Chapter Twenty-two

"You coldhearted son of a bitch."

Pritkin looked up from perusing the stained piece of paper posing as a menu and gave me what he probably thought were innocent eyes. They weren't. I didn't think that was an expression he was all that familiar with. "Is there a problem?"

"You feed me tofu while you've been eating *here*?" I gestured around at the cracked Formica, orange Naugahyde and grimy windows of what had to be the greasiest greasy spoon in Vegas.

"No one eats healthy all the time."

"That's not what you always say!"

"And do you listen to what I say?"

"Yes." He just looked at me. "Sometimes."

"Which is the point. If I told you to eat well merely most of the time, then you'd do it occasionally at best."

I started to reply to that, and then realized I didn't have one. "So why bring me here now?"

"Because some days, everyone needs pizza."

That, at least, we could agree on. He ordered for us, which normally would have annoyed me, but there wasn't much of a menu to choose from. This wasn't so much a restaurant as a dive, and you either ordered pizza and beer or you went home.

Unless you ordered ice cream. I decided on a chocolate

shake instead of more beer, and although Pritkin didn't say anything, his expression was eloquent. "You're going to run it off me anyway," I pointed out.

"Anything else?" he asked drily. "Onion rings? Pie?"

"They have pie?"

"No." It was emphatic.

I was in too good of a mood to argue the point. The seat was sticking to my thighs, a broken spring was stabbing my left butt cheek, and the air-conditioning, while present, was completely inadequate for August in Nevada. But I was out. I'd won this round. And tonight, I'd take what victories I could get.

"Are you going to explain what's going on?" he asked, after the waitress left. "When I tried—"

"Wait a minute."

There was an old jukebox in the corner, with dirty glass and yellowed titles, not one of which was less than twenty years old. But it had Joan Jett's entire repertoire, so I fed it a couple of quarters and punched in a selection. The sound quality wasn't the best, but that wasn't my main interest, anyway.

"It's Mircea," I said, when I rejoined him. "He's got this crazy idea that you're a danger."

Pritkin's jaw tightened. "I know."

"You know? Has he said—"

"He didn't have to. But you may assure him that I am no threat in that regard."

"I have," I said impatiently. "But when these things keep happening—"

"They do not keep happening. It was one time."

I frowned. "One time?"

For some reason, he flushed. "Of any consequence."

"Well, excuse me for thinking they were all pretty important!" Any time something was trying to kill me, I took it seriously.

Pritkin ran a hand through his hair, which didn't need the added torture. "I didn't mean to downplay the significance of what occurred—"

"I would hope not!"

"—merely to assure you that it won't happen again."

"You can't know that."

Green eyes met mine, with what looked like anger in them. "Yes, I bloody well can!"

I just sat there, confused, as he abruptly got up and went over to the jukebox. He received a glance from a woman in a nearby booth on the way, and it lingered. He was still in the same jeans as earlier, having just thrown a gray-green T-shirt over the top. Although you couldn't see much of it because of the long leather trench he wore to cover up the arsenal all war mages carted around.

But he'd somehow jammed everything under there without noticeable bulges, because the dark brown leather fit his broad shoulders sleekly. Likewise, the soft, old jeans hugged a rock-hard physique, and the T-shirt brought out the brilliant color of his eyes. Pritkin would never be conventionally handsome; his nose was too big, he missed six feet by at least three inches and he only remembered to shave about half the time.

But I didn't have any trouble understanding why she was staring.

"This is what you listen to?" he demanded, his back to me as he perused song titles.

"It's 'I Love Rock 'n Roll.' It's a classic."

That got me a dark glance thrown over his shoulder, but he didn't say anything. He just dug a couple of quarters out of his jeans and made a selection of his own. And oh, my God.

"Johnny *Cash*?"

"What's wrong with Johnny Cash?" he asked, sitting back down.

"What's right about him?"

"Country is based on folk music, which has been around for centuries—"

"So has the plague."

"—longer than the so-called 'classics.' For thousands of years, bards sang about the same basic themes—love and loss, lust and betrayal—and ended up influencing everyone from Bach to Beethoven."

"So Johnny Cash is Beethoven?"

"Of his day."

I rolled my eyes. That was just so wrong. But at least "Ring of Fire" covered the conversation pretty well.

I leaned forward and dropped my voice. "I wasn't trying to be rude a minute ago. I just meant that, to the vamps, a demon seems like the most likely culprit, and Mircea's decided—"

"Demon?"

"Yes, demon."

Pritkin frowned. "What do they have to do with this?"

I stared at him. "Well, what are we talking about?"

"I'm not sure."

I took a breath. "Mircea thinks you're a warlock," I said, slowly and clearly. "He's decided that's how you've lived so long, why you're as strong as you—"

"Is that what he told you?"

"Yes. Why?"

He looked away. "No reason."

I waited, but he didn't say anything else. And after a pause, I soldiered on. "*Anyway*, that's why he told Marco to lock you out for the night. He was afraid you'd call up something else—"

Pritkin snorted.

"—while I couldn't shift away."

"Yes, I'm sure that was his main concern."

"Is there something you want to tell me?" I demanded.

"No." He didn't say anything else, if he'd planned on it, because the waitress returned with our drinks. He poured beer, tilting the glass to minimize foam, because this wasn't the kind of place where the waitstaff did it for you. "If you were merely instructed not to see me until tomorrow, why go to these lengths?" he asked, after she left. "Why not simply agree?"

"Because I couldn't. V—" I caught myself. The jukebox had gone quiet, and I was kind of afraid of what he might select next. So I settled for modifying my language. "They will push and push, to see where your boundaries are. And if you knuckle under once, they'll expect you to do it every time."

"Meaning?"

"That if I hadn't left, next time it wouldn't have been, 'It's only for tonight, Cassie.' It would have been 'It's only for this week,' or this month, or this year. . . .'"

"And they chose to push when they knew you were vulnerable." He sounded like he expected nothing less.

"They didn't choose," I said, frowning. Because Pritkin always assumed the worst about vampires. "They probably thought I'd sleep all night and it would never come up. But it did, and in their society, you can't afford to ignore a challenge like that. If you do, you'll be labeled weak, and that's a really hard thing to undo."

Pritkin looked confused. "Are you trying to say that Marco *wanted* you to defy him?"

"This isn't about Marco. He was just following orders."

"Then *Mircea* wanted you to defy him?"

I laughed. "No."

Pritkin was starting to look exasperated. "Then what—"

"Mircea wants me to do what I'm told. He'd love it if I did what I'm told. But he wouldn't *respect* it. He wouldn't respect me."

I took a moment to work on my shake, which was thick and rich and headache-inducing cold. I'd sort of given up explaining any vamp to any mage, much less Mircea to Pritkin. But he'd asked, and I owed him one, so I tried.

"Mircea didn't give that order expecting me to ever know about it," I said. "But he *did* give it, and once he refused to rescind it, it became a direct challenge."

Pritkin's eyes narrowed. "And you couldn't ignore it because it would have made you look bad?"

I had to think for a moment about how to answer that. It was surprisingly difficult sometimes to put into words things I had accepted as the natural order since childhood. But they weren't natural for Pritkin, or for most mages, other than for those who worked for the vampires themselves. And they didn't talk much.

"It wouldn't have made me look *bad*," I finally said. "It would have made me look like what he was treating me as: a favored servant. Someone to be petted and pampered and protected—and ordered around. Because that's what servants do: they take orders. But that isn't how one of his equals would have responded."

"But he wouldn't have tried that with one of them."

I snorted. "Of course he would. They do this kind of thing all the time, testing each other, seeing if there are any chinks in the other person's armor, any weaknesses that maybe they didn't notice before. And if they find one, they'll exploit it."

"It sounds as if you're talking about an enemy, rather than a . . . friend," he said curtly.

I shook my head. "It's part of the culture."

"That doesn't make it right!"

"It doesn't make it wrong, either. It's how they determine rank. If you knuckle under to some other master's demands, especially without a fight, then you're accepting that he or she outranks you. And afterward, everyone else will accept that, too."

"But you're not a—" Pritkin caught himself. "You're not a master."

"But I have to be treated as one."

"Why?" He looked disgusted. Like the idea that any human might actually want to fit into vampire society was unfathomable. For a moment, I thought about telling him just how many humans were turned away each year by courts much less illustrious than Mircea's. But somehow, I didn't think it would help.

"Because there's no alternative," I said instead, as our artery-clogging pepperoni pizza was delivered. It was New York style, which meant the pieces were so big I had to fold one over to eat it, and a trickle of grease ran down my arm. I sighed happily.

Pritkin started working on his own meal, but to my surprise, he didn't drop the subject. "Explain it to me."

"There are only three types of . . . us . . . as far as they're concerned," I said, in between bites. "Servants, prey and threats. There's no category for ally or partner, because that requires viewing us as equals, and they just don't do that."

"They are allied with the Circle, at least for the duration of the current conflict," he argued.

"Yeah, well. Words have different meanings to different groups," I hedged.

"And what does 'ally' mean to the Senate?" Pritkin demanded predictably.

I hesitated, trying to think of a phrase that wasn't "cannon fodder." "Let's just say I don't think that they're planning on a real close association."

"They had better be," he said grimly. "We need strong allies. We have enough enemies."

There was no arguing that.

"My point was that, right now, I'm seen as an especially useful servant, like the humans who guard their courts during the day or cast their wards for them. And as long as I follow orders, accept restrictions and do what I'm told, that's how it's going to stay."

"Then defy them!"

I gestured around. "What does this look like?"

He shot me a look. "You're eating pizza. That is hardly defiance."

"It is by their standards."

"I meant, get out." He gestured sharply. "Tell them to go to hell. You could go—"

"Where?" I demanded. "To the Circle? Where who knows how many of Saunders's buddies are still hanging around? To my lovely court?"

"You're going to have to set up your court sooner or later."

"Later, then. After the alliance."

I reached for the grated cheese, and he frowned. But I guess my health wasn't the cause, because what he said was, "What alliance?"

"Of the six senates? What Mircea's been working on all month?"

"What does that have to do with you?"

I shrugged. "Having a vamp-friendly Pythia is the trump card in his argument. It's something the vamps have never had. They've always felt like they were on the outside of the supernatural community, that the Pythia was part of the Circle's arsenal, not theirs."

"And now they think the opposite."

"They're coming around." They knew Mircea. And when they looked at me, twenty-four and fresh off the turnip truck, I doubted they had any trouble believing that he could wind me around his little finger. That wasn't a problem for me as long as it helped us get the alliance.

And as long as he didn't start believing it, too.

"But if you were suddenly removed?" Pritkin asked. "If you were killed, for instance?"

I shook my head. "I know what you're thinking, but that can't be it."

"Why not? You said it yourself—you are the only Pythia the vampires have ever felt was theirs. Your replacement would likely come from the Circle's pool of Initiates—"

"Which wouldn't make them happy. But they're not talking because of me. They're here because of the war and because Apollo showing up scared the shit out of them. I'm just something to sweeten the deal."

"But if someone didn't know them well enough to know that—"

"Then they wouldn't know why they're meeting in the first place. They've been using the coronation and some other stuff as cover while they hash out the details. Like who gets to lead—"

"And Mircea is attempting to use you as an argument for his consul."

"'Attempting' would be the right word."

Pritkin swallowed a bite of fatty goodness. "Why? You just said—"

"That I'm seen as a vamp-friendly Pythia, yeah." I shrugged. "But it takes a little more than that. Half the senators aren't convinced that I know what the hell I'm doing. It's easy for them to imagine me being under Mircea's thumb; it's a little harder for them to believe I'm strong enough to be a real asset."

"And without believing it, they're bickering and feuding over leadership instead of doing anything about the war."

"Pretty much, yeah."

"Typical."

I didn't say anything; from what I'd seen, Circle politics were no different, but I wasn't in the mood to argue about it. "Anyway, the point is that I'm better off where I am right now—"

"That's debatable."

"—but to be able to work with the Senate, I have to be accepted by them, and not as a servant. A servant takes orders; she doesn't give them. But that's sort of my job now, isn't it?"

He looked at me with exasperated eyes, brilliantly green in the harsh lights of the diner. "The former holder of your office gave orders, and they were obeyed."

"Were they?" I munched crust. It was slightly burnt on

the bottom and chewy, with little dough bubbles here and there. Perfect. "How often did Agnes persuade the Senate to do something they didn't want to do?"

"I'm sure there were any number of times."

"Name one."

He scowled.

"Yeah. They might have fiddled around a little, debating some issue they didn't really give a damn about, and then let her think she'd had a victory. Particularly if they wanted something in return. But to actually give up part of their sovereignty to someone they viewed as being in the Circle's back pocket?"

"The Pythia is supposed to be neutral."

"Try telling that to a vamp." I caught his hand as he reached for more red pepper flakes. "Seriously?"

"What?"

I nodded at his current piece of pizza, which was almost completely red—and not because of sauce. "You're going to give yourself heartburn."

"I don't get heartburn."

"What? Never?"

"No."

I let him go. That was completely unfair. I ate antacids like they were candy.

"Anyway, we weren't at war in Agnes's reign, so it didn't matter as much," I said, digging a half-finished pack of Rolaids out of my shorts. "It does now."

Pritkin cocked an eyebrow. "And you think that going out for the evening is going to make them respect you?"

"More than staying in would have." I chewed a couple of tablets while he thought that over.

"It still sounds like something an enemy would do," he said. "Pushing you, testing you—"

"An enemy would use the information to hurt me," I pointed out. "Mircea would never do that. At least, he wouldn't *intend* it that way. But burying me under a stack of guards, restricting who I can see, where I can go . . . it *is* hurting me."

"It's also safer," Pritkin said, looking sour. Probably because he was being forced to agree with a vampire.

"You can say that after the last few days?" I sat back against the seat. "Nowhere is safe. Nowhere has ever been safe. I'll take reasonable precautions, even unreasonable ones sometimes. But I'm not going to live like a prisoner."

"It's only been two months—"

"It's been my whole life!" I said, harsher than I intended, because nobody got that. Not Mircea, not Pritkin, not Jonas, who would have loved to add a couple dozen war mages to the crowd of guards already milling about the suite. Nobody understood that ever since I could remember, I'd been locked away. Like I'd done some crime I didn't recall, but kept having to pay for.

It was getting really old.

"You're talking about that other v— Your old guardian," Pritkin said.

I nodded and popped another antacid. Tony had that effect on me.

"But you ran away from him." Pritkin sounded oddly hesitant suddenly, as if he were sure I wouldn't talk about this, that I'd shut down, shut him out. Maybe because that's what he'd have done, if the situation were reversed. He was the most closemouthed person about his life of anyone I'd ever met—okay, barring a certain vampire—and while I knew more about him than most people, I didn't know much.

But I didn't mind telling him. In fact, I wanted to, wanted someone to finally get it. "I ran away twice, actually. But I never really got away. Tony was always there, at least in my mind, right on my trail."

"Because you set him up for what he did to your parents."

I nodded. "I tried to ruin him, to get him on tax fraud, because I didn't know how to kill him. It didn't work, but I knew he'd never forget it, never stop looking for me."

"And part of you didn't want him to."

I had been scraping a fingernail over the label on Pritkin's empty beer bottle, but I looked up at that. Because until he said it, I hadn't fully realized it myself. "Maybe," I said slowly. "Maybe part of me did want that showdown I never got. But I don't know what I'd have done if he'd come looking for me. I'm not a trained assassin, and even if I had been . . ."

"You're not a killer," Pritkin said flatly.

"Sometimes, I really, really wanted to be."

He didn't ask, didn't say anything. But I could tell he wanted to. I hesitated, because I hadn't planned to talk about this. I never talked about this. But there was no way he'd understand without it.

"Eugenie," I finally said, and I was proud of myself. It came out pretty steady.

"Eugenie?"

"My governess. Tony told his people that she'd helped me escape, that she knew where I was. But he lied. I knew that even before I saw his face as she lay there in pieces, bleeding out at his feet."

"He killed her for no reason?" Pritkin asked carefully.

I laughed and ripped the label off. "Oh, he had a reason. He was a miserable, sniveling, cowardly, vindictive bastard who was furious that some little human had come so close to bringing him down. Somebody had to pay for that. Somebody had to bleed. And if it was somebody whose death he knew would hurt me, so much the better."

And it had hurt, as much as if I'd been there, bleeding myself. But even worse was the crippling fear that had followed. I went from being somebody who had risked everything just to watch him fall to being too scared to leave my own apartment.

"The first six months after I left him were the worst in my life," I said. "Because he wasn't keeping me a prisoner anymore—I was doing it to myself. I was so sure he'd find me, so sure I'd end up like Eugenie, that I didn't do anything. I didn't go anywhere, except to look for work, buy groceries—just what I had to do. And then I went straight back home. People in actual prison probably have more human contact than I did."

"But you had a roommate," Pritkin said.

"That was later. After I started going places again, meeting people . . . after I figured it out."

"Figured what out?"

"That this was my life now. And that I could let some bastard decide how I was going to live it, let fear decide or I could decide. And I decided; I wasn't going to give Tony that kind of power. I wasn't going to give him any more of my life."

"You just woke up one day and stopped being afraid."

Pritkin's expression hadn't changed, but for some reason, he sounded almost angry.

I flashed on my performance a day ago, slumped in a sniveling heap on the bathroom floor, and grimaced. "No. I mean, you don't, do you? At least, I never have. And I kind of think it would have happened by now if it was going to."

"Then what do you do?" He'd leaned over the table, close enough for me to map the ring of jade around each iris, and the pale amber-green layer that darkened to golden brown around the pupils. There were striations, spokes of gold, and specks of brown and emerald, all of which blended to just green at any distance at all.

Beautiful, I thought randomly—for a second, until he abruptly pulled back and looked away.

"You go on, anyway," I said, after a pause. "And, yes, you're scared sometimes. But it's better than being scared all the time. Better than letting your life be about fear and nothing else. So, no, I'm not going to let them shut me away 'for my own good.' I'll take precautions, as many as I can. But I'm going to live."

Pritkin ran a hand through his hair. "Yes," he said brusquely. "You are."

Chapter Twenty-three

We walked out a few minutes later to find a trio of vamps loitering in the parking lot, next to a shiny black SUV. Pritkin swore, but I wasn't exactly surprised. I had at least three trace spells on me that I knew about, and two of them were the Senate's. The point of leaving hadn't been to get away; it had been ... well, to make a point.

Which I obviously hadn't done, or they wouldn't be here.

It was late or, to be more accurate, really early, and the lot was dark. A lone streetlamp leaked a watery yellow puddle in one corner, illuminating cracked pavement and a sagging chain-link fence. But alongside the building, most of the light came from the flickering sign outside the diner. It cast a ruddy tint across the vamps' faces, enough for me to see that they weren't looking too happy.

That was especially true when Pritkin strode over and grabbed one of them by the collar. It was the good-looking blond who had complained about the phone. I guess baby-sitting me was his penance.

Or maybe that was being slammed against the side of their SUV.

"Are you trying to get her killed?" Pritkin snarled, about the time a brunet got him in a choke hold.

"Break his and I break yours," the brunet said matter-of-factly. "And I know who's gonna recover first."

Instead of answering, Pritkin pulsed out a small section of his shield. It was only a vague blue iridescence against the night, as filmy and insubstantial-looking as a soap bubble. But the brunet's arm flew off his neck like he was giving a salute.

The blond didn't struggle; his expression clearly said it was beneath him. He looked at me, past Pritkin's shoulder. "Would you call off your pit bull? Please? I just bought this suit."

"And they'll bury you in it if you don't answer me!" Pritkin told him harshly.

"Too late," the vamp said, baring glistening white fangs.

"Stop it!" I said. "Pritkin, they're just standing there."

"And putting a neon sign over your head in the process!"

I didn't understand that, but apparently the blond did. "What do you take us for?" he sneered. "Amateurs?"

"Well, technically, I am," a mousy little vamp said. He was perched on the hood of the SUV, feet drawn up, watching the scene with big eyes.

Everybody ignored him. He kind of looked like he'd expected it.

"Did anyone follow you?" Pritkin demanded, giving the blond a shake.

"Bite me!"

Pritkin didn't seem to like that answer, judging by the way the blond's eyes suddenly bulged. He rotated them at his buddy. "Are you just going to stand there?"

"What do you want me to do?" the brunet asked in Italian.

"Shoot him!"

A muscular shoulder rose in a shrug. "Won't get through the shield."

"Then help me drain him!"

"Girl might object."

"Yes, the girl might!" I said in the same language.

The dark-haired vamp looked mildly surprised. "Your Italian is not so bad."

"I grew up at Tony's court," I reminded him.

He grinned, a sudden flash of white in a handsome olive face. "That would explain the accent."

Pritkin was starting to look apoplectic, which experi-

ence had taught me usually precipitated pain for someone.
"Would you please answer him?" I asked.

The vamp stole a cigarette from the blond, who was in
no position to object, and took his time lighting up. He
was tall, with black hair cut short to minimize a tendency
to curl, judging by a few at his neck. That wasn't so
odd—a lot of the younger vamps wore their hair short,
including plenty of those who belonged to Mircea. But
they didn't also have five o'clock shadow or a tribal tat
decorating one bicep, or dress in jeans and tight black
muscle shirts.

"We're new—we flew in last night," he finally said, taking a drag. He blew out a breath and regarded Pritkin
through the smoke. "Mage, why would anyone follow us
when they don't know who we are?"

Pritkin thought about that for a beat and then finally
released the blond. The vamp took his time straightening
up, brushing out the wrinkles in his silver-gray suit. Then
he looked at me. "You need him on a leash," he said
viciously.

"Would somebody please explain what is going on?" I
asked.

"What is going on is that your safety depends on no one
knowing where you are," Pritkin told me, still glaring at the
vamps. "And considering how we departed, no one should.
We exited directly into a ley line, under cover of the hotel's
wards, and didn't leave it until halfway across the city. No
one saw us—a fact that does little good if someone leads
your enemies straight to you!"

"Well, we didn't," the blond snapped, rubbing his neck
under the pretense of adjusting a rumpled burgundy tie.

"That's why Marco couldn't come after you himself,"
the brunet informed me, leaning back against the SUV.

"What is?" I asked.

The cigarette glowed against the night as he waved a
negligent hand. "The paparazzi have marked him. He was
waylaid outside the hotel a couple of days ago by a mob
shouting questions, wanting photos. . . ."

"Of him?"

"Of you. You're front-page news. Haven't you seen the
papers?"

"Not recently." And considering what they'd been

printing the last time I did look, that was probably for the best. "But I haven't seen any reporters—"

"They're not allowed in the hotel."

"And you don't exactly use the front door," the blond added. "I'm Jules, by the way." He extended a slim hand, which I took after a brief hesitation. If they intended to stuff me into the SUV, they could do it whether I cooperated or not. "And this is Rico and Fred."

"Fred?" I looked at Mousy, because no way was the brunet a Fred. He smiled weakly.

"I get that a lot," he said. "I'm thinking of changing it. What do you think about André?"

I thought I'd never seen anyone who looked less like an André.

"So Marco's afraid of the paparazzi?" I asked skeptically.

"More the other way around." Rico grinned.

"He threatened to do something anatomically impossible to one of their men," Fred told me.

"Not impossible," Rico blew out a thoughtful breath. "The camera could be made to fit, although the case—"

"What about the tripod?"

"I don't think he was serious about the tripod."

"The paparazzi aren't the issue," Jules interrupted, shooting them a look. "But if they've managed to figure out that Marco's your bodyguard, more dangerous types could have done the same. He couldn't risk leading anyone to you, so he sent us."

"To do what?" I asked, pretty sure I already knew.

"You want it verbatim?"

"Minus the profanity."

Sculpted lips pursed. "Well, that would shorten it a bit."

"What. Did. He. Say?"

"To paraphrase? 'Let her finish her pizza and then drag her back here. By the hair, if necessary.' "

"Doesn't he get it?" I demanded. "That's the kind of attitude that forced me to leave in the first place!"

"Oh, he gets it," Rico said. "He just doesn't want it."

"I don't give a damn what he wants! He has to understand—"

"He understands that you're twenty-four," Jules told me, swiping his cigarette case back from his friend.

"What's wrong with being twenty-four?"

"Nothing. Unless you're dealing with a guy who's well over a thousand."

I blinked. "What?"

"Marco," he confirmed, tapping a cigarette on top of the case. "Saw the fall of Rome, or so they say."

"The fall of—" I stopped and stared. "Gladiators, Colosseum, guys in leather miniskirts—*that* Rome?"

"That would be the one."

"I wouldn't mention the miniskirts," Rico advised. "Marco used to be in the army."

"Have to wonder how anyone took them seriously," Jules said.

"I think if you laughed, they cut your balls off."

Jules paused, halfway through lighting his cigarette, the flame dancing in wide blue eyes. "That would do it."

"But . . . but why is he working for Mircea?" I asked. Vamps that old were Senate members or headed up powerful courts. They didn't work for masters a third their age.

Jules shrugged. "You'd have to ask him; I was always afraid to. But you can see why he doesn't react well when someone he considers a child—"

"A fetus," Rico put in.

"—ignores an order."

"An order he had no right to give!" I said heatedly.

"Technically, the master gave it—"

"Who also has no right to order me around!"

"I like this one," Rico said. "Feisty."

I shot him a glare, which had no effect, except to widen his smile.

"I guess Marco figures, if he still has to take orders after all this time, why not you?" Fred asked.

"Because I'm Pythia," I said, striving for patience.

He blinked at me, obviously confused. "And?"

I threw my hands up.

Jules frowned at him, but not on my account. "Stop it."

"It's driving me nuts," the little vamp said, tugging at the polyester monstrosity around his neck.

"You'll get used to it."

"I don't want to get used to it. And why do I have to wear a tie, anyway? Rico doesn't," he looked pointedly at the brunet.

"Rico is a law unto himself," Jules said drily.

"Well, I'm not used to this."

"What are you used to?" I asked, wondering where a guy like Fred fit into Mircea's somewhat more . . . glossy . . . family.

"I just wear clothes, you know?" he said, pushing wispy brown hair out of his eyes. "I mean, nobody cares what an accountant looks like, as long as the books balance. Not that we use books anymore, but you know what I—"

"You're an accountant?" Pritkin asked sharply.

Fred jumped and then regarded Pritkin warily. "Why shouldn't I be an accountant?"

"Because you're supposed to be a bodyguard!"

"Well, I am." Pale gray eyes shifted. "I mean, I am at the moment. I mean—"

"He means that it's none of your business," Jules interjected.

"Well, it is mine," I pointed out. "What is he doing here?"

I didn't get an answer because Rico's head snapped up. He didn't move otherwise or even tense, as far as I could tell, but there was suddenly something dangerous about him.

Pritkin must have thought so, too, because his expression tightened. "Accountant?"

"Never said I was," Rico said, his eyes on the empty street.

"Then what are you?"

"You could say I'm on the troubleshooting squad."

"Troubleshooting?"

He put a hand on the back of his waistband. "I see trouble, and I shoot it."

"Well, don't shoot them," Jules said irritably. "We have enough problems."

"Shoot who?" I asked.

"Circle," Rico told me, to the accompaniment of a car screeching around the corner and into the lot.

It was actually a limo, the kind that carted high rollers, honeymooners and anybody with a wad of cash all over Vegas. They were almost as ubiquitous as taxis, and often used back streets like this one as a way of avoiding clogged thoroughfares. But the ten or more grim-faced people pil-

ing out were too muffled up and too bulging with concealed
weapons to be anything but the Circle's favorite sons.

"Aren't we supposed to be past this?" I asked Pritkin, as
a familiar six foot five inches of pissed-off war mage got out
of the limo and strode across the lot. The imposing mountain of muscle in the long leather trench had coffee-colored
skin, a military-style buzz cut and a handsome face—when
he wasn't looking like he'd like to rip someone else's off.

This wasn't one of those times.

"What the hell?" he demanded in his deep voice, before
he'd even reached us.

"Hi, Caleb," I said, resigned.

"I was asked to get her out; I got her out," Pritkin said
obscurely.

"You were told to bring her in!"

"Bring me in where?" I asked.

"HQ," Pritkin said. "After Jonas found out about this
latest attack, he insisted—"

"And instead, you bring her here!" Caleb gestured
sharply. "Middle of goddamned Vegas in the middle of the
goddamned night—"

"She's perfectly safe—"

"—with one fucking bodyguard—"

"What do we look like?" Jules demanded.

"—and half the world looking for her!"

"I think the term is 'chopped liver,'" Fred said.

"They're looking for her at the hotel," Pritkin snapped.
"Not here."

"How the hell do you know?" Caleb demanded. "You
don't know what this thing is—you told the old man as
much yourself!"

"You called Jonas?" I asked, deciphering that.

"To ask if he had any ideas about what attacked you,"
Pritkin said. "After what David Dryden told us, I had a suspicion, but this isn't my area of—"

"Suspicion about what?"

"What we're dealing with." He pulled something out of
his coat and handed it to me. It was a pencil sketch, heavily
shaded, that looked a lot like—

I looked up. "Where did you get this?"

"I had one of the Circle's artists do it, from some old
drawings."

"Old drawings of what?"

"The Morrigan."

"The what?"

"The wife of the Dark Fey king. After the description you gave me of what you saw, and what David said about the High Court dialect, and what your servant mentioned about the gods having the ability to possess . . . well, I thought it possible. Particularly in light of the name."

"What about the name?"

"It's a Celtic title. Some translate it as 'Great Queen' or 'Terrible Queen.' But the oldest version, and, I believe, the correct one, is 'Phantom Queen.' The ancient texts speak of her being able to take both physical and spectral form."

"But . . . this is Fey?" I asked, looking at what appeared to be a raven caught in a thunderstorm. A really wicked, pissed-off raven.

"Yes and no. Her mother was Dark Fey, but her father was one of the old gods."

I felt my stomach sink. *Please, please, please—*

"Would you care to guess which one?" he asked.

"Not really."

"Cassie—"

"This doesn't have to be about Ragnarok," I said stubbornly. "The Dark Fey king isn't my biggest fan—you know that. Maybe he sent her—"

"It's possible. But the fact remains that the Morrigan was worshipped by the ancient Celts as a goddess of battle, because her father was believed to be—"

"Don't say it."

"—the Celtic god Nuada—"

"I'm not listening."

"—who is associated with the Romano-British Mars-Nodens—"

"I'm begging you."

"—who many scholars equate with the Greek god Ares."

"Goddamnit, Pritkin! Jonas can't be right, okay? He can't!"

"I am not saying that he is. However, it seems strange, if, in fact, this was caused by animus, that she would apologize and tell David that 'they' were making her do it."

I dug out another antacid.

Caleb cursed. "And yet knowing that this thing might be after her, you still bring her out here!"

"Better than somewhere it would be likely to look!"

"Wait," I said, crunching chalky cherry crap and trying to think. "Is David sure that's what she said? Didn't he say he was lousy with the language?"

"Yes. Which is why I had one of our linguists visit him. She couldn't be certain, not having heard the words herself, but she said David seemed to have the gist of it."

"Okay, but still. 'They' made her do it." I held out the scary-ass image. "Who makes something like this do anything?"

"Her father, presumably."

Damn it, I'd known he was going to say that.

"But Ares isn't here! None of the gods are here!"

"Well, it looks like this one is," Fred pointed out. "And how's that work, exactly? I thought all of them were kicked out way back when."

"They were," Pritkin told him tersely. "But demigods have a human, or in this case, a Fey, parent, giving them an anchor in this world. The spell banishing the gods did not affect them."

"Yet knowing a god or half god or whatever the hell might be after her, you bring her out here anyway," Caleb said, beating that dead horse for all he was worth. I had to give it to the guy; he gave new meaning to "single-minded."

"Where she's completely defenseless!"

"She is hardly defenseless—"

"Thank you," Jules said indignantly.

"I'm with her. And whatever that thing was, it can pass right through wards. Meaning she would be no safer at HQ than at the suite. I told Jonas I would ask Cassie where she wanted to go and—"

"Yeah," Caleb said sourly. "And he told me he wants her someplace secure!"

"She will be—"

"As soon as we get her back to the suite," Jules butted in.

"She's not going back to that death trap of a suite," Caleb snapped. "And that's final!"

"It's not a death trap," I protested.

"It is if you can't shift away! As I explained to that thickheaded vampire, leaving you in that place, much less drugged and insensate, was virtually asking for another—"

"You talked to Marco?" Pritkin said sharply.

"Yes, we—"

"When?"

"A few minutes ago. I—"

"On the phone?"

"No, we—"

"How, then?"

"Would you let me finish a sentence?" Caleb said angrily. "When you didn't show up with the girl, Jonas assumed you hadn't been able to get her out of the suite. He sent us to assist, but that damned vampire wouldn't tell us—"

"You went by the hotel?"

"Yes—"

"And then you came here?"

"Shit," Rico said, and grabbed my arm.

And the next thing I knew, I was in the SUV.

It was almost like shifting—I didn't remember moving, the car door opening or sitting down, but there I was anyway. I blinked at Rico, who was in the driver's seat in front of me, for about a second. Until he was snatched out of the still-open door and sent flying.

"Lasso spell," Fred said, as his buddy slammed into the open top of a Dumpster, halfway across the lot. "I hate those things."

I peered into the front, to find the little vamp ensconced in the passenger's seat. "When did you get in?"

"A minute ago. I figured we'd be leaving soon."

"I didn't notice."

"Yeah." He sighed. "I get that a lot, too."

"I wish I had that problem," I muttered, watching Pritkin and Caleb yelling at each other outside, while a trash-covered Rico crossed the lot in a blur. A second later his assailant went flying into the side of a truck. And a second after that, four war mages jumped Rico.

I sighed and started crawling over the seat.

"Is it always like this?" Fred asked, as Jules started forward, a fake smile plastered on his face and a placating hand raised—only to have someone use it to sling him into the SUV. I flinched back when he hit the windshield headfirst, that handsome profile making an impressive set of cracks in the supposedly shatterproof glass.

"No," I told Fred, as Jules shook it off and leapt back into the fight. "This is pretty calm, actually."

"What are you doing?" he asked, watching me check the cushions, the floor and then the visor over the driver's side. The keys were under the visor, and they fell into my lap.

"Putting a stop to this. If they're going to act like children, they can at least do it out of sight of norms."

"And you think they're gonna listen?"

"No. But if I leave, they'll have to follow."

"Well, I don't know how you're gonna get out. They've parked that big-ass limo of theirs right across the exit. And the fence goes right up to—"

He cut off as a metallic shriek rent the air, bouncing off the surrounding buildings and echoing down the street. "What the hell was *that*?" he demanded, staring around wildly.

I didn't answer. I was too busy watching the limo rise into the air, its long body twisting and writhing as if in pain, metal screeching, car alarm screaming and window glass popping. A windshield wiper flew off like an arrow, spearing the old sign above the diner and sending a wash of sparks across the pavement.

"*What is this?*" Fred yelled, gripping my shoulder as the limo was wrenched in two, the violence of the movement sending half of it crashing into the building opposite.

And the other half spinning straight at us.

"How things usually go," I told him, and floored it.

Chapter Twenty-four

The engine must have caught at some point, because we shot ahead, the luxury projectile missing us by inches. I swerved and stomped on the brakes, avoiding another car but slinging us into the fence. I barely noticed, because I was sure the limo had just taken out the diner and everyone in it.

Only it hadn't.

I stared through the cracked and bloody windshield at the limo's backside, which was sticking, cantilevered, out of a wavering field of energy. Unlike Pritkin's seamless blue shields, this one was a patchwork of colors and textures that ran and muddied together as they fought each other and the car. But somehow, they'd stopped it. Like a fish caught in a net, the huge hunk of twisted metal hung there, eight or nine feet off the ground, quivering and shaking—and leaking.

Something was dripping from the tail end, enough to form a puddle on the ground below. It reflected the sparks still shooting from the ruined sign, which were showering both the car and the puddle. It took my half-frozen brain a second to realize what I was seeing, and then I was fumbling with the gears, shoving the SUV hard into reverse.

"What now?" Fred demanded.

"Gas!" I said, stomping on the pedal while the war mages scattered, shields retracting around their owners or being thrown in front of the diner in a last-ditch attempt to protect the people inside. And the car—

"Shiiit!" Fred screamed as it exploded midfall, sending a cloud of lethal projectiles scattering in all directions.

I ducked—there was no time for anything else—only to find the floor already occupied. I covered my head as we bounced backward, still moving but not fast enough to avoid the spear of metal that obliterated the remains of the windshield. Glass exploded through the small space, stinging my arms and sending a wet trickle sliding down my temple. But thanks to the dash, the rest of me fared better.

Although not as well as Fred, who had been cowering on the floorboard.

"You're supposed to be a bodyguard!" I said, hitting the brake.

"I am."

"Then what are you doing down there?"

"I'm not a very good bodyguard."

"Get up!" I yanked him off the floor, intending to use vampire vision to help me spot Pritkin in the chaos. But before I could get a word out, the scene in front of us tilted, the diner skewed wildly to the left and then disappeared entirely, replaced by a dizzying view of darkened buildings and a star-flung sky.

"What's happening? What's happening?" Fred demanded hysterically, grabbing me as I grabbed the steering wheel to keep from sliding through the missing windshield.

I didn't reply, because it was taking all my concentration not to lose my grip while spinning in a kaleidoscope of falling glass and debris. Like the limo, the SUV had risen into the air; unlike the limo, it was slowly flipping end over end, slinging the headlights in a wide parabola that intermittently highlighted the escalating fight below.

"Where're the controls?" I yelled at Fred, as we tumbled around like two sheets in a dryer.

"What controls?"

"For the charm!"

"What charm?"

"The one you just hit!" I said furiously, as half a dozen mages suddenly went flying.

It looked like they'd been blown sky high by some sort of explosion, only I hadn't seen one—or much of anything else except for Fred's size-nine shoe. But something scary was down there. Because the man who rocketed by the windshield had the closest thing to fear I'd ever seen on a war mage's face.

I knocked Fred's foot aside and started frantically searching under the dash.

A lot of cars in the supernatural community are equipped with levitation charms to access the ley lines, many of which don't follow the ground. But those usually belong to mages, who are the main users of the earth's magical highway system. Vampires tend to avoid areas that can incinerate a person in seconds without proper shields, which even masters don't have.

As a result, I'd come into contact with the lines and the vehicles that used them only recently. And it hadn't been in the kind of leisurely way that allowed for a lot of questions— like what the damn charm was supposed to look like. But if it wasn't so goddamned dark—

I'd barely had the thought when a blow interrupted the spin cycle, sending us sailing backward on a wash of heat and light. That turned out to be a good thing, since the space we'd been occupying was suddenly filled with diner. We slammed into a building across the street in a crunch of whiplash-inducing speed, and the chrome roof of the restaurant shot spaceward, shedding burning detritus like a Roman candle rocket ship out of an old Buck Rogers film.

The car scraped off the bricks and drifted back into the street, listing a little to the left like an old drunk, while the diner arced impossibly high above us. It trembled against the night for a long moment, as if it really intended to leave gravity behind. And then it plunged back to earth in a hail of bricks and old floor tiles and flaming orange Naugahyde.

"Shit," Fred said faintly.

And then we both had to grab the dash when the SUV was battered by a billowing cloud of dust and debris. I tried to spot Pritkin in the chaos, but it was impossible. But at least it looked like the Corps had evacuated the diner before the explosion. Panicked people were scattering in all directions—including a blond racing just ahead of a line of cars parked along the street.

She was petite and busty, with short hair that was closer

to brown than my strawberry blond. It also didn't curl like mine, and we weren't dressed the same, but I guess the resemblance was close enough. Because something was knocking cars out of line left and right behind her.

Yet, amazingly, no one seemed to have noticed. Amid the choking dust and the burning lot and the blaring car alarms and the screaming people, the blond's predicament had attracted zero attention. And by the time it did, my doppelgänger was going to be toast.

I started working to get the stalled-out car started again.

"Did you ever see anything like *that*?" Fred demanded.

"Uh, maybe a few things."

"Well, I haven't. I mean, *damn!*" He stared at the lot, the fires reflecting in his wide gray eyes. "I guess a spell must have hit a gas main or something."

"Yeah, maybe."

"Maybe? What else could it have been?"

"We're about to find out," I told him, as the reluctant engine finally caught.

I hit the gas and we careened across the road, still listing a little, but moving. The girl ran straight under the car, so panicked that the sight of a levitating SUV didn't even register. I flicked on the brights and the emergency lights and sat on the horn, staring around for some glimpse of what I was taunting. But all I saw was the carnage, not what was causing it.

An invisible fist caved in the side of a nearby delivery van, knocking it on its side and sending it skidding back a dozen yards. An old VW Beetle gave up the ghost in a fiery crash with a new Lincoln. And someone's motorcycle took an Evel Knievel–type leap over the rest of the cars before flaming out against the side of a billboard, setting the whole thing ablaze.

And then nothing.

The metal massacre suddenly stopped, the invisible cause pausing as it assessed the oddity of a battered, airborne SUV lit up like a Christmas tree. And a blond behind the wheel who actually looked like she wanted to be caught.

I beeped the horn again, just in case it had somehow missed us, and Fred gripped my arm. "What are you doing?" he asked shrilly.

"Getting some attention."

"Getting some— *Why?*"

"Because whatever's out there went after the limo and then the diner and then the blond. It's looking for me."

"Well, of course it's looking for you!" he said, shaking me. "That's why we need to get out of here!"

"We're about to," I said, as something huge and dark forgot about the girl and shivered through the air toward us, visible in movement as it hadn't been before.

I still couldn't tell much about it, just a vague shadow that dimmed but didn't obscure the city lights behind it. And I didn't have time for a closer look. I mashed the gas pedal to the floor at the same time that something lashed out at us with the speed of a striking cobra.

It would have hit us full on, but we'd scooted forward enough that it only caught our rear end. But that was enough to send us spinning like a roulette wheel into the chain-link fence. We hit backward, bowing out the mesh, and the car tried hard to die on me. But I punched the gas and, with a sputter and a groan, it leapt forward, tearing across the lot and down the street like we'd been shot out of a gun.

I kept my foot against the floor, hard enough to feel the blood pounding in my leg, but something was wrong. The back of the car was dragging badly, pulling the nose so far up that I could barely see anything over the hood. And considering how close together buildings were in this part of town, that was a very bad thing.

"What's going on?" I asked Fred, who was peering back through the seats with his mouth hanging open.

"Oh, shit."

"Oh, shit *what*?"

"Oh, shit, we have passengers!"

I whipped my neck around, but there was nobody in the car but us. And all I saw outside was a lot of night—and a huge shadow that was eating up the air faster than we were. It wasn't entirely dark, after all; there were flashes here and there, like glints of sunlight through a storm, or a veil with rents in it that gave glimpses of the face underneath. But it didn't look like Morrigan, or whatever had attacked me before. It was too big, for one thing, and the little I could see looked more like it was covered in scales than—

And then Fred screamed, and I realized that maybe this wasn't the best time to take my eyes off the road—so to speak. I snapped my head back around in time to see us plummeting toward a parking garage. There was no time to stop, barely even time to course correct so that we flew into an opening instead of splattering onto rock-hard concrete.

Something else wasn't so lucky, hitting the side of the building with the force of an earthquake. Gray chunks flew off the walls and scattered across the floor, but it looked like whatever was after us was too big to fit through the narrow opening. Because no dark ripple followed us into the glaring lights of the mostly empty space.

We barely made it ourselves, blowing out a tire on the ledge and scraping the floor, courtesy of our sagging rear end. But it wasn't sagging as badly as before, and suddenly I could reach the gas pedal and see at the same time. Which would have been great, except that what I saw was a pylon heading straight for us.

I swerved but we still clipped the edge and went skidding around in a circle on a great wash of sparks. But at least I figured out what Fred had meant. Because clattering along behind us was what looked like half a mile of fencing, some of it with the posts still attached.

And trying to hang on to the bouncing, bucking, twisting mass was a very pissed-off war mage.

I blinked, sure I was seeing things. But if I was, I was still seeing them when I opened my eyes. It was Pritkin, and he wasn't alone.

Three other guys were hanging on with him, and they looked pretty normal—jeans, dark jackets, dark hair—as far as I could tell in the brief glimpse I got before they slammed into the wall. But I didn't think they were. Because while one hit an open space and catapulted over the side of the garage, the others acted like crashing into concrete at fifty miles an hour was a minor inconvenience.

They jumped back to their feet and, a second later, they jumped Pritkin.

I'd have thought they were using shields, but I didn't see any, except for Pritkin's—right before it popped. I stared, getting a really, really nasty feeling of déjà vu all of a sudden. And then I grabbed Fred with my free hand. "Do you have a gun?"

"What?"

"A gun! A gun!"

"Of course I have a gun. I'm a bodyguard," he said, with no irony whatsoever.

"Then shoot them!"

"I . . . I'm actually better with a sword—"

"But you do know how to shoot, right?"

"Well, you know. Sort of—"

"Damn it!" I grabbed a gun out of the holster under his arm and thrust him into the driver's seat. "Drive!"

Pritkin saw me as we careened back toward the fight, listing badly now thanks to our blown back tire, and his eyes widened. He ducked a punch that cracked a pylon and then shook his head violently, shouting something that I couldn't hear over the ear-piercing screech of metal on concrete. And then he threw himself to the ground as I squeezed off a shot.

It must have missed, because the mage I'd been aiming for didn't so much as flinch before throwing out a hand—and a spell. But the very familiar red lightning bolt crashed into the ceiling instead of our heads, due to Pritkin swiping the guy's legs out from under him at the last second. A choking cloud of dust and rubble poured down from above, along with pieces of mangled rebar and the front half of a Nissan Sentra. And then a spell from the other mage took a man-sized chunk out of the floor, spraying concrete hail in my face.

But none of that seemed to intimidate Fred, who had apparently decided to solve the problem by just running everybody down. At least, I assumed that was why we were suddenly headed straight for the trio and picking up speed. They paused, staring at the mangled SUV with the flapping tire and the crazy vamp driver and the dust-covered woman brandishing a gun like she actually knew how to use it.

And then they abruptly hurled themselves to either side.

"What are you *doing*?" I yelled at Fred, who looked at me wildly.

"Did I mention that I don't know how to drive?"

"No!" I said, as we pelted off the side of the garage, snatching Pritkin along for the ride.

The charm caught us before we'd fallen more than a story, sending us dipping and bobbing and listing in a circle, heading back in exactly the wrong direction. I grabbed the wheel and wrenched it to the right, but it was too late. The two mages launched themselves off the side of the garage, one grabbing the fence in midair, and the other—

"Crap," I said, as heavy boots dented the top of the SUV.

And then my gun was up and I was firing.

There was no way I missed him this time. I emptied a clip into the roof, saw bullets punch through felt and metal, knew they must have connected. But no body hit the roof or fell over the side, and a second later a spell slammed down through the middle seat, crumpling the roof like aluminum foil and knocking a two-foot hole through the bottom of the chassis.

The next one would probably have knocked a hole in me, too, but we suddenly streamed under an overpass, missing the clearance by pretty much nothing at all. It was close enough to skin the top of the SUV, to pop the headlights and to bathe the car in a shower of sparks. Close enough to have me hunkering down, seriously afraid that the roof was about to cave the rest of the way in.

Close enough to smash our assailant face-first into concrete.

I stared at Fred as we exited the other side, sans unwanted passenger. "I thought you didn't know how to drive!"

"I don't!"

"Then what was *that*?"

He stared at me, confused. "What was what?"

I didn't answer, too busy vaulting over the seat to stare down through the smoking hole. I spotted Pritkin getting dragged along underneath, clinging to the fence and staring up at me with a bone white face. And then smacking into a pylon and yelling something that looked really profane.

I seconded the emotion, because three mages were somehow still dragging along after him.

"Son of a *bitch*!"

"What is it?" Fred demanded.

"There's three more mages down there!"

"What? But there should only be one!"

"Tell me something I don't know," I snarled, as one of them tried to sling another spell at us, only to have Pritkin all but wrench his arm off. One of the others responded by trying to do the same to Pritkin's head, but he must have gotten his shields back up, because it didn't work. But shields wouldn't last long, not against these guys.

I crawled back up to Fred. "Change of plan."

"We have a plan?"

"We do now."

Pritkin's shields might not work against the mages, but they worked well enough on most other things. I just had to find the right other things. Fortunately, there were plenty of options.

"Aren't you taking this thing?" Fred demanded, as I got a knee up on the seat so I could see outside.

"No, you're driving."

"Didn't you hear me? I don't know how!"

"You're doing fine so far. Just hold the gas pedal down and keep the steering wheel steady. I'll correct if you get off course."

"Gas pedal," he said, looking panicked. "Which one is that?"

"The one your foot is on."

"And which is the brake?"

"You're not going to need the brake," I told him, and yanked the wheel hard to the right.

We zipped back toward the garage and the row of buildings it serviced, the fence streaming out behind us like the tail on a very strange kite. "You can see, right?" Fred asked nervously.

"Yes."

"Good. 'Cause with this damn hood in my way, I'm almost— Auggh! What was *that*?"

"It's okay, you're doing fine."

"But I hit something!"

"You should probably get used to it," I told him, staring out the back window.

The mostly flat-topped Vegas roofs are nothing like the slick fronts presented to the public. Along with the usual clutter of satellite dishes, old antennas and solar cells, they also house the city's massive air conditioners, since sand clogs up the works if they're left on the ground. And I made sure that we didn't miss a single one, hurling the mages back and forth between giant units like very unhappy Ping-Pong balls.

Pritkin was still yelling, but I couldn't hear him over the

wind and Fred's cursing and some weird noises coming from overhead, like leather sheets caught in a hurricane. But at least no one was trying to kill him right now. They were too busy hanging on for dear life.

And, unfortunately, they were hanging on pretty damn well. The mage near the end went flying when we tore around a corner, snapping out the wildly bucking fence like a towel in a locker room. But the other two were higher up and they grimly held on, despite smashing through a greenhouse, skimming across a pile of old bricks and then slapping face-first into a wall.

"I don't believe this!" I said, as we dragged them over the top of the wall and through somebody's patio set.

"These guys really want you dead," Fred said, staring in the rearview mirror.

I didn't answer, because one of those lightning-bolt spells sheared off the passenger-side mirror, rocking the car violently. It didn't look like the rooftops were providing enough in the way of distraction. If we wanted to lose these guys, we were going to have to get a little more extreme.

I nudged the steering wheel slightly to the right.

Within seconds, smoke billowed up in front of us, like a dark curtain held against the sky. It felt like we'd been in the car half an hour, but it couldn't have been more than a couple of minutes. Although I heard sirens in the distance, no emergency vehicles were yet parked around the crash site.

"Is the diner still burning?" Fred asked, frowning.

"Not exactly," I said, as we plunged for the middle of the fiery billboard.

The motorcycle must have had a full gas tank, because the entire huge surface of the sign was now covered in flames. The paper had already burnt away, leaving an old wooden frame and heavy support beams to feed the blaze. And they seemed to be feeding it pretty well, judging by the heat that smacked me in the face, even this far away.

In seconds, the conflagration had filled the whole length of the missing windshield, the smoke-laden air whipping my hair around my face and making my eyes water. I glanced behind us, and it looked like the mages had seen it, too. They were staring through the lattice of the fence, watching the approaching inferno in disbelief.

And not watching the deadly war mage above them.

Pritkin lashed out with a heavy boot, snapping one man's head back and then kicking him viciously in the chest. He went flying, his head lolling at a very unhealthy angle, and Pritkin turned on his companion. But he wouldn't get a fight there. The last mage just let go of the fence, falling on purpose into the surrounding smoke.

"I guess he doesn't like fire as well as concrete," I said in satisfaction, before noticing that Pritkin hadn't budged. "What the hell is he doing?" I asked Fred, who was looking at me apprehensively.

"What fire?"

"He's just holding on." I climbed over the seats to stare out the back, but even a full field of vision didn't help much. Pritkin's shields could definitely cushion a fall from this height, but he wasn't jumping—or climbing or doing anything but staring, and not at the billboard.

"What fire?" Fred asked, a little more forcefully.

I flicked my eyes in the direction Pritkin was looking, but didn't see anything, aside from a lot of smoke. Part of which seemed to have taken on a very weird form. I blinked, but it was still there a second later, the hazy outline of an impossible shape set against the brilliant skyline.

And headed straight for us.

"Oh, shit. Fire!" Fred screamed, and we crashed into the middle of the sign.

Chapter Twenty-five

Luckily, the smaller support struts were already half char-coal, and they exploded harmlessly in a sizzle of black ash. But something a hell of a lot bigger hit the pylons under-neath, sending smoking posts the size of tree trunks spinning into the night. We managed to dodge most of those, since they shot out below us, but we weren't so lucky with the spell that burned through the air a second later.

It had come from below, where I guessed one of the mages had survived the fall. Red lightning crackled over the dash, raised goose bumps on my arms and caused Fred's wispy comb-over to wave around madly. It didn't hurt, at least not us. But the SUV did a sudden, vomit-inducing one-eighty in midair—and stalled out.

I screamed, Fred screamed and we hit the roof, which wasn't so bad.

And then we tumbled through the missing windshield, which was.

I felt myself start to fall, arms outstretched but nothing to grab. And this time, there was no parachute above me, no strong arms to catch me, no anything but wind and air and a long, long way to fall. Which I did—for about a sec-ond, before being jerked around in a parabola that had the city lights streaming in a dizzying dance of color that con-fused my already confused brain even more.

Until I realized that my scream had turned into a duet

with Fred's, who was clutching me against his chest. He had one arm under mine, holding me face out like a sack of potatoes. And the fingers of the other wedged, white knuckled, between the lattice of the fence.

The one we were now hanging off of.

For a moment, I just hung there, panting and staring at the sight of hotels, casinos and LCD montages. And then I looked up at Fred, his completely freaked-out face backlit by the distant neon. "Thanks," I squeaked.

He didn't say anything. He also didn't move, breathe or even blink. I was grateful for the assist, but it was less than reassuring to find myself gripped by a Fred statue who was apparently having the vampire version of a panic attack.

"Fred?"

Nothing.

I licked my lips, trying not to give in to the real desire to join him and just zone out for a moment. Because I didn't think we had one. I didn't see the creature, which was, presumably, ahead of us somewhere. But a glance up showed that the back bumper of the SUV was now hanging half off the vehicle.

Which was a problem, since that's what the fence had managed to tangle itself around.

It obviously wasn't designed to take this kind of abuse and didn't look like it was going to be doing it for much longer. I looked down at Pritkin, who, instead of climbing, was slinging spells at something I couldn't see off in the smoke. I didn't know what he was doing or why, but he wouldn't be doing it in a minute if we didn't move. Now.

"Okay, Fred? Fred, listen," I said, trying to make eye contact. That would have been easier if his hadn't looked kind of dead—set and glassy and not really focused on anything. "We need to climb back up, Fred."

Nothing.

"And when we need to do that is now."

Nada.

"Our weight is dragging the fence off the car," I told him tightly, forcing my voice to stay composed, because screaming at an already panicked person didn't help. And because if I started, I might not stop. "If we don't get off, you and me and Pritkin are going to be in free fall in about a minute. Maybe less."

That got a slight eye twitch, but nothing more.

"And while I'm pretty sure that Pritkin can save himself if that happens, I think you and me *are fucked, Fred*."

"And we're not now?" he asked hoarsely.

"Not if you do exactly what I tell you."

He shook his head and then froze again, as a gust of wind caused the fence to shimmy like a showgirl. "I can't."

"Yes. Yes, you can."

He looked down for the first time, and his face paled. Which was impressive, as it had been pretty pasty already. "Oh, God."

"Fred," I said, sharply enough to snap his wide gray eyes back to me. "Fred, listen. You're going to get us out of this."

"And if I *can't*?"

"You can. I know you can."

"But I'm not . . . I'm just an accountant. I don't—"

"You're not 'just' anything," I said harshly. "You're a master vampire, and we both know what that means."

"Yeah, well, in my case, it doesn't mean as much as you might—"

"And you're my bodyguard. You're the Pythia's body-guard. Which means you must be pretty damn badass."

He licked his lips. "I'm . . . badass?"

"You wouldn't have been assigned to me otherwise, would you?"

"Well, actually, they said they needed my room for the—"

"Fred!"

He nodded, swallowing. "I'm badass," he whispered, looking up.

And then his arm tightened around my waist, his body tensed and he *jumped*. I don't know what he used for leverage, because the only thing available was the fence, and that probably would have ripped it the rest of the way off the car. But we nonetheless shot up at least a half story, all the way back to the rear door of the SUV.

Which would have worked better if it had been open.

My head hit the door hard enough to stun me, so I didn't see how we got back inside. But judging from the fact that the next time I looked, the SUV didn't *have* a back door, I thought it might have had something to do with vampire strength and extreme motivation. Either way, a moment later we were sprawled on the dented inside of the roof, our butts in the air and our stomachs—at least mine—roiling.

I clutched a dangling seat belt for a moment and concentrated on trying not to lose my dinner. And people wondered why I lived on antacids. The pizza and beer and milk shake were doing some really unpleasant alchemy in my stomach, which was even truer when I saw what glided up alongside the window.

My first thought was that it was beautiful, all sleek, powerful lines that blended almost seamlessly with the night. A river of ebony scales flowed down a heavily muscled form, from a huge head to a vast rib cage to great, talon-edged claws to a long, barbed tail. They were hard and dagger edged, like shards of obsidian, and shared its color, too. Deepest midnight, they seemed to pull all light into them, reflecting nothing of the fire or the moonlight or the far-off, flickering neon. Only the eyes glowed, like living jewels, gold shading to green to pale chartreuse around catlike, elongated pupils.

I got a good look at them when the great head slowly turned my way.

I stared back at it, knowing what I was seeing. But my mind simply refused to name it. A few minutes ago, I'd been standing on a cracked sidewalk outside a greasy diner, arguing with the usual suspects. It was a little hard to make the transition to being pursued through the air above Vegas by something out of a fairy tale.

Something that was now dropping to come underneath us.

"Fred?" I said calmly.

"What?"

"Move!"

He didn't ask questions this time. He scrambled under the backseat and I scrambled under him, which was lucky, because a second later, there *was* no backseat. It had been ripped out as easily as if the SUV was made of paper, crushed in the massive jaws of the thing behind us, along with most of the rear end of the vehicle.

Including the fender.

I twisted around, clutching the middle seat, and stared down at Pritkin, who was still dangling from the fence. A fence that was now hanging from the mouth of something out of a nightmare. He was two-thirds of the way up, which put him close enough that I could see his expression. And the stark panic on his face as he stared up at me wasn't reassuring.

And then the creature shook its head violently, sending its mouthful of SUV spinning away into the night. I didn't scream, because Pritkin didn't go with it. Instead, he slung around in a large arc and then came trailing after us just like before, only this time without any sort of visible support.

"I didn't know mages could levitate without a platform," Fred said, his voice preternaturally calm.

"They can't!"

"Then how's he— Oh, I see."

"See what?" I asked, heart in my throat. I couldn't see anything—except the creature coming up fast, ponderous wings beating the air, great maw gaping for another bite. And then veering off at the last moment for no obvious reason.

"He's using his shields like a rope." Fred pointed up at the chewed-off floor, to where a faint glimmer of blue was wrapped around the drive train. "He must've slung it up here when he got close enough."

I stared from the flimsy lifeline to Pritkin and back again, paralyzed by a fear that made my previous panic seem like nothing. Because no mage could project more than one shield at a time. And if Pritkin was using his like a rope, he wasn't using it to protect himself.

The thought broke my panic fast enough to leave me dizzy. "Keys!" I screamed, grabbing Fred.

"What keys?"

"Our keys!"

"Car keys?"

"Yes!"

"Oh, I don't know where those—" Fred said, before I threw him aside and lunged for the steering wheel.

The keys were still in the ignition. I ducked under the driver's seat, forcing myself not to panic, but I was shaking so much, it took two hands to turn them. I mashed my hand to the overhead gas pedal, but for a long second, nothing happened, not even the ominous clicking of a dead battery or a flooded engine. Goddamnit, *please*—

And then it caught.

"Is it working?" I rasped.

"Is what— Oh," Fred said. "It's pulling him up. That's really—"

He broke off as Pritkin slammed into the drive train and the creature slammed into us, almost at the same moment. And for a brief, horrible second, there was nothing but shrieking metal and screeching creature and a car literally exploding from the inside, as everything behind the front seat disappeared in another huge bite.

I grabbed the back of a seat, staring at the sight of the thing hanging in midair, powerful wings beating madly as its outstretched claws ripped at something above us. I craned my neck, but I still didn't see anything but black sky and a sliver of moon, looking serene and ethereal in the midst of the chaos. But a moment later, a huge gash was ripped in our attacker's wing, and it gave a screech that I felt all the way through my skull.

And then I saw them, Caleb and four war mages I didn't know, hanging over the edge of Pritkin's beat-up jalopy, firing spells and bullets that bounced off the impermeable hide, appearing only to be making it mad. But not for long. The great tail lashed out, sending both cars tumbling backward, and in the case of the convertible, end over end. But I didn't get a chance to worry about Caleb.

Because the creature was coming straight at us.

It turned in a sinuous, flowing movement like an eel in water, all sleek muscle and shining scales, and then it dove, the bulk of it blocking out the sky. Breath caught in my throat, my chest, spiked heavy through my lungs. I tried to swallow, but my throat was too dry. Fred was babbling something incoherent beside me, or maybe I just couldn't understand him. Not with beautiful death slicing through the air toward me.

And then Pritkin grabbed me and a gun and before I had time to wonder what he thought he was going to do with that, he fired. But not at the creature. Instead, he aimed at the mass of crumpled metal still clamped in its huge maw.

Including one shiny, like-new gas tank that he nailed dead center.

The tank ignited in a whoosh of deadly flame, and since

it was halfway down the creature's throat, that's where the majority of the blast went, too. For a split second, fire boiled under its skin, red and orange and roiling, glowing between those glittering scales. It was strangely beautiful, separating each into a single, perfect diamond of polished ebony for one last, trembling instant—

And then the creature exploded, sending bones and blood and dark, wet meat flying everywhere—along with about a thousand knife-edged scales.

Pritkin had gotten a partial shield up, which saved our bodies, but the SUV was sliced to ribbons around us, peeling away even as the blast hurled us backward. One second we were kneeling on the curve of the mangled roof, staring out at a beautiful nightmare. And the next we were falling, his arms around my waist, my legs wrapped around him to keep him close, cinders and smoking ash stinging my skin.

I saw Fred get snatched out of the air, a lasso spell grabbing him by the ankle and jerking him up like a great elastic band. I saw part of a wing go spinning into the night, visible because of the fire eating its way across the surface, highlighting the delicate tracery of veins. I saw the ground rushing up at us with impossible, deadly speed—

And then something caught us with a lift and a jerk, sending us hurtling back up on a great wash of air.

At first I thought it had to be a lasso, that Caleb had somehow gotten one around us, too—only he hadn't. I looked up to see an amorphous mass of blue over our heads, like a shield chute, only not. It was flat instead of rounded and lumpy instead of smooth, with thinner areas here and there that the dark showed through. It was also sort of wedge-shaped, with filaments that had reached down to attach themselves to Pritkin's arms and—

"You can *hang glide*?" I asked incredulously.

"It isn't . . . recommended."

"Why not?"

"Steering problems."

"Steering problems?"

And then I didn't have to ask, because a building was coming straight at us. Pritkin tried to miss it, but apparently he was right—shields weren't designed for aerial acrobatics. We sluggishly moved to the left, but the arc was too faint and the wind was wrong and we were going to be bug splatter on the bricks before we could turn or land or—

And then a spell detonated against a window in front of us, sending an explosion of shards inward as we burst through what was left, slid across someone's desk, tore through a flimsy partition, and took out half a dozen cubicles. Right before something the size of a semitruck came crashing through the wall after us. I got a glimpse of a huge head and glowing eyes, and then a wash of flame obscured them both as Pritkin flung us through the fire door.

It must have been pretty highly rated, because it actually lasted a couple of seconds before bursting out over our heads. But by then we were down a story, jumping over the railing and landing painfully. But not as painful as burning to death, I thought wildly, as we tore down the stairs, taking three and four at a time and barely touching down, almost fast enough to qualify as flying again.

Only it wasn't fast enough.

Pritkin slammed us back against a wall, just in time to avoid a column of crimson fire that ripped down through the middle of the stairs. I only got a glimpse of our attacker through the flames, but that was enough: blackened, smoking bones, some still burning, ruined wings with one tip missing, great rib cage half gone and outlined with gory flesh, huge maw edged with cracked, charred teeth that were nonetheless still hideously sharp—

I stared at it in utter disbelief. It was dead; it had to be dead. When the gasoline ignited, the car parts in its mouth had turned to deadly shrapnel, literally ripping it apart from the inside. Nothing could have survived that amount of damage. Nothing.

And yet there it was.

And for some strange reason, the emotion uppermost in my mind wasn't terror or even incredulity; it was outrage. I felt cheated, bitter, furious. You killed the dragon and *you got to go home*. It was some sort of rule—dead dragon=game over. Every video gamer, Hollywood producer and six-year-old kid knew that.

Only it looked like my life hadn't gotten the memo.

And then the firestorm ended and we were running again, through a door and down a hallway, four tons of pissed-off dragon crashing through the wall behind us.

For something so huge, it was ungodly fast, maybe because it didn't bother with little things like hallways. It just tore through the walls, as easily as if they were cardboard, judging by the sounds coming from behind us and the huge cracks running ahead of us. I glanced behind once to see doors flying through a storm of drywall, and then I was yanked through a door and into an office.

And a dead end.

I stared around frantically, but there was nowhere to run or even to hide, not that that was likely to work, anyway. No windows, no closets, not even a bathroom cubicle. Just a fake wood desk, a sickly plant and gray industrial carpet tiles, several of which needed a change.

They're about to get one, I thought blankly, and then Pritkin grabbed me by the shoulders. "We have to split up!" he yelled over the sound of the building imploding.

"What?"

"I hit it with a spell to blind it. I doubt it took entirely, but its vision should be blurry. If we can get it off our tail, I can lead it away—"

"First of all, no. And second of all, *hell* no!"

"This isn't a discussion!"

"The hell it—"

I cut off when he flung something against the floor and then flung us against the wall, his battered shields taking another blow as an explosion blasted a chunk out of the floor. And then we were sliding through the new exit into the office below, which, apparently, took up the entire story. There were no halls here, just a ton of cubicles with plants and family portraits that I really hoped nobody was all that attached to, because a second later, something tore through the ceiling after us.

And suddenly, there was nowhere left to go. The space was huge and the creature was in between us and the stairs. The only other door was impossibly far away, and I doubted we'd have made it even if there hadn't been a maze of tasteful gray partitions in the way. We couldn't punch through to the next floor with it right on our ass, and judging by the desperation on Pritkin's face, I didn't think his shields were going to hold up to another firestorm.

It really is game over, I thought, and then he threw us out the window.

We burst back into the night along with a storm of paper and a suicidal watercooler. It kamikazied someone's car below, caving in the roof like a body would, just as Pritkin's makeshift glider caught us. And then it caught a draft, wafting up the side of the building just as a swell of fire burst out below, incinerating the mass of fluttering paper midair.

The creature paused on the window ledge, looking even more impossible when framed by modern glass and steel. And then it threw back its head and gave another screeching cry, loud as a foghorn, loud enough that I thought my eardrums might burst in my head. Loud enough to shiver the mirrored side of the building across the street, making its reflection shudder.

I watched it ripple like a stone thrown in water as we rode a circular air current a few stories above the creature's head. Pritkin wasn't even trying to move away from the building, and I didn't have to wonder why. If we couldn't outrun that thing on land, we sure as hell couldn't in the air. Not in something that had little steering and no propulsion.

Seconds ticked by as it peered around, its firelit eyes searching for us in the darkness, the nauseating smell of half-cooked flesh mixing with the ozone taste of its magic. I held my breath until I was dizzy, while my heart tried its best to beat through my chest. Because all it had to do was crane its head; all it had to do was look—

And then it spotted us, and I didn't even have time to draw a breath before it launched itself into the sky, huge wings carving the air with deadly precision. It's still strangely beautiful, I thought dizzily. Streamlined and elegant, a magnificent instrument of death, even in its ruined state.

Right up until it crashed into the opposite building.

And our reflection.

It hit like a bullet before exploding like a grenade, pieces of the once-powerful body flying off in all directions. I saw what remained smack down amid a waterfall of glass, saw it flatten a car like a pancake, saw the spatter fly up three stories high. And then I didn't see anything else, because we were falling, too.

Pritkin's overtaxed shield gave out a few seconds too soon, sending us tumbling through the air, with me desperately trying to shift, even knowing it wouldn't work. And all I could think in those last few, furious seconds was that we'd won, against all odds we'd *won*, damn it, and it still wasn't—

And then we were jerked up, so hard I thought my bones might separate.

I just hung there for a moment, bouncing on air, too dazed to feel much of anything except some blood slipping ticklishly down my spine. Then I noticed Caleb overhead, leaning dangerously far over the side of the convertible, something close to terror on his habitually calm face. And his hand outflung in an odd gesture.

I thought that might have something to do with the faint golden glimmer wrapped around Pritkin and me like—well, like a lasso. *Nice catch,* I didn't say, because my mouth didn't seem to work. Until Pritkin slumped against me, his face slack, his body a deadweight in my arms, and I got a good look at his back.

And screamed.

Chapter Twenty-six

"What happened?" Caleb demanded, as two mages carefully hauled us over the side of the car. Caleb had hold of me, but I threw him off and pushed through to where they were laying Pritkin facedown on the backseat. "Cassie!"

"It was that last blast," I said numbly, staring at him. God, it looked worse from this angle. Red and black and white all mixed up together, blood and burnt leather and bone—

"This wasn't caused by fire," someone said.

I didn't even look up to see who it was. I was watching them carefully pull away the remains of his coat. It was spelled to repair itself, but I didn't think that would be happening this time. A few filaments were gamely trying to knit themselves back together, but there wasn't enough left to work with. Despite the armor spells woven into it, almost the entire back of the coat was simply gone, eaten away in huge, bloody holes with little more than leather "lace" between them. And the body underneath—

"My God," someone said as the remains of the coat were peeled back, taking some of his flesh along with it. The stars spun dizzyingly around me.

"Dragon blood," Caleb spat, and somebody cursed.

I looked up. "But that can't . . . we were nowhere near—"

"It must have spat it at you before you escaped," he said roughly. "Get us to Central. Now!" he ordered the driver.

"He's not going to last that long," one of the other mages

argued. "We have medical staff on the scene. They just arrived—"

"And you think they're going to be able to handle *this*?"

"If they don't, he's gone. I'm telling you, we can't—"

"Get out," I said softly, my eyes on the ruined map of Pritkin's back.

"And if we try the emergency unit and they can't do anything?" Caleb demanded. "We'll have lost any chance of—"

"There's no time for anything else!"

"I said, *get out*!" I snarled, pushing at the nearest mage. "All of you, except for Caleb!"

"What?" the mage who'd been arguing with the boss, a young Hispanic guy, turned to look at me. "What are you—"

"If you want him to live, get the hell out of here!"

"Do it," Caleb rasped, watching my face. I don't know what it looked like. I didn't care.

"Drive," I told him.

The mages bailed over the side, taking a protesting Fred along for the ride. Caleb climbed into the front seat and I bent over Pritkin. The stench of burnt leather mingled with the metallic tang of blood was bad enough, but there was something else there, too, something dark, something wrong.

"Don't touch him," Caleb said harshly. "The stuff's like acid. You get any on you and it'll eat through you, too."

I ignored him. I couldn't do this without touching. I wasn't sure I could do this at all. Pritkin was part incubus, which meant he could feed off human energy, almost like a vampire. It was the part he hated most about himself, the part that had once resulted in the death of someone he loved. But it was the only thing that might save him now.

I'd fed him once before, in a similar situation, but I'd had one major advantage then: he'd been conscious and an active participant. I didn't know what to do with him out cold. If he'd been a vamp, I'd have opened a vein for him, held it over his mouth, made him take what his body desperately needed. But he wasn't.

And incubi fed only one way.

I slid down to the floor by the seat, so that our faces were on a level. And realized that I had another problem.

He was lying on his stomach, his head turned toward me, and there was precious little undamaged flesh that I could reach. I ran a hand through his hair, and as always it was soft, despite the dust and sweat that currently matted it.

I combed my fingers through it anyway, before trailing them over his equally dirty brow, down the too-large nose, across the too-thin lips. He hadn't shaved today, maybe not yesterday, either, and the bristles rubbed my fingers as I smoothed over his cheeks, his jaw. My hand began to tremble as I reached his chin. The adrenaline that had kept me going for the past half hour was wearing off, but that wasn't the only reason my hand was shaking. Part of it was fear for Pitkin, but part of it—

Part of it was fear *of* him.

I'd only seen him feed the one time, and he'd been oh, so careful. And with cause. The power he possessed could not just take some of a person's energy; it could take all of it. Not that he would, not if he was awake and in his right mind and able to think clearly. But he wasn't now. And while I'd never seen an incubus drain someone, I'd seen master vampires when they were seriously injured, seen what they left behind when they—

I cut off, breathing hard. Panic and exhaustion vied to put me down for the count, but I pushed them away angrily, along with my stupid, stupid cowardice. Pritkin would risk it for me. *He'd do it for me.*

I bent and found his lips with my own.

The kiss, if you could call it that, tasted like dust and ashes. I felt his breath on my face, faint and warm, but nothing else. There was no response at all.

I pulled off my tank top and unhooked my bra.

"What the hell are you doing?" Caleb demanded. "I told you not to touch—"

"Caleb. Whatever you see, whatever you hear, you forget," I said harshly. "That's an order."

"Have you gone completely—"

"And here's another one. Shut up."

I picked up Pritkin's hand, limp and lifeless but so familiar. I knew every bump, every callus, every line. These hands were the ones that had taught me the right way to hold a gun, that had corrected my stance in martial arts, that had done their best to teach me to throw a proper punch. And for a few, brief moments once, they had held me in passion.

I really, really hoped some part of him remembered that now.

I held his hand to my breast and kissed him again.

There was still no response, at least not from him, but I felt something, a brief tremor of sensation when his calluses dragged over sensitive flesh. Incubi raised lust in their partners because it was how they tapped into human energy. It was the conduit they used to feed, as blood was for vamps.

But if my brief sensation awakened anything in Pritkin, I saw no sign of it.

It didn't help that I'd never felt less sexy in my life. It wasn't the dirt or the exhaustion or the audience, although that sure as hell didn't help. It wasn't even the blood. Mostly it was the panic. The growing certainty that I was going to lose him if I couldn't do this made it that much less likely that I could.

"If you can hear me, stop being a stubborn son of a bitch," I whispered desperately. *"Help me."*

I didn't get a response, and we were running out of time. I could see it in the pallor of his face, hear it in the shallowness of his breath, sense it in some undefined way I couldn't have named, but knew just the same. Tears of frustration welled in my eyes as I kissed him again, pushing it deeper, willing him to feel something, *anything*—

"That has to be the most pathetic display I have ever seen," someone said, and my head jerked up. Because it hadn't been Caleb's voice.

I stared up at the glimmering outline of a man shot through with stars, perched casually on the back of the seat. He was barely visible against the night, but then we slipped into a ley line and the jumping blue energy bent around a familiar set of features. They were the same ones as on the body I held, but they looked so very different with that particular mind behind them.

"Rosier," I spat, feeling my flesh crawl.

"What?" Caleb asked, and since he was still driving and not lunging over the seat with weapon drawn, I assumed he couldn't see the demon who had somehow hitched a ride.

"I told you; just ignore everything," I said roughly, as the deadly creature bent over his son. "Don't hurt him!"

"Hurt who?" Caleb asked, confused.

"Just drive!" I snapped, trying to push Rosier away. He had a body when he chose, but he obviously wasn't using it tonight. Because he was as insubstantial as a column of mist, and my hand went right on through.

"It seems you've done well enough on that score yourself," Rosier said drily. "I always said you'd be the death of him."

I felt tears welling up, of frustration, of anger and of mind-numbing fear. It made it hard to think, hard to breathe. Because he was right. I should have stayed in the damn hotel suite, should never have left it. This was my fault, completely and utterly, as much as if I'd put a gun to Pritkin's head. He was going to die and I couldn't help him, and I was going to have to sit here and watch it happen—

Just like Eugenie.

The very thought paralyzed me in horror. "No," I whispered.

"Why are you sitting there, blubbering?" the demon demanded. "We've work to do."

I looked up to find the pale outline more blurred than before, and forced myself to focus. I dashed angry tears away. "Why should I believe you want to help him? You tried to kill him!"

"Him, no. I tried to kill you, if you'll recall."

"You sent the damn Rakshasas after him!"

Rosier shrugged, as if sending a hit squad of soulless demons after his own son was a minor issue. "They were meant as a scare tactic—they couldn't touch him while he was alive, after all."

"They touched him plenty!"

"Only because you insisted on pulling him outside of his body. But do let's discuss this while he finishes slipping the mortal coil, shall we?"

I stared at Rosier, the hateful, lying, deceitful bastard that he was, and just didn't know. Pritkin hated his father, and while I didn't know all his reasons, I assumed they were good ones; I had plenty of my own. Trusting him now—

"My dear girl," he said, with a patient drawl in his voice. "If I wanted him dead, why would I be here at all? A few more minutes in your tender care should take care of things, with no interference from me."

And he was right. Despicable as he was, he was right. I was sitting here mourning the man, and he wasn't even dead yet. But he would be, would be very soon, if I didn't get my shit together, if I didn't figure something out. I pushed at Pritkin's inert body, trying to turn him on his side, to gain more access, but he was heavy and I didn't see how this was going to—

"Oh, for the love of— *What* he sees in you, I will never know," the demon said, in evident amazement.

"What do I do?" I asked frantically.

"If you want someone to eat, you must first prepare the meal. And he is hardly in a position to do it for you. Here," he said, with a sigh. "Let Daddy help."

And without warning, something snapped in the air around us. It felt like an electric current, only softer, warmer, infinitely more enticing. It pulsed through me like a wave, making my skin flush, my nipples peak and my heart beat harder in my throat. I stopped pushing on Pritkin and curled up next to him instead, sighing as my hands slid into the front of his coat, seeking warmth, seeking skin.

I slipped them under his T-shirt, feeling hard muscle and soft hair, and kissed his neck. That didn't get me anywhere, but when I gently bit the knob of his Adam's apple, I felt it bob faintly under my lips. So I did it again, before moving up to take his lower lip between mine. It gave under my teeth, a damp, swollen heat, and somebody moaned, but I wasn't sure which of us it was. I didn't care.

Except about one thing. There were too many straps and buckles and obstacles in the way. There were holsters and belts and vials and guns, when I craved skin on skin.

But that wasn't a problem for long. I watched in bemused fascination as a buckle on his shoulder slid out of its loop all on its own, the little prong popping loose from its leather jail, before the whole thing slithered to the floor. The same was happening with the belt around his waist, which turned loose and then jerked out from under him, tossing itself into the front seat. And then the zipper on his jeans slid open, as if an invisible finger was pushing it down.

I don't remember much of the next few minutes. Everything went fuzzy, a warm, golden haze that caught the seconds, stretching them like taffy. I do remember a man's chest, hard muscle under my hand, a sweeping ladder of ribs, the smooth rise of a hip ... and Pritkin jerking back, his breathing heavy, his jaw like iron.

His weapons were gone, and most of his shirt, too, although, oddly, he still wore one arm of his coat. The jeans were also still in place, but they were sagging in front, showing off a ridged abdomen and a light brown treasure trail. I pushed at them impatiently, got them mostly off his hips, before a hand grabbed mine and forced it back against the seat.

"You don't want this," he told me harshly.

I didn't say anything; I couldn't think clearly enough to put into words just how wrong he was. I'd never wanted anything more in my life.

I slid the other hand behind his neck, tried to pull him down to me, only to have the same thing happen. My other hand hit the seat, trapped in his as securely as in a manacle. Pritkin wasn't touching me otherwise, but he was right there, bare chest heaving, skin damp and moist, his one bare arm corded with muscle as he held me against the seat, helpless.

My body liked that, liked the fact that his eyes had bled black, with only a thin ring of emerald fire around the iris. But it liked a lot less that he was just staying there, wasn't moving away, but wasn't coming closer. It hurt not to touch him, an actual, physical ache, to see the rivulets sweat had carved down all those muscles, the swirling patterns it had made in his body hair, and not be able to trace them with my fingers, with my *tongue*. ...

He was saying something, but I didn't listen. Didn't care. My hands were fixed to the seat, but in holding mine, he'd immobilized his own as well. And we were close, so very close, that he couldn't stop me from winding a leg around him, from arching up to rub my cheek against the soft fur on his chest, from finding a peaked nipple and biting—

"Cassie, *please* ..." It came out choked, desperate, but to me it sounded like encouragement.

I bit down a little harder, and he cried out. I let my tongue lave the small mark I'd made, and his whole body shook in pleasure. It rippled into me, banishing the pain, but increasing the hunger. It felt wonderful, touching this much flesh, feeling his heart beat hard under my lips. But I wanted more, wanted to feel all that velvet skin on mine, wanted everything.

And so did he. Whatever he said, his hunger radiated down through his skin and into mine, making me cry out, making me crazy. I arched up and his chest barely brushed my erect nipples, but the shock of pleasure was intense, overpowering, magnifying the craving by a power of ten. I writhed against his hold, *needing* the pressing weight, the fierce cadence of skin on skin, the—

"Cassie!" A hand gripped my face, turning my eyes up to his, making me focus. Green eyes blazed down into mine, no longer black but strangely, unearthly bright. "You've been influenced. Do you understand? Remember how it felt before?"

A memory tugged at my mind, but it was vague, uninteresting. I pushed against his hands, throwing everything I had into it, but it was like fighting a statue. I cried out in pain and raw, unfulfilled need.

Pritkin cursed, but not at me. "What did you do to her?"

"What do you think?" someone laughed. "You know, you really should help the poor girl."

"Stay out of this," Pritkin snarled, and the tone was enough to send tongues of flame licking at pleasure points deep inside me. I whimpered.

"If I had, you'd be dead," the other voice commented. "You're welcome, by the way."

He may have said more, but I didn't hear. Because those warm hands had released me to close over my feet, gently sliding off my shoes before smoothing possessively over my calves. The sensation was exquisite, torturous, had my whole body jumping like a sensitized nerve ending. I started to reach out, to touch, to stroke, and immediately the hands were removed.

"No. Stay still."

It was Pritkin's voice, the one he used for command, the one I rarely heard but automatically obeyed. Usually because it meant that bad people with nasty weapons were aiming them at my head. I didn't know what the cause was this time, but I fell back against the seat, breathing hard. And the hands returned.

Callused palms brushed the soft undersides of my knees, then slipped around to warm the outsides of my thighs. They smoothed all the way up my body, encountering no barriers until they reached the thin material of my track shorts. Rough skin caught on the smooth nylon as he slid his hands over my hips, fingers slipping just under the elastic of the waistband.

They just stayed there for a moment, and our eyes met in the almost dark. Pritkin's held the same fierce, focused intensity they did when he was bending over me in the training salle, a sword resting hot against my neck. Only there was something more there tonight, something fierce and hot and possessive. I was shocked to feel myself start to tremble.

The feeling intensified as those big hands slowly spread against my skin. For a dizzying moment of clarity, I could feel everything: the fingers smoothing over the line of stitching running up each side of the shorts, the faint scratch of the tag against my skin, the sweat-damp material sticking to the small of my back. And then those hands began smoothing, oh, so slowly, back down my body. And they took the shorts with them.

I heard myself make a sound, nothing I recognized. And then time seemed to slow again, going soft and liquid. To the point that I could feel every inch of the thin, silky material as it skimmed over my belly button, glided past my hips, drifted across my pelvic bones and then stroked down my thighs.

Somewhere along the line, a spiraling, falling feeling took over my head, banishing any kind of rational thought. I didn't fight it. It was something I needed badly— something that let me forget what we were and where we were, and all the reasons why this was a very, very bad idea.

The silky cloth brushed over my feet as he pulled it completely away from my body. He never said a word. But as I lay there, bare except for a brief thong, I slowly realized that he was shaking. The tremors were almost imperceptible, as controlled as everything else about him. But I felt them.

I tried to tell him it was all right, that I trusted him, that this wouldn't change anything. But then warm hands found my skin again and slid up my legs. And all I could manage was a low sound, deep in my throat, as he slowly pressed my thighs apart.

He bent his head, not hurrying, but with an intensity on his face that made my brain start to short-circuit. Warm breath ghosted over me as he tracked up my body, pausing here and there for long seconds, as if breathing me in. But never stopping, never *touching*. His lips were millimeters from my flushed skin, so close that every breath raised goose bumps. And that's where they stayed, until I thought I would scream.

I wanted to touch him; I needed to *move*. But I couldn't seem to do anything but writhe in helpless counterpoint to that merciless nonassault. Within seconds, I was biting my tongue to hold back something perilously close to a whimper. Then those hands slid up my sides and that mouth finally made contact, closing on the tender flesh just above the bow on my thong.

I gasped at the warm, wet sensation, so different from the feel of hands. And suddenly it was much easier to lie still, my whole body going heavy and languid. I sank back, surrendering to the weight that settled between my legs, the cool feel of his hair and the shockingly intimate caress of lips and tongue on sensitive skin. Satisfying a months-old craving, I laced my fingers deep into the soft mane, feeling his head move under my hands.

The tender mouth went on to feast on my thighs, drawing another sound of startled pleasure from deep within me, a sound that turned to a groan when the hot tongue found the crease where thigh met hip. It made me want to touch him again, to flow against him like water, to slide along that muscled warmth and return pleasure for pleasure—

"Stop," he said mildly, nipping lightly at my hipbone. And my body reacted with a sweet, surprised rush.

He slowly tracked across my skin until I melted, becoming a malleable creature of pure response as the warm, wet onslaught moved over my hips, my stomach and then lower. His tongue ran around the top of the thong, tracing the lace, catching on the small satin bow. I couldn't see what he was doing; his head was in the way. But I felt it when a warm mouth closed over that small scrap of material, brushing my skin as he started tracking back down my body. And pulled it off with his teeth.

I stared at him blankly for a moment. All my fantasies, and still I'd never guessed, never known that *this* man simmered all the time below those grumpy looks, that stubborn-set jaw and stiff-necked control. Or maybe some part of me had known, and known the risk. . . .

And then I couldn't watch him anymore. I lay back against the seat, panting, as I was stripped bare to the warm night's breeze. Rosier was gone, or at least I couldn't see him. I couldn't see Caleb, either, because of the seat back, but wasn't sure if the opposite was true. At the moment, I didn't care. I didn't care about anything but the golden head now working its way back up my body.

He was drawing light patterns with his lips, his tongue, runes and symbols I was too far gone to read but that burned through my skin. The sensation was so intense, so overwhelming, that it felt like my body couldn't contain it. He stopped at a point where, had I been wearing panties, he would have been below them, feasting on skin I'd just waxed a few days ago. But he wasn't low enough, not even close, and that all-consuming need was building again.

I sank my hands into his hair, trying to direct that head to where I so needed it to be. But he ignored me, continuing to nuzzle softly against my flesh with that same deceptive gentleness. Until a stab of longing tore through me, so strong that I thought the emptiness might kill me if it went on much longer.

I did whimper then, a ragged, involuntary moan that didn't even sound like me. It would have been embarrassing if I'd been capable of caring about such things. But I wasn't and I didn't, not about that, not about anything but the almost unbearable intensity of need. I gasped out his name on a sob.

And finally, *finally*, he dropped that last inch. Warm lips closed over me, a wet tongue circled me. And a fierce, spiraling ache of need shot down every nerve I possessed. *There. Oh, there, yes, there.*

A faint shudder ran through him and his breath caught audibly. *"Yes,"* he hissed, so soft it might have been my own imagination. But the hands on my hips tightened convulsively, and that tongue became demanding, forcing me open, learning me intimately, discovering what I needed.

And then I couldn't think anymore. It was sensory overload, hearing the sounds he made deep in his throat, smelling that peculiar mix of sweat and gunpowder and magic that may as well have been his signature cologne, feeling the assault of that mouth, all wet, silken heat and fiery passion, nothing safe, nothing sane—

And then he gently bit down.

And oh, dear *God*.

Pleasure racked me, a deep, primal shudder of response followed swiftly by a surge of pure, molten lust. The rush of heat started in my belly and swept outward in an unexpected, uncontrollable wave, the raw force of it wrenching a cry from my throat. Merciless, he sucked me deeper and did it again. And my body simply couldn't take any more.

Ecstatic release flashed like chain lightning through my lungs and thighs and every place in between, right down to my toes. It rippled into Pritkin, tightening his hands, causing his fingers to dig into my flesh. And the sound he made, deep and vulnerable and desperate, made my body shudder harder, as if trying to come again even in the middle of mind-shattering release.

"God—" I heard myself choke, and didn't know if it was a plea for mercy or a prayer of thanks.

When it was finally over, I clung to the heavily muscled body, the skin fever hot with the thrum of magic pulsing just under the surface, gasping. A hand crushed my head to his chest, fingers tangling in my hair. I didn't even try to move; didn't think I could. I just stayed there, listening to his heartbeat pound strong and sure, if a little erratically, under my ear.

And then the car touched down, bumping asphalt, somewhere outside Vegas.

Chapter Twenty-seven

The shape I was in didn't really hit me until I stumbled out of the car. And face-planted onto something hard. I didn't know if it was the afterburn of adrenaline or being a snack for a half-incubus war mage, but I was completely wiped. To the point that the concrete under my cheek actually felt pretty damn inviting. I was all for sleeping wherever the hell I was, but somebody picked me up. I didn't have the strength left to protest.

Those same hands gently wrapped me in a blanket. It had to be three, maybe four a.m., but Vegas in August is stifling even at that time of the morning, and the blanket was scratchy and hot. I decided not to care, because it was easier.

We started across a cracked parking lot toward a brightly lit aluminum building with a couple of trucks and, incongruously, a limo parked outside. I squinted at it blearily. If that was war mage HQ, color me disappointed. It looked like it ought to be warehousing shoes. But I guessed it was more interesting inside, because a couple of leather-coat-clad guards were roaming around, giving us the hairy eyeball.

I didn't care about them, either.

I did care a few minutes later when I was put down on something puke green that smelled like cigarettes and old shoes, but decided I could live with it. I went to sleep. And then woke right back up at the furious, whispered conversation going on over my head.

"They called ahead; told them to expect you. What the fuck am I—"

"Tell them whatever you like. I am more concerned with getting a healer in here."

"You'd best be concerned with your job!"

"I could care less about—"

"Then how about your *neck*? Because that was assault, and assault on the Pythia carries a mandatory death sentence, as you damn well—"

Which was when I sat up. "No doctors," I croaked.

"Cassie!" We were in a small office, with Pritkin crouched beside what could best be described as an anti-sofa. Besides the unfortunate color and the more unfortunate smell, it was also hard and lumpy and stained, and had sad little tufts of stuffing dribbling out of one of the cushions. Kind of the Platonic ideal turned on its head.

Two sets of startled eyes looked at me, so I guess I'd said that last part out loud. "What? I read."

"Are you all right?" Caleb asked, crouching down beside Pritkin. Which gave me nowhere to put my legs. I thought about drawing them up, but then I'd probably go back to sleep again, and that was a bad idea for some reason that currently escaped me. I sat there and blinked at them, and waited for it to come.

"She needs a healer," Pritkin said harshly, and started for the door.

That was it. "No doctors," I said again.

And then I flopped over.

"You heard her," Caleb said, as Pritkin paused, his hand on the knob.

"Damn it, Cassie—"

"I'm just really, really tired," I told him, wondering why the fake wood paneling behind him was bleeding over into his body space. And then I realized that my eyes were crossing. "Do you have any booze?" I asked Caleb.

"You probably shouldn't drink," Pritkin said, looking conflicted.

I thought about that. There was a phrase I was looking for, but my brain was really not cooperating right at the— Oh yeah. "Fuck it," I said brightly. And then I sat up again, because the antisofa seriously reeked and because Caleb was coming over with a paper cup in his hand.

It was the kind you get out of watercoolers, small and cone-shaped, but it held some really fine whiskey. Really, really fine, I decided, tossing it back, all smooth and peaty.

And then it hit the party going on in my stomach and oh, shit.

"Trash can," I said thickly.

"What?" Caleb looked at me.

"Trash can!"

Pritkin cursed and grabbed one, just about the time everything I'd eaten that night paid a repeat visit. Whiskey, pizza, milk shake, beer—and a lone, half-dissolved gummy bear, which was a surprise, since I couldn't actually recall having eaten any. Fun times.

I finally finished, and was rewarded with another little paper cup, only this time filled with water. "Keep it coming," I said hoarsely as Pritkin held my hair back from my face and Caleb handed him a box of tissues.

Cleanup took a while, since I'd been pretty damn dirty to begin with. During which Pritkin kept bitching about a doctor and I kept saying no, until I got pissed. "You're not putting your head in a noose when I'm fine," I croaked. "I'm just tired. For God's sake!"

He finally shut up, maybe because he realized he was giving me a headache. Or maybe because he had one himself. He looked like nine kinds of hell. He'd had the presence of mind to leave the shredded coat in the car and to toss a blanket around the two of us, which had hidden the fact that he had no shirt and his jeans were acid-washed and not in the fashion sense. His face was drawn and pale, despite the feed, there was dried blood on his chest and his hands shook. And the less said about his hair, the better.

But then, that was always true.

"You need clothes," Caleb said roughly.

"There are some in my locker," Pritkin told him. "Two twenty-one. Or there should be. I don't remember what I—"

"I'll get them. Stay here."

Caleb looked at me sharply, why I don't know. Like I was actually up to shifting us out of there. Or walking out. Or sitting up.

I slumped back against the stinky couch and stared at Pritkin, who stared mutely back. I didn't know if it was because he'd fed, but his eyes were a little freaky. Almost neon green, bright and burning. And full of some dark emotion I couldn't read, but could guess at pretty well.

"I volunteered," I reminded him.

"To be used!" His hand tightened on the sofa cushion, until the knuckles bled white. "He wouldn't have cared if I'd drained you!"

"He'd have probably preferred it," I said, staring at that hand. "Save him some trouble."

"How can you—" He stopped and closed his eyes, and just breathed for a few moments. That wasn't a good sign; Pritkin was better when he was yelling and stomping around. But maybe he didn't have the strength right now. I could sympathize.

I moved my hand over the top of his and he immediately pulled back, something close to horror on his face. It seriously pissed me off. "That's a little hypocritical, don't you think?"

"It isn't—" He looked away. "It isn't you."

"I know it isn't me. What? Am I stupid?"

That got an eye blink, and I grabbed his hand again and tugged at him. I was too weak for it to have much effect, but he came anyway, sitting beside me. I held on to the hand, partly to be an ass, but also because, for some reason, it made me feel better. And right then, anything comforting, I'd take without question.

"I'm sorry," he said, after a moment. His jaw was tight enough that it looked like it hurt. I sighed.

"For what? For saving my life? For almost getting killed in the process? For not dying nobly? What?"

His brow tightened into a familiar frown. "You're in a mood."

"Yes. Yes, I am. I have had a *day*, and I am in a *mood*. So what are you apologizing for, exactly?"

"For . . . taking it that far. But I didn't see an alternative. He'd put you under a strong compulsion, and that kind won't break without—without completion."

"Completion." It took my tired brain a few moments to work through that one. And then another moment, because the only answer I was getting didn't make sense. "Okay, let me get this straight. You're apologizing for giving me a mind-shattering orgasm?"

Caleb slammed in the door. "I didn't hear that."

"Damn straight."

He had clothes, plain gray sweats and sneakers for Pritkin, and an oversized navy T-shirt for me. "It's mine," he told me. "I figured it'd work as a dress on you."

"Thanks." At this point, anything was better than the scratchy blanket. "Is there a shower?"

"Yeah. Over by the gym." He looked at Pritkin. "Gonna wash her back?"

And Pritkin growled—literally. Rabid pit bulls don't make that kind of noise when going for the jugular, although that seemed to be the plan, since he was out of the seat and lunging for Caleb faster than I could blink. Only to stop when I kept a grip on that hand.

Good idea grabbing it, in hindsight.

"Not the time, Caleb," I said briefly.

He nodded, looking a little freaked. I guess he hadn't heard that particular tone before, either. I struggled to my feet.

I'd actually been asking about the shower for Pritkin, who looked like he could use some hot water downtime. But clearly, leaving the two of them together was a no-no. And I was sort of afraid that maybe the couch wasn't the only thing stinking in the room.

Pritkin threw on the new sweats, which pretty much negated their status as clean, but which meant that I got to keep the whole blanket. I drew it around me until I was pretty sure I wouldn't shock anybody, and grabbed Caleb's tee. And then peered out the door.

Thankfully, the halls outside were as deserted as you'd expect at something o'clock in the morning. There wasn't even a janitor pushing a mop around; just a shadow behind a frosted glass door and a guy doing laps in the gym. Not that it was a gym, per se. Just an area carved out of the huge complex by some plywood partitions, and fitted out with a track, some treadmills and a lot of iron in the form of weights lining the walls.

A Fey would go nuts in here, I thought vaguely, and felt slightly more cheerful.

We followed a line of lockers to the back, where two

bathrooms were situated side by side. Pritkin got me a towel and a squeeze bottle of something out of his locker that had no discernable scent but that I assumed was soap. I said thanks and he said nothing at all, and we went our separate ways.

The shower part of the bathroom was, like the rest of the place, extremely utilitarian. I guessed it made sense—until a month ago, the Corps had been based at MAGIC, aka the Metaphysical Alliance for Greater Interspecies Cooperation, aka the supernatural version of the UN. At least it had been, until the war left it a glass slick in the desert. That had forced the Corps to find a new home, and trust them to make it as Spartan as humanly possible.

There were no cubicles—privacy was so damn girly—just an even dozen showerheads and a sloping floor with a drain in the middle. The tile was white and the fixtures were shiny, but only because they were new. I doubted that the shoe warehouse had come equipped with bathrooms this big, so they'd probably been a recent add-on. And yet, despite the newness, the place managed to be really ugly in the tradition of institutional spaces everywhere.

I scrubbed and scrubbed and scrubbed some more, and since the soapy stuff seemed to double pretty well as shampoo, that included tackling my hair. And damned if I didn't manage to finally soak the green out. Should have asked Pritkin for something before, I thought blearily, resting my head on the water-slick wall.

I felt exhausted, clammy and vaguely nauseous—the same as when I fed Billy a little too much. I wasn't completely drained; Pritkin had stopped short of that. In fact, Billy had left me feeling worse than this a time or two—with one exception. Feeding Billy had never left me with a burning little knot of guilt under my sternum.

And that's exactly what this was, too: guilt. Not overwhelming or paralyzing or crushing, but guilt all the same. I'd experienced enough of it in the past to have no trouble identifying it. I just didn't know what it was doing there.

This wasn't the first time Pritkin and I had gotten close; it was the second. The first had been about a month ago during the final battle with Apollo. Pritkin had been seriously injured and his incubus abilities had saved him, with a little help from me. Very little, compared with today, but the basic idea had been the same: I'd provided the energy, he'd done the healing, the end.

And it really had been the end. Our relationship had gone back to the usual and I hadn't even thought that much about it afterward. There had been so much other stuff going on that it had seemed, well, just one of those crazy things. Like almost drowning myself in a bathtub or being chased by a dragon through an office building. Crazy shit like that happened all the time lately, and that's the folder it had gone into in my brain. If anything, I'd just been grateful it had worked and that we'd both come out of the battle with a whole skin.

So what was different now?

Was it because I'd enjoyed it? Because I had; there was no point in denying it. Not the first few minutes—those had been pretty damned horrifying. But later . . . yeah. I'd enjoyed it. Kind of a lot. Okay, a hell of a lot. But then, I'd enjoyed it the last time, too. And, seriously, Pritkin was the son of the prince of the incubi. What the hell did my brain expect? That I'd hate it? I mean, what were the odds?

And the fact was, I'd have helped him whether I'd gotten any pleasure out of it or not. The guy was *dying*. I wouldn't have let that happen, regardless. And I sure as hell wasn't sorry he was alive. So no, I didn't think the pleasure thing was the problem.

Was it maybe because I was dating Mircea now, and I hadn't been before? I mean, Mircea had claimed me a while ago, but master vamps had a habit of simply taking whatever they wanted, as I knew from long experience. It hadn't surprised me, but I also hadn't considered us married just because he said so. I hadn't considered us as having any status romantically at all until we started dating, and that had been after the last little incident.

So was that it? Was I feeling like I'd cheated on him? I thought about it for a while, but that didn't feel quite right, either. It wasn't like this had had anything to do with romance. If Pritkin had been a vampire, I'd have given him blood; as it was, I'd given him what he needed to heal. And considering that he'd almost died in both instances because of me, I'd sort of owed him one.

And yet, for whatever reason, this one felt different. I hadn't had any trouble meeting Mircea's eyes after the last time. I didn't know if that would be true now, and it pissed me off that I didn't even know why.

However, I did know one thing. I wasn't going to get any absolution—not that I needed any, damn it—because I couldn't tell him. Not because I didn't think he'd understand. Vampires tended to be a lot more pragmatic than humans, and if I could explain that it had been a life-or-death situation . . . well, there was a chance Pritkin wouldn't lose too many limbs. The problem, of course, was that I couldn't.

I couldn't tell Mircea anything, because if I told him why, I'd also have to tell him what—specifically what Pritkin was. And if I told him what he was, I might as well tell him who he was, since there'd only ever been one human-incubus hybrid in all history.

And I didn't think the magical community was quite ready to hear that Merlin had returned.

Of course, I didn't know that they would hear about it. I didn't think Mircea would plaster it all over the front pages, for instance. But he'd do something with it. He wouldn't be a vampire if he didn't.

And I really didn't want to find out what that something would be.

After a while, I sighed and gave up. I'd figure it out later when maybe I didn't feel like I was about to fall over. The water had stayed hot, but my knees were starting to get wobbly, so I shut it off.

God, I was tired.

I dried off and pulled Caleb's shirt and a half over my head. The "short" sleeves came down past my elbows, and the hem almost hit my knees. I decided it would do and padded back outside.

The jogger had gone off somewhere and no one had taken his place, so the cavernous space felt kind of creepy. I looked around for Pritkin, because it would be perfectly in character to find him pumping iron even after being almost dead half an hour ago. But I didn't see him.

The gym was big but it was also pretty open, with no real obstacles in the exercise area and only industrial fluorescents overhead. So it wasn't like I could have missed him. For one, brief, panic-filled moment—or it would have been panicked if I'd had any panic left—I thought he might have

gone back to pick a fight with Caleb. But then I heard water
running.

I debated it for a couple of seconds, in case it was the
runner who had decided to have a sluice down. But I was
really too tired to be embarrassed, and war mages tended
to take things in stride. I decided to risk it.

The guys' bathroom looked exactly like the women's,
other than being larger and having a line of urinals. I
walked past the bathroom stalls and into the big shower
room in back. There was no door—of course—so it didn't
take me long to find him.

It took me a little longer to figure out what to do.

For a guy who was as loud as Pritkin, he really didn't
lose it very often. Maybe all that yelling served as a release
valve; I don't know. But no matter how bad things got, he
kept his shit together better than most people I knew, including me. Not that that was saying much. I was usually
the run-screaming-at-the-first-sign-of-danger type, but Pritkin was Mr. Cool under Pressure.

Which was why it was a little strange to find him standing in the spray, staring at a bar of soap with the air of a
man who has forgotten what he's supposed to do with it.

It didn't look like he'd used it. There were streaks of
blood on the powerful legs, oil or something black on the
broad back and livid bruises pretty much everywhere. The
black stuff had run, dripping down the multicolored skin,
making him look like some kind of avant-garde painting or
vandalized sculpture. *The Thinker* in yellow, purple and
green.

The hair was wet and plastered to his skull. It made the
bones of his face stand out more, and his nose look bigger
as he turned his head to me. It wasn't with his usual rapid
reflexes, but in a bewildered kind of way that really worried
me. Not that an assassin was likely to be sneaking up on
him at war mage HQ, but still. I had the disturbing impression that, if I *had* been an assassin, Pritkin would have just
stood there and let me kill him.

Okay, then.

I walked over, despite not knowing what the hell I was
supposed to do. Growing up at Murders 'R' Us, I'd seen a
lot of nasty stuff, and my visions had shown me a lot more.
Pretty early on, I'd learned to distance myself from incon-

venient feelings, from anything I couldn't easily handle. And by now, I was tops at the Scarlett O'Hara school of emotional distancing. I always thought about the uncomfortable stuff tomorrow, and, as everyone knows, tomorrow never comes.

And despite what psychologists would have you believe, living in denial actually works pretty damn well. At least most of the time. It had worked for me, keeping me functional, keeping me sane—more or less—long after anyone could have reasonably expected.

It wasn't working so well right now.

It meant that I didn't know how to talk to Pritkin about his shit, whatever his shit was, because I rarely talked about mine. I didn't know how to tell him it was going to be okay, because I wasn't sure that it was. I didn't have anything useful to say at all, so I didn't try. I slid my arms around him from behind and held on.

The water was still warm. I supposed that was something.

Pritkin didn't say anything, either, so we just stayed like that for a while. I found that I was in no real hurry to move. I was bone tired, but he was warm and solid and easy to hold on to. I got this weird kind of floaty feeling after a while, a combination of exhaustion, relief and the thrum of his heart under my ear.

He hadn't bothered to turn on the lights, so the only illumination was whatever filtered in from the bathroom or through the open top of the shower area. It wasn't much, and the water hitting the tile sounded like rain, the kind Vegas rarely got. I pulled him closer and felt my eyes slip closed.

I thought maybe I'd just sleep here.

"Her name was Ruth," he said hoarsely. And then he stopped.

His back was warm against my cheek. I could feel the column of his spine just under the surface. I didn't say anything.

"My wife," he added, after a while. I nodded, but he couldn't see it, so I just tightened my grip for a moment. I'd kind of thought that might be it.

I wasn't an expert on Pritkin's past, but I knew a few things. Like the fact that, more than a century ago, he'd married a woman he'd presumably loved a lot. I didn't know much about her, because that was one topic that got a very swift conversation change. But I knew the important thing: I knew how she'd died.

It had happened on their wedding night, when the incubus part of Pritkin got out of control—seriously out. For some reason, instead of simply feeding, which would have been normal under the circumstances, it had decided to drain her—dry. Pritkin hadn't been able to stop the process, and it had killed her.

Or, rather, he had killed her, because as the only half-human incubus, the two parts of his nature were forced into an uneasy cohabitation. It was like being Jekyll and Hyde, only at the same time, all the time. Other incubi could leave their bodies behind when they weren't feeding, since they'd only borrowed them from a human anyway. But Pritkin couldn't.

I didn't know if that had something to do with why he'd lost it that night or not. Because he'd told me those few hard facts and nothing else. It had been around the time we'd started to notice an attraction, and I guess the idea had been to scare me off.

It had worked like a charm.

The idea of ending up a straw-haired, desiccated corpse had proven a real incentive in ignoring any inconvenient feelings. Pritkin and I were together a lot, often in circumstances that got the blood pumping, if not spurting. It was only natural that there might be an occasional spike of something. It would have been strange if there hadn't been, really.

But we'd ignored them by mutual consent, because, clearly, they weren't going anywhere. I was dating Mircea, and Pritkin . . . Well, as far as I knew, Pritkin didn't date anyone. Ever. I'd gotten the impression that he wasn't going to risk whatever had happened happening again.

I suddenly found that really sad.

Someone cursed behind us, but I didn't jump. I was too tired, and anyway, I knew that voice. I looked over my shoulder and saw Caleb's big body outlined in the doorway for a second before he disappeared.

But a moment later he was back with a couple of large towels. He shut off the water, wrapped one around me and threw one at his buddy. Or former buddy, given the scowl marring those handsome features.

"Out," he said roughly, pushing us at the door. "It's getting too close to morning. There's going to be people showing up soon, and we got enough to explain as it is. And that vampire's on the phone, fit to be tied."

"Which one?" I asked, pretty sure I already knew.

"Marco. Said you either call him or he's accusing us of kidnapping you."

He handed me a phone and I took it with a sigh. I punched in the suite's number and it was picked up on the first ring. "Cassie, what the *hell*—"

"You know what the hell. Am I still a prisoner?"

"You know damn well you aren't!"

"Then I'll be back. Now stop calling." I hung up.

Caleb just looked at me. "That was it?"

"That was it until I figure out what story I'm using."

"I know the feeling," he snarled, and pushed us toward the office.

Chapter Twenty-eight

We walked back into the little space and Caleb slammed a bottle of Jack down on the desk. "Talk about whatever the hell it is you need to talk about, and get your story straight. I have to make out a report before the bosses show up, and it needs to be tight. You feel me?"

I nodded. Caleb left.

The air conditioning was on and my makeshift dress was clammy. I pulled it off and draped it over the back of Caleb's desk chair, and wrapped myself in a towel instead. When I turned around, Pritkin had pulled the sweats back on and sat on the stinky sofa. He had his arms crossed in front of him, like a man who doesn't want company, so I took the hard plastic chair in front of the desk.

I poured the Jack, but not because I wanted any. My stomach felt like it might be fine without anything in it for a year, maybe two. But if a guy had ever looked like he needed a drink, Pritkin was him.

"We don't have to talk," I told him. "I mean, I don't mind listening, but it's . . . I don't need an explanation."

"But you deserve one."

"Do I?" I kind of thought we were even. He'd saved my life; I'd saved his. But it didn't look like he agreed.

I handed him the whiskey and he threw it back like a pro, not even wincing. He noticed my expression and smiled faintly. "Compared to what I grew up on, this is . . . fairly mild. And yes, you do."

I was wondering what the hell he'd grown up on—the Celtic version of rotgut? But I didn't ask and he didn't offer. He just sat there, cradling the empty paper cup gently in his hands.

They were still long-fingered, still refined. But they looked more like they belonged to a war mage tonight. Along with the ever-present potion stains, there was a smudge of dark brown that the shower had missed—dirt or dried blood—in the crease between the left thumb and the palm. It had run into the cracks, highlighting them like strokes of charcoal on a sketch. I had a sudden urge to reach over and wipe it off, but I didn't.

And then he started talking, and I forgot about everything else.

"I told you once about Ruth. About . . . how she died."

I nodded.

"But I didn't give specifics. We hadn't known each other long at the time and it didn't . . . I assumed that you would never need to know." He paused for a moment, staring at the fake wood paneling on the opposite wall, as if it held some kind of fascination for him. "I think perhaps you do now."

"Okay."

"Ruth had a small amount of demon blood. Ahhazu, a minor species, from her paternal grandmother. She was an eighth, or some such amount."

"You didn't know?"

"I knew. I knew as soon as I met her. But I assumed that, as she was living on Earth, she must feel the same way about the demon realms that I did. That they have their pleasures, but they are ultimately corrupting to whoever ventures there. Stay long enough and you lose yourself—your ideals, your values, everything you are—all in the pursuit of mindless pleasure. And in the end, there is no pleasure in that."

"But she didn't see it that way?" I guessed.

"No. By comparison to the glamorous, glittering courts she had occasionally glimpsed, Earth was squalid, disease-ridden and poor. It didn't help that she was born into the middle of the Industrial Age, when, in fairness, those things were often true. The Thames stank like an open sewer, and very nearly was. The new industrial cities like Birmingham and Manchester were littered with overcrowded, filthy, rat-ridden tenements, filled with people dying of overwork, pollution, disease.... Even Prince Albert died of diphtheria, because of the filthy drains at Windsor. It was an ugly age, and she hated it, all the more for the brief glimpses she'd had of worlds beyond human imagining."

"But she didn't tell you this?" I didn't need to guess on that one. I couldn't see Pritkin having much in common with someone who had loved the world he hated.

"She told someone, but it wasn't me."

"Rosier." I don't know how I knew. Maybe because Pritkin only got that particular look on his face when he discussed his father.

A curt nod. "She went to see him, gained admission by mentioning my name. He later told me that she said she'd lived her life like a child in a candy store—one without any money to purchase anything. Able to see the beauty of her other world, but unable to gain access to it."

"Because of her mixed heritage?"

"No. Demons aren't like some of the Fey, jealously guarding their bloodlines, afraid of any impurity. They regularly mix races, among themselves, other types of demons, humans, Weres, Fey—anyone who has an attribute they think might be useful. Anyone who might give them an edge over a rival."

"Then why couldn't she just change worlds if she wanted? If she didn't like it here—"

He shook his head. "It shouldn't be difficult for you to understand. In that regard, as in others, your vampires are very similar to demonkind. What is the only thing that really matters to a vampire?"

I hesitated, not sure where he was going with this. "There are a lot of things—"

"Are there? In that case, why is your friend Raphael not the head of his own family? He is arguably one of the greatest artistic talents the West has ever produced, and yet he serves a sniveling, wretched nobody like that Antonio."

"He doesn't anymore. Mircea broke Tony's hold."

"But he did until recently."

"Not by choice. Rafe is a master, but he isn't that powerful—"

"And there you have it. Power. The one thing, perhaps the only thing, your vampires respect. It is the same with demons. And Ruth had almost none."

"But she was part demon—you said so."

"Yes, but demons are like any other species. Mix the genetics and you never know what will come up. Even full blooded Ahhazu aren't that strong, and in her case . . . she may as well have been the human she pretended to be."

"But you're part demon and part human. And you told me yourself that the incubi aren't considered one of the more powerful species, either. But you—"

"Yes, but my other half was magical human; hers was not. And that, or the small amount of Fey blood I inherited from my mother, or the way the genes combined—something worked to boost my abilities. I ended up stronger magically than I should have been, instead of weaker. If I had not, I doubt I would have ever known who my father was. He would have rejected me as another failed experiment and moved on. And the same was true for Ruth. Without power, she was of interest to no one."

"No one except you."

Pritkin was silent for a long moment. And when he spoke his voice was different from usual, softer, almost tentative. As if he had to find the words because he never spoke about this and didn't have them ready.

"She saw me, I think, as an entrée into a world she could only imagine. She knew I was part demon from the moment she met me. It is difficult to hide that from another of our kind, but it is also difficult to tell which species one belongs to if the human side is dominant. I think—I would like to think—that she didn't know until I told her. That her affection for me had some basis other than the fact that my father was the prince of one of the most magnificent of the courts. It is far from the most powerful, but in opulence, in decadence, in wealth . . . it would be difficult to name another more entrancing. Certainly, it entranced her."

"I'm sorry." I couldn't think what else to say. No one liked to feel they were wanted only because of what they had, or, in his case, who they were.

"As am I."

He was quiet for a while, the whoosh of the air conditioner and the faint buzzing of the overhead light the only sound. It was peaceful, and the small office was oddly cozy. It felt like an island away from the craziness of our usual lives, another moment stolen out of time. Maybe that's what did it, or maybe, like me, he just wanted to tell someone. Have somebody understand.

"Demons do not . . . have relations . . . the same way humans do," he finally said. "Or, rather, they can—the more humanoid of the species, in any case—but it isn't considered a real joining. That comes only from merging with another, gaining power by feeding off their energy, having them feed off yours. . . . If done between two full demons, it can result in an exchange of power, enabling both to grow stronger. Some matings are done specifically for that purpose, to allow beings with complementary abilities to enhance them, possibly even mutate them into something neither had experienced before."

I frowned, trying to grasp what he was telling me. "So instead of making a new life, you . . . remake yours?"

"In a way. Of course, a joining can result in both outcomes, although that's exceedingly rare. But demon lives are long and experimentation is . . . almost a universal hobby. It is like the human fascination with genetics, the attempt to make oneself better through whatever means are available."

"And Ruth wanted to do that with you?"

He nodded curtly once, and then went still. When he finally spoke it was harsh, clipped. "She didn't tell me. She told my father, asked for his advice—why I don't know. He would be the last person to give anyone selfless advice, but perhaps she assumed he would want the best for his son." His lips twisted in savage mockery.

"And he told her to go ahead?" I asked.

"I don't know what he told her. I know only what he said—*after* I found out on my own that she had been to court. He swore that he had informed her of the risk, but he had every reason to do precisely the opposite. He hated the idea of my 'wasting' myself on a human, and a nonmagical one at that, with barely enough demon blood to mention. He wanted me mated to full demons, powerful ones, influential ones."

"Why? Why would he care—"

"Because it would lend him influence with the courts. Most demons have a very limited pool of partners with whom to experiment, because most are restricted in what kind of energy they can absorb. Incubi, however, are the . . . the O positive of the demon world. We can feed from virtually anyone and transmit energy to anyone, anyone at all."

I stared at him for a moment, sure I'd misunderstood. But as crazy as it sounded, I didn't see what else he could have meant. "He was going to *pimp you out*?"

Pritkin shot me a glance, and something of the tension went out of his shoulders. His face relaxed, not into a smile, but into something less forbidding. "If you could see your expression."

"How else am I supposed to look? You're his son!"

"Which makes me a bargaining chip. Or was supposed to. I don't know what he envisioned—someone like him, I suppose, handsome, charming, ready to bed whomever and whatever was needed for the good of the clan. He did as much himself when it would help his negotiations. But while he could offer a power exchange, he couldn't give the other races what they truly wanted."

"And what was that?" I asked, almost afraid to find out.

"Children. Progeny who might carry the traits of both parents, thereby enriching the line with new blood for eons to come. Full demons have an incredibly low reproductive rate. They live for so long, if anything else were true, they would face mass starvation. But humans . . ."

He paused, but I didn't push it, didn't say anything. I just sat there, torn between horror and outrage. But he saw, and that same quiet came over his face, as if my anger somehow lessened his own.

"It is the greatest strength humans have, and their greatest asset in the struggle to survive. Despite living far longer, other sentient species can't touch the human reproductive rate, can't even come close. Rosier spent centuries trying and failing to father a child with other demonic races. But it wasn't until he switched to human partners that he managed it. And even then . . ."

Pritkin trailed off, but I knew he was thinking about the countless children Rosier had fathered on his quest and who had died—and had taken their mothers along with

them. I'd never known if that was because of the terrible
rate of death in childbirth among ancient and medieval
women, or if it was the fact that the babies were half-
incubus, a species designed to prey on human energy, that
had been the cause. But none had lived. None until him.

"So he wasn't pimping you out," I said harshly. "He was
putting you out to stud."

"In a manner of speaking. Half demons aren't overly
fertile, either, but in comparison . . . And any demon race
would give more—much more—for a power exchange, if
even an outside chance of a child came with it."

"And I thought I hated him before," I said grimly. "How
could he expect you to agree to that?"

"Because a full demon would have, without question.
Would not have concerned himself with the futures of any
children he helped to create, or the use Rosier was putting
to the influence he gained. He would have viewed it as an
honor, as a way to help the clan and to increase his own
status at the same time. But needless to say, I felt differ-
ently."

"I'd hope so!"

"My refusal caused the first major breach between us,
although there had been others. But it was what finally convinced me to leave it all behind, to rejoin the human world,
to build a life free of him, of the courts, of the constant
scheming and power plays."

"And he let you go?"

Pritkin finally smiled, and it wasn't a very nice one. "I
forced his hand, you might say. But in the end, it mattered
little, as his ambition for me remained the same. And a mo-
nogamous marriage to a nonentity would do nothing to
service it. He said he warned her, but he does nothing counter to his own interests. Nothing!"

I didn't say anything that time, because I had finally
caught on to where he was going with this. At least, I was
afraid that I had. But I don't think Pritkin noticed. He was
staring at the damn paneling, but his face was . . . somewhere else.

"I will never know for certain what went on at that
meeting," he said. "I know only what she did. On our wedding night, she initiated the exchange of power. I believe
she hoped it would strengthen her own magic, make her

acceptable in the eyes of the courts. And had she been fully demon, even half, it may well have done so. May have given her entry into that world she wanted so badly. But she wasn't, and she didn't understand. . . ."

He paused, and for a moment, I thought that would be it. But then he spoke again. And it was so raw, so bitter, that the very tone hurt to hear.

"The exchange of power is designed to be exactly that. But I suppose she never wondered what would happen if one partner had no excess power to give. Had nothing but the energy she needed to live. And I was . . . distracted. . . . I didn't notice what was happening, not for a moment, because incubi typically feed in those instances. But not that much, not that *fully*. And by the time I realized, it was too late. Before the cycle could even properly begin, she was—" His lips tightened. "She never received anything back. She never had time. She gave and gave and then it was over . . . so quickly. . . ."

He trailed off, for which I was grateful. Pritkin had described what happened once before, and I remembered the conversation in vivid detail. It was a little hard to forget, as he hadn't spared himself. He hadn't told me the reason his wife ended up a dried-up shell of a creature, shriveled and desiccated, barely recognizable as human. But he had made sure I knew who had been responsible, at least in his mind.

He might have hated his father because of what he knew or suspected.

But he hated himself a lot more.

Again, I didn't know what to say. Except the obvious. "It wasn't your fault," I said quietly, only to have him give me a look of incredulous disbelief.

"I've just explained—"

"That you tried to stop it and you couldn't. What else could you have done? You didn't know—"

"I should have! There must have been signs, clues to what she intended—and yet I saw nothing!"

"Maybe there was nothing to see. Maybe she was careful—"

"Maybe I was a blind fool!" He got up and poured more whiskey. "I should have realized what was going on, should have noticed how giddy she suddenly was, how happy . . . but I put it down to the forthcoming wedding. Women like weddings, all the . . . the decorations and the gowns and the . . . And I was busy searching for a home for us. I'd lived in bachelor quarters until then, but they wouldn't do for her, and—"

He broke off and went back to the sofa. He took the whiskey bottle along. I really couldn't blame him.

"That night . . . I should have been able to shut things down before they progressed that far. But I couldn't, because I'd refused to mate with demons, had restricted myself to humans, and therefore knew little about the process. I knew what was happening, but not how to stop it. And obviously, neither did she. I'd kept my lofty principles, thwarted my father's wishes, and in doing so, left myself ignorant in the one area that mattered. And he knew that. Knew he had the perfect way to punish me for daring to tell him no—"

"Which is my point," I said, leaning forward, because I couldn't stay quiet any longer. "Rosier set you up. If you want to blame someone, blame him!"

"I do! But he wasn't there. He didn't drain her, he didn't steal her life away, didn't feel her crumble in his arms like—"

He cut off, breathing hard, and put his head in his hands. I went over and sat beside him, not hugging him because those moments in the shower had been an aberration, and I somehow knew he wouldn't appreciate it now. Maybe because of the nervous energy that was thrumming through him, like a grounded lightning rod. I could feel it, just sitting there, an electric charge jumping under his skin.

I didn't know what to say to Pritkin. When you hated and blamed yourself for something for years, it became truth, your truth, whether it actually was or not. And technically, we were in the same boat. What had happened to Eugenie wasn't my fault, at least in the sense that I couldn't have prevented it.

And that was exactly no fucking comfort at all.

After a while, I pulled my feet up and grabbed the whiskey, drinking straight from the bottle. My stomach wasn't too happy about it, but my stomach could go to hell.

"The worst part," he finally said, his voice hoarse, "was that I enjoyed it. Emotionally, mentally, I was horrified. But physically ... it was the same as tonight. When I woke in that car, it was to terrible pain, but also to indescribable pleasure. You held nothing back, your power was *right there*, and I ... I could have ..."

"But you didn't. You didn't drain me."

"I came damn close!"

I shook my head. "No, you didn't. You took a lot, but I know drained, okay? I've fed ghosts, vampires and now a half demon—twice. And both times—"

"I was conscious last time!" he said savagely. "I kept control for nearly the entire process, and you had a place to run when I lost it. None of that was true tonight!" Green eyes blazed into mine. "Do you understand that? Do you realize the risk you ran? You were trapped and there was no one to help you and—"

"And nothing happened." I didn't even bother to get annoyed at his tone; yelling at me for saving his life was typical of the man. "Besides, there *was* someone to help me."

He snorted. "Caleb? Do you have any idea how inadvisable it is to disturb a demon when it is feeding? And I am more powerful than most because of who sired me. If he'd interfered, the only damage would have been to him!"

"I wasn't talking about Caleb," I said evenly.

"You couldn't access your power. You couldn't have shifted—"

"Damn it! I'm not talking about me, either. And if you say Rosier, I swear I'll hit you."

"There was no one else there."

I rolled my eyes. Maybe I'd hit him anyway. It was starting to look like the only viable option.

"There was you. I knew I would be okay because I was with you. I knew you wouldn't—"

"Then you're a fool," he rasped. "For one moment, I didn't know where I was, who you were—I didn't know anything, but how good pulling on all that power felt. And a moment is all it takes!"

"But *you didn't do it*," I repeated, because he didn't seem to get that. Which was odd, because for me, it was kind of the main point here.

"But I could have! I felt it, the hunger, the burning, the *need*." His fists clenched. "I didn't *want* to stop—"

"But you did. I remember when you pulled back. You'd

have stopped it right then, as soon as you fig̲ ̲ ̲ ̲
was happening, if your father hadn't laid that̲ ̲ ̲

"You don't know—"

"And even then, it's not like you did all̲ ̲ ̲
said, talking over him, because it was the onl̲ ̲ I̲
word in edgeways with Pritkin sometimes.

He had filched the bottle back to take a̲ ̲ ̲
that he lowered it and looked at me, his ey̲ ̲ ̲
next to the amber liquor. "What?"

"I just meant, it wasn't all that and a bag̲ ̲ ̲
know?"

He blinked at me.

"No offense," I added, because he was lo̲o̲ ̲
poleaxed. Like maybe he hadn't had a who̲ ̲ ̲
plaints before. Which was, frankly, pretty dam̲ ̲ ̲
able. But I feigned indifference. "I mean, it̲ ̲ ̲
been that bad if—"

"Bad?"

"Well, not *bad* bad."

He just looked at me.

"I mean, I came and everything, so that h̲ ̲ ̲
some—"

I cut off because I was suddenly envelop̲ ̲ ̲
pair of arms, and my head was crushed to a̲ ̲ ̲
chest that appeared to be vibrating. It took̲ ̲ ̲
ments to get it, and even then I wasn't sure̲ ̲ ̲
kin's face was buried in my hair. But I kind̲ ̲ ̲
impossible as it seemed—that he might be . . .

physically . . . it was the same as tonight. When I woke in that car, it was to terrible pain, but also to indescribable pleasure. You held nothing back, your power was *right there*, and I . . . I could have . . ."

"But you didn't. You didn't drain me."

"I came damn close!"

I shook my head. "No, you didn't. You took a lot, but I know drained, okay? I've fed ghosts, vampires and now a half demon—twice. And both times—"

"I was conscious last time!" he said savagely. "I kept control for nearly the entire process, and you had a place to run when I lost it. None of that was true tonight!" Green eyes blazed into mine. "Do you understand that? Do you realize the risk you ran? You were trapped and there was no one to help you and—"

"And nothing happened." I didn't even bother to get annoyed at his tone; yelling at me for saving his life was typical of the man. "Besides, there *was* someone to help me."

He snorted. "Caleb? Do you have any idea how inadvisable it is to disturb a demon when it is feeding? And I am more powerful than most because of who sired me. If he'd interfered, the only damage would have been to him!"

"I wasn't talking about Caleb," I said evenly.

"You couldn't access your power. You couldn't have shifted—"

"Damn it! I'm not talking about me, either. And if you say Rosier, I swear I'll hit you."

"There was no one else there."

I rolled my eyes. Maybe I'd hit him anyway. It was starting to look like the only viable option.

"There was you. I knew I would be okay because I was with you. I knew you wouldn't—"

"Then you're a fool," he rasped. "For one moment, I didn't know where I was, who you were—I didn't know anything, but how good pulling on all that power felt. And a moment is all it takes!"

"But *you didn't do it*," I repeated, because he didn't seem to get that. Which was odd, because for me, it was kind of the main point here.

"But I could have! I felt it, the hunger, the burning, the *need.*" His fists clenched. "I didn't *want* to stop—"

"But you did. I remember when you pulled back. You'd

have stopped it right then, as soon as you figured out what was happening, if your father hadn't laid that damn spell."

"You don't know—"

"And even then, it's not like you did all that much," I said, talking over him, because it was the only way to get a word in edgeways with Pritkin sometimes.

He had filched the bottle back to take a drink, but at that he lowered it and looked at me, his eyes very green next to the amber liquor. "What?"

"I just meant, it wasn't all that and a bag of chips. You know?"

He blinked at me.

"No offense," I added, because he was looking kind of poleaxed. Like maybe he hadn't had a whole lot of complaints before. Which was, frankly, pretty damn understandable. But I feigned indifference. "I mean, it couldn't have been that bad if—"

"Bad?"

"Well, not *bad* bad."

He just looked at me.

"I mean, I came and everything, so that has to count for some—"

I cut off because I was suddenly enveloped in a strong pair of arms, and my head was crushed to a hard chest. A chest that appeared to be vibrating. It took me a few moments to get it, and even then I wasn't sure, because Pritkin's face was buried in my hair. But I kind of thought—as impossible as it seemed—that he might be . . . laughing?

Chapter Twenty-nine

"I'm glad you two are having such a swell time," Caleb said, slamming back in a minute later.

I barely heard him. I was too busy watching Pritkin, who had slumped over with his head on the sofa arm, shoulders shaking helplessly, and what looked suspiciously like tears leaking out from under his closed eyes. "Not that bad," he muttered, and then he was off again.

Caleb looked at him like he thought the guy might have totally gone around the bend. I wasn't sure he wasn't right, because Pritkin rarely smiled, and he *never* laughed. But he was doing it now, and for a moment, I just absorbed the image. Of all the strange things that had happened on this very strange day, I thought that might just take the prize.

And then Caleb was jerking me out the door.

"Are you lucid?" he demanded.

"Pretty much."

"Good. Then maybe you can tell me—" He stopped, because a door closed somewhere down the corridor. Caleb's head whipped around like a guy's in a spy movie, and then he hauled me across the hall and into another office.

This one had boxes lining the walls and stacks of files teetering dangerously high on the only desk. There was also a trench coat on a hook on the back of the door and he grabbed it, shoving it at me. "Do I want to know what happened to my T-shirt?"

"It was wet."

"And why was it— No, wait. Don't answer that."

"Because I wore it in the shower!" I said, getting into the coat, which was about five sizes too big. "We just talked, Caleb!"

"Then talk some more. Like about what we're supposed to do."

"About what?"

"About the fact that John may have lost his ever-loving *mind*, but he's physically doing pretty damn good for a guy who was almost dead an hour ago! And people *saw*, okay? And by now they've talked—"

"Talked to who?"

"How the *hell* do I know? We had maybe a couple hundred people on the ground, with most of 'em still there."

"Why so many? Can't you just go with 'gas leak' or something?" It was Dante's default excuse for the not-so-occasional weirdness that went on.

"For the restaurant, maybe. It may even be partly true in that case. But that's still leaves us with two wrecked buildings, a trashed parking garage and four thousand pounds of *dragon flesh* bleeding out in the middle of a—"

"Okay, I get it. We made a mess."

"A *mess*? Do you have any idea how many memories, how many video monitors, how many—"

"I said, I get it."

"I don't think you do! But right now, I'm not even worried about all of that. Do you know what has me freaking the hell out? Would you care to take a wild fucking guess?"

I didn't say anything.

"Let me give you some help," he said savagely, beginning to pace around the tiny space between the desk and the door. "I keep going over and over it, trying to find another explanation. Telling myself I must be crazy. Telling myself I must be wrong. But two plus two equals four. And incubus plus human equals—"

"Stop right there."

"Like hell I'll stop!" He whipped around to face me, surprisingly fast for such a big guy. "Do you have *any* idea what's going to happen when everyone else does the fucking math—"

"They're not going to do it."

"Oh, really? Let's go through it, shall we? John gets hit with a crap load of dragon blood, enough to take out a fucking platoon. The usual spells for stopping shit like that aren't worth a damn, and every single person in that car knows what's what. I do, too, but I've known him a long time, so I'm gonna see to it that he gets back here, even if it's only to have the docs hang a damn toe tag on him!"

"Caleb—"

"I figured that's what you were doing, too, and when you ordered those men out, I guessed you just wanted to give him some privacy in his last moments. Thought that 'if you want him to live' shit was just to get 'em moving or to give yourself some hope or something. But lo and behold. What happens?"

"*Caleb*—"

"You start putting the moves on what is basically a *corpse*, and then talking when there's nobody there, and then some weird-ass shit starts going down with sparkly light and heat and John comes back to life and jumps your goddamn *bones*—"

"Technically, he didn't—"

"And the next thing I know, he's doing just fine. He's fucking dandy. And you're the one who looks like a corpse and almost are one—"

"I was not."

"And he's all energized with creepy, glowing eyes and enough power radiating off him to take on an army, *and there's only one way he got it*, okuy?"

"He could be possessed by an incubus," I argued. "He doesn't actually have to be—"

Caleb looked disgusted. "Sell it somewhere else. Everyone knows John is half demon—it's not the kind of thing you can hide from the sort of work-up the Corps does on its recruits. But we didn't know what kind. He told us Ahhazu—"

"Imagine that."

"—but they're minor-level functionaries. They can't do that kind of shit. And a demon can't possess another demon—or a half, for that matter. So two plus two, okay? His other half ain't Ahhazu, it's incubus. And there's only one half human, half incubus ever been recorded—"

"Maybe Pritkin's birth wasn't recorded."

"Bull*shit*. You know damn well who we got—"

"Don't say it."

"—next door, and John Pritkin ain't his—"

"I'm warning you."

"—name. It's motherfucking *Mer*—"

"Say it and spend the rest of your life in the *Jurassic*," I hissed.

We just stood there and breathed at each other.

"You gonna tell me I'm wrong?" Caleb finally said.

"I'm not going to tell you anything. Which is exactly what you're going to tell everyone else."

"Okay." He ran a hand over his buzz cut, which was too short for him to tear out. Which was probably just as well, judging from his expression. "Just for the hell of it, let's say I don't want to rat him out. Let's say I've worked with him long enough that maybe I don't want to see what'll happen after everyone finds out he had another name once. Let's say I'm on your side. What the fuck do you expect me to do? I already told you, too many people *saw*. And there's gonna have to be a report, and—"

"They didn't see what happened in the car. They only know—"

"That he's alive when he shouldn't be. And that's more than enough to pique some goddamned curiosity!"

"All right!" I said. "Give me a minute."

"I hope you don't need much more than that," he said grimly. "We got lucky when we came in, with almost everybody on shift called out to that disaster you left. But they're going to be back soon, plus the first day crew is going to be coming on and—"

"How long?"

He glanced at his watch. "Less than an hour before the day crew shows up. And probably nowhere near that long before the first groups start coming back from Disaster City. They're gonna need to make out reports before they go off the clock, and that takes—"

"So how long do we have?"

Black eyes met mine. "Minutes."

"Then we had best make good use of them," Pritkin said, opening the door behind us. "And you forgot a silence spell."

Caleb cursed. "I'm losing it."

"With cause."

"Damn straight with cause!" Caleb gazed at his friend, his eyes scanning the familiar features, as if he expected him to have suddenly sprouted horns.

"What is it?" Pritkin asked stiffly.

Caleb didn't answer for a moment; then he shrugged. "Nothing. Just never met a legend before."

"A legend is merely a man history decided to bugger," Pritkin said harshly. "I'm the same person I always was."

"Yeah, maybe. It's gonna take some getting used to."

"Then get used to it."

"Don't take that tone with me when I'm risking my ass—"

"Then don't look at me as if I'm a laboratory specimen on a slide!"

"Well, forgive the hell out of me for being a little fucking *traumatized*—"

"Will you two *shut up*?" I yelled.

They both turned to look at me. I hadn't actually intended to shout, but it seemed to have worked. And Pritkin was right; we needed to figure something out before Jonas showed up with his fussy little ways and his too-sharp blue eyes and his seemingly innocent questions, and we were screwed.

"We need to deal with this," I told them.

"I think that's been established," Caleb said nastily. "But unless you know—"

"What I know is that people like simple explanations for things. Especially weird things—"

"According to who?"

To every vampire I ever met, I didn't say, because it wouldn't have helped. "It's a fact of human nature," I said instead. "People don't like complicated answers. They like simple, easy-to-imagine ones. Ninety-nine times out of a hundred, if you give them two solutions—a really complex truth or a really simple lie—they'll take the lie. It's just easier."

"Okay, so what's our simple lie?"

"That I did it." I glanced at Pritkin. "We'll say I bubbled you. Like with the apple."

"But you can't do that yet."

"So? They don't know that."

"I am fairly certain that Jonas does," Pritkin said drily. "We need to come up with something else."

"We don't *have* anything else! And we don't—"

"What are you talking about?" That was Caleb.

"A trick," I said, glancing at him. "Or, really, it's not a trick; it's something Agnes could do with her power—speeding up time in a small area. I've been practicing—"

"And you can do that?" he interrupted.

"In theory."

He cursed.

"Look," I said impatiently. "The point isn't whether or not I can do it—"

"Then what is the point?"

"That I'm *supposed* to be able to do it! That a real . . . that a well-trained Pythia could do it. And it will be a lot easier for people to imagine that than a legend coming back to life and hanging out in their damn cafeteria!"

"*If* you could do it," Caleb said. "Maybe so. But you can't, and the old man knows you can't. So how is that—"

"He knows I *usually* can't, but that's not the same thing. I *can* do it, just not on demand. But occasionally I luck out and my power works for a change. And that's almost always in a crisis or when I'm pissed off or—"

"Which makes little sense," Pritkin said, interrupting me.

I looked at him. "What?"

"You said it yourself: you *can* use the power. You have proven that on a number of occasions—you prove it every time you shift. And the power is the power; it doesn't change. Merely your perception of it does."

"Meaning what?"

"That if you can use it under duress, you should be able to use it all the time. You should be able to use it at will."

"But I *can't*. I told you before: once in a while I get lucky, but most of the time—"

"Then perhaps you have been trying too hard. Did you not tell me that Lady Phemonoe said the power would teach you, that it would show you what it can do?"

"Yes, and I keep waiting—"

"And it has been showing you things, has it not? Or did Niall somehow teleport himself to that desert?"

"Niall?" Caleb asked.

"Jonas shouldn't have told you about that!" I said, flushing.

"He didn't do it to embarrass you," Pritkin said. "But as an example of your progress."

"Niall Edwards?" Caleb persisted.

"I'm not making progress!" I said furiously. "I haven't made any in weeks!"

"Not since the last crisis."

"What does that have to do with—"

"Niall I-fell-asleep-at-the-beach-and-that's-why-I'm-lobster-red Edwards?" Caleb asked.

Pritkin ignored him. "In a crisis, you forget to tell yourself that you can't do something. You forget your anxieties and your fears, your nervousness and your self-doubt, and you reach for your power. And it responds. It has been doing so since the first. I believe you have always been able to do what you need to do. You simply have to learn to get out of your own way, so to speak."

"If it was that easy, do you really think Initiates would need years of training?"

"There's more to being Pythia than manipulating the power, Cassie. You've primarily been dealing with that end because you've had no choice. From the beginning of your reign, we have been at war. I doubt Lady Phemonoe fought as many battles in her entire time in office as you have already done. But that is not normally the case, and a Pythia in peacetime has a number of other functions—"

I didn't say anything, but Pritkin cut off anyway. I guess my face must have spoken for me. "You *can* do this," he said simply.

I just stared at him. I wished that were true. I really, really did. But the fact was, I wasn't Lady Phemonoe, beloved Pythia. I wasn't even Elizabeth Palmer, heir extraordinaire. I was just Cassie, ex-secretary, lousy tarot reader and all-around screwup.

And coronation or not, I had a terrible, sneaking suspicion that I always would be.

"This is all very interesting," Caleb said. "But can we get back to the—" He broke off when a door slammed somewhere down the hall. Booted footsteps started coming our way, a lot of them, echoing loud on the cheap laminate tile. "They're back," he said, pretty unnecessarily.

Pritkin looked at me. "What are we going with?"

I spread my hands. "What I said. It's all we've got."

"Then we got nothing," Caleb said. "Speeding up healing might work on a cut or bruise or broken bone. But something like this? If you sped up time, it might speed up his healing, but it would also speed up the action of the corrosive. He'd just die faster!"

"But not if she slowed it down," Pritkin said thoughtfully. "You can say—"

"*I* can say?"

"Well, I can't be seen here in perfect health," he pointed out impatiently. "Not for a few days, until I could reasonably have been expected to heal. And Cassie is hardly up to an interrogation at the—"

"So you guys sneak out the back, and what? I stay here and lie my ass off?"

"Yes. Is there a problem with that?"

"Is there—" Caleb broke off, face flushing. "Oh, hell, no. Why would I possibly—"

"Good. Then all you need to say is that Cassie slowed down time around the car, except for you and her."

"Which would have made you die slower and nothing more!"

"Not if you used the opportunity to clean out the wound."

"With *what*? That stuff eats through everything it touches!"

"But some things take longer to dissolve than others," Pritkin said, looking pointedly at Caleb's shabby old leather coat.

Caleb clutched a lapel possessively. "No."

"Have you a better idea?"

"Yeah! I'll say we used your damn coat!"

"You can't. Too many people saw the shape it was in. There wasn't enough left to work with by the time—"

"Well, we're not using mine!" Caleb said angrily.

"I'll buy you another one—"

"I don't want another one! I've had this coat for twelve damn years—"

"Then perhaps it's time for an upgrade," I pointed out, grabbing a sleeve.

"Like hell! I just got it spelled the way I like—"

"I'll help you spell a new one," Pritkin told him, tugging at the back.

"Get off me!"

"Caleb," I put a hand on his arm. "Please?"

He looked at me and his lips tightened. "You're damn right you will," he told Pritkin. "And none of those little pansy-ass spells, either. I want the good stuff."

"You can make me a list."

"Fuckin' A I'll make you a list," Caleb muttered, and stripped off his coat. "You know, legend or not, you're still a royal pain in my ass."

Pritkin nodded approvingly. "Now you're getting the idea."

Chapter Thirty

Five minutes later, Pritkin and I were haring across a dark parking lot that was rapidly becoming less so as sunrise toyed with the horizon. But nobody was around, and we had enough darkness left to get away clean and things seemed to be looking up. Until I put a hand on the door of his beat-up jalopy—and froze.

Draped over the passenger seat and trailing halfway onto the floor was Pritkin's battered old potion belt. It was just a strip of worn leather, darkened in places from handling, with the nicks and scratches you'd expect from long use. A few enchanted vials filled with sludgy substances were still in place, like oversized bullets on a bandolier. Others had been used in the fight, leaving lighter places on the leather, like a toddler with missing teeth.

There was nothing remotely sexy about it. But I had a sudden, visceral image of the last time I'd seen it, arcing against the night as it was thrown over the front seat of the car. And I shivered, hard.

Pritkin glanced at me sharply, and his face tensed. "It will pass," he said roughly, and threw the belt in back.

I bit my lip and nodded, which was pretty much all I could do with a sensory memory of pleasure ripping through me. It tightened my body, blurred my vision and sent goose bumps washing over my skin in waves. It was . . .

shockingly realistic. He was on the opposite side of the car, not touching me, not even close. But suddenly, I could smell his scent, taste his sweat, feel his lips on my skin. They were warm and soft, unlike the hard fingers digging into my hips as he held me in place, as he—

I made a small sound and shuddered again, my breathing picking up, my hand tightening on the side of the car hard enough to hurt. I prized my fingers off and wrapped my arms around myself and rode it out. I was suddenly really grateful for the trench, which was too thick and too loose to show any inconvenient signs of my little flashback.

After a minute, I got in, not because it had stopped, but because cars were starting to come back in larger numbers, popping out of the ley line in strobes of blue-white light, sending cracks like thunder echoing against the building. Pritkin put the car into gear and we pulled out the normal way, I guess to avoid the metaphysical traffic jam. We eased through a fence, a ward rippling around us like water, and slid into the empty streets of predawn Vegas.

This far out, it was mostly asphalt and industrial buildings, in between empty lots of hard-packed red soil, a few desert plants and blacktop. It didn't look much like the glitzy, glittery city of the tourist brochures, but it had a stark kind of beauty nonetheless. Distant scarlet veils of dust turned the sunrise spectacular and painted the buildings in black and gold. I watched the landscape pass by blearily, so tired I could hardly keep my eyes open, and so aroused I wanted to scream.

Yeah, this was fun.

"This didn't happen last time," I finally said, mostly as a distraction.

"I didn't feed as completely last time," Pritkin told me, as I tried to control my breathing and failed utterly.

I swallowed. "How . . . how long?"

"Usually five or ten minutes. Do you want to stop?"

"No!" The only thing keeping me from grabbing him was the fact that he was driving.

He didn't say anything for a moment, and I concentrated on not writhing against the seat. It didn't go so well. I wiped my hands on the skirt of the trench and left sweaty palm prints on the beige fabric. I stared at them, teary-eyed and hurting and desperate. God, if this didn't stop soon, I was going to go *completely*—

"After Ruth died, I went somewhat mad for a time," Pritkin said suddenly.

I blinked, because that had come completely out of the blue. And almost read my mind. "Y-you did?"

He nodded. "My memories of those days are hazy at best, but apparently I attempted to kill my father. I suppose I blamed him for her death, although I can't say I recall the exact thought process. I do remember a strong desire to feel the bones of his neck breaking under my hands, however, which may give some indication."

I licked my lips. "But you didn't succeed."

"No, but I came damned close. So close, in fact, that, along with several past . . . indiscretions . . . it convinced the demon council that I was an intolerable threat. They sentenced me to death."

"Death?" I turned to look at him, shocked for a moment out of everything else. "But . . . but you didn't succeed. And you said yourself you weren't sane—"

"None of which matters under demon law."

"But you're still alive."

"Yes, due to my father's interference."

"Your father?"

Pritkin smiled slightly. "He was livid. I don't recall much about those days, as I've said. But I do recall him storming into the council chamber and accusing them of attempted robbery—of his only physical child. He said that the damage had been done to him, and therefore he, as a member of council, should be allowed to set the sentence. They agreed."

"And what was the sentence?" I asked, almost afraid to find out.

"I was to return to court and take up my proper duties as his heir. The ones I had flatly refused to carry out before. He assumed, I suppose, that I would prefer that over death. He assumed wrong."

"Wait. You chose to *die*?"

"Better that, I thought, than to live for centuries as his slave. And at the time . . . at the time I can't recall caring very much if I lived or died. I told them to carry out the sentence and be done with it. They were about to comply when he intervened again—with a compromise."

"What kind of compromise?" I asked warily. Because I knew it couldn't be anything good.

"That I would be banished from the demon realms, unable to return, under pain of death."

I frowned. "Banished where?"

"Here. To Earth."

"But . . . but that doesn't seem like much of a sentence. You'd been living here anyway."

"That is what the council said. They pointed out that many full demons would give a great deal to be 'banished' to this world, where they can feed like nowhere else in the demon realms."

I nodded. Pritkin had told me before that one of the main reasons the council existed was to regulate the numbers of demons allowed on Earth at any one time. Otherwise, there would have been a free-for-all.

"So why did they allow you to come back?"

"They were persuaded by my father's argument that there can be few punishments more severe than sending a starving man into a banquet hall—and not allowing him to eat."

"Not allowing—" I stopped, unsure I'd understood. But I'd seen Pritkin eat plenty, so I knew we weren't talking about regular food. "You mean . . . you can't . . . at *all*?"

"The agreement I made was simple: no sex, of the demon or human varieties. Else I would forfeit my 'parole' and be returned to my father's court, forever to remain under his absolute authority."

"That's . . . but . . ." I looked around in a panic, why I don't know. Like Rosier would be chasing us in a car. "Is he coming for you *now*? After what we did?"

Pritkin shook his head. "Feeding to save my life was specifically exempted. My father does not want me dead, as you saw. He wants me alive and in his service, and I think he was afraid that not allowing me to feed in emergencies would ruin his plan."

"He didn't think you could do it," I said slowly. "Stay here, I mean."

"No. He was certain I would break, that I would be back

within the decade, two at the outside. And either is a trifling amount of time for the demon races. He had waited hundreds of years already. What were a few more?"

"He underestimated you."

"I believe there were wagers made at court as to exactly how long I would last, all of which have now expired."

"But ... did you know what it would be like when you—"

"No." Pritkin huffed out a humorless laugh. "No."

"But you must have thought—"

"At the time, I don't believe I was capable of much thought of any kind. But insofar as I was ... I truly did not believe I would ever want intimacy again. The very idea was repulsive, on every possible level. I was horrified at what I had done, at what I had become—"

"You didn't become anything! It was your father's fault, your wife's decision. It had nothing to do with you."

"Other than the fact that I was the instrument of her death."

"Yes, which makes you the victim here, not the ... the monster!"

"Not in the eyes of my fellow monsters. Unlike most of the other races, the incubi have a reputation for showing ... some consideration ... for their partners. It is often selfish, of course; it is easier than constantly finding new prey. But nonetheless, there were those at my father's court who shunned me after what happened. Creatures I had long held in disdain were ashamed—*ashamed*—to be associated with me. And I didn't blame them. I felt like I would never want to feed again."

"And later?" I asked softly. It was none of my business, but I just couldn't imagine what it must have been like. I didn't know too many humans who could shun all intimacy like that, much less someone whose body was specifically designed to need it.

"Later ..." His lips twisted. "I began to understand why my father had been willing to make that deal. I had understood intellectually from the first, of course, but the reality was ... somewhat different."

"You still feel like this, don't you?" I asked, in shock. "What I'm feeling now—all the time?"

"Not all the time, no. It was almost constant for more than a decade—"

"A *decade?*" He shot me a glance, and for some reason, it was amused. Because clearly, the man was *insane.* "How—"

"I am ashamed to say that I became rather addicted to a number of substances during that time, in an attempt to ... to survive, I suppose you would say. It didn't help much, nothing did, but the struggle became easier over time, as the demon part of me became weaker. And I obtained an outlet for my energies in hunting down those who had done as I had—only on purpose."

I didn't say anything for a moment. I watched the sand turn mauve and crimson and honey as the night slowly retreated before the sun. And thought about what it would be like to have a part of yourself literally starving to death and yet unable to die. And to know that if you gave in, even once, to the constant, gnawing hunger, you would forever forfeit your freedom.

"Your father is a son of a *bitch*," I said, with feeling.

"I wouldn't argue the point," he said drily. "However, from his perspective, he feels cheated. He spent a considerable amount of time over the centuries trying and failing to have a physical child. And when he finally managed it, against all the odds, the result was not ... quite what he'd expected."

"Too damned bad! A lot of parents have children who aren't exactly what they thought they would be. But they learn to love them anyway."

"Most parents aren't demon lords. And love was never the issue."

"It should have been."

"For someone who deals in it, or its physical manifestation, as much as my father, he knows astonishingly little about it."

Pritkin was quiet for a few moments, and I knew I should probably drop it. But he opened up so rarely, I fully expected tomorrow to come and the lid to be clamped down again, tight. If I didn't ask now, I might never have a chance. And it wasn't like the guy was shy. If he didn't want to talk, he'd tell me. Probably pretty bluntly.

"Is that why you're a health nut now?" I asked. "To make up for those early days?"

"No, it was more an attempt to compensate slightly for the power loss I had sustained when I stopped feeding."

"What power loss?"

"As I told you, I had never merged with other demons, never tried to enhance what I was born with, as it would have merely made me more useful to my father. And him that much less likely to let me go. But much of my strength had nonetheless always come from . . . my other half, if you like. And once it was incapacitated, I had to find other ways to compensate."

"Like the potions."

He nodded. "I was never greatly interested in them before. But they became a way of balancing the power loss. And I find making them to be . . . calming. Some of the more deadly require utter concentration, and I discovered that when I was focused on something so completely, it helped to curb the hunger. Do you not agree?"

I didn't know what he meant for a second, until I realized—the flashback was gone. My breathing was normal, my heart rate steady, my hands still sweaty, but only as a leftover. I relaxed back against the seat with a sigh.

"Thank you." It was heartfelt.

"One learns coping mechanisms over time—"

"Or one goes insane?"

"Some would say I already am."

"They'd be wrong."

We slid to a stop at a crossroads, and Pritkin turned slightly in his seat to look at me. "And how would you know?"

We were close enough that I could see his long, sandy eyelashes, almost close enough to count the whiskers of the end-of-day beard shading his jaw. He hadn't had a chance to torture his hair yet, and it was looking soft and oddly flat, and was blowing slightly in the breeze coming across the windshield. It made him look younger somehow, gentler, sweeter. . . .

I mentally rolled my eyes at myself. Yeah, sure.

Pritkin was annoying, stubborn, secretive, impatient and rude. He had the tact of a Parris Island drill sergeant and the charm of a barbed-wire fence. He regularly made me want to slap him and other people want to shoot him, and that was without even trying. I'd probably yelled at him more than anybody else in my entire life, and I'd known him less than two months.

And yet he was also loyal and honest and brave and weirdly kind. Most of the time, I didn't understand him at all. But I knew one thing.

"I grew up with some genuinely crazy men," I told him harshly. "You're not one."

"Then what am I?"

I pushed a strand of wildly waving hair out of his eyes. It just wouldn't behave for shit, would it? Kind of reminded me of the man.

"Pritkin," I said simply. It sort of summed up the whole, crazy package.

His lips twitched. "Do you know, no one else calls me that?"

"What about the guys in the Corps?"

"They usually call me by my given name if they know me, or by my rank if they do not."

I thought about that. For some reason, it made me happy. "Good."

He shook his head, refusing to let the smile out. I don't know why. Like it might damage something.

"Where do you want to go?"

I sighed. "Back to the suite."

"Are you sure? We can make other arrangements, and there's the fact that . . ."

"That what?"

"That Jonas won't like it."

I raised an eyebrow. "Does it matter?"

He did smile slightly then, and put the car in gear. "Now you sound like a Pythia."

Chapter Thirty-one

I guess I fell asleep in the car, because I didn't remember getting back. Or getting into pink-striped shorty pj's. Or falling headfirst into bed. But I must have. Because I woke up tangled in my own sheets, the pillow half over my head and sunlight leaking in through a crack in the drapes.

I rolled over, feeling groggy and thickheaded and gritty-eyed and yucky. It was so much like yesterday that, for a minute, I thought it had all been a dream. But even my dreams weren't that bizarre. And then I tried to move, and immediately knew it had been real enough.

Because I got the charley horse from hell in my left calf.

I didn't shriek—it wasn't that loud. But to a vampire's ears, it must have been loud enough, because the bedroom door burst open and Marco rushed in, gun in hand and face pretty damn scary. He looked around wildly, I suppose for something to shoot, and when he didn't find anything, he grabbed me.

"What is it? What's wrong?"

I stared up at him, still half-asleep and disoriented from the pain, and didn't say anything.

"Cassie!"

"Charley horse," I finally managed to gasp, only it didn't seem to do any good. Because he just stared at me, uncomprehending, as the room quickly filled up with vamps.

And then he blinked. "Did you say *charley horse*?"

I nodded tearfully.

Marco said something profane and shoved his gun into the small of his back. "Get outta here," he told the others, who melted away into the shadows, looking absurdly grateful.

He sighed and sat on the edge of the bed. "Where does it hurt?"

"Everywhere."

It wasn't an exaggeration. It felt like my entire body had whiplash. I was beginning to understand why Fred had said he hated lasso spells. Of course, the one that had made me feel like shit had also saved my life, but that wasn't all that comforting at the moment.

I held up my left leg, which was cramped so badly I couldn't even straighten it out. Marco's big hand smoothed gently over the muscle, and then he applied a little pressure. I gasped in pain and then in wonder, as the muscle suddenly released. It still hurt like a bitch, a dull throbbing that mirrored the racing of my heart. But at least I could breathe.

"You know, I've lived a long time," he told me, massaging the calf more firmly now. "And I met a lot of people. But I ain't never met a woman made me want to beat her to death as often as you."

"Sorry," I choked out, and tried to pull away, but his hand held me firm.

"You're not going anywhere," Marco said. "Not until we have a little chat."

But he didn't chat; he didn't talk at all. He just continued the long, soothing strokes with those big fingers, so clumsy-looking but so deft in movement. And after a few moments, I felt my body slowly relax. "You're good at that."

"Had a lot of practice."

"Really? Where?" I asked, less because I wanted to know than to postpone the bitching-out I was about to get. Usually, I held my own pretty well, even with the vamps. But right now, it didn't feel like I had anything left.

Marco shot me a look that said he knew damned well what I was doing, but then he shrugged. "The lanista I worked for had me ready the men for combat. They fought better if they were loose, or so he thought."

"Lanista?"

"Guy who owned a bunch of gladiators."

"I thought you were in the army."

A bushy black eyebrow rose, but he didn't ask. "I was. Worked and scraped my way up to centurion, just in time to see the empire crumble around me. I was almost dead after a battle, when some men dug me out of the blood and the muck and carried me off. Turns out they worked for a vampire with an entrepreneurial streak, and he liked ex-army."

He added a little extra pressure, and I moaned, but not because it hurt. That leg felt better now, although it just highlighted how sore the rest of me was. It was like I hadn't been able to concentrate on all my other aches and pains until the big one got taken care of. And now they were all clamoring for help.

Marco just shook his head at me. "Turn over."

I turned over, and those big hands got to work on my back. I stifled a whimper in the pillow, because Marco's idea of a massage bore no resemblance whatsoever to the relaxing spa variety. There was no lavender oil, no soothing music, no hot towels. Just an all-out assault on cramped muscles, until they cowered in surrender and turned to Jell-O.

"Why did this vampire like ex-army?" I gasped after a few minutes, mostly to give myself something else to think about.

"Fortunatus was in the business of providing gladiators for the rich. Politicos who wanted to play up to the crowds, or fat cats trying to outdo each other in private events. The best money came from fights to the death, but it cost him a lot to train a gladiator well enough to put on a good show. Having him die in a death match one of the first times he fought wasn't good business, even at the prices he charged."

"So he picked people who were already trained?"

"No, he picked people who were already trained, and then he made 'em vampires. That way, the crowds could watch us 'die' over and over, but he didn't have to constantly replenish his stock. We—" He stopped when I turned over and stared at him. "It was a long time ago."

"That's horrible!"

"That's life. If his men hadn't seen me on that battle-field, hadn't decided that a centurion was just what the boss had ordered, I never woulda made it. I almost didn't any-way. Took him two months to nurse me back to health so he could kill me."

I swallowed. "I hope you weren't with him long."

"A century, give or take."

"A *century*?"

"Until the games were outlawed." Marco pushed me back down and started on my shoulders. "Christianity didn't approve, maybe 'cause a few too many of their peo-ple had ended up in 'em, and not by choice. You know?"

I nodded.

"And once it started to spread, the politicians stopped financing matches, because they started to cost them votes 'stead of the other way around. And then the emperor con-verted and passed a law against it, and while some people still held them illegally, there weren't enough to make it worth Fortunatus's time. He traded me to another master who needed a bodyguard, and I just got shuffled around after that."

"And ended up with Mircea."

"You know the score. Gotta belong to someone."

"But you're a senior master." I pointed out. "You could have a court of your own, if you wanted."

"Yeah. And have all the expense and the headaches and the diplomatic shit to deal with, and still have to answer to somebody. Everybody's the same; can't wait to move up, to hit fifth or fourth or third level, and strike out on their own. Only to find out the same thing."

"And what's that?"

His hands stilled on my back. "That there's no freedom in our world, Cassie. If I left Mircea, I'd have to ally with some other high-level master in order to survive. And then I'd be dragged into his life, his fights, just like now. Every-body answers to somebody; everybody has restrictions they got to put up with. Even senators. Even Mircea."

I was starting to see why Marco had been willing to get on this topic. I sighed and buried my head in the pillow. "Even Pythias?"

"Everybody takes orders from somebody," he repeated.

"Mircea takes 'em from the Consul, and believe me, some-times, he really don't like it. But he does it."

I turned over and regarded Marco tiredly. "Yes, and why does he do it?"

Marco frowned. "It's his job."

"And she's his boss, his superior."

"Yeah."

"And there's your answer."

"There's what answer?"

I sighed. "Mircea does what the Consul orders because he's her servant."

"Yes?"

"But I am not his."

I got up and went to the bathroom.

Of course, Marco followed. "You are not his."

"His girlfriend, yes. His servant, no. I can't be and do my job."

"You've done it pretty well so far. What the hell do you think Mircea's gonna ask you to do?"

"I don't know. But that's not the point, is it?" I started running hot water in the tub.

"Then what is the point?"

"That he can *ask* whatever he wants. I'll probably even do it most of the time. I'd have done it last night, if it had been a request. I'd had the day from hell; I really didn't want to go anywhere. But it wasn't a request; it was an or-der. And if I start taking orders from a senator—any senator—I may as well forget having anyone take me seri-ously."

"The Consul takes Mircea seriously."

"As a valued servant, yes. But she knows that, when she pushes, he'll do what she wants. He owes his job to her, so he can never be truly impartial. But I have to be, or the Circle will ignore me as a vampire pawn, and the Senate will ignore me because they can order me around, and it'll be . . . the Tony Syndrome all over again. And I won't live like that. I just won't!"

Marco sat down on the side of the tub, making the por-celain creak. "What's the Tony Syndrome?"

Somebody had restocked the bath salts, and I threw half the jar into the water. "Most seers see both sides of life," I told him. "They see the baby somebody has been hoping for, or the long-overdue promotion, or the love of their life, right around the corner. It helps balance out the bad stuff, the stuff nobody wants to see. The earthquakes and the bomb plots and the fires and the car crashes. But I never had that balance. I don't see the good stuff. I never did."

"That's rough."

"It's . . . exhausting. It's depressing. It keeps you from enjoying a lot of life because, even when you're having a good day, suddenly you'll see someone else's pain, someone else's grief. And the record scratches, you know?"

He nodded.

"Eventually, I learned how not to see things. But for a long time, I didn't have that ability. The only way I could deal was by telling myself that the stuff I saw was in the future, and that maybe some of it could be averted. That maybe I could change things, at least for a few people. And Tony promised me he'd get the word out."

"And he lied."

"Of course he lied. But I was a kid and I believed him, maybe because I wanted to believe him. When I finally figured it out and confronted him, he just shrugged and told me that there was more profit in tragedy."

"That sounds like that fat little weasel." Marco regarded me narrowly. "You're saying you expect the Senate to go around averting tragedies?"

"No. But if I see something coming, something potentially disastrous for our world, I expect them to listen to me. I expect them to trust me. And right now, I don't know that they respect me enough to do that."

Marco sighed and looked at me, his elbows resting on massive thighs. "Look, I'm gonna tell you something, and if you repeat it, I'll deny it. But the master shouldn't have given that order. He ought to know you well enough by now to know what was gonna happen. But he did it anyway, because he's scared and he's stressed and he don't always see so clear where you are concerned. But that don't mean he don't respect you."

"Well, it sure doesn't mean that he does!" I said, swirling the soap around, a little more forcefully than necessary.

"He talks about you a lot in the family. He's proud of you—anybody can see that."

"Anybody but me."

"He may not say it to you, but that's the truth."

"Then why doesn't he say it to me? Right now, I feel like . . . like one of those floozies you talked about—"

"I never used the word 'floozy'—"

"—who is supposed to hang around, shopping and doing her nails and waiting for her lord and master to show up! That's how he treats me, so why shouldn't I believe that's how he sees me?"

"Because he probably does like the thought of you shopping and doing your nails instead of the kind of shit you usually get up to! And because he's a politician and don't want to give up an advantage."

"Advantage in what?"

"In the power games you two got going—"

"This isn't about power."

"The hell it's not."

"It isn't! I don't want to order Mircea around. I don't want to order the Senate or the Circle around. I just want them—"

"To take you seriously. To listen to you. To be guided by what you tell them. And that translates into power, don't it?"

"It translates into doing my job."

Marco looked at me for a moment and started to say something, and then he just shook his head. "I thought I'd never meet somebody as bullheaded as the master," he told me. "But what do you know."

"I'm not trying to be stubborn."

"I know. It's like with Mircea; you don't got to try. It comes naturally."

I sighed. "I guess I need to talk to him."

I don't know what my expression looked like, but Marco laughed. "Yeah, but you get a reprieve. He said he'll call you tonight, late. He's got a thing all day."

"What kind of a thing?"

He shrugged. "Senate stuff, I guess. You'll have to ask him."

"What about Jonas?" I might as well get one awkward conversation out of the way.

"He called a while ago, while you were asleep. Said— Hang on." Marco fished a notebook out of his back pocket and flipped it open. "Said he thought he might know what attacked you last night. He's not sure, but thinks they could be something called the Spartoi."

"Spartans?"

"No—that's what I thought, too, but he spelled it for me. And it's Spar*toi*. There's supposed to be five of them, sons of Ares and some dragon—"

I looked up from shutting off the water. "Dragon?"

"Yeah, one of the Fey. They can shape-shift, you know?"

"Yeah," I said slowly. And that would explain why the damn dragon had been so hard to kill. I'd seen Pritkin and a friend of his, Mac, take on one before, and it hadn't been anything like that. But then, that other dragon hadn't been a half god, either.

"Anything else?" I demanded. "Like how we're supposed to fight these things?"

"I think the idea is not to," Marco said drily. "He said for you to stay in the hotel today. He's tripled the guards, so nothing should get in here. He needs to do some more research, but he'll talk to you tomorrow." Marco flipped over a page in his notebook, but must not have found anything, because he flipped back. "And that's it."

I kind of thought that was enough. Apparently, Marco did, too, because he was looking a little worried, like he was afraid I was about to break down on him again. I wasn't. I was too pissed off. It looked like the other side didn't worry about little things like playing fair. One not-so-great clairvoyant against five freaking demigods seemed a little one-sided to me. No wonder it had almost gotten Pritkin killed!

"You okay?" Marco asked.

"Yeah." I forced a smile, because none of this was his fault. "I was just thinking—I have all day with nobody bitching at me."

He grinned. "Well, I can, if it'll make you feel better."

"You just did!"

"Naw, that wasn't bitching. You should hear me when I get going."

"I'm afraid."

"Hold that thought." Marco ruffled my hair and left. I stripped and got in the tub, sinking down in the water up to my chin.

It felt good. It felt better than good, and not just because of my sore muscles. Three days ago, something had tried to drown me in this very tub, and now I was back, relaxing in it. I had a stinky charm around my neck and a vampire probably listening at the door, but still. That was progress.

My feet floated to the top of the water and I stared at my poor, chipped toenail polish. I thought about redoing it. I thought about making Augustine's life miserable. I thought about going to the salon and seeing if any of the guys could do something about my hair.

But none of that had much appeal. It was hard to concentrate on my to-do list with the sword of Damocles hanging over my head. It felt like I was just marking time, waiting for the next attack. And that was getting really old.

I was sick and tired of playing defense. But to play offense, I needed some help, and I didn't know where to get it. Or, rather, I did, I just didn't know how.

Assuming Jonas's crazy theories weren't quite so crazy after all, I needed to find a goddess—fast. And I thought there was a tiny chance that the one I needed was still hanging around. It had been her spell that banished the other gods, after all, so maybe it hadn't affected her. And maybe she hadn't wanted to go back to a world filled with a bunch of pissed-off fellow gods. In fact, the more I thought about it, the more it seemed like helping humanity might have stuck her with us. If she had gone home, wouldn't her fellow gods have forced her to lift the spell by now? They obviously wanted back in pretty badly, and she could hardly have stood up to all of them. And gods were supposed to be immortal, weren't they? So if she hadn't gone home, it was at least possible that she was still here.

But even if that was the case, she hadn't been seen in three thousand years. And anyone who had hidden that long had probably gotten pretty good at it. Barring a vision with a map, I had no freaking clue where to start looking. And without a clue, I wasn't likely to get a vision. It was a vicious catch-22.

I needed somebody who could point me in the right direction.

I needed somebody who knew about gods.

I needed *a* god.

Fortunately, I knew three of them.

Chapter Thirty-two

For a hotel designed to look like hell, Dante's wasn't so bad. It had been themed to within an inch of its life by someone who subscribed strongly to the "more is more" concept of decorating. But this was Vegas, where tackiness passed for ambience and vulgarity was all part of the fun.

But this wasn't fun. This was just plain sad.

"You let guests come down here?" I asked, gazing around at what passed for a bus entrance. A few sickly topiaries guarded a cracked cement floor covered with oil and gas stains. There was trash in the corners and dirt on the walls, and the whole place smelled like pee.

"Nobody comes to Vegas on a bus," Casanova, the hotel manager, said while feeling around inside his suit coat. It was a pale wheat color, one of his favorites because it set off his Spanish good looks. But it was a little incongruous in this setting, like an Armani model who had taken a wrong turn and ended up on skid row. "At least, no one who stays here."

"So why have it at all?"

"Because some people want to take tours—Grand Canyon, Valley of Fire, Hoover freaking Dam," he said impatiently. "And they get pissy if there isn't a place for them to be picked up on-site."

"And this is what you came up with?"

Casanova shot me a look out of sloe-dark eyes that would have been attractive if they'd had a different mind behind them. "If they're taking a bus, they're leaving the casino."

"So?"

"So they're not going be spending any money here."

"So screw 'em?"

"Exactly."

His hand emerged with a slim-bodied flashlight, which he shone around. There were fluorescents overhead, but they weren't on. A spill of late-afternoon daylight leached away part of the gloom on either side of the echoing space, and some electric light spilled down the nonfunctioning escalator behind us. But that still left the main part of the garage a dark cavern.

"I don't think anybody's down here," I told him, halfway hoping that was true.

"Oh, they're here, all right," he said grimly. "Took my boys the better part of two weeks, but they finally managed to track them. Now come on."

I pushed limp blond hair out of my eyes and followed him into the gloom, feeling a trickle of sweat slide down my back. The place was hot as an oven—apparently airconditioning was another thing bus-loving tourists were denied. And despite the fact that we'd been down here only a few minutes, the back of my blue tee and the waistband on my jean shorts were already soaked.

"Why do people come to Vegas in summer?" I complained. "It's the biggest tourist season, which makes no sense. It has to be a hundred twenty degrees out."

"The kids are out of school."

"But most people don't take kids here. That whole family-friendly thing kind of fell flat."

"Exactly." His flashlight bounced off the ceiling, as if he thought our prey might be clinging to the rafters like bats. It didn't help my mood that, for all I knew, they could be. "The kids are out of school, so parents need a break from the little bastards."

"It's a good thing you don't have children!"

Nervousness had made my voice harsh, but Casanova didn't seem to take offense. "One of the best things about being a vampire. Now stop talking and start looking."

We edged farther into the darkness and my hands started to sweat, and not just from the heat. He was right about one thing: most of the people flooding into Vegas these days were adults, with fully half of them seniors. Which might explain why the three old crones we were after hadn't been attracting the attention they deserved.

Well, that, and the fact that they were ancient demi-goddesses with more than one trick up their sleeves. That was what had me clutching the slim black box I carried hard enough to leave my fingers white. It was a magical trap, the kind that had once imprisoned the trio known as the Graeae long enough for their story to fade into legend.

I suspected that they didn't want to go back in.

That was fine with me, because I didn't want to put them there. I just wanted to ask them some questions, assuming we ever found them. But Casanova wasn't exactly an altruistic kind of guy, and I'd had to fudge a little on my motivations.

"I don't know why you're being so helpful all of a sudden," he said suspiciously, as if he'd heard my thoughts.

"I'm always helpful."

"You're never helpful! You drop problems in my lap all the time and then disappear somewhere and leave me to deal with them."

"Name one."

"Those blasted kids you swore would be out of here two weeks ago!"

He was referring to some magical orphans he had less than charitably taken in until we could find other homes for them. The casino had more than a thousand rooms, but the two the kids were occupying preyed on his shriveled little soul. He acted like it was causing him actual pain.

"Tami is working on it," I said, talking about their de facto foster mother. "It's hard to find a house big enough for that many people that's reasonable to rent."

"And why bother when you can stay here and eat me out of house and home?"

"They don't eat that much."

"In comparison to what? Starving marines?"

I rolled my eyes. "Well, they'll be out soon—"

"That's what you always say."

"—and I'm helping you today, aren't I?"

"About damn time, too," Casanova muttered, stopping to peer into a curbside drain as if he seriously thought someone might have squeezed down there. I looked in along with him until my brain conjured up a memorable scene from *It*, and I shied back nervously. He glanced over his shoulder, an annoyed frown creasing those handsome features.

"What is wrong with you?"

"Nothing." I didn't really think there were any homicidal clowns down there—or any ancient goddesses, either—but you never knew. This was Dante's. Crazy was what we had for breakfast when we ran out of Corn Flakes.

"Good, because this is all your fault," he complained. "You are *not* going to come up with another reason not to help me."

I didn't say anything, because technically, he was right. I'd sprung the gals from jail, and nobody seemed to care that it had been an accident. Least of all Casanova, whose beloved casino had become their favorite stomping ground.

"Why are you so interested in getting them out of here?" I asked, as we moved onto a loading dock. "They've been out for almost six weeks, and the worst thing I've seen them do is rip apart a slot machine." And anyone who had ever played the one-armed bandits on the Strip could certainly sympathize with that.

"Well, one little thing would be that they keep breaking into the upper-level suites," he said acidly. "The Consul came out of her bedroom the other day to find them swimming in the pool on her balcony!"

I grinned.

"It's not funny!"

Considering that it had once been *my* balcony, before she'd pulled rank and kicked me out, I kind of disagreed. "Did they eat all her food?"

"There wasn't any food. But they drank all the booze and beat up the guards she sent to remove them. They were there almost three hours before they went off to terrorize someone else. She wants them gone!"

"And God forbid anybody should inconvenience her," I said sourly.

To my surprise, Casanova agreed. "I'm losing money every day that the damn Senate stays in residence. They're using half of my suites—for which I've yet to see a dime in payment—co-opting my staff, taking over the conference rooms and eating me out of house and home!"

"This is only temporary. They'll be gone soon."

"Yes, leaving me with a trashed hotel, a ruined conference schedule and debts out my ears!"

"Mircea will understand—"

"Mircea doesn't give a shit about this hotel," Casanova said viciously. "Mircea cares about the damn war. If I drown in red ink, it's all the same to him. He writes it off as a tax loss and transfers me to some dead-end job where I can molder away for another century or so." He suddenly rounded on me, shining the light in my eyes and making me wince. "And that's not going to happen, you understand? This is my one shot at the big time. Those old crones aren't going to ruin it for me, and neither are you!"

"I'm not trying to—" I began, but he was already pushing forward again, muttering something indistinct in Spanish.

I scowled and started to follow, when a grizzled head popped out of nowhere in front of me. It was hanging upside down, the long, gray curls streaming earthward like moss on a plantation. It was Deino, the one who had always had a soft spot for me—at least until I started hunting her.

Like all the girls, she had a scrunched-up dried apple of a face with enough wrinkles to make a shar-pei jealous. It was a little hard to read the expression that was probably buried under there somewhere. But she wasn't smiling.

Her chin dipped toward the trap I still clutched, and a few more wrinkles appeared on the weather-beaten face. "Um," I said awkwardly.

It was hard to know what to say, since I'd been caught red-handed. And how much English she understood was problematic, anyway. But it didn't matter, because before I could figure it out, she suddenly leaned over and kissed me on the cheek.

"Heh," she said, and popped back out.

And so did the box.

I whipped my head around, but I didn't see anything. Except for Casanova looking behind some stacked crates. "Uh, we may have a problem," I told him nervously.

"What's wrong now?" he demanded, brushing at a cobweb that had dared to sully his formerly pristine linen.

I didn't answer, because I was staring at another ancient crone who was prowling toward him over the tops of the crates. Her movements weren't remotely old, ladylike or, for that matter, particularly human. Enyo had gotten her hair cut, I noticed irrelevantly, right before Casanova winked out of existence.

For a moment, I just stood there while she bared toothless gums at me and cackled. Then she held up the black box and shook it suggestively. There was no doubt at all what had happened to the vampire.

"Oh, shit," I said. Enyo cackled again and then paused, before holding the box out like a gift. I eyed it suspiciously. "You're giving him to me?"

She nodded, grinning like a fiend. I suspected a trap, but, then, if the girls had wanted me in that box, they could have managed it easily enough. So maybe they were just trying to teach Casanova a lesson.

I tentatively took a step forward, then two. I put out a hand and almost had my fingers on it when Enyo flicked her wrist, tossing it over my head to Pemphredo, the third member of the trio. She was crouched on top of a nearby van, wearing grizzled pigtails and a "Vegas Made Me Do It" T-shirt, and peering at me out of the one eye they all shared.

She watched me silently for a moment, then slowly held out the box. Like I was actually going to fall for that again. "No, I don't want to play," I told her. "Really."

That was too bad, because it looked like I was in the minority.

"I want him back," I said. Pemphredo shot me a look. "Okay, maybe not actually *want*, but you know how it is."

She tilted her head inquiringly. Clearly, she didn't know. That was a problem, because I didn't, either.

"See, it's like this," I said, trying to come up with a reason why they should let him go. "He's annoying."

The girls nodded. This, apparently, we could all agree on.

"And . . . and obviously he had no right to try to trap you like that. I mean, it's not like you've been doing anything wrong."

More nods.

"It's just . . . um . . ." I stopped, trying to recall why *I* wanted the guy back. I thought about it while they all waited politely. I gave up. "Look, I don't really have a good reason for you to give him back," I said honestly. "He's a crabby, self-centered, egotistical, money-grubbing snob. His own employees don't even like him much. But it could be worse. If you cart him off somewhere, they'll have to get a new manager. And he might be a lot more of a hard-ass."

They exchanged glances.

I didn't know if that was a good sign or not, but I decided to push ahead anyway. "And if you let him out, I'll talk to him for you. Maybe if he gives you a suite, you can promise not to go breaking into the others anymore?"

Further glances were exchanged.

"A nice suite?"

Enyo made a little come-hither movement with her hand. It looked like I was getting warm.

"With room service?"

Ding, ding, ding, we had a winner. At least I guessed so, because she handed me the box.

I tucked it under an arm instead of letting him out, because I didn't want to deal with the drama right now. "I, uh, I had another reason for coming down here," I told them.

Pemphredo had been about to crawl off, but at that she came back and settled down, brushing off her filthy shorts. Deino crossed her legs. Enyo stopped picking at her fingernails with a knife and put it politely away.

I kind of felt like I should be serving tea.

"It's like this," I said. "It's starting to feel like Grand Central around here for demigods. You know what I mean?"

They nodded.

"First it was this Morrigan person. She's this half-Fey child of Ares who tried to possess me. And that really sucked."

More nods.

"But it didn't work, so then she possessed this mage who tried to kill me and almost succeeded."

That got me a little pat from Deino.

"And then, last night, a bunch more demigods showed up. A guy I know thinks they may be something called the Spartoi, which would make them also children of Ares. Plus, I think they were also after my mother way back when—at least, they fought the same as those other guys and . . . Anyway, I don't think these attacks are just going to stop, you know?"

Nods all around.

"I'm pretty sure I'm going to have to deal with them, only I don't know how. But there's this prophecy that says I can get help if I find a goddess. The one they used to call Artemis back in Greece."

Deino frowned.

"I know the gods were all banished. But I thought that maybe, since it was her spell, she might still be around somewhere—"

The others just looked at me, but Deino slowly shook her head.

"You're sure?"

A nod.

Damn. So much for that theory.

"Okay, then how about this? The prophecy said that Artemis and Ares were supposed to fight, but he isn't here, either. It's his kids who have been causing the trouble. So I was thinking, maybe I need to find *her* kids, you know?"

The girls exchanged some looks.

"I mean, she was supposed to be this virgin goddess, but I gotta think after a few thousand years, that's gonna get kind of old. So I thought maybe—"

I broke off because the girls' heads jerked up, all at the same time, like they were on a string. I hadn't heard anything, but when I looked back over my shoulder, I saw a mob of Casanova's security guards heading for us at a dead run. They must have been watching on CCTV, or maybe they felt it when the boss went pop. Either way, not good.

"No!" I yelled. "Don't—"

That was all I got out before they were past me, ruffling my hair with the unnatural speed of vampires in a hurry. They didn't ruffle the Graeae's, because the girls were no longer there. I'd been looking at the vamps, so I hadn't seen them move. But there was suddenly nothing where they'd been, except for a few gray hairs drifting slowly earthward.

The vamps stopped, realizing that their prey was gone, about the time that a piercing whistle from the other end of the garage caused all our heads to jerk back around. Silhouetted against the fading daylight were two stooped, wrinkled forms. One of them was waving, while the other held up Casanova's box.

I hadn't even realized it was gone.

Pemphredo turned around and dropped her filthy shorts, showing the guards a wrinkled white ass. Deino waggled the box some more and pointed. The challenge was clear: *come and get him.*

"No, wait," I told the guards, glancing around for Enyo. She was the scariest of the three, and she was currently AWOL. "One of them is missing. We need to—"

I might as well have saved my breath, because they didn't even hesitate. They started back toward the gals at full speed, just blurs against the gloom—until a plastic-wrapped pallet went sailing through the air like a Frisbee. Half the guards hit the wall with a sickening crunching sound. The other half turned, snarling, and came after Enyo.

Or, at least, they tried. But the bus depot contained one of the main loading docks for the hotel, which explained all the stuff sitting around. Including a case of produce that Enyo had just popped the top on, repurposing the contents as veggie grenades. Or make that fruit, because the first ten or twelve she threw in rapid-fire succession were cantaloupes. They spilled their slippery guts all over the floor, right about the time the vamps ran across it—and promptly ended up on their vampy asses.

But they were still sliding in our direction, and now they were really pissed. On average, a vampire would prefer to have his body wounded rather than his pride, which at least would leave him bragging rights among his peers. Losing a food fight with three old women, on the other hand, didn't do a lot for the image. They were going to have a tough time spinning this unless they caught the girls.

Suddenly, the hunt became personal, and that really wasn't good.

That was especially true because I didn't think Casanova had bothered to tell his boys what they were facing. If the legends were to be believed, the trio had been created as ancient versions of the Incredible Hulk. Sweet—kind of—as long as they weren't crossed, they morphed into scary with a little scary on top when threatened.

I'd seen Enyo's alter ego before, and was really okay with not seeing it again. And it was looking like I'd get my wish. Because she was still in little-old-lady mode, just standing in front of a parked semi, as if asking to be caught.

For some reason, that made me more nervous than the reverse. But the sticky, pissed-off vamps didn't appear to feel the same way. They lunged for her, and for a moment, I thought it was all over. Until I looked again and they were suddenly gone.

For a second, I thought she must have had another trap. But then a fist-shaped bit of metal bulged out of the side of the semi, followed by a lot of cursing. And laughter, because Enyo was on her knees, slapping the dirty ground and cackling.

"It isn't funny," I told her, as four or five other fist- and shoe-shaped bulges appeared.

She looked up at me, tears streaming down the crags on her face. Obviously, she begged to differ.

"I'm serious. They're probably calling for backup right now. This could get really—"

I didn't get a chance to finish, because the girls suddenly took off for the escalator. I ran after them, cursing vamps in general and one in particular, because that way led to the lobby. And just on the other side of that was the main casino floor, packed with people escaping the heat and working on tomorrow's hangover.

And most of them didn't have a vampire's ability to throw off severe injury.

There was no point trying to catch the girls on foot, so I didn't try. I shifted into the corridor in front of them, popping out of space in time to see a bunch more vamps running down the hall. It looked like backup had arrived.

There was no sign of the girls until I turned around and spotted them haring down the corridor toward me. They took in the guards in front of them and then glanced over their shoulders at the ones coming up behind. And then they took off—into a corridor branching to the left.

And, shit. That was the back way to the lobby, a shortcut used by the staff. I shifted again, appearing behind the main desk in time to freak out the nearest clerk and to see little, wrinkled streaks I assumed were the Graeae zip past, headed for—

"Oh, crap."

I scrambled after them, but of course they beat me to the bridge. It spanned the River Styx, which wound through the stalactite-infested lobby, carrying boatloads of tourists happily on their way to hell. The bridge was for those who wanted a faster way to damnation, or at least bankruptcy, and was usually busier than the riverboats.

It was still fairly early, though, and Dante's never really heated up until after dark. Security blocked off access to each side of the bridge, but let me through. I walked up to Deino, who was dangling the trap over the water. That wouldn't have worried me so much if there hadn't been a big-ass drain right underneath this bridge. A drain Enyo was currently prizing up.

I sighed and leaned over the railing. The water was dark, because the bottom of the concrete channel was painted black. It reflected the overhead lights, which wavered in the ripples Enyo was making sloshing around down there. So I couldn't read what was written on the drain. But I was pretty sure I knew where it went.

I turned my head to look at Deino.

"I'd consider it a personal favor if you didn't drop him down the sewer."

She looked thoughtful.

"Today," I said.

She grinned.

Something caught my eye and I looked back down at the water. One of the reflections from the overhead lights was drifting upward. It was a testament to how my week had been going that I didn't so much as blink when it broke the surface and floated into the air, like a small glowing balloon. Only this one had familiar shadows drifting over the surface, one half of which was dark, and the other a blinding, brilliant white. I reached out a hand to touch it, because it looked so solid, so real.

But as soon did, it just sank into my hand and was gone. And a moment later, so was Deino. She hared away across the bridge with her sisters, leaving me with a cursing, livid, doused vampire flailing around in the dirty water below the bridge. And the feel of cool, cool mist on my fingertips.

Chapter Thirty-three

I heard the yelling as soon as I popped back into the suite, a vaguely familiar voice screeching in one of the back rooms. I paused in the foyer, wondering if I cared. I decided on the negative, and was about to pop back out again, but I waited too long.

Somebody grabbed me.

"Cassie!"

I looked down to find a panicked-looking Fred standing at the bottom of the short flight of steps and gripping my sleeve.

"What now?" I asked, resigned.

"It's . . . I . . . Marco is off duty and I don't want to have to call him. It makes it look like I can't handle things."

"What kind of things?"

Fred waved a hand toward the interior of the suite. "That thing. He stormed in a few minutes ago and demanded to see you. And, of course, I had to tell him that you weren't in and I didn't know when you'd be back. And he went off—"

"He who?"

"—and started going though your stuff. I told him he couldn't, but—"

I didn't have to wonder what he meant for long, because a second later, a tall, enraged blond emerged from the hall. He was wearing a glittering green brocade tailcoat that, with his height and overall skinniness, made him look like a particularly fabulous praying mantis. "You!"

A long, bony finger was pointed, and of course it was at me.

"I've been wanting to see you," I told him, but I may as well have saved my breath. Augustine wasn't listening.

"Who are you wearing, and don't lie to me!"

"What?"

"A month of my life—a month. Do you understand?" The finger was shaking now, and so was he, but I didn't think it was in fear of the circling ring of vamps. In fact, I got the impression that Augustine didn't even see them. His eyes were fixed on me, and if blue eyes could burn, they were doing it. "I have slaved—*slaved*, worked myself into a frenzy. My masterpiece! Do you understand?"

"No."

"My masterpiece," he screeched. "The finest gown I have ever made. It's almost ready, and what do you do? *Who are you wearing?*"

"Okay, no touching," the redhead guard told him, prying long, bony white hands off the front of my shirt.

"You set me up!" Augustine's usually perfect complexion was an ugly, mottled red. "You planned this all the time!"

"Planned what?" I asked, staying calm because I thought there was an outside chance the guy might actually have a heart attack right there.

"It isn't ready! Do you understand? Another day, even two—but not by tonight!"

"Tonight? What is tonight?"

"Don't give me that! We started getting requests this afternoon, but I didn't think anything of it. It's normal that people would want to pick up their dresses in advance. They are accustomed to dealing with inferior tailors, people like that Claude, who can't fit a gown to save his life, or that ridiculous Tyndale. Tyndale—what kind of name is that for a—"

"Augustine—"

"But they kept on coming, didn't they? Request after request, and do you know how many gowns I have left now? One! *The* one. The one in comparison to which all others are garbage—*garbage*. Do you understand? Except for mine, of course, but even they—"

I grabbed him. And I guess that was okay, because none of the vamps interfered this time. "Are you trying to tell me that the dresses for the coronation went out today?"

"You know damned well they did! Which means they changed the date, didn't they? But no one bothered to tell me, and it isn't finished! It isn't—"

I didn't hear what else it wasn't, because I'd already shifted.

You know it's not going to be a fun party when a serial killer answers the door. Of course, I'd been assuming that anyway. Crashing a vampire ball to which you've been specifically uninvited pretty much ensures that the evening will suck.

The killer in question leaned against the doorframe and looked me up and down, the pallid face stretching into a rictus. "Cassandra Palmer. And just when I thought the evening would be a frightful bore."

I pushed fake black hair out of my eyes and glared. I'd been hoping for a nice human or even a lower-level vampire—someone who might have been fooled by the glamourie I'd used to give my too-round cheeks a little definition and to tint my blue eyes brown. So of course I ended up with a master vamp who thought he was funny.

"How did you recognize me?" I demanded.

"You have a style all your own."

I looked down at the disguise I'd had to assemble on the fly. I'd been going for high-end waitress, but Dante's wasn't exactly known for good taste. As a result, I'd ended up with a cross between naughty French maid and *The Rocky Horror Picture Show*: ratty green velvet, torn fishnets and an Elvira wig that kept falling into my eyes.

I looked back up. "Ha. Ha."

He leaned closer, his nostrils flaring. "And your scent is really quite . . . distinctive."

I tried not to flinch or to let the fact that he knew what I smelled like gross me out.

But I must not have done a great job, because that horrible smile emerged again. Someone should mention that it wasn't a good look for him. Of course, it was hard to think of anything that would be.

He dressed like an old-fashioned mortician, his hair was the flat black of a bad dye job and his fangs were always out and always yellow. I had no idea why he chose to look like that. Anyone who had been a vampire since the Victorian era had definitely had time to get it down pat.

He kept leaning in until I could feel his breath on my throat. "I would know you in the dark," he whispered.

And then he licked my neck.

I stumbled back, fighting revulsion, and lost my grip on the tray of hors d'oeuvres I was carrying. I grabbed for it and for my ridiculously short skirt at the same time and caught only one. My butt hit the bottom of a short flight of cold, wet steps just as the door slammed shut above me.

"Jack!"

There was no response.

I hauled myself off the ground, pulled my thong out of my ass and stomped back up the steps. I peered through the door but didn't see much. The frosted glass in the servant's entrance showed me only vague shadows, one of whom I was pretty sure was laughing at me. "I'm not going to just go away, you know!"

Nothing.

"It's *my* goddamned party!" I yelled, and kicked the door. All I got for my trouble was a stubbed toe and a warning thump from the house wards.

I cursed and went to retrieve my tray. The blinis were no longer edible, having been scattered all over the grass, but I needed them for my disguise. Assuming I ever got inside to use it.

But that was looking less and less likely. My power couldn't even feel the house, much less get a grip on it. Every time I tried, it slipped through my metaphysical clutches like a wet piece of glass, leaving me holding nothing. It didn't feel like a spell or like I was being blocked somehow. I'd had that happen before, and this was different. I could see the house, could reach out and *touch* the damn thing, but as far as my power was concerned, it just wasn't there.

"Told you that wouldn't work," Billy said, lounging in the air beside me.

"I didn't hear you come up with any better ideas," I pointed out, just as I noticed a new tear in my hose. Goddamnit!

"You shoulda just come in jeans. All the servers I saw are male—and vampire."

"You mean I dressed like this for nothing?"

"Well, you look cute," he offered, trying to look up my skirt.

"Stop that! And find me a way in."

He shook his head. "That's what I came to tell you, Cass. There *is* no way."

"What are you talking about?"

"I figured it out when I tried to float through a window and I couldn't. I couldn't do it!"

"So? Maybe it's warded."

"It shouldn't matter. I'm a ghost. There's never been a ward invented that works on me."

"Well, obviously, there is."

He shook his head. "No, there isn't. It took me a while to figure it out, too. I probably wouldn't have, but a couple of the guests were talking about it. Apparently, they don't do it often and the mages are having a collective magicgasm over the whole—"

"Billy!" I said impatiently.

"I couldn't go through the wall because it wasn't there," he said simply.

"Come again?"

"Near as I can figure out, they've turned the whole inside of the house into a portal. The outside is still here, but they've transported the inside . . . somewhere else."

"Where?"

"I don't know. There're only two doors that work—the front and this one—and none of the windows do. I guess when you go through one of the working doors, you go through the portal to . . . well, wherever they've taken the place. And when you come out, you're back here."

"That's why I can't shift," I said slowly. "They've taken the house outside this world, and my power only works here."

"That would be my guess, yeah. So, like I said, you're not getting in."

"Oh, I'm getting in." This only made me more determined. Not only were they having my coronation without me, but they were having it somewhere my own power didn't even work. And, apparently, no one saw the irony in that.

Billy crossed his arms. "Okay, say you do. What then? Most of the major players in the sup world are in there. If something big is about to go down, let them handle it."

"They can't handle it if they don't know what it is."

"You don't know what it is."

"And I'm not going to if I'm stuck out here. Now get back in there and get me something I can use!"

Billy sighed and faded away, muttering something, while I stared in frustration at the ultramodern sphere looming overhead. It looked vaguely like aliens had crashed into the side of the mountain, leaving half of their flying saucer sticking out. Much of the visible part of the house was glass, I suppose to take advantage of the panoramic view of the tree-lined valley below and the snow-capped Sierra Nevadas beyond.

It was gorgeous, sleek and impressive, much like its owner. With a shell just as maddeningly hard to crack. But I had to figure something out or this was going to be one memorable evening—for all the wrong reasons.

I was still standing there when a couple emerged from the darkness. The man had a seventies nerdstache and eyes as cold as a new razor blade. The woman adjusted a spill of mink over her shoulder and tried not to look like she'd been feeding a vampire in the woods in the middle of the night. Neither paid any attention to the snack carrying snacks as they mounted the stairs.

The man rapped imperiously on the door, which promptly opened. His lip curled as his eyes took in Jack's complete dearth of sartorial elegance. "Even tonight, you couldn't make an effort?"

"An effort?" Jack inquired, deliberately disingenuous.

"You know what I mean! Half the guests are human!"

"And half are vampire." Jack ran a bony finger under the guy's too-wide polyester tie and gave it a flip. "Do you think for a moment that fine clothes and a pretty face make them forget what we are?"

"Not with you wearing that ridiculous costume!" the

man snapped with a total lack of irony. He and his dinner swept inside.

Jack laughed. It looked no better on him than the smile, but the sound was surprisingly full and rich. "Everyone here is in costume," he called after them. "Some are even smart enough to know it!"

"Everyone except you," I said.

His eyes slid back to me, reflecting the gaslight from beside the door. It made flames dance in his pupils, like he needed the added creepy. "I beg your pardon?"

"That's how you really look, isn't it?" Judging by the brown lace of his cravat and the frayed cuffs on his coat, they might have been Victorian originals. And his pale face and limp, lifeless hair looked that way because he was exerting no power to make them appear otherwise. I was in disguise; the other vamp was in disguise. But Jack was just Jack.

I hadn't really expected an answer, but he suddenly bent forward, his breath raising goose bumps on the still-wet skin of my neck. "Tell me, little one, do you know why vampires find the Hollywood stereotype so loathsome?"

"Bad dialogue and worse acting?"

"Because it shows us stripped bare, exposed and naked in our brutality—in other words, as we really are. We're all monsters, under the skin." He grinned at me. "Even the beautiful ones."

I ignored the jab at Mircea, who most definitely fit that description. "Is that why they stuck you guarding the back door? Because you embarrass them?"

"They're afraid of what I might say if allowed to mingle with all our fine guests." His tone was light, but there was something dark in his eyes.

"Same here," I said, trying to find common ground.

His gaze met mine, and there was the tiniest glint of laughter in those beetle black depths. He knew he was being played, but he was bored and pissed and he didn't care. "I thought they were afraid that their precious asset might get her soft, white throat cut."

I swallowed, resisting a strong urge to cover up the vulnerable skin in question. "That's what they say, because it sounds better. But I think they're ashamed of me. I grew up in a vampire's court, but it wasn't the *right* court. You know?"

He nodded. It was no secret that Tony had been the vampire equivalent of white trash. It was one reason why I was starting to suspect that I would never fit in with vampire society. That and not actually being a vampire.

"We outcasts should stick together—is that your contention?" he asked.

"You're the one who said this party needed livening up."

"So to speak."

"Are you going to let me in?"

"My orders were to stop you."

"That wasn't what I asked."

Jack beamed like the owner of a dim-witted puppy that has finally done its first trick. "No, it wasn't, was it?"

"Well?"

His eyes narrowed thoughtfully. "You are about to become Pythia."

I crossed my arms. I knew what was coming. "And?"

"And you may have an opportunity to do me a small favor in the future."

"What kind of favor?"

"Nothing too disturbing," he murmured.

Since this was Jack, that didn't reassure me much. "I'd have to approve of whatever it is," I said reluctantly. It felt like I was making a pact with the devil, which wasn't far from the truth. But I *had* to get in there.

"Agreed," he said, so quickly that I knew I was going to regret this. But he flung open the door with a flourish. "I look forward to seeing Lord Mircea's reaction to your presence."

"That makes one of us," I muttered, and hurried inside.

Chapter Thirty-four

Jack had set up a stool at the end of a walnut-paneled hall-way just outside the kitchen. There was a mirror on the wall, probably for the servers to use to check themselves out, so I did—and got a shock. My strawberry blond curls were still hidden by the wig, but it was my own tip-tilted nose and wide blue eyes staring back at me.

"Antiglamourie charms," Jack murmured, watching me with amusement.

Great. And the green velvet did not, as I'd hoped, look black in the low lights. I tried pulling up the too-low top, but that merely raised the skirt to indecent levels, so I stopped. "Anything else I should know about?" I demanded.

"Almost certainly," he said cheerfully.

I shot him a look, which did no good at all, and headed down a corridor. It let out onto a vast foyer with a sweeping staircase, heavy with aged wood and hushed elegance. And another half dozen guards.

That was a problem, because a couple of these guards I knew. Tall, blond and impassive, they were like perfectly matched bookends, right down to the sleek black tuxes and eerie golden eyes. I ducked behind a porphyry vase taller than I was and silently cursed.

No wonder Jack had let me in so easily; he knew I wouldn't get ten yards. And he was right, damn it. There

was no way they weren't going to recognize me. Those two
had been assigned to my bodyguard detail until this little
shindig took precedence, and ancient eyes didn't miss
much. Even worse, the staircase ended not two yards away
from them, meaning I couldn't even try to find another entrance without being nabbed.

I was about to double back and see if there was another
exit through the kitchen when the front door burst open,
letting in a swirl of rain and a couple of glittering corpses.
They must have been important, because half the guards
jumped to greet them and the rest were staring like star-
struck teenagers.

No one was looking at me, so I went forward with the
rest, hoping to edge around to the ballroom while the
Amazon who had just come in provided a distraction.
Easily seven feet tall, the voluptuous redhead was gleaming in a silver sheath and enough mink to send PETA into
paroxysms.

Or at least she was before she shrugged it off and tossed
it over my head.

"Meercha! I vant Meercha. Vere is dat beautiful scoun-
drel?" she demanded.

"In the ballroom, my lady," someone murmured. Or
maybe they said it normally; I couldn't tell. The damn coat
was heavy enough that I almost went down, and left me as
little more than a mink-covered lump.

"Lyubov Oksinia Donskoi is a grand duchess; her correct title is Illustrious Highness," the small, bald man said
diffidently, as I fought my way free.

"My apologies," the guard said, only to be bopped on
the head with a jeweled fan.

"Vell? Vat are you vaiting for?"

"My lady? I mean, Your Illustrious . . . ness?" he guessed.

The bald man nodded slightly, but his companion didn't
look like she gave a damn. She raised long, white-glove-
clad arms, like an opera star about to sing an aria, showing
off breasts like the prow of a ship and enough diamonds to
make a person wince. "Tell heem to come greet his Ly-
ubochka!"

The guard just stared for a moment, looking suitably
dazzled. Then he swallowed and manned up. "I would,
but . . . but he is with the Pythia at the moment, madam."

"Ze Pythia?" Carmine lips pursed. "Vat is dees?"

"The new seer," the bald man said. "You remember, Lyly—the coronation?" She looked blank. "The reason we're here?"

"I am heer to see Meercha." Slanted hazel eyes looked down at the guard, which appeared to make him nervous. He was over six feet tall, so I suppose he wasn't used to it. "Do you not know vere your master ees?"

"The ballroom, Your Illustriousness," he repeated, starting to look worried.

"Zen eef you know vere he is, vhy are you standing here?" She gave him a playful smack on the arm that sent him staggering.

"Yes, my—your . . . Right away."

The vamp scurried off and I scurried after him, trailing about a hundred pounds of mink. And neither of the guards gave me so much as a first glance, much less a second. Then I entered the ballroom and stopped worrying about the vampires behind me. I was more concerned by the one who lay ahead.

I spotted him almost at once. He stood in the middle of a cluster of people, near the patent leather shine of a piano, looking like something out of a '40s movie. Tall, dark and handsome, he was the perfect foil for the blond perfection on his arm. Every hair in his companion's upswept chignon was in place, except for the ones artfully arranged to curl around her ears. The low-cut, midnight blue evening gown she wore was likewise flawless, somehow managing to hug every curve without being vulgar.

She looked too good, I decided.

No way was anyone going to believe that was me.

"Zat?" I jumped at the sound of a booming voice right behind me. I turned to find the principessa or scrinissima or whatever the hell her title was standing less than a yard away, checking out my doppelgänger through a pair of specs on a stick. "Zat ees ze new Pythia?" she demanded, of no one or everyone; it was hard to tell.

The little man at her side said something I couldn't hear over the conversation and music and sounds of people stuffing themselves. But it didn't seem to sit well with Lyly. "Common," she announced in a tone that said it ended the matter.

And was about as loud as the announcer at a football game.

Not surprisingly, everyone in the vicinity stopped to stare at us—including Mircea, whose eyes slid off Lyly and latched onto me before I could bolt. They narrowed and his lips tightened, which for him was the equivalent of a hissy fit. Then just as quickly the expression blanked and he turned back to his date, laughing with her about something.

And then I didn't see any more because I was being propelled out of the room by another vamp wearing a tux and a scowl.

Kit Marlowe was the Senate's chief spy. He was known for laughing dark eyes, messy brown curls and an easy smile—and a reputation at odds with all of them. Most of the time, I found it difficult to see the dangerous vamp everyone swore was under the handsome exterior.

I wasn't having that problem tonight.

"I want to talk to Mircea," I told him, as I was hustled toward the back.

"You are talking to him," he said, his voice clipped. "And it might look a little odd, don't you think, if he suddenly left the side of the Pythia-elect to chat with a servant girl?"

"She isn't the Pythia. She's a sitting goose who's about to be cooked. There's going to be an attack, Marlowe!"

"Very probably."

I dug in my heels, trying to slow him down, which didn't help a lot on the highly polished floor. I don't even think he noticed. "If you're so certain, why the hell are you doing this?"

"Because it's tradition. Because the damn mages insisted. Because no one is going to sign the infernal alliance without at least meeting the new Pythia."

"And if she gets killed, are they going to sign then?" I demanded, as Jack thoughtfully opened the back door.

"No one is going to be killed tonight, I assure you. We've taken precautions. It's perfectly safe."

"If it's so safe, why can't I stay?"

"Because you're tired and you want to go back to the hotel," he said with enough power behind the suggestion to leave me light-headed.

"That doesn't work on me!" I told him furiously.

"Then how about this?" he asked. And for the second time that night, the door was slammed in my face.

"Marlowe!"

After a moment, when it became obvious that he wasn't joking, I sat down on the steps. They were cold and clammy, like the mist that surrounded the house. It was August, but this high in the mountains, summer was just a concept.

I glared at the thin veil of stars overhead and a spattering of rain hit me square in the face. I didn't bother to wipe it off. It fit my mood.

Was this what it was going to be like? Locked out or locked up? My whole life spent spewing out predictions, with no say in how they were used or even if they were?

It sounded like Tony's all over again. It *was* Tony's all over again, just with the Senate in his place. Don't expect to influence anything; don't expect to control anything; don't expect to make any decisions.

Just stay in your corner and do what we tell you.

Just wear the pretty dresses and smile.

Just behave yourself, little girl.

And I had. I'd done what I was told until I found out what Tony was doing with the information. The people he was hurting. The lives he was ruining. And then I'd gotten out, because I wouldn't be responsible for hurting or maybe killing other people, even by proxy. Because I wouldn't be a part of a system I knew nothing about. Because I had had enough.

When had I forgotten that?

The door cracked open, but I didn't turn around. Somebody came down the steps and a jacket was placed around my shoulders. It smelled like rich spices and dark forests and Mircea. I hugged it around me automatically.

"You said it wouldn't make a difference," I said without looking up.

Mircea didn't pretend not to know what I was talking about. "It did not. This has nothing to do with our personal relationship."

"Doesn't it?" I looked up, feeling angry and betrayed and hurt and powerless.

He came around in front, and since I was sitting on one of the higher steps and he was standing on the ground, when he bent over and took my hand, we were almost eye to eye. I remembered something I'd read once, about executives making sure their seats were higher than their subordinates', so they would have some kind of psychological advantage. Mircea didn't use tricks like that. Mircea didn't need them.

"No, it isn't. We have two relationships, Cassie. You know this. It can't be otherwise. And this was a professional decision—as was last night's."

"Professional," I said bitterly, staring into beautiful dark eyes. They reflected the gaslight, just like Jack's. And yet managed to look so very different.

"Yes."

"Then let's talk professional," I said quietly. "A month ago, you promised me you wouldn't interfere with me doing my job."

"A month ago, Apollo was dead and I thought the worst was past us."

"So you lied."

"No. I said I would try. And I have. But this is not about your job."

"It's my coronation!"

"It's a *formality*. One that has made me nervous from the beginning."

To my surprise, he sat down on the wet step beside me, getting his Armani-covered tush wet. I guess he could just go change; this was his home, after all. Not that I'd ever had a chance to see it.

"I would have had you here long before this," he said, with that uncanny ability of guessing my thoughts. "But we were attempting to make it secure. We knew the coronation would be an obvious target, but it was impossible to forgo it. The people need to see you—"

"Only, apparently, they're not going to."

"We had planned for you to be here; all along, that was the intent."

"Then what changed?"

He looked at me in amazement. "The past week changed. Three attempts on your life in as many days changed! The chance of an attack went from a possibility to a probability to a certainty, and the risk was deemed too high. It was determined—"

"Yes, it was," I cut him off. "It was determined. Without consulting me, without even telling me—"

"And if we had told you? If we had said, 'We have decided to hold the ceremony with a doppelgänger in your place for security reasons.' What would have been your reaction?"

"What the hell do you think?" I said angrily. "I've told you a hundred times—it is not okay for someone to die for me!"

"And I have told you that sometimes it is necessary. She is a professional; she takes risks such as this all the time. It is her job—"

"And this is mine!"

We stared at each other, and Mircea's face reflected the frustration, even some of the anger, that I was feeling. I was surprised he'd let me see it; his facade was flawless when he wanted it to be. I searched his face, wondering if this was a trick, if this was some way to manipulate me into feeling guilty for causing him more problems, for taking him away from his duties, for being a pain in the ass once again.

If so, it was doing a pretty good job. I did feel all those things, along with a nagging suspicion that he had a point. The problem was, so did I. And he couldn't see that, couldn't see anything but that little eleven-year-old girl cowering in her room. I wasn't that person anymore; I hadn't been for a while now, but I didn't know if he'd ever be able to see that, to see *me*—

My thoughts scattered as something knocked me broadside. It wasn't an attack, or if it was, my own power was doing it. Something like a fist knotted in my being, jerking me, tugging me, trying to drag me somewhere, somewhen else.

Mircea was talking, saying something that probably sounded logical and reasonable and charming all at the same time, and it might have been really persuasive, except that I was a little too busy to listen right then. And then the tug became a heave and the pull became a wrench, and it was like before I became Pythia, when the power had just tossed me around here and there, wherever it needed me to go. And it must be needing something pretty damn bad, because fight as I would, I was losing.

Mircea must have finally noticed something wrong, because he grasped my shoulders. "Cassie! Cassie, what—"

"Fair warning," I told him through clenched teeth. Because his hands were gripping my arms, and if I went before he let go, he was coming along, like it or not.

"What?"

"Fair warning!" I yelled, trying to pull away. Because I didn't know where my power was taking me, but judging by the intensity of the pull, it wasn't going to be anywhere fun. "Let go!" I told him, but his hold merely tightened, fingers digging into my flesh.

And the next moment, we were gone.

Chapter Thirty-five

Time twisted, colors ran and the bottom fell out of my stomach. And the next thing I knew, I was bouncing on the lap of a tuxedo-clad man in the back of one of London's iconic black cabs. I stared at him and he stared back, brown eyes big and astonished. After a second, I leaned back and checked him over.

His tux didn't tell me much, but the wide-eyed woman clinging to his arm was wearing a cute bob and a flippy little piece of chiffon that practically required rouged knees. "Twenties?" I guessed, because for some reason my time sense was seriously messed up.

"Sixties," Mircea told me, staring out the back of the cab as it crept along through a snarl of traffic.

I adjusted my position so I wasn't actually straddling the speechless guy's leg. "How do you know?"

"Because they didn't have miniskirts in the twenties." He nodded at a nearby giggle of girls in tiny outfits.

"Are you sure?"

"Believe me, *dulceață*, the advent of the mini is forever emblazoned on my mind."

I scowled; it would be. But under the circumstances, I preferred some confirmation. I poked the girl, who jumped and gave a little screech. "What year is it?" I asked, but she only stared at me.

"Che anno è?" I tried.

Nada.

"En quelle année sommes-nous?"

Uh-uh.

"What are you doing?" Mircea asked.

"I don't think they speak English."

"I think it more likely that they are merely startled."

"Okay. But they've had time to get over it now."

"N-nineteen sixty-nine," the woman finally whispered.

I frowned. "Then why are you dressed like that?"

"We're on our way to a fancy dress party, if you must know," her date said, finally finding his voice. "Now, who the hell are you and how did you—"

"There!" Mircea cried, pointing at something in the crowds outside.

"Thanks for the ride," I told the partygoers, as we climbed over them to get out of the cab.

Outside, snow was swirling down out of a black sky, gilded by the lights that poured out of shop windows and glittered from stacks of multicolored signs. It looked vaguely like Times Square, except it was more of a circle, with a tipsy Cupid presiding over what looked like the Christmas rush. Hanging nets of illuminated stars hung across every street, swaying lightly in the wind. A wreath dangled drunkenly off a nearby lamppost. And half the people filling the sidewalks and dodging the street traffic were carrying shopping bags.

I looked at Mircea. "Is this—"

He nodded. "Piccadilly."

That meant nothing to me, except that this was where my mother had dropped us off on our last little trip into time. And now, for some reason, we were back. And so was she, judging by the Victorian coach that was lying on its side across one lane of traffic, causing a major jam.

The horse was still in place, bucking and rearing at the smell of smoke from the burnt-out hulk behind it. My heart clenched; why I don't know. I was still alive, which meant my mother had to be, too. But I didn't see her or the kidnapper or anything else in the rapidly growing crowd.

But I guess Mircea did, because he grabbed my hand and took off.

"I think I left a shoe in the cab," I told him, struggling to keep up as we wove through the human obstacle course at a breakneck pace.

"Considering how often that happens, perhaps you should consider ankle straps."

"They're dangerous."

He tossed a disbelieving look over his shoulder. "*That* is what you consider dangerous?"

"You can break a foot."

"And we wouldn't want that," he said, sweeping me up in his arms as we came to the entrance to a tube station.

I stared around as we were swallowed up by London's steamy underbelly, but I didn't see anything but coat-clad torsos, all of which appeared to be in a hurry. Finding one hustling couple in the wall-to-wall crowd wouldn't have been easy at any time. But doing it while being buffeted by pointy elbows, harassed mothers and kids with the hyperactive look of the overly sugared was pretty much impossible.

"I'm not tall enough," I told him, only to be hoisted up onto a strong shoulder. I put a steadying hand on the grimy wall and tried to spot a tall woman in an electric blue evening dress. The mage's tux blended with the standard city uniform in any era, but that color would be hard to miss.

Only apparently I was missing it, because I didn't see them.

"Did they shift again?" Mircea asked, as I desperately scanned the crowds.

"No, I'd have felt it."

"Are you certain?"

"She's the heir, but I'm Pythia. I'm certain."

And a moment later I spotted her, wearing a shabby brown overcoat that wasn't quite long enough to cover an eye-searing hem. The mage was by her side, a lanky figure in a tan trench hiding his formal blacks, but it was the right guy. I saw him clearly when he turned from the ticket counter, a panicked look on his face and that damned suitcase in his hand. And then he dragged his captive back into the crowd and down a hallway.

I hopped down and we took off after them, Mircea hoisting me over turnstiles and then forging ahead to clear a path. It was still tough going, but the crowds parted for him a lot better than they would have for me, and my bare toes got stepped on only a few dozen times before I limped onto a platform behind him. And stopped in confusion.

There were maybe three dozen people sitting on benches or leaning against walls, waiting for the next train. But a quick scan showed that none of them were the two we were after. "They didn't shift," I said, wrinkling my nose at the pungent smell of pot and body odor.

They were coming from a busker in beads and buckskin who was standing beside the platform, shaking his filthy hair and doing an enthusiastic rendition of "Proud Mary." At least he was until Mircea thrust a bill into his hand. "Woman in a brown coat and blue dress; man in a trench. Where did they go?"

I was about to protest the bribe—not in principle, but because you never knew what seemingly little thing could alter time. And there'd been enough done to this era already. But then the hippie smiled the smile of the happily buzzed and pointed at the yawning mouth of the train tunnel.

And my protest turned into a curse.

I started toward the side of the platform and the dropoff to the tracks, but Mircea pulled me back. "I'll go."

"And if they shift again?"

"I'll come back and get you."

"And if there isn't time?"

"I'll be quick."

I shook my head, hard enough to cause my wig to slide over one eye. I threw it down in annoyance. "I don't know how the link between us works. If I get too far from them physically, I may not be able to follow if they shift again."

"That seems unlikely. If the power is meant to retrieve the heir, it couldn't be that restrictive."

"I can't risk it!"

Mircea's brown eyes narrowed, like a man who was prepared to argue indefinitely, but I didn't give him the chance. I kicked off my other shoe and jumped down beside the tracks, feeling the collected muck of who knew how many years squelching between my toes. And a second later, he landed lightly beside me, a scowl on his face and a penlight in his hand.

I assumed the little flashlight was for my benefit, but it didn't help much. Neither did the work lights set into the walls here and there, which did little more than stretch the shadows. I couldn't see squat once the brightly lit station had faded behind us.

Not that there was much to see. The tunnel itself was claustrophobically small, to the point that it seemed impossible that trains actually ran through this. It was also warm and damp, and reeked of dust and mildew. I was kind of glad I couldn't see details. I could hear, though, and it wasn't helping my nerves.

There were odd rumblings of trains that shook the ground under our feet and seemed to come from every direction at once. There was a weird echoing effect that threw our footsteps back at us, making it hard to listen for others up ahead. And then there were some very suspicious squeaks.

"I think there may be rats," I said, my grip tightening on Mircea's arm.

"At least one," he said softly, about the time I saw the dim glow of another light bouncing off the concrete walls ahead. It was surprisingly distant, considering that we couldn't be more than a couple of minutes behind them. But if they got far enough ahead to break the fragile connection, that lead might well become permanent.

I started to run.

And almost bumped into the kidnapper booking it from the opposite direction. I hadn't seen him in the dark until he was right on top of us, but suddenly there he was, his blue eyes wild, his hair sticking up everywhere and his mouth open in the O of *Oh, shit*. He almost knocked me down with the damn suitcase, gangly legs churning up the dark as he and Mother headed back toward the platform at a dead run.

"What the—" I didn't get a chance to finish before Mircea grabbed me around the waist and flung us at the wall.

I hit hard, bruising my knee and smashing my cheek against the filthy concrete. But I didn't complain. Because at almost the same instant, a bolt of red lightning sizzled through the tunnel, electrifying my hair and raising gooseflesh on my skin. Goddamnit!

"They're supposed to be dead!" I said, furious.

"Perhaps this is a different group."

"Jonas said there were only supposed to be five!"

"Yes, we'll have to mention that to him when we return," Mircea said grimly, as a bunch of pissed-off demigods blew past us.

I thought there were four, not five, but I couldn't be sure. It was hard to see anything at all with bright green afterimages leaping across my vision. And then it was impossible, when so much spell fire lit up the tunnel that it looked like a sophisticated security system had been installed in there.

Laserlike spells bounced off walls and ceiling, crisscrossing each other in a deadly web of crimson fire. They turned the small, round space into something straight out of hell, and gave me plenty of light to see that the spells weren't the kind meant to stun. Everywhere they hit, they blackened the heavy concrete, sparked off the rails and sent a thick layer of dust from the floor billowing into the air.

Mircea cursed and pulled me behind him, which would have been fine, except that a bolt slammed into the wall just down from us a second later. It must have hit an electrical line, because a great shower of sparks spewed across the tunnel, a few flaming out against my dress. Mircea cursed again and pulled me back the other way, near the still-smoking blast mark from the previous spell.

"Get out!" he rasped.

I stopped staring at the fireworks long enough to stare at him. "What?"

"Shift out of here! Now!"

I shook my head. "We've been through this. If they kill her, I'm dead anyway! Why do you think my power brought me back here?"

"I'll deal with it!"

"You can't! Mircea—"

He pushed me against the wall, his body shielding me, his eyes reflecting the sparks. And their expression was pretty damn scary.

"Why are you doing this?"

"Because I don't know how to keep you safe."

"I don't expect you to."

"What?" He looked at me like he thought I'd gone mad.

"Would you protect the Consul if she was here?"

"Of course not!"

"What would you do?"

"Whatever she needed—"

"You would help her."

"Yes!"

"Then help *me*."

"You are not the Consul, Cassie! She has abilities you cannot possibly—"

"—understand. I know." And from the little I'd seen of them, I was really okay with that. "But I have abilities she doesn't. She can survive a direct hit from one of those blasts; I can shift out of the way and miss it. It's the same—"

"It is not the same! You are this." He gripped my arms, hard enough to bruise. "You are flesh, soft and sweet and yielding and *vulnerable*. You need protection, but I can't—"

"Mircea! They've been trying to kill me for three days and *I'm still here*."

"Due to luck!"

I stared at him. "Then I must be the luckiest person alive!"

He just looked at me, and I'd never seen that expression on his face before, like he was really going to lose it. There was something going on here, some issue I didn't understand. But there was no time to figure it out.

"I have to fix this," I told him, as clearly and calmly as I could. "If you want to help me, then help me. Don't shield me, don't protect me, don't bury me alive. *Help me*."

He stared at me a moment longer and didn't move. The fight was escalating and also getting farther away from us, back toward the crowded platform. And I didn't think the Spartoi cared much how many people they killed, as long as my mother was one of them.

"Mircea, *please*!"

"What do you need?" It was harsh.

"To touch her. That's all I ever needed. One second and we're gone—all of us—and this is over."

He nodded briefly and let me go.

I pushed off the wall and back into the corridor, trying to get a glimpse of my mother. I only needed to touch her for a second to shift her away, but I couldn't just appear beside her. Spatial shifts required me to see where I was going, or risk ending up in a wall or a ceiling or part of a mage.

And right now, I couldn't see shit.

Except for billowing clouds of dust, crisscrossing spells—and the crazy-ass kidnapper, erupting from the fray and screaming bloody murder.

He was headed straight at us, but he wasn't running this time. Instead, he and Mom were levitating on something I couldn't see, thanks to their flapping coats. But I felt it just fine when it slammed into my stomach, picked me up off my feet and sent me careening backward into the far reaches of the tunnel.

And now there were two of us screaming, me and the mage, as we pelted into darkness, him trying to push me off and me holding on for dear life, struggling to reach behind him, to grab her, to touch—

But either he figured out what I was doing, or he was the worst damn driver in history. Because we went weaving across the narrow space, bouncing off the sides and scraping across the ceiling, red bolts of spell fire following us into the gloom. And then he got smart and tipped over, dumping me ass-first onto the hard gravel between the tracks.

I cursed and scrambled back to my feet, about the time that a blinding radiance flooded the air. It sent wildly leaping shadows dancing around the walls, disorienting me almost as much as the deafening sound of a horn and the tracks vibrating under my feet and the dirt shimmering like gold dust in the air—

"What's happening?" I screamed.

"Train," the kidnapper shrieked.

I stared up at him. "Train?"

"Train!" Mircea yelled, flinging one of the Spartoi against the side of the tunnel. And then the guy's friends leapt for Mircea and he leapt for me and I leapt for my mother—

And grabbed a handful of something soft and rubbery and gelatinous instead, completely unlike human flesh. That wasn't surprising, because the bastard of a mage had flung a shield around the two of them and I'd grabbed a handful of that. It stretched, encasing my arms like thick latex as I tried to punch through, and Mircea tried to keep the mages from incinerating us all, and the damn kidnapper tried his best to kick me in the head.

He gave me a glancing blow on the temple, but I stubbornly held on, as the rattling around us grew worse and the horn sounded again, deafeningly close, and my hand finally closed over one of my mother's. For a second, I stared at her and she stared back, her wide blue eyes reflecting the approaching light. But while I could feel the fingers under mine, could trace the bones of her hand, could grasp her wrist, I couldn't actually touch her. A thin membrane of the shield still separated us, and as long as it did, I couldn't shift—

And then I couldn't anyway because something smacked into us with the force of a Mack truck.

We went shooting down the tunnel like we'd been fired out of a gun, bounced off a wall, hit the floor and then went tumbling head over heels over head. I had the mage's shield in a death grip and I didn't let go, even as it careened around the small space like a Ping-Pong ball on acid. It absorbed some of the damage, and Mircea absorbed most of the rest, throwing his body over mine until something scooped us up and carried us along like a—

Well, like a speeding train.

The train must have been pretty much automated. Because the driver had been tipped back in his seat, reading a magazine and enjoying a cup of tea. The latter was now all over his natty blue uniform as he stared in wide-eyed disbelief at the knot of yelling, fighting and kicking people rolling around in the air just outside his front window.

And then Mircea grabbed the kidnapper, getting a hand around his neck despite the shield that still encased him. I tried to remember what Mircea had said about how long it took to drain someone through a shield. But my brain was a little busy and I couldn't remember, and then it didn't matter anyway, because the next thing I knew, they were gone.

I ended up with my butt half on, half off some type of levitating luggage and my face smashed against the train's front window. It gave me a perfect view of the mage dragging my mother through the narrow cabin and into the next compartment. Damn it!

I grabbed for the door leading into the driver's cabin, but my hand slid off something hard and glasslike. It took me a second to realize that the mage had flung a shield over the front of the train, and then another second to bypass it, shifting into the cabin right on his heels. Only to have the door he'd flung open slam back and hit me in the face.

That turned out to be kind of lucky, because I staggered back against the front window, and a glance up reminded me that I'd forgotten something. Namely Mircea, who was pelting down the tunnel just ahead of the barreling locomotive. I didn't see the Spartoi, who I really hoped were the train version of roadkill by now, but he was using vampire speed to stay out in front.

Sort of. It actually looked like he might be losing ground, which would explain the expression on his face when he turned to look at me over his shoulder. *Cassandra,* he mouthed, and, okay, I deserved that one.

Sorry! I mouthed back, staring frantically at the buttons and dials and thingamajigs on the driver's console.

There were a lot of them, but none that were all lit up in red and conveniently marked STOP. And I couldn't just shift back outside and grab him without my added weight sending both of us plunging to the tracks. I grabbed the driver instead.

"How do I stop this thing?" I demanded, only to have him turn that blank stare on me.

I shook him as Mircea slowed down or we sped up, and he slipped within inches of oblivion. But shaking didn't do any good. So I slapped the man, which turned out to be the wrong move, because it broke his paralysis, but then he started shrieking like a little girl. I cursed inventively and stared around, out of time and ideas both, and caught sight of the lightly bobbing suitcase.

It had shifted inside with me, maybe because I'd been sitting on it at the time. It was old and worn and vaguely trunklike, like something out of another era. But the spell the mage had cast was obviously still in decent working order, making it the closest thing to a life preserver in sight.

I grabbed it under one arm, shifted outside and grabbed Mircea with the other. And after a terrifying few seconds flailing around a hairsbreadth in front of a few hundred tons of speeding metal, we landed back inside in a heap of arms and legs. And as a bonus, we managed to trip up the driver, who had been about to run into the compartment behind us.

Mircea snaked up an arm and grabbed him, jerking the guy down to eye level with less than his usual calm. "Forget," he told him harshly, and the man suddenly stopped hyperventilating. He docilely sat back in his seat, looking bemusedly into his empty teacup, as we scrambled unsteadily to our feet.

"Sorry," I told Mircea again, only to have him smile grimly.

"We'll discuss it later," he told me, somewhat ominously. "For now, where are they?"

"That way," I said, and we ran.

Chapter Thirty-six

It should have been easy enough to spot them, but it was the holiday rush, and there had to be a couple hundred people wedged into the next car, along with bags and boxes and a guy hugging a full-sized Christmas tree. It had the whole car smelling like pine, which would have been great if the damn stuff didn't give me hay fever. I searched the crowd for my mother, shoving branches out of my face and sneezing my head off.

"Did they shift again?" Mircea asked, as we plowed our way down the car, through the connecting doorway and into the next one. Some people were looking at us like we were crazy, because the space between sections of the train was pretty open.

I felt like telling them to try the front seat for a while.

"No." I shook my head. "I'd have felt it."

"You're sure? If they shifted in the middle of all that—"

"I'm sure." The main reason I'd left him hanging was that every nerve, every sense I had, was focused on that tenuous link with my mother. I had it in a mental death grip, prioritized ahead of everything else. There was no way she'd shift an inch and I wouldn't know.

"But why haven't they?" Mircea demanded. "Staying in a limited, enclosed space when they know they're being pursued makes little sense—"

"Unless they don't have a choice."

He shot me a look. "You think she's getting tired."

"It depends. If this is the same day as the party—"

"It is."

"How can you be sure?"

"I could smell the alcohol on him when he passed by— the champagne you spilled."

I always forgot: vampire senses. "Then she's tired. In fact, she should be passed out cold by now. I don't know how she's still able to do anything. Taking someone else through time is exhausting, even if it's only once. And she's done it—"

"How tired are *you*?"

"I'm fine, not that it matters. It's not like we can stop for a rest."

"It matters," he said, gripping my arm. "Because it determines how aggressive I need to be. I am trying to be cautious and alter this time as little as possible. But if you are nearing the end of your strength—"

"I'm okay," I told him.

He shot me another look, but I was telling the truth. If this thing was shaping up to be a race to see who ran out of gas first, then the kidnapper was shit out of luck. I would never stop chasing her. I would fall over with a fucking aneurysm before I stopped chasing her.

"I *am*," I insisted.

And I guess it must have been convincing, because Mircea nodded. "When you begin to reach exhaustion—"

"I'll let you know." Although I really hoped it wouldn't come to that. I kind of didn't want to know what Mircea's idea of "aggressive" was. His idea of "cautious" was pissing off enough people, as we pushed, shoved and elbowed our way toward the back of the train.

I had no idea what the mage's plan was, or even if he had one. But we finally caught sight of him in the second-to-last car, where he was trying to get the connecting door open to the final one. But that wasn't going so well, thanks to an enraged old woman. A shopping bag lay at her feet, with shards of some kind of porcelain spilling out the top. Which might explain the umbrella he was currently taking upside the head.

I could have kissed her, but didn't have time. Because my mother was standing to the side, talking to him urgently, although the beating he was taking made it unlikely he was paying much attention or that he had shields up—around either of them.

There were people packed all around her, and no place to shift closer, so I just started pushing forward, climbing or crawling or jumping over anyone in my way. Outraged voices rose all around me, and several people pushed back, but I barely noticed. Mircea had gone for the mage at the same moment, and if he could distract him for just a couple of seconds—

And then the train rocked hard around us, sending people staggering left and then right as it almost left the tracks. I didn't know what had happened until the back window exploded in a wash of bright red energy. And not just the back one. The metal body of the car must have acted like some kind of conductor, because window after window burst in a long line, like firecrackers on a string.

Glass pelted the screaming crowd, which surged to its feet, people scrambling after bags and umbrellas and jostling me on all sides. Then the lights blew out, plunging the entire train into darkness. And that was it for the passengers, who collectively rushed away from the chaos and toward the only door out.

Which happened to be the one we'd just reached.

I jumped for my mother, but someone stepped on my instep and someone else elbowed me in the ribs, and then I was knocked backward entirely, shoved into the side of the car. My head hit hard enough for me to see stars, but I struggled back to my feet anyway, mainly to avoid being trampled. The people in the last car were pushing into this one, the ones in this one were pushing into the next, and the ones in the next were putting up the kind of fuss you'd expect with three or four hundred crazed passengers trying to stuff themselves into an already overstuffed area.

But the commotion meant that I couldn't hear Mircea, and the lack of light meant that I couldn't see him. Or the mage. Or my mother.

Goddamnit, I'd had her! I'd *had* her. If I didn't get another chance, I was going to—

Freak out at the sight of a man slithering in the missing window beside me.

An emergency light had come on and was flickering

dimly at the front of the car, giving me an intermittent look at his face. But for a moment, I didn't believe it. Because it wasn't a face I'd expected to see again.

I had assumed that the Spartoi had ended up underneath the wheels, because there had been nowhere else for them to go. There was almost no clearance around the train, not on top, where the roof almost skinned the ceiling of the tunnel, and not on the sides, where the curved walls were streaming away maybe six to eight inches from the windows. It was physically impossible for a grown man to squeeze into a space that small; hell, I couldn't have done it, and he had at least seventy pounds on me.

But he was coming in anyway.

I watched, torn between fascination and horror, as his body seemed to shrink, to elongate, to flow with an almost serpentine movement. He could have broken out the rest of the glass in the window, giving himself a bit more space. But he didn't bother. He just oozed through the small opening like he'd suddenly gone boneless, an amorphous mass of skin and flesh and distorted, running features, including a patch of floating hair with no skull to give it definition anymore, and two round eyeballs swimming in the gelatinous mass of his face.

Eyeballs that were nonetheless looking straight at me.

I made a sound between panic and revulsion and stumbled back, and he oozed the rest of the way through the window. And as soon as he did, he started to solidify, bones and muscles and assorted free-range body parts all snapping back into place, like a balloon inflating. And I suddenly stopped worrying about losing my lunch and started worrying about the rifle he was aiming at the crowd.

Or, more precisely, at the back of my mother's head. I didn't know why he was concentrating on her with me standing right there, but at that moment, I didn't care.

I could see her in the next car, her copper hair gleaming under the emergency lights as she looked around frantically, as if trying to find someone. She started pushing forward, calling out something I couldn't hear over the sound of the screaming crowd and the rattling train and my own blood rushing in my ears. And then I grabbed the long barrel and forced it down, even as he fired.

I didn't see if I'd been fast enough. I didn't see anything, because a vicious blow sent me skidding backward, until my head stopped me by smashing into a metal railing. In the next compartment.

For a moment, I couldn't move, too stunned to do anything but lie there as the car swam sickeningly around me. Two head blows in quick succession had me trying to decide between passing out and puking up breakfast, or possibly doing both at the same time. I rolled over, glass crunching under my hands, but some old clubbing advice about never passing out on your back got me onto my hands and knees. I looked up, dazed and disoriented.

In time to see the gun leveled at my head.

I stared at it for a split second, my eyes crossing, and then I tried to shift. But my head wasn't clear enough, and even if it had been, panic makes shifting difficult. And nothing panics me quite so much as staring down the wrong end of a gun. I tried again anyway, but the mage squeezed off a shot at the same moment, and I knew I was dead.

Only for some reason I wasn't, despite the sound of the shot and the smell of gunpowder in the air. It told me I hadn't shifted, but I couldn't figure out how else he'd missed me from all of two yards away. And then I looked up and bumped my head on the suitcase, which was still bobbing about despite having had a smoking chunk carved out of its butt.

I didn't know where it had come from, since I hadn't brought it with me. But I didn't ask questions, just grabbed the thing for a shield I didn't need because Mircea had arrived. And he was no longer looking so interested in caution.

He snatched the Spartoi's gun out of his hand, the metal squeezing up through his fingers like Play-Doh. The demigod looked from his ruined gun to the enraged vampire and back again, and for some reason, he seemed more perplexed than frightened. And then Mircea used the gun to thwack him into the opposite side of the now-empty compartment.

The blow had looked effortless, almost casual, like someone swinging a golf club on a Sunday afternoon when he really doesn't give a damn if the ball goes into the hole or not. And yet it sent the Spartoi far enough into a metal side panel to bow it outward in the shape of his body. And I decided that my estimate of the clearance must have been about right. Because we were suddenly treated to the nails-on-a-chalkboard sound of metal being dragged over concrete, as his steel-covered ass scraped along the tunnel wall outside.

He didn't move, and I thought he was done for, was sure of it. To the point that I whipped my head around to see if my mother was all right. But the movement was too fast for my aching skull, folding my knees under me after a half-hearted attempt to stand. Mircea moved to help me, and therefore he also wasn't watching when the Spartoi peeled himself out of the panel and jumped—straight at us.

Mircea did sense him in time to turn, to get an arm up—which the Spartoi used to throw him the remaining length of the car. I stared as he busted through the shattered back window, twisted in midair, caught the bottom of the jagged windowpane and propelled himself back inside. Only to get hit with a spell that sent him sailing what looked like half a mile down the tunnel.

All that took far less time to happen than it did to say, and then a blast hit the suitcase I was clutching hard enough to toss me back like a rag doll. I felt something scrape across my back and something else rip what felt like a chunk out of my scalp, and then I was tumbling end over end into almost pitch-darkness. Until my back hit a wall, hard enough to knock the air out of my lungs, to cost me my grip on my floating life preserver, and to send me tumbling to the floor.

My knees hit gravel and my hands hit steel and blood was cascading into my eyes and I couldn't breathe. So it took me a second to realize that I'd been tossed back into the tunnel. But that somehow, I was still alive.

I had to be. Death didn't hurt this much.

But I didn't understand why until I looked up to see the Spartoi walking toward the next compartment as the train sped off. He didn't bother to look back, didn't even wait until I was safely out of sight before turning away. Like he hadn't bothered to waste power disposing of me.

Blood trickled into my eyes as I sat there, understanding flooding me along with something that made my hands shake and my cheeks burn. Mircea had been a threat, and had been dealt with accordingly. But in the Spartoi's eyes, I wasn't worth pursuing. I wasn't worth killing. I was just some minor nuisance to be taken care of on his way to murdering my mother, and I didn't *think* so mother*fucker*.

I grabbed the suitcase and leaned forward, and the little platform shot ahead like a bat out of hell. Mircea grabbed me around the waist a second later, appearing out of the darkness and vaulting up behind me. He said a really filthy phrase in Romanian that I probably wasn't supposed to know.

I couldn't have agreed more.

The train had disappeared around a bend and we leaned left and followed, scooting around the corner at what had to be fifty miles an hour. We didn't bother discussing a plan, because the plan was simple: find him; kill him. I actually wanted that bastard's head more than the kidnapper's, who at least didn't appear to want my mother dead.

Right after we took out the goddamned Spartoi.

I leaned forward a little more, to the point that I risked tipping over, trying to milk every ounce of speed out of the spell. It should have been insanely frightening, rocketing into a pitch-dark tunnel with seemingly no end in sight, and no way to know if we were about to take a header into a wall. But apparently fear and fury don't work together, because I didn't feel anything but *hurry, hurry, hurry* thrumming through my veins and echoing in my ears, along with the growing rattle of the train up ahead.

And then light flooded the tunnel and we passed a station filled with people staring in the opposite direction, probably wondering why the hell the train had just barreled by without stopping. Or maybe they were wondering about something else. Because a couple of seconds later, we zipped into the tunnel's mouth and almost ran into three figures streaking along ahead, barely discernable against the gloom.

It looked like the remaining Spartoi had arrived a little late to the party. But they were catching up fast, courtesy of some motor scooters they'd commandeered from somewhere and levitated. Two were on one and one was on another and they were tearing down the tunnel at a rate of speed that left them little more than blurs against the night.

I stared at them, horrified, because I'd just seen what

one of these things could do. There was no way we could let three more get to that train. Just no way.

"Mircea—"

"I know. Get me close," he said, like I had a choice. The damn tunnel was twelve, maybe thirteen feet across, and they were right in the middle of it. Which meant that anywhere I went was going to be close.

"Why?" I asked anyway.

And then we shot in between them, and I found out why.

Mircea savagely kicked the guy on one scooter, sending him crashing headfirst into the wall. And then he leaned over and kept him there, as we and the scooter and the guy shot ahead. Or, at least, most of the guy did. I was thankful that the headlight on the thing was jumping around, so that I didn't get much more than a glimpse of the black streak left by his head as Mircea ruthlessly ground it into solid cement.

And then kicked him off and jumped on his scooter. The body went flying, tumbling back into darkness, and the scooter ricocheted away from the wall. And straight at the one driven by the other two guys.

It looks like caution is kaput for this round, I thought blankly.

But we'd had the advantage of surprise on the first attack, and we definitely didn't now. One of the Spartoi jumped onto the front of Mircea's scooter and then flung himself to the side, trying to tip him over. But Mircea flexed his thighs and stayed seated, which meant that they shot down the tube spinning sideways, over and over, as there was no inertia in midair to stop them.

I couldn't help because the other Spartoi had spotted me and was right on my tail. I felt a bullet brush past my shoulder and another graze my thigh, leaving a line of searing pain all the way up to my hip. But it could have been worse—and probably would have been, but the suitcase steered like a wounded buffalo and was bouncing around all over the place.

But that wouldn't help for long, and I didn't have time to come up with something that might. Other than the definite impression that being the one in front was not a plus here. I pulled back on the suitcase, the Spartoi shot by me, and then I hurled myself ahead, getting right on his tail for a change.

The Spartoi spun, gun in hand, just as I aimed my bracelet at him and two ghostly daggers arrowed in his direction. They looked brighter than usual in the dim light, but had all of their usual enthusiasm for any kind of violence. I flung myself to the side to avoid any more bullets, so I didn't see them land. But I did see the headlight from the scooter sling wildly around the tunnel, heard it crash into the wall, felt the heat when its engine decided "to hell with this" and exploded in a ball of orange fire.

I slowed down, the case turning in a wide arc as I stared at the flames licking up the side and roof of the tunnel. And felt vaguely sick. I hadn't had a choice; I knew that. But it didn't make me feel a hell of a lot better. I could count on one hand the number of lives I'd taken, and I wasn't thrilled about increasing the number.

Only it looked like I hadn't yet.

Because someone walked out of the flames, charred and burned and leaving blazing bits of himself behind on the tunnel floor. His clothes were mostly burnt off, his hair was on fire, his skin was cracked and charred and running, and fiery light was gleaming on the blood cascading down his body. But he was on his feet, acting like he didn't even feel it.

And he was smiling.

Chapter Thirty-seven

I'd like to say that I planned what happened next, but I'd be lying. All I could think about was getting the hell out of there, but the Spartoi went for me at the same time. I started to turn back in the direction of the train, and he leapt in my path and grabbed the suitcase.

Although, in retrospect, that turned out to be okay, because the spell was a strong one and I was leaning forward with everything I had. And instead of stopping me, he was dragged along underneath, his feet making rhythmic *bump, bump, bump* sounds on the crossties.

At least, they did until a very alive-feeling hand gripped my thigh right over the bullet wound and I almost whited-out in pain. My body jerked and the scarred piece of luggage went shooting into the floor, hitting down hard and then scraping the Spartoi's entire body across gravel.

I hadn't planned that, either, but I damn sure kept the pressure on once it happened, knowing from personal experience exactly how sharp that gravel was. The chunks were big and there had never been any rain down here to wear off the knifelike edges. They were also coated with a layer of black grit or dirt or dust or whatever the hell— anyway, it was finer than sand, as it proved by flying up in a choking cloud all around us, leaving me gasping for air and the demigod cursing inventively beneath me.

But he still didn't let go. Instead, he pushed off the

ground, trying to use his extra weight to flip us, I guess to give me a taste of my own medicine. Which might have worked if we hadn't hit a bend in the tunnel, which neither of us saw coming, thanks to the Underground's idea of adequate illumination. I might not have seen it, but I felt it when we hit, and heard it when something of his went crunch.

It was alarmingly satisfying.

It was also useless, because the next moment, he flipped us anyway, using the wall for leverage, fighting and scratching and kicking as best as possible from two different sides of the case.

"Just fucking *die*," he snarled, and I actually saw the expression through the diffuse light sifting in from somewhere up ahead.

I tilted my head back and saw the body of the train, which had either slowed to a crawl or was stationary. And either way would do.

"You first," I snarled back, and flipped us one last time. Last, because a second later we slammed into the back of the train.

Or, to be more precise, he did.

Being on top, I sailed through the missing back window to experience the joys of rug burn on a whole new level. Which, all things considered, was better than smashing into a hunk of steel face-first. Although it wasn't feeling so much that way at the moment.

I rolled to my knees after I rolled to a stop, almost to the door at the far end of the compartment. My body was crying out for rest, for oblivion, but my brain was telling it sternly to shut up. But it kind of looked like the body might win, because when I tried to stand, I staggered and wobbled and went back down. And not just because of pain and dizziness and a distinct desire to throw up.

There was something wrong with my feet.

I managed to focus bleary eyes on my filthy, bloody soles, and the glass, gravel and God knew what sticking out of them. Clearly, the Underground was not the place to go barefoot. I doubted I could walk, much less run, in this state.

And then the Spartoi's head poked up over the serrated edge of the window. He would have looked like he was doing some kind of old vaudeville act, the kind that makes people wince these days at its deliberate racism. Except that blackface didn't usually involve a ton of blood, a half-missing scalp or a bunch of gravel embedded in the raw flesh all along one side of the face.

I screamed, and he grinned and flopped another arm over the ledge. And this one held a gun. And I discovered that—surprise—I could run after all, a scrambling, hobbling gait that got me through to the next compartment just before bullets started strafing this one. I stared at the back of the seat in front of me as it was quickly shredded and tried to think, only that wasn't going so well. My brain was frozen in horror and seemed to be stuck on a loop screaming *no, no, no, no* over and over, which was less than useful.

I told it to get a grip, and it told me *no, no, no, no,* and I screamed again, because it was do that or lose my mind.

And for some reason, it seemed to help.

For one, the barrage stopped, maybe because the Spartoi thought he'd got me. And for another, I could sort of think again, only all that came to mind was that my knives weren't likely to be a big help against a guy who could walk out of a burning inferno. Among other things.

But I couldn't let him get past me. I couldn't let him get to my mother. And there was only one way to ensure that he didn't. I was going to have to grab him and shift him out of here, and then try to shift back before he could kill me. Which was not sounding like fun for so very, very many reasons, including the fact that I would have to touch him, and I thought that that might just send me the rest of the way to Crazytown and—

And then Mircea walked through the far door. He strolled down the aisle like a guy looking for a good seat, despite the fact that the barrage had started up again. Half a dozen bullets hit him in quick succession, blooming bright against the white of his shirt. But he didn't seem to notice any more than the demigod had, just held out a hand like that would stop the hail of bullets.

And then it stopped the hail of bullets, or something did. I peered around the corner in time to see the Spartoi slump over the window ledge, the gun falling from his limp hand. "You killed him," I said in disbelief. I'd started to think that wasn't possible.

"For the moment," Mircea said grimly.

"What does that mean?"

"It means that these things don't stay dead," he said, giving the Spartoi's body a vicious kick. "I killed the creature I chased in here, but within thirty seconds he was alive again."

"Alive . . . You mean he was a zombie?"

"No, I mean he was alive. I just now drained him for the second time. It is virtually the only thing that works with these things—and it doesn't work for long."

"Then . . . then however many times we kill them, they're just going to continue chasing her?"

"Unless you can help." The quiet voice came from behind me. I turned to find my mother in the doorway, the mage behind her.

"This is crazy," he told her urgently. "I told you—"

"And I told you, did I not? We can use tricks to elude them, as we did before. But they'll keep coming. Or we can end this, now, once and for all."

"But you weren't there! You don't know—"

She took his hand. "Hush now."

He stared at her, obviously frustrated. And then he transferred that stare to me. And if looks could kill—

"Right back at you," I said dizzily.

My mother had turned to look at him, but now those lapis eyes swung back to me. "There is little time," she said simply. "Will you help?"

"I . . . there's . . ." I had about a million questions, but looking into her face, I couldn't seem to remember a single one. And a glance at the dead demigod showed that he was already stirring, flesh flowing along his body like water, jagged wounds pulling together, raw red flesh retreating, the whole turning into a seamless garment of pale olive skin. Any minute now, his heart was going to start to beat and his eyelids were going to open and . . . and I really didn't want to be here when that happened.

I looked back at her. "What do you want me to do?"

Thirty seconds later, we were still on the Underground, still rocketing through a dark tunnel, but things looked a little different. There were plush bench seats of padded leather, posh lights overhead and shiny wood panels on the walls.

And the passengers all looked like they were going to the same fancy dress party as the people in the cab.

Or they would have, if they hadn't been shrieking in shock at seeing a group of people pop out of thin air in front of them. Or maybe it was more the fact that one of those people was mostly naked and completely dead. Again. Mircea pried his hand away from the creature's throat, and he hit the floor like a sack of rocks.

I stared down at the man's sightless, staring eyes, shimmering in the gaslight. They were blue. I swallowed. "What the hell is he?"

"Spartoi," my mother confirmed. "Ares mated with one of the dragon kin long ago, and they were the result."

"That's why they can transform into one?"

She nodded. "Yes, but not here. The tunnel is too small; it would trap them. And without that ability, much of their power is lost."

"That's why you came down here, isn't it? You knew—"

"Yes."

"How?"

Those beautiful eyes met mine. "They have been hunting me for a long time."

I didn't get a chance to ask anything else, because screams and gunshots came from ahead of us. I looked up in time to see another red lightning bolt take out a connecting door a couple of cars away. I couldn't see what was going on next door because of all the smoke, but there were more screams and more terrified people bursting through into our car. And then, over their shoulders, I got a glimpse of two more Spartoi tearing down the length of the train.

And then we were shifting again, sort of.

This time, it wasn't so much like we went anywhere than as if the scene shifted around us. The train stayed pretty solid, except for the ads on the walls, which bloomed and faded in bright spots of color. But mostly the people changed, morphed, flowed into each other and then into new people, like they were liquid, along with the time stream barreling us along. Days, weeks, months of passengers spilled around us, flickering in and out as we were probably doing in their view as we ran forward, through space and time and back through the compartments.

My feet hurt, my body ached and I was half-convinced I had a damn concussion. And I barely noticed. I had a vague impression that I was staring around with my mouth hanging open, but I didn't care about that, either. I'd never seen anything remotely like it.

Of course, that went for most of the stuff that had happened lately. I wondered if this was what training was like, real training, the kind I was never going to get. I thought Agnes would have liked setting me some crazy obstacle course, making me run after her, challenging me to keep up or have my ass left behind in some other place, some other time.

Only this wasn't training; it was real. And getting left behind here wouldn't mean an inconvenience or an embarrassing return; it would mean never returning at all.

From what I understood after all of a half minute of explanation, the Spartoi had managed to get some kind of spell on my mother that caused their state to mirror hers. That meant that they piggybacked along whenever and wherever she shifted. It also prevented her from using any of the tricks I'd seen at the party—stopping time or slowing it down—where they were concerned. She could still slow down time, but if she was immune to it, they would be, as well.

Until, presumably, she ran out of gas and they killed her.

I had no idea why they wanted to kill her, or where the kidnapper fit into all this, or much of anything else. But I knew the main thing. I knew how she planned to break their spell.

She and I weren't using our own power to shift; we were borrowing it from the same source—the enormous well of energy left to the Pythias by Apollo. That put our magic on the same wavelength, for lack of a better term, and was how I was able to track her. My magic "felt" it whenever she used hers, and could follow it to the source.

The idea was to use that similarity to confuse the Spartoi's spell. I was to keep up as she shifted, to stay right alongside her, until our spells merged, overlapping to the point that the piggyback spell got confused and latched on to both of them. Then we were to shift in opposite directions, ripping our spells apart in the process and hopefully destroying theirs, as well.

If we timed it right, if we did it in the middle of a shift, that should leave them in the same position I'd accidentally almost ended up in a few days ago—scattered on the winds of time, never to be reassembled anywhere or anywhen. It wasn't death, because these things couldn't be killed. But it was damn close, and I'd take it.

Assuming I didn't pass out first.

This was hard. This was really, really, goddamned hard. The shifts were so close together that it wasn't like a series of them at all, but more like one long, continual slide back into time, one that was taking everything I had just to keep up.

It wasn't helped by the fact that the maniacs behind us kept firing, even while we were in the middle of the shift. It didn't look like it was doing much good—most of the spells and bullets vanished into the weird liquid time we were passing through, seemingly without connecting to anything. But not all of them.

Every so often, we were solid a split second too long and some of the barrage got through. Mostly, it hit the kidnapper's shields, because he and Mircea were behind us at the moment. But they couldn't shield us completely, and that left Mom and me in the line of fire more than once.

I felt a couple of bullets whiz by me, one of which took out a window somewhen and probably scared a bunch of passengers to death. Another must have been fired just as we shifted, because it raced right alongside my head as time sorted itself out, before vanishing like smoke. I didn't care.

I didn't care about anything, except—please, God—not falling over. But my hands were shaking and sweat was coursing down my face and I couldn't hear anything anymore but my heart hammering in my ears. I think the only thing that kept me upright was Mircea's hand on my arm and a healthy dose of pure rage.

Goddamnit, I was supposed to be good at this! The *one* thing, the *only* thing, that had ever come naturally to me in this whole, crazy job. Yet here I was, panting and swearing and falling through time, nothing like Mother's elegant, effortless shifting, power boiling around her as she calmly walked ahead, as though this were nothing, just an afternoon's stroll through the park.

And *that* is a Pythia, I thought, staring in awe and pride and pain and more than a little disbelief. Agnes had boasted of mother's abilities, but I'd never understood what she meant until now. Until I saw how she made it seem so easy. How she made it seem like breathing. Commanding time, not being thrown around by it, not tripping and stumbling and almost falling as the room blurred around us.

A smooth white hand cupped my face, cool to the touch, unlike my overheated skin. Concerned lapis eyes stared into mine, and I cringed at the thought of what she must be seeing. Frazzled hair sticking to my sweaty face, filthy clothes and panicked eyes, as I fought what was rapidly becoming clear would be a losing battle.

"Almost there," she told me softly, and I nodded, no breath to talk, nothing to say anyway, nothing that would help, at least.

Then the pace picked up, and what had been torment became impossible. I didn't know how I was keeping up, or even if I was. I couldn't think, couldn't see, couldn't even be sure that my feet were moving forward anymore because I couldn't feel them. Days became months became years became decades, time flipping by like pages in a book, a book that was smearing and fluttering and shredding before my eyes, and I screamed in pain and fury. Because I wasn't strong enough, because I couldn't keep up, because I was about to fail at the thing I was supposed to be good at, and I *couldn't—*

Suddenly, there was a horrible wrenching, like my body was coming apart at the seams. Only it wasn't me. It was our magic pulling and tearing and ripping as she veered one way and I fought the current of her power to go the other. But she was so strong, so unbelievably strong, and I didn't have anything left, and I felt myself stalling and flailing and starting to turn—

And the damn Spartoi saved me. They had started firing more wildly, sending panicked people scrambling away from them—and straight at us. It didn't help that the crazed crowds usually disappeared before they reached us. I kept flinching back, expecting a collision, and the near panic made it impossible for me to concentrate well enough to keep shifting.

I felt myself falter, my grip on time shaking along with my concentration. And I suddenly—belatedly—realized that I didn't *have* to shift away from her. All I had to do was remain stationary somewhere, and *she'd* shift away from *me*.

And then a big guy in an old-fashioned suit and a bowler hat barreled right into me, sending me sprawling. We went down in a pile of tweed and leather and outraged pink skin, and there was an umbrella in there somewhere, too, because it was stabbing me in the backside. And then Mircea pulled me up and I realized that something wonderful had happened.

We'd stopped.

Chapter Thirty-eight

I guess I passed out. Because the next thing I knew was waking up in a strange bed, in a strange room, with a strange city view outside a small balcony. But the man standing in front of the window, leaning on the open French door, was familiar. Mircea's dark hair was blowing in a slight breeze, the same one that was ruffling the thin silk of his dressing gown as he turned his head toward me.

He didn't say anything, and neither did I. He just walked over and sat on the edge of the bed, leaning to brush my sleep tumbled curls out of my face. "Are you cold?"

I shook my head. I wasn't wearing anything under the comforter, but it was thick and warm except for my feet, which were sticking out of the covers. They were a little chilly, but also pink and whole and perfect, a gift from Mircea, I assumed. The rest of me felt pretty good, too; tired, but also warm and whole and clean and alive.

I decided I didn't mind the temperature. It felt good to feel cold. It felt good to be able to feel anything.

Mircea must have thought so, too, because he pulled me in a little more, until he could rest his chin on the top of my head. I usually disliked that; there wasn't enough hair up there to cushion the bone. But tonight . . . tonight I didn't mind.

"Your mother was an extraordinary woman," he murmured, after a moment.

"Hm."

"Much like her daughter."

I thought about that for a moment and then twisted my head around, so I could see his face. "I thought I was just ... lucky."

Mircea's lips twisted. "I am not going to be allowed to forget that, am I?"

"Probably not." At least not anytime soon.

He pulled me back against him and ran a hand through my pathetic hair. "I have never doubted you."

"Mircea—"

"It's true."

"Then what was all that in the tunnel? What has been going on all week?"

He didn't say anything for a moment, and I thought maybe he wouldn't. Master vampires weren't in the habit of having to explain themselves, except possibly to their own masters. And Mircea had never had one of those.

"We talked about my parents," he said, after a moment. "A few days ago. Do you remember?"

I nodded.

"Did I ever tell you what happened to them?"

"I know what happened to your dad," I said. "Sort of."

Mircea's story about his father's death and his own near miss changed depending on the circumstances When I was a child, he'd made it sound almost comical: crazy nobles trying to bury him alive when—surprise—he'd been cursed with vampirism more than a week before. Later, I'd heard a less amusing version, including a late-night flight barely ahead of the torch-wielding mob who had killed his father and blinded him, before leaving him six feet under.

Mircea had crawled out of his own grave and gotten away, still half blind, his newly vampire body struggling to heal itself with no food, his mind reeling from shock and horror. He'd had no master to help him, no one to go to for advice or shelter. And yet, somehow, he'd survived.

"I know all I need to know," I told him, tilting my head back to look up at him.

His hand tightened on my arm. "No," he said softly. "I don't think you do."

He drew the covers around us, probably on my account. It takes a lot to get a master cold. And then he told me the whole story. The one I doubted he'd told too many people before.

"In 1442, the pope decided to call for a new crusade against the Ottoman Turks, who had conquered much of the Middle East by that time, and were making inroads into Europe. It was felt that someone needed to bring them to heel, and the king of Poland was elected. He had dreams of glory, but at barely twenty, little battlefield experience. He relied on the guidance of a soldier of fortune named John Hunyadi."

I didn't have to ask if Hunyadi was the bad guy. Mircea's tone was the same one a devout Catholic would use to say "Satan." "I take it you didn't think much of him."

Mircea's hand ran lightly up and down my arm, causing a wave of goose bumps to chase his fingers. "Hunyadi did have military skill," he admitted grudgingly. "But his ambitions often overruled his judgment. Such was the case when he and Ladislas—the Polish king—met with my father on their way east. Napoleon famously said that God fights on the side with the largest battalions. That was centuries later, but it fairly sums up my father's opinion. Which is why all his diplomatic skill could not keep the horror off his face when he saw their 'army.'"

"It was that bad?"

"It wasn't an army at all. The idiots had brought a totality of fifteen thousand men with them. As my father told Hunyadi, the sultan often took that many on hunting expeditions!"

"I'm assuming this Hunyadi guy didn't listen."

"He informed my father that a Christian knight was worth a hundred of the sultan's 'rabble.' Rabble!" Mircea's voice was bitter. "When the Janissaries, Murad's elite military corps, were among the best-armed, best-trained soldiers in the world. They were trained from the time they were children—Christian children whom the Turks took as *devshirme*, a sort of tax, on areas they conquered."

"I wouldn't think slaves would be all that thrilled about fighting for their masters."

"These weren't slaves in the American sense. The Janissaries were among the elite of Ottoman society, respected and feared, even by free men. They had known nothing but military service their whole lives. They ate and drank it. At that time, they didn't even marry, for fear it would distract them from their work. They threw all of their passion into warfare, and these were the soldiers against whom Hunyadi was taking a paltry force under an untested king!"

"Didn't he know this?"

"Of course he knew. But he was a pompous, arrogant ass, and worse, a zealot. A cardinal, Cessarini, was traveling with the army, a papal appointment to see to it that God was on the battlefield." Mircea lips twisted, but not in a smile. "If he was, he was fighting for the other side."

"They lost?"

"We lost. Or, to be more precise, we were obliterated." His hand stilled on my arm.

"We? You mean you were there?"

"Yes. Leading four thousand cavalry from Walachia."

"But if your father knew it was a lost cause—"

Mircea sighed. "That was precisely my argument. But my father was in a difficult position. He owed his position to King Sigismund, his old mentor, who had loaned him the army he had used to seize the throne. Sigismund was dead by this time, but Ladislas had succeeded him, and he reminded my father of his obligation. There was also the fact that my father was a member of the Order of the Dragon, a Catholic military organization started for the express purpose of combating the Turkish threat."

"So it was a religious thing?"

"It was a political thing. My mother was the devout one in the family; my father put his faith in a strong arm and a good sword, and he had need of one. There were many competitors for his throne who would have liked to do to him what he had done to the cousin he dethroned. If he gave the surrounding Catholic leaders a reason to distrust him, they might lend one of them an army, as Sigismund had done for him."

"Then why didn't he lead the forces himself? Why send you to do it?"

"He would have preferred to go himself, if one of us must. But he had signed a treaty with the Turks forbidding it."

"But . . . I thought they were the enemy."

"They were. But they also had an army far larger than our tiny force. Had it come to invasion, we would have

fought bravely, but we would have lost. As it was, after the
Turks made a raid, we would find whole villages nailed to
crosses or impaled, or find pyramids made out of the
bleached skulls of the dead."

"Why would they do that? Why not just plunder and
leave?"

"Because they wanted to be bought off, and they made
sure my father had little choice. In the end, he had to sign a
treaty agreeing to pay them ten thousand gold ducats a
year and to refuse to lift his hand against them in battle.
And to guarantee his good behavior, he had to give two of
his sons as hostages."

"That's how your brothers ended up in a Turkish dungeon." I'd known that Vlad, the brother better known to
the world as Dracula, had gone insane in a Turkish prison.
But I hadn't known the details of how he got there.

Mircea nodded. "My father went for the treaty discussion under a flag of truce, taking my two younger brothers
with him. They were supposed to be safe, but they were
seized and put in chains as soon as they arrived. Vlad and
Radu were carried away before the treaty was given him to
sign. He knew if he failed to do so, their lives would most
certainly be forfeit."

"So he signed."

"Yes, and was therefore put in an impossible position
when Ladislas demanded his loyalty as a member of the
Order, to fight alongside him on his damn fool crusade. My
father couldn't refuse without risking his throne, but agreeing would likely mean the death of his sons. He therefore
agreed to send the smallest acceptable force with Ladislas,
but chose me to command it, thereby keeping the letter of
the treaty, if not the spirit."

"By not lifting a hand against the Turks himself."

"Yes."

"I assume it didn't work?" I really didn't have to ask. I
could read that much from Mircea's expression.

"Nothing worked. At the battle, we were outnumbered
three to one, and then that foolish, foolish king decided to
make a dash for glory along with five hundred cavalry—
and predictably ended with his head on a pike. The Turks
paraded him around like the trophy he was. And as soon as
his army saw it, they broke and ran. My forces stayed to-

gether and managed an organized retreat, which is probably why most of us survived. Virtually everyone else left
their bones bleaching on the battlefield—including the cardinal, who was stripped naked by the victors and left for
the carrion birds. Hunyadi, of course, escaped, as such men
always do."

"And your brothers?" I asked softly.

Mircea lay back against the bed, his hair spread out
around him. I combed my fingers through it, fanning in out
on the pale blanket, because it was beautiful. But also because I couldn't do anything else to erase the sadness from
his face. It had all happened so long ago, but it looked like
I had been wrong. At least for one vampire, the past hadn't
faded at all.

"Before the defeat at Varna, they had been hostages, yes,"
he told me. "But very well-treated ones. They were kept at
Adrianople, the capital, were given food and clothing worthy of their station, were well educated and even received a
good bit of freedom within the city itself. After the debacle,
they were imprisoned in a filthy dungeon, beaten on a daily
basis and half starved. It is a wonder they survived."

"And your father couldn't do anything? Pay a ransom
or—"

"No. The Turks weren't interested in money, not after
Varna left all of Eastern Europe open to conquest—or so it
looked at the time. They groomed Radu, who had proven
to be the most malleable, to be a puppet prince for when
they annexed Walachia. Vlad, who fought them at any and
all opportunities, they mistreated terribly, but kept alive
because his hatred for them paled in comparison to his
loathing for their mutual enemy, Hunyadi."

"Because he'd caused him to be imprisoned?"

"No." Mircea got up abruptly. "Because Hunyadi mur-
dered his entire family."

I sat there blinking while Mircea disappeared onto the
balcony. I wrapped the comforter around me and followed,
a little hesitantly, because I wasn't sure I was wanted. I
found him lighting up a cigarette, one of the small, dark,
spicy ones he preferred, which wasn't a great sign. Mircea
only smoked when he wanted to settle his nerves, or to give
himself something to do with his hands besides wrapping
them around someone's neck.

But I guess that someone wasn't me, because he pulled me back against him, adding his warmth to the comforter's, making the otherwise frigid balcony almost cozy. It looked like this hotel was connected to a train station, because there were a ton of people coming and going far below, all looking like extras out of Dickens. Maybe *A Christmas Carol*, because a bunch were singing on the sidewalk in the middle of the mad rush. The songs drifted up to us in snippets, blown around on the breeze.

For a long time, Mircea smoked and I just enjoyed the feeling of those arms around me. I didn't get it very often these days, with negotiations and Senate duties and the damned coronation taking up so much of his time. I laid my head back against his shoulder; it was always a surprise how good he felt.

"My father was livid with Hunyadi," he finally told me, letting out a breath of sweet-scented smoke that drifted up, ghostly pale against the blackness. "He had warned the man, had almost begged him not to go, and now fifteen thousand good men were dead, his sons were imperiled and *nothing* had been gained. If anything, the crusade had only served to show the Ottomans our weakness, and he knew them well enough to know they wouldn't hesitate to exploit it."

"What did he do?"

Mircea shrugged, a liquid movement against my back. "What he should have done. He imprisoned him when the man passed through Walachia, intending that he should answer for his crimes. But Hunyadi had powerful friends, and they immediately began petitioning my father to release him."

"And did he?"

Mircea was quiet for a moment, but his arms tightened around me almost imperceptibly. "They called me Mircea the Bold then," he said quietly. "Due to my actions in battle. But I was too bold on that occasion. Furious and grieving, and still in pain from wounds received at that disaster of a crusade, I was rash. I spoke out in open court, told how I had seen Hunyadi's arrogance firsthand, that I knew his ego and ambition would drive him to find a scapegoat for his failure. He could hardly blame the martyred king or the saintly cardinal, leaving us as the obvious targets. I begged my father to kill him, warned that if it was not his head on the chopping block, it would be ours."

"And did he listen?"

"No. But someone else did. I don't know—I never knew—who told Hunyadi. But somehow, my words reached his ears. And after my father bowed to pressure and released him, Hunyadi vowed to do precisely as I had said: to see us all dead. He put together a force and attacked us—his former allies—barely three years later. My family was forced to flee for our lives, but it did little good. *Boyars*—the local nobility—in his pay hunted us down. It was about this time of year when they caught up with us."

It was a little incongruous, standing there warm and safe, listening to Christmas carols and smelling the cold, crisp air and Mircea's funky little cigarette. And imagining the horror he must have felt. "They killed . . . everyone?"

"Everyone they could reach. They slit my mother's throat, tortured my father and buried me alive. It is ironic, but the only thing that saved my brothers was being in Turkish hands. They were far safer in Adrianople than they would have been at home in their own beds."

I turned to look at him. "Why did you tell me this?"

Cold hands slid inside the coat, caressed my bare flesh, made me shiver. "So that you would understand. I caused the deaths of my entire family once—"

"You didn't!"

"Shh." His hands curved around my waist, then dropped to settle on his favorite spot—my bare ass. "I have had five hundred years to come to terms with what I did. I was young and hotheaded and foolish, and Hunyadi might have done the same even had I said nothing. I will never know. What I do know, what I learned from that one tragic mistake, was never again to risk the ones I love."

I looked up at him to find the dark hair dusted with snow. It clung to his high, arched brows, trembled on his lashes. "You love me?"

He just looked at me for a moment. And then he reared back his head and laughed, a rich, mellow sound, unreserved and unashamed. "No, not at all. I regularly battle gods for women I dislike!"

I just stood there, snow melting on my cheeks like tears.

"What is it?" he asked, after a moment.

"I— Nothing." Except that no one had ever said that to me before. Not Eugenie, not even Rafe. They had acted like it, had shown it in a lot of little ways, but no one had ever said it.

No one at all.

Mircea pulled me against him, and I laid my head on his chest.

He was silent for a moment. "I have had ... difficulty ... with this season, ever since."

"Perhaps you need a good memory in place of the bad ones."

A corner of his lips quirked. "And where would I obtain such a thing?"

I buried my head in his chest. "I think we can figure something out."

Chapter Thirty-nine

"You brought that thing?" I asked the next morning, sitting up in bed. I was looking at a battered old suitcase with a burn scar on its bum that was hovering near the foot of the bed.

"I could hardly leave it, *dulceață*," Mircea said, pouring coffee at a little table by the window. "The charm still works."

"Sort of." It was drooping like a week-old bouquet or a half-deflated balloon. I pushed it with a finger, and it bobbed a little in the air, giving off a nasty smell. I wrinkled my nose, wrapped a sheet around myself and went to see what was for breakfast.

Watery sunlight was leaking in through the glass, gleaming off white china and solid silver, and a wire basket that was leaking mouthwatering smells. Fresh scones. Yum.

Mircea handed me a cup of coffee. "And I thought you might want to keep it, as it belonged to your mother."

"What, the suitcase?"

He nodded.

I shook my head, mouth full of scone. "It was the mage's."

Mircea raised a dark brow. "Not unless he used her perfume."

I swallowed and pulled the little case over. I didn't smell

anything but charred leather and smoke, but I trusted Mircea's nose. And sure enough, there was a pile of lingerie and a few obviously female outfits inside. A pair of shoes a size too big for me. And tucked into a pocket along the side, a bunch of old letters.

"But . . . how would she have had time to pack?" I asked, sorting through them. "It's not like she knew she was being kidnapped!"

"If that was, in fact, what we saw."

I looked up. "What do you mean?"

"*Dulceață*, I have seen many people under a compulsion, and without fail, they are blanks. Almost robotic in their movements, their speech . . . they do not make decisions; they wait for orders. And they do not tell their captors to hush."

"You're saying . . . she went with him on purpose?"

"It would seem the only answer."

"But . . . why? How would she even *know* someone like that? She was the Pythian heir!"

"Perhaps the letters will tell you."

I shook my head, opening one after another. "No. These were all written by my father. It looks like he'd been writing to her for a while and she'd kept them. . . ." I frowned. "But that doesn't make sense, either. Jonas said that my parents barely knew each other a week before they ran away together. And these . . ." I checked a few more. "They go back more than a decade."

Mircea hesitated. I wouldn't have noticed, but I was looking right at him. And he definitely started to say something and then stopped.

"What?" I demanded.

"I could be wrong," he said carefully. "It has been many years, and I had no reason to pay particular attention at the time—"

"Attention to what?"

"To your father's individual scent."

I frowned harder. "What does that have—"

"I did not notice it at the party. Things were too fraught and there were too many other scents in the vicinity. But last night, when I was standing by the mage, I thought I recognized—"

"No." I looked at him in horror.

"—the same tobacco, the same cologne, the same brand of hair pomade—"

"No!"

That damned eyebrow went up again. I was starting to hate that thing. "Would you prefer to have been sired by a dangerous dark mage?"

"Yes! If the alternative is . . . is *him*. He was—"

"Quite capable."

I stared at him. "Are you— Did you *see*?"

"I saw him protect your mother from four demigods for a protracted period of time."

"He did no such thing! *She* was driving the carriage—"

"Yes. Because it is difficult for anyone other than war mages to keep up a shield and to concentrate on anything else at the same time."

"I didn't see a shield."

"No more did I. But I saw several direct hits bounce off of something. He wasn't able to keep it up for the entire chase, but he certainly helped. And last night—"

"All he did was enchant a suitcase."

"And it proved useful, did it not? The Spartoi must have had them cornered, but he broke through their ranks—"

"Because he was acting like a crazy man!"

"—and protected your mother during a firestorm of spells such as I have rarely seen."

"He was screaming the entire time!"

Mircea's lips quirked. "It is only in the cinema that heroes have to look a certain way. I have been in many battles, *dulceață*, and can tell you from experience that what matters is what works. Ladislas's charge looked heroic banners streaming, armor glinting, five hundred horses galloping in one great wave—but it was the height of folly. Your father's tactics were . . . less impressive . . . but they succeeded. Which is the most heroic, in the end?"

"But he didn't look anything like that!" I said, grasping for straws. Because Mircea could say whatever he liked, but being related to that guy . . . no. Just no. "The kidnapper was tall and blond and you said my father was—"

"I told you how he appeared to me. But he was in hiding; it would not be surprising if he used a glamourie. In fact, it would have been more so if he had not."

"But you said nothing was supposed to happen at the

party—that your men had checked! If he was my father, if he was supposed to be there, to elope with my mother or whatever the hell they were doing, wouldn't your people have known?"

"By all accounts, the party was supposed to be uneventful," Mircea agreed. "I would hardly have taken you there otherwise. Your mother was not reported missing for several months."

"There. You see? He can't be my father!"

"Yes, but, *dulceață*, the important term is 'reported.' My people were not at the party; they did not see for themselves. They were going on the official reports. Reports that may well have been . . . adjusted."

"Adjusted? But why—"

"To give them time to find her." He waved a hand. "The Pythian court likes to appear infallible, mysterious, all knowing. This is not a reputation that would be enhanced by losing their heir to a set of circumstances none of them foresaw. It would not be surprising for them to wait some time before admitting that they had lost her. They would want a chance to locate her and bring her back without anyone realizing there had ever been a problem."

"You think they lied about when she left."

He shrugged. "I think it possible, yes. I always found it odd that they maintained that your father knew her for such a short time before they eloped. Eight days is not much in which to persuade the heir to the Pythian throne to leave it all behind for a life on the run!"

"But . . . but at the party, he was trying to disrupt things! That's what the Guild *does*," I insisted.

Mircea cocked his head. "But if that were the case, why not focus on Lady Phemonoe? She was Pythia; your mother was merely the heir. And one due to disappear soon, in any case. Removing her from her position a few months early would hardly seem likely to make a huge impact on history."

"No! There were spells everywhere—"

"Yes, thrown by war mages attempting to shield your mother and the Pythia."

"How do you know that?"

"Because the spells were frozen, *dulceață*. If your father

had thrown them, they would not have been trapped in time any more than he was."

I shook my head. "My father was a member of the Black Circle, not the Guild."

"Is there any reason he could not have been both?"

I sat back in my chair and glared at him. "Okay. So he's part of some crazy cult that wants to change the world, but then one day he gets bored and decides—just for the hell of it—to join the most infamous group of dark mages around and try to take them over? And when that doesn't work, he thinks, oh well, and elopes with the Pythian heir? Is that what you're saying?"

Mircea laughed. "I thought your father was an interesting man. I just had no idea how much."

"He isn't interesting; he's a nut. And he isn't my father."

Mircea shook his head. "As you say. But perhaps we can discuss it later, in our time?"

"You just want to see how badly the guests trashed your house."

His lips quirked. "With representatives from five of the six senates in attendance, it is a concern."

"All right." I drained my coffee and grabbed another scone. "But we hit the suite first. I need some clothes."

"And afterward, if it remains standing, I will show you around the house."

"Deal," I said, grabbing his hand. And shifted.

And knew immediately that I was in trouble.

One clue was the slick, wet feel of damp grass under my feet, instead of the suite's plush carpet. Another was the Cheshire cat grin of Mircea's glass ballroom, glowing gold against the night—a night that should have been over. And a third was the fist slamming into my jaw, hard enough to send me sprawling.

"Pathetic, weak, idiot *child*. *You* killed the great Apollo?" Something reached into my brain like a rain of quicksilver, clean and cold, but burning down all my nerves. *"Obscene."*

I couldn't see what was attacking me—the transition from watery daylight to thick darkness had left me half blind—but I really wasn't that curious. I reached for Mircea, intending to shift us out of there, but I didn't find him.

His strong grip was no longer on my hand, and I doubted that he'd have just let go. For one thing, I couldn't remember him materializing with me. And for another—

For another, he usually objected when people kicked me in the ribs.

The pain was breathtaking, like a dagger through my flesh, robbing me of breath and bringing tears to my eyes. But it wasn't bad enough to keep me from shifting. That was something else, grabbing me, jerking me back the second I tried.

"Oh no. Not this time, little Pythia." A booted foot came down on my wrist, crushing it into the dirt, sending pain lancing up my arm—and trapping my daggers against the ground. My hand spasmed, still holding a warm scone, which tumbled into the mud.

"This time, there won't be any running away—or any powerful friends to save you. This time, I have you all to myself."

I looked up to see boiling, dark clouds laced with distant lightning, backlighting a face. It blurred across my watering eyes, or maybe that was the rain, which was still coming down. But for a moment, I couldn't tell what I was looking at.

And then my vision cleared and I still couldn't.

On the surface, it was a sharp-faced brunet with slicked-back hair, thin cheeks and a long nose, vaguely familiar although I didn't . . . and then it snapped into place. Niall, the officious pain-in-the-ass from the publicity department. It had taken me a second to recognize him, because while the face was the same, the eyes—

The eyes were horrible.

No, not horrible. They would have looked perfectly fine in the face of his alter ego, the dragon that had chased Pritkin and me through an office building. But seeing those same firelit orbs in a human's face, complete with elongated pupils and reptilian, nictitating membranes . . .

A wave of visceral revulsion washed over my skin, making every hair stand on end.

I guess I knew where the fifth Spartoi had gone, I thought wildly, even as I panicked and tried to shift again. But the same thing happened—I was slammed back onto the dirt at his feet, hard enough to hurt, like I'd been grabbed by one of the Circle's lassos. But I didn't think that was it. Because the creature standing over me held something up.

Lightning flashed off a slim gold chain, and the familiar charm dangling from the end of it. "Recognize this?" Niall asked pleasantly. "I took it off your good friend the war mage. I told him Jonas had sent me after it, but he didn't seem to believe me."

I stared at the innocuous-looking little thing, swinging slowly to and fro, and remembered with a lurch that I hadn't seen Pritkin today. I hadn't thought about it; had assumed he was resting. But what if instead—

My blood ran cold.

"What—what did you do?" I asked thickly. Blood dribbled down my chin. I didn't bother to wipe it off.

"Let's just say, I don't think you should count on having him come to your rescue yet again. Or anyone else, for that matter. The coronation has begun; the lockdown is in place. And by the time it ends"—he smiled—"I do not think there will be much left to rescue."

"I wouldn't bet on that," I snarled, and shifted.

Of course, I didn't go very far. The damned necklace that I was going to grind into *powder* if I got out of this saw to that, jerking me back almost immediately. But that got my arm free, and when I rematerialized, I was a couple of yards away—behind Niall.

He spun, some sixth sense warning him of danger just as two ghostly daggers shot out of my bracelet. They looked brighter than usual in the dim light, but had all of their normal enthusiasm for any kind of violence. As they demonstrated by slamming into his torso with enough force to send him hurtling back into a tree—and to pin him there.

For about a second. His hands were free, but he didn't bother to use them. He just leaned forward, against the knives, which disappeared into his blood-drenched shirt up to the hilts. And then vanished completely when he simply *walked right through them*. There was a little pause as the hilts caught on something—his heart, his rib cage; who the hell knows?—and then he tore free with a sucking, squelching sound that left me a little dizzy, even before I saw the knives quivering in the wood behind him.

Then I blinked and he was on me, bearing down on my

already injured wrist until I felt something pop. A dagger of pain shot up the length of my arm, making me gasp. And that was before he rotated his foot slightly, causing bone to grind against bone.

I screamed, trying not to curl around my broken wrist, trying to shift again. But God, it hurt, it *hurt*, and I couldn't *focus*—

Couldn't do anything, not even cover myself. My towel had ended up a few yards away, leaving me naked except for a lot of mud. But I didn't think Niall cared. There was no lust in those horrible eyes as he looked me over, no heat, no human emotion at all. Just cold assessment, the same spine-shivering stare he'd given me in the air.

"You know," he said mildly. "I think I will enjoy this."

"This is about revenge?" I gasped.

"No, you foolish child. That will be a bonus. This is about the end of a chase that started long before you were ever born. When that damned bitch Artemis turned on her own, banishing the gods from what was rightfully theirs. Using her power over the pathways between worlds to slam a door shut in their faces, and her power over the hells to keep it there."

"The hells?"

"Earth is an upper hell. How else could demons travel here so easily? She was a queen in her castle; no one could touch her. No one but the children the gods left behind."

"You—you're looking for Artemis?" Small world.

"Not looking; found. We hunted her for millennia, and nothing—*nothing*! But we were patient, because we knew, queen or no, this world doesn't feed her kind. Every century that passed made her weaker, sapped her strength. Why do you think she had to form the Circle, to fuel her spell? Could not a goddess power it herself?"

"I . . . never really thought about it."

"No. Neither did they. Never wondered why she had to rely on the humans she loved so much—because her own power was failing. We watched and we waited, knowing that, sooner or later, she would be forced to go to the only source of the gods' power remaining in this world."

It took me a moment to get it, because of the pain and because it felt like something was pounding on the back of my skull. "The Pythian power."

"Yes. Her own brother's legacy. How she must have hungered for it, lusted after it, more and more each year as her own vast store of power faded and thinned and drained away. And at last, after three thousand years, she broke and we had her. *We had her!*"

"You killed her?" I said, even knowing that wasn't right. Knowing something . . . the pounding in my head was getting worse.

"We tried. Oh, how we tried. For you see, little Pythia, there is no spell that can block off a world. No word, no enchantment, no charm has that kind of power. The only way even she could manage it was to weave a piece of herself, a piece of the very fabric of her being, into her spell. She became part of it, an integral part. And what happens, little Pythia, when you remove a vital component of a spell?"

"It falls," I said blankly.

"Yes. So we tried. But we missed her. An idiot mage helped her, something we hadn't expected. And she disappeared again like smoke. But her power was weak—so weak! We knew we were close. We redoubled our efforts, worked tirelessly day and night. And finally, five years later, we found her again."

The pounding was a hammering thrum now, like a thousand running horses.

Or one, pulling a crazy carriage through a distant street.

"The mage had hidden her away—with a vampire, of all things! And by the time we finally tracked her, the vampire had already taken care of the situation. He had been cheated by the mage on a business deal, or so he said. And had taken the most final possible revenge."

The drumming was so loud, I could barely hear. Hard and fast, like the pounding of my heart, like the blood drumming in my ears, like the crest of a wave, about to break—

"He swore to us that she was dead, and after some checking, it appeared that he was telling the truth. And yet the spell hadn't fallen! She had been blown to a thousand fragments by the vampire's bomb, but it was as solid as ever. And that was when we realized—she must have left something of herself behind."

"No."

"Oh yes. But the vampire lied to us. He never mentioned

a child, wanting to keep his little cash cow alive and well and working for him. And to our discredit, the idea never so much as crossed our minds. Why would it? She was the famous virgin goddess. There were no gods here, no one worthy of her, so who would she have taken to bed?"

"No!"

"Yes, horrifying, isn't it? That ridiculous creature—but we should have known. It was all there in the name. Garm was Hel's faithful companion in all the old sagas, was he not?"

I nodded slowly.

"But did you know? 'Garm' in Old Norse . . . is 'Rag.'"

I shook my head. That didn't mean—

He saw and smiled. "Ragnar Palmer—that was your father's real name, wasn't it? Before he changed it? And 'Ragnar' means 'warrior of the gods' in Old Norse."

The wave broke, crashing over my brain, whiting out all thought for a moment. And when I could think again, it was a succession of images, clues, things I should have seen and totally hadn't. My mother overriding Agnes's spells at the party, something no heir should have been able to do. Her unbelievable stamina, leaving her stronger at the end of a fight than I was at the beginning. Her saying that the Spartoi had chased her for "a long time." The look on Deino's face when I asked about the child of Artemis.

I finally recognized it for what it was: stunned incredulity.

I could sympathize.

"After your parents died, the trail went stone-cold," Niall told me casually. "We had no choice but to work on other avenues. Five times we painstakingly amassed the power to go back in time, to attack her when she was weakest. And five times we failed, dying over and over as those damned spells misfired and backfired and ripped us to shreds!"

The face lowered until I could feel the hot breath on my face, warm—too warm—to be human. Not that there was any chance of that with those eyes staring directly into mine. I stared back at them, paralyzed less by fear than by sheer disbelief.

This wasn't happening. This wasn't happening. This wasn't—

"Having the ability to be resurrected by one's brothers does not mean one does not feel pain *in the dying*," he hissed. "I bled, my brothers bled, over and over again. For *nothing*. Until a month ago, when that idiot Saunders came to me, wanting a little favor. It seems the vampires have a golden girl, a shiny new Pythia, whose name he would like me to blacken. Oh, and by the way, you'll never *guess who her mother was*."

That last was a scream, but I didn't even flinch. I was way too far gone for that.

"Must have been a shock," I said blankly.

"It was ridiculous! That one stupid little girl could be so much trouble. Before you came on the scene, Myra was well on her way to destroying the Senate. Our allies among the vampires were posed to take over what was left. Our people had infiltrated the Circle, removing Marsden and substituting a greedy, duplicitous idiot in his place, who could be manipulated and blackmailed at will. Weakened on all fronts, with no allies and nowhere to turn, the Circle would have fallen to our forces in a matter of weeks, and Artemis's damned spell along with it.

"But at the ninth hour, what happens? A stupid, bumbling, ridiculous *child* stumbles onto the scene and ruins *everything*. In a matter of a few months, you destroyed Myra, reinstated Marsden and are on the brink of uniting the vampires! Oh yes, we know what they're really doing up there," he said, gesturing at the house. "But that isn't going to happen, Pythia. You're going to repair the damage you've done. This ends now."

Chapter Forty

He jerked me to my feet, and I finally realized what he'd been waiting for. The house lights had extinguished, leaving the once glowing ballroom dark and silent. I couldn't see very well, but from what I could make out, a solid wall of people stretched across the glass opening, their heads blacking out the lighter walls beyond, their jewels occasionally catching the light.

It's like stadium seating, I thought blankly. Only what they were watching tonight wasn't the latest football game. It was an execution.

"They can't help you," he told me. "But they can watch—as all their plans and schemes and useless alliances go up in smoke. You die, the spell fails and my father returns. And the last legacy of that traitor is gone forever."

I didn't answer, mainly because he backhanded me and I went sprawling. But then, I didn't have to. Because the darkness suddenly faded, the trees whispering to one another as the pale smudge of a moon, like a coy lady, glided up over a hill. And immediately, everything changed.

The dark sky flooded the color of polished silver, the wet grass sparkled like diamonds, the hills and the trees and everything around us was bathed in a brilliant white light. It reflected in the puddle I'd landed in, a luminous, wavering orb like the one Deino had offered me, but that I hadn't understood. I'd never seen anything so beautiful.

Not since the look of mingled joy and pain and disbelief on my mother's face as she gazed at me.

My mother, who, if the Spartoi hadn't hounded her, wouldn't have had to flee, wouldn't have ended up with Tony, wouldn't have died. They may as well have killed her. They'd driven her into the hands of the one who had.

But they hadn't killed her. They hadn't been *able* to kill her. She might have lost her power over the centuries, but she'd never lost her courage. She'd taken on four of these things twice over and won. And she'd done it all while drawing from the same well of power I did, power that was hers by right of birth.

As it was mine.

My power wasn't some alien thing, I thought, watching the sky in wonder. It wasn't borrowed from another or stolen from a better candidate. There *was* no better candidate; there never would be. It had flowed away from Myra as soon as it saw me, like the tide when the moon comes out. Because it was mine—it was mine; it knew it was mine.

I was the one who had taken a little time to catch up.

I rolled over on all fours, gathering strength to stand. I was a little wobbly, and my wrist felt like it might just be on fire. But I got into a crouch on the balls of my feet.

The Spartoi looked me over. "You would duel me?" he asked, amused.

"That's the idea."

"To what end? Even were you somehow to win, my kind are immortal. My brothers would simply resurrect me."

"You know," I told him. "I wouldn't count on that."

"And why is that?"

"You sent them a sixth time after my mother, didn't you? To hedge your bets."

"Yes?"

"It didn't go well," I said, and threw out a hand.

A time wave flowed across the grass, churning up the dirt as it flowed toward him. He transformed in an instant, surging up from the ground on a rush of air that almost knocked me down as the wave flowed underneath. A group of trees behind where he'd been standing suddenly shot up, ten and twelve feet in seconds, but he was twice that high, huge wings blocking out the light as he banked and turned and dove—

The ground around me exploded in fire even as I shifted. I landed in a nearby copse of small trees, hoping for cover. But he must have anticipated that. Because almost immediately I had to shift again, as the trees burst into flame, flooding the landscape with garish light and sending strange shadows writing over the ground.

I could see them from the other side of the hill, where I'd landed behind a rocky outcropping. They backlit the huge form of the transformed Spartoi, which was hovering in the air, powerful wings churning up the air. His back was to me because he was still facing the trees. But I couldn't stay where I was. He was already spiraling up to get a better look. Any moment now, he'd spot me—

A wave of fire came my way, before I'd finished the thought. And it wasn't a narrow stream that I might have been able to dodge. It was a wall of flame that blistered the air, like a tidal wave, if they came in crimson and gold.

I shifted again because I had no choice, but I couldn't keep doing that. I had my mother's power, but not her stamina. I was already panting—that time wave had been a bitch—and another few shifts would have me close to exhaustion. I had to make the shifts I had left count. Which is why, when I shifted again, it was back in time.

Normally, I wasn't good at judging short time shifts. A day I could do, or even twelve hours or so, but anything less was tricky. Sometimes it worked; sometimes it didn't. Okay, most of the time it didn't. So I was pretty surprised to land on the right side of the Spartoi at roughly the same moment that it set the trees on fire.

But not as surprised as having a second dragon pop out of the air right over my head.

I froze, hiding in the shade cast by my pursuer's own body. I guessed I knew what that quicksilver feeling had been earlier. He must have put the same spell on me they'd used on my mother.

Which meant that I couldn't time shift, or I'd take the asshole with me.

Perfect.

The only thing that saved me was that he'd been looking outward instead of straight down and didn't immediately spot me. Maybe because he was too busy screaming a warning to his former self. I didn't know what language they used, but if he told him where I was about to shift to, former me would soon be dead. Meaning present me would be dead. Shit!

Luckily, everything had happened so fast that his alter ego didn't have time to capitalize on the information. He went screeching toward former me, my Spartoi spiraled up looking for present me, and I decided to hell with this. Despite the cold, my hair was sticking to my cheeks, my palms were sweaty and my heart was drumming in my ears. I thought I had maybe one more time wave in me, if I was lucky.

This one had to work. And as fast as these things moved, there was only one way to ensure that. I gathered my power and shifted—

Onto its back.

I'd hoped it wouldn't notice an extra hundred and twenty pounds for a few seconds, considering it had to weigh something like seventy times that. I was wrong. I'd no sooner rematerialized than it let out a bellow of rage that echoed off the surrounding mountains and almost deafened me. And then it did a barrel roll.

I screamed, with nothing to hold on to but rain-slick scales that tore at my palms even as I grasped for them. But I launched my last time wave, even as I fell. I saw it veer off course, saw it slice into one of the great wings, saw it miss the body. But I didn't have time to curse.

Because the next second, I was hitting down—hard.

I landed on my side, and, of course, it was the side with the injured wrist. A wave of pain engulfed me, so fast and so hard that it froze a scream in my throat. Or it would have, if it hadn't already been knocked out of me. I writhed in the mud, too crazy with pain to do anything else, including think, for a long moment.

And when I did manage to gather some thoughts, they were nothing I wanted.

I told myself I'd just had the wind knocked out of me, that I'd only fallen maybe two stories, and onto soft ground that had just been churned up by the talons of those two beasts. In a minute, I'd get my wind back, I'd gather my strength, I'd get out of this. There was nothing to worry about, no need for panic.

And if I'd had any breath, I'd have laughed. Because if ever a situation called for panic, this was it.

I did finally manage to drag in a shaky breath, but by then it was too late. A shadow fell over me, a human one, because the Spartoi had transformed back. I suppose he didn't think he needed the extra power to take out a half-dead body, and it didn't help that I kind of agreed with him.

He stopped beside me, staring down out of those horrible eyes. "You forgot," he said gently. "My father was Ares, god of war."

And my mother was death, I didn't say, because I didn't have the breath. I just stepped out of my body and grabbed him.

I don't know if he could feel my dim, insubstantial hand around his throat, but he acted like he felt something. He staggered back, flailing and tearing at nothing. Because what I was, he could no longer touch.

But I could touch him, although for a long moment, it didn't seem to matter. Nothing was happening, just like with the damn apples. And then, slowly, almost imperceptibly, his face began to change.

Liquid skin pulled away from flesh, from muscles, from bone. Eyes rolled in sockets, hair grayed and whitened and then fell out as the skin holding it in place rotted away. The tongue, a bloated black thing lolling in his mouth, tried to move, to speak, to curse, before suddenly deflating and disappearing, withdrawing back into the skull like the eyes, like everything, until the bones cracked and splintered and the whole thing dusted away on the breeze.

For a moment, I just stared at the imprints of his feet in the soft soil, which were quickly filling up with rain. That had worked. I couldn't believe that had worked. I'd ... I'd *won*? I didn't feel like I'd won. I felt dizzy and sick and more than half crazy, like I wanted to run screaming around the hillside. Only I couldn't. I didn't have feet anymore, either.

I didn't have anything, I realized, except for the tiny bit of life force I'd torn away with me when I came out. And after using up most of it on the battle, it was fast running out. I turned, feeling misty and jumbled and oddly . . . disjointed, like parts of me were already trying to float away. . . .

And saw the small pale slash of my body lying almost halfway across the still-burning hillside.

It was so far. How had we come this far? I didn't remember moving much at all. Of course, I didn't remember much of anything except watching the Spartoi's face peeling back.

A breeze came by, blowing some burning cinders through me, and I flinched. I didn't feel them, was starting to have trouble feeling anything. Or concentrating . . .

I needed to move. I needed to get back. I needed to get back *now*.

I started forward in a vague, streaming motion completely unlike walking. And that was wrong, wasn't it? It hadn't felt this way before in the apartment, had it? I couldn't remember. But it was wrong somehow, a halting, dragging feeling, slowing me down, pulling me back. I turned, half expecting to see that a piece of myself had caught on something, stretching my metaphysical form behind me like taffy.

But I didn't. I saw something worse.

A seething cloud of blackness had boiled up behind me, blocking half the sky. It looked like a storm cloud, except storms are laced with lightning, not iridescent feathers. And they drop rain, not tendrils of odd, black smoke.

"No," I whispered, knowing what it was. And that, without a body, I was nothing more than a tasty snack for any passing spirit.

And then it was on me.

I screamed, expecting it to hurt, but it didn't. It didn't. But the draining sensation ramped up a few dozen notches, causing my hand to shimmer in front of my face as I reached out, trying to part the thick, blue-black clouds to see. But it didn't want me to see. If I could see, I could find my way back, and once inside my body, I would have not only its protection, but that of Pritkin's talisman, as well.

Pritkin. The name caused pain, caused my tenuous concentration to wobble, and I felt a stinging slap to a face I no longer had. Sentiment . . . sentiment in battle got you killed. Not once in a while, not occasionally, but almost every single fucking time. *You do not stop to cry or whine or mourn, not in battle, never in battle. That's for later, when you're safe, when you're home. Do you understand?*

I'd understood. I'd told him I understood. I'd promised, and now I had to . . . I had to . . . *concentrate.*

Yes, I had to concentrate. I had to get back to my body . . . my body. Where was my body? I couldn't see. And now it did hurt some as the draining sensation picked up and—

Blue-black clouds were everywhere, almost completely cutting off any vision. I surged forward, hoping I was going in the right direction, only able to catch glimpses, here and there, of stars and trees and my body, which seemed to be constantly changing position. I knew it wasn't moving, knew I was the one getting off course, but I couldn't seem to stop it.

I raised a hand, dim, so dim, almost transparent now. I could see the mist through it, like it was almost a part of it, like it was floating away . . . and maybe it was. Maybe it already had. Maybe I had. Things were getting dimmer, harder to see, and I didn't know if that was the clouds getting thicker with stolen power or my sight getting dimmer, but either way, it was very bad news. Because I couldn't see at all now.

I stumbled on anyway, hoping I would literally stumble into my goal. Would I know it? I thought I would know it, but what were the odds? It was a huge hillside and my body was small and I couldn't *see—*

"Cassie!"

The sound was vague and indistinct, like my form, like everything. I wasn't even sure I'd heard it, but then it came again, a faint, echoing sound, but stronger to the right. Was it? I thought so, and instinctively moved in that direction.

"Cassie!" It came again, nearer now, or so it seemed, maybe . . . I couldn't really tell. I didn't have ears; how could I hear without ears? Wasn't sure I had much of anything now, and I had a feeling a coherent thing like a body might be too much for me to maintain at this point. I had a flash of a dim silver ball, a little twinkling light against a wall of clouds, bright, so bright, against the darkness. But I was probably just making that up. I couldn't see, after all. I didn't have—

"Cassie!"

I jerked, because that had been close. Really close. Close, close, somewhere ...

There.

I felt a body, not mine, but familiar. Warm. So full of life. Hurt.

Why was it hurt?

"Cassie! Listen to me. You have to merge with your body. You have to do it now!"

My body. Yes. I had to get back to ... but where was it? I put out a hand, or what would have been a hand if I had hands left, a tendril of power, anyway—

And then snatched it back, mewling in pain, after something took what felt like a bite right out of it. God, *that* had hurt. But it cleared my mind, or what was left of it, because I suddenly remembered. My body ... was on the ground.

I dove, and something screeched in my ear, a furious, screaming cry, full of hunger and pain and desperation —

And then I was back, filling myself not in one quick rush as I had before, but in tiny trickles here and there. Funny, it didn't feel that different, being back. It didn't feel that different at all.

I stared up at the sky, at the rain falling almost straight down, highlighted here and there by stray beams of moonlight. It wasn't enough to obscure the stars, which were winking with pinprick brightness through the trees. Or the moon, riding a sea of clouds overhead, silvering the landscape. Beautiful.

I wondered if I was dreaming. And then I knew I was, because he was there. Strong arms went around me, pulling me up. *Beautiful,* I thought, looking into clear green eyes.

He gathered me in, folding me under his chin, and I thought there was something . . . something strange about ...

He had on a shirt too light for the weather, thin cotton with the sleeves rolled to the elbows, showing the tendons in his forearms. His forearms ... that was it. I could see the arms he'd wrapped around me because he wasn't wearing his old, battered coat. But Pritkin always wore ... didn't he? Some reason floated here and there, darting across my mind like a butterfly ... but I couldn't ... couldn't catch it. ...

"Cassie." Warm fingers trailed down my cheek, my neck. So warm, so warm. Was he healing? I couldn't remember him being this warm. But it felt good. It felt . . .

A sigh leaked out like blood.

We sat like that for a moment, his chest hard at my back, his arms hard around me, so solid, grounding, when I felt like I could float away. My head lolled back against his shoulder. It seemed too hard to hold it up anymore. His hand came up, burying itself in my hair, clenching.

And then releasing as he carefully laid me down on the grass again.

His face swam into view over me. He looked different, and it wasn't just the coat. His hair was a rumpled, silky mess. His eyes were hot, the lines around his mouth deeply etched. He was breathing hard. I watched it curl out of him, silver air on a silver sky. . . .

Maybe I'm dreaming, I thought vaguely. Maybe he wasn't here at all, just some shade I'd conjured up because I didn't want to die alone. But he looked real, sharply defined by dark shadows, highlighted at the curve of his neck, the breadth of his shoulders, by moonlight. Substantial, undeniably *there*. My fingers curled around his, and he caught them in a hard grip.

I thought I could write a ten-page paper, with illustrations, on all the ways Pritkin's features differed from the usual standards of beauty, but that didn't change anything about what I saw when I looked at the man.

"Beautiful," I whispered. He closed his eyes.

Overburdened clouds broke open with a rumble and a sigh and rain fell like a veil across the horizon. I was watching it, mesmerized at how it blurred the distant mountains, at how it—

Pritkin's hands framed my face. He bent closer, until his lashes brushed my cheek, until his lips touched mine. "Kiss me."

Or, at least, that's what I thought he said. But it was hard to hear. Something like voices murmured in my head, like a hive full of lazy bees, inarticulate and insistent, waxing and waning. I wished they'd shut up.

"Cassie," his fingers tightened. "Like you mean it."

And then he was kissing me, lips soft and slightly chapped on mine, the scratch of a three-day old beard against my skin, the smoothness of teeth, of tongue. He tasted like coffee and electricity and power, so much power. It filled my mouth like whiskey, like the best drink I'd ever had. It flowed down my throat, burned along every limb, snapping nerves back to life, filling veins, sending my heart racing in my chest.

Suddenly, I could breathe again, not shallowly, but fully, deeply. Only I didn't want to breathe. I wanted him. My hands came up, burying in his hair, holding him, drinking from him, desperate and sloppy and greedy and ravenous. All warm and good and power and, God, oh, God, *so good*.

I groaned and rolled on top of him, so hungry, so hungry. His hands settled on my waist, not stroking, barely touching. Just holding me in place as I took what I needed. I could see it in my mind, like I saw the Pythian power sometimes, a glittering golden stream flooding out of him and into me, so *good*. And then his hands were clenching, holding me, bruisingly hard, for one last, brief instant—

And then there were people, people everywhere, running and yelling and pulling—on me. Pulling us apart. I tried to fight them and my limbs actually seemed to work now, to respond to my commands. But they were vampires and so strong and—

And he was gone. The hillside was spinning, people's faces and the streamers of smoke and the rain all blurring together into a kaleidoscope of don't care, because I didn't want them; I wanted Pritkin. I struggled up, and someone tried to push me back down, and I snarled at them and they let me go.

I stumbled to my feet, naked and muddy and bloody and half crazy, but he wasn't there, he wasn't there. And in a flash, I knew why. He'd told me himself—*human or demon varieties*. I'd given him power to save his life, and now he'd returned it. And while that didn't mean anything in human terms, except emergency and necessity and the only possible way out, in demon terms it meant—

It meant—

"What have you done?" I screamed to no one, because he wasn't there.

I dropped to my knees, screaming in fury, and the earth

shook. A time wave boiled under the soil, causing roots to fly out of the ground, pushing up boulders, sending a cascade of mud and debris spilling down the hill and forcing several vamps to jump wildly out of the way. So much power, I thought dully.

And it did me no good, it did me no good, it did me no good.

"Now zat," someone said approvingly, "is a Pythia."

And then blackness.

Epilogue

I woke up in bed to find a vampire in my room.

He was sitting in the chair in the corner, flipping through a newspaper. The front page was turned to me, and the headline was a little hard to miss. One word, in huge black letters: GODDESS.

I stared at it for a long minute, feeling empty, feeling nothing. The vampire turned over another page. "You're not supposed to be here," I told Marco roughly.

A pair of bushy eyebrows appeared over the paper. "You kicking me out?"

"No," I said. And then I burst into tears.

He came over and gathered me up. He was big and warm and smart enough not to say anything. I cried his shirt wet. I was hard on his shirts.

"I got more," he told me, and gave me a handkerchief. It was big, like everything about him. I just held it.

I didn't give a shit what I looked like.

"What happened?" I asked, after a while.

Marco's big chest rose and lowered in a sigh. "Well, as I understand it, you showed up to your coronation naked, rolled around in some mud, dusted a dragon and then made out with the mage. Nobody really knows what happened, but it impressed the shit out of the senates. They signed the alliance early this morning."

"Okay."

"Also, they caught that thing that attacked you. You know, the Morrigan?"

"Uh-huh."

"She claims she was forced into it because the Green Fey invaded and kidnapped her husband. Guess they're working for the bad guys now, only nobody seems to really know. Anyway, she said she's willing to let bygones be bygones if we help her get him back."

"How generous."

"Yeah. That's what I said. But that Marsden guy is considering taking her up on the offer."

I tilted my head to stare up at him. "Why?"

"He was here all morning, reading your dad's letters. It turns out that that spell everybody's been worried about—the one that keeps the so-called gods out of here?"

"The ouroboros?"

"Yeah, that's the one. Looks like it wasn't linked to you at all. Even if that Spartoi had killed you, it wouldn't have done any good."

"But something is keeping it active. And if my mother isn't here—"

"I didn't understand everything the old man said," Marco told me. "But it seems she did something to merge her soul with your dad's before she passed on—as insurance, you know?"

I sat up and turned to look at him. "But he died with her."

"Yeah, but his soul stayed here."

It took me a moment to get it. "Because Tony trapped it in his damned paperweight."

"Yeah. And it's still here. Or in Faerie, somewhere on this side of the spell. Anyway, Marsden figures we got to find the fat little weasel before he figures out what he's got, and if he's in Faerie, we're gonna need help."

I nodded slowly, but I wasn't thinking about Tony. I just sat there for a moment, a couple of dozen emotions washing through me. But the one I finally settled on was pride—fierce and glowing.

She must have known they would never stop coming for her, had to realize they would find her, sooner or later. She was weak, possibly dying, because I couldn't see her going to the Pythian Court in less than dire need, not knowing what stalked her. She'd had almost no one she could trust, for even at court there were those like Myra who would have sold her out. But still, she'd found a way. She'd found a way and beaten them all.

I wiped my eyes, got up and started going through my dresser.

"So Marsden said he needs to know if you got any ideas where to start looking for the paperweight," Marco told me. "And there's a lot more stuff in your dad's letters he wants to talk over with you. Plus, Pritkin hasn't checked in and he keeps asking if I've seen him. I told him what I could, but it wasn't—"

I looked up. "What did you tell him?"

"That he came through here last night, covered in blood and ranting like a madman. He demanded to see you, and when I told him we thought you'd gone to the coronation, he cursed at me, ran for the balcony and threw himself into a ley line. That's the last any of us saw of him."

I thought I could fill in the rest. Niall had left Pritkin for dead, but he hadn't counted on his demon blood—or his sheer stubbornness. Pritkin's body had healed enough for him to swim back to consciousness, to realize that the necklace was gone and to understand what that meant. He'd come here looking for me, probably to warn me not to shift, but I was already gone. So he'd gone after me.

He'd gone after me and he'd saved me. He'd said he'd rather die than go back there, into slavery, into his father's tender care. But he'd saved me anyway.

Like Mom, he'd found a way.

I grabbed a tank top and a pair of shorts and went to the bathroom.

"That was a couple of minutes before the master popped back in," Marco said. "Only without you. Things got a little crazy after that, because nobody knew where you'd ended up. And we couldn't reach the house by phone and we couldn't even contact anybody mentally 'cause they were all in that portal thing. But nobody'd seen you here, so we finally went out there, only to find we'd missed all the excitement."

I ran a comb through my hair and didn't comment.

"The master wanted to keep you at the estate, but Marsden threw a fit, so they compromised and we brought you back here," Marco continued. "The master'll be back as soon as he can shake the senators, and Marsden said he'll be checking in tonight. But he wanted to know if you have any idea where Pritkin is."

"Yes." I scrubbed my face and started to get dressed. Pritkin's little talisman bumped my skin as I pulled off the pajama top. I put a hand on it, squeezing hard, and something greasy leaked through the material and onto my palm. I didn't wash it off.

There was no question where he was, but Jonas couldn't help him. As soon as he'd exchanged energy with me, the thing that called itself his father had jerked him back, "revoking his parole," as Pritkin had put it. And I didn't think it was going to be easy to pry him loose. I wasn't sure it would even be possible. I didn't understand much about the demon realms, didn't know what, if anything, could be done.

But I knew who to ask.

"By the way, your dress arrived," Marco told me.

"What dress?"

"For the coronation."

I stuck my head out the door. "We already had that."

"No, you had a mud bath. Seems they want to do it over, do it right, this coming Saturday—"

"No."

"It's gonna be here, instead of at the estate—"

"No."

"It's a nice dress."

I pulled on the shorts and came out. Marco was standing by something that was a little better than "a nice dress." It was a delicate, shimmering piece of art. A few crystalline lines sketched out the form here and there, like the ones connecting stars in a constellation. They delineated the soft drape of the skirt, the low-cut back, the plunging neckline. And between those was . . . nothing. Or, at least, what was there wasn't cloth.

It was completely transparent, with a faint tinge of teal, like a dress made out of ice or glass—or the light that glimmered along fiber-optic filaments one minute and was gone the next. It was suspended a few feet off the floor and was slowly rotating, shedding softly glowing particles as it went. They lingered for a moment after the dress had turned, like a train of stars, before they disappeared.

I'd have been a little worried about the transparency thing if I didn't think Augustine had done some sort of trick, like with Francoise's ribbon. And if I hadn't already gone full monty in front of most of the leaders of the magical world. And if I planned to wear it.

"It's beautiful," I said honestly, and Marco sighed.

"You ain't coming, are you?"

"Let my double do it. She's probably better at these kinds of things anyway."

"And what are you going to do?" he asked, watching with disapproval as I shoved my feet into a pair of old sneakers.

"Raise some Hel," I told him. And shifted.

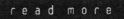

KAREN CHANCE

TOUCH THE DARK

The first novel in the Cassandra Palmer series

Cassandra Palmer can see the future and communicate with spirits – talents that make her attractive to the dead and the undead. The ghosts of the dead aren't usually dangerous; they just like to talk . . . a lot.

The undead are another matter.

Like any sensible girl, Cassie tries to avoid vampires. But when the bloodsucking Mafioso she escaped three years ago finds Cassie again with vengeance on his mind, she's forced to turn to the vampire Senate for protection.

The undead senators won't help her for nothing, and Cassie finds herself working with one of their most powerful members, a dangerously seductive master vampire – and the price he demands may be more than Cassie is willing to pay . . .

KAREN CHANCE

CLAIMED BY SHADOW

The second thrilling novel in the Cassandra Palmer series

A recent legacy made Cassandra Palmer heir to the title of Pythia, the world's chief clairvoyant. It's a position that usually comes with years of training, but Cassie's circumstances are a little . . . unusual. And now she's stuck with a whopping amount of power that every vampire in town wants to either monopolize or eradicate – and that she doesn't dare use.

What's more, she's just discovered that a certain arrogant master vampire has put a *geis* on her – a magical claim that warns off any would-be suitors, and might explain the rather . . . *intense* attraction between them. But Cassie's had it with being messed around and anyone who tries it from now on is going to find out that she makes a very bad enemy . . .

read more

KAREN CHANCE

EMBRACE THE NIGHT

The third novel in the Cassandra Palmer series

Recently named the world's chief clairvoyant, Cassandra Palmer still has a thorn in her side. As long as Cassie and a certain master vampire – the dangerously sexy Mircea – are magically bound to each other, her life will never be her own . . .

The spell that binds them can only be broken with an incantation found in an ancient text, the Codex Merlini. The Codex's location has been lost in the present day, so Cassie will have to seek it out in the only place it can still be found – the past.

But Cassie soon realizes the Codex has been lost for a reason. The book is rumoured to contain dangerous spells, and retrieving it may help Cassie to deal with Mircea, but it could also endanger the world . . .

KAREN CHANCE

CURSE THE DAWN

Cassie Palmer is the world's chief clairvoyant but this, as she knows to her cost, is often more trouble than it's worth.

After coming close to an agreement with the Silver Circle – an organisation that's been trying to kill her for years – Cassie gets kidnapped by one of its more embittered members. She escapes, but to protect herself against further harm, she invests in a magical device: a statue that grants wishes.

What her clairvoyancy *doesn't* tell her is that the statue grants wishes according to its own wicked whims. And when she wishes to shift herself and her companion Pritkin out of a sticky situation, the statue does something so bizarre that Cassie and Pritkin's lives will never be the same again . . .

read more

KAREN CHANCE

DEATH'S MISTRESS

Dorina Basarab is a dhampir - half-human, half-vampire - and the only way she can stay sane is by unleashing her sometimes uncontrollable rage on demons and vampires that deserve killing.

After the fortunate demise of her insane uncle Dracula, Dory is back home in Brooklyn, hoping that life will calm down for a while. But then two visitors arrive: her friend Claire, asking for Dory's help in finding a magical Fey relic, and the gorgeous master vampire Louis-Cesare, desperate to find his former mistress, a vampire named Christine.

Dory and Louis-Cesare soon discover their problems may be connected: the same master-vampire Christine is bound to is also rumoured to be in possession of the relic. But they soon realize there's more at stake when Christine's master turns up dead. Someone is killing vampire Senate members, and if Dory and Louis-Cesare can't stop the murderer, they may be next . . .

read more

KAREN CHANCE

MIDNIGHT'S DAUGHTER

Dorina Basarab is a dhampir, the daughter of a vampire and a human woman. Subject to uncontrollable rages, most dhampirs are born barking mad and live very short, very violent lives. So far, Dory has managed to maintain her sanity by unleashing her anger on those demons and vampires who deserve killing.

But now Dory's vampire father has come back into her life. Her uncle Dracula, notorious even among vampires for his cruelty and murderous ways, has escaped from prison, and her father wants Dory to work with the gorgeous master vampire Louis-Cesare to put him back there.

Vampires and dhampirs are mortal enemies, and Dory prefers to work alone. But Dracula is the only thing on earth that truly scares her, and when Dory has to go up against him, she'll take all the help she can get . . .